EXPERIMENTAL HEART

SECRETS

BOOK 3

SHANNON PEMRICK

Secrets
Experimental Heart | Book Three

Copyright © 2017 Shannon Pemrick
www.shannonpemrick.com

Cover Illustration by Jackson Tjota
Cover Typography by Amalia Chitulescu
Editing by Sandra Nguyen and Cody Anne Arko-Omori

ISBN 978-1-950128-19-8 (paperback)
ISBN 978-0-9912213-9-4 (hardcover)
ISBN 978-0-9984464-4-8 (e-book)

To Joe
For unwavering support. Without you, Eira and Raikidan's story would
have never gotten this far.

And

To Sammie, Taryn, and Frank
Without you three, this story would have never been so exciting.

BOOKS BY SHANNON PEMRICK

EXPERIMENTAL HEART

Destiny

Pieces

Secrets

Exposed

Surrendered

ORACLE'S PATH

Prophecy of Convergence

Prophecy Tested

Prophecy Chosen

LOOKING FOR GROUP

Spellbinding His Ranger

Protecting His Priestess

Summoning Their Elementalist

My body ached from the torture I had endured. Two soldiers dragged me back to my cell, each holding me by an arm, and dropped me every so often to remind me how powerless I was. I didn't utter a sound when they tossed me on the stone floor of the holding cell. I just waited for them to leave before I struggled to pull myself to my feet and drag myself to my corner.

I didn't acknowledge anyone as I curled up. I didn't deserve the sympathy they'd try to give. The only thing I deserved was their hatred for what I had done. So I closed my eyes and remembered the memory the soldiers had interrupted. I'd remember, even though I knew other memories would also follow.

CHAPTER 1

Dead leaves crunched under the hooves of my mount as we traveled through the dense forest. Birds chirped their late afternoon songs and insects chirred. A light breeze rustled the leaves in the canopy, and a brook babbled in the distance. I gazed around, tucking loose strands of my violet hair behind my ear, and inhaled the petrichor odor still clinging to the air from the remnants of a rainstorm earlier this morning. I had no idea where I was, but Tla'lli had assured me this black elk knew the way, so I trusted her words and this creature to bring me to my destination.

The elk halted suddenly and exhaled. Glancing around, I slid off the giant elk's back and removed the bridle and reins from the elk's face. Giving him a quick scratch on the nose, I stuffed the tack into a small bag sewn into the cloth saddle. The elk huffed at me before heading back the way we had come.

Now alone, I had no real idea where I was. Tla'lli assured me the elk would bring me to the edge of their territory, but that didn't help me get back to the campsite if I was lost. Inhaling deeply, I caught the faint scent of Raikidan. Breathing in again, I assessed the odor to be a few days old, and not far from my current location. Making sure my bag was secure on my back, I headed out.

We had traveled nearby when we had been searching for the burial site. *If I head north from here, I should end up at the campsite.* It was strange traveling back alone, but it was for the best. The moment I had woken up, I spent little time waiting. I had eaten with my men, gave last-minute orders, and headed out, all before Raikidan had woken up. I didn't need him or his little games around. I had real lives on the line and real problems to deal with. Raikidan could take his boredom and waste someone else's time.

I halted when a large shadow blocked out the sun briefly. I looked up but saw nothing. Shrugging it off, I continued on until the shadow appeared again, but this time it lasted longer. I stopped walking, but didn't look up even when the shadow left. Instead, I listened. *Wing flaps.* Large ones that could support the size of the shadow I saw.

When the shadow appeared for a third time, I glanced up and was taken by surprise by the sight of a black dragon descending from the sky. What would a black dragon want with me?

The dragon's head turned, revealing a red stripe running down the center of his head and back. *It can't be…* Still several feet above me, the Dragon shifted into a nu-human shape. His muscles rippled under his tan skin upon impact of the ground. He ran a hand through his black and red hair before he peered at me with his piercing sapphire eyes.

"Raikidan…" I wasn't sure what to think of him being here.

"You left without me," he accused.

"Leave him here and be on your way," the haunting malevolent voice in the back of my head said.

I turned on my heels and continued heading north. "I told you to go home."

"And I told you I wasn't going anywhere." He followed me. "You don't understand—"

I whirled around. "I don't understand? How the hell am I supposed to understand when you don't tell me?"

Raikidan looked down. "It's… it's complicated…"

I snorted. "I'm sure it is."

"Good, don't believe his lies."

Raikidan grabbed me by the arm as I turned to continue on my way, forcing me to look him in the eye. I could see it there. How complicated it was for him, but that didn't excuse him.

"Don't believe it. It's an act."

"Do you just not trust me?" I asked.

"Do *you* not trust me?"

I grunted and turned to continue on. "Let's go, then."

"Not that way."

My brow rose. "This is the way we came. It leads us directly back to camp."

"I found a faster way," he said. "Trust me."

"Don't trust him."

I sighed and followed. "You'd better not be pulling my leg. I'll kill you while you sleep if you are."

Raikidan chuckled. "Well then maybe I shouldn't sleep for the next few days just in case."

"Raikidan!"

He laughed. "I'm kidding. Just trust me on this one, okay?"

I frowned. "Fine."

My eyes cautiously took in our surroundings. The sun had sunk low in the sky and Raikidan stopped walking, though not by choice. We stood before the mouth a large cave. It sent an unsettling wave through me. "I'd rather go a different way."

"Scared?" he said, a teasing smile on his stupidly handsome face.

I snorted. "No. I just don't see how a cave can have an exit."

"It does," he insisted. "I told you, I checked it out before I came to find you. Besides, we need to get to the higher ground above—or did you forget we had to scale a cliff to get down here? It took you forever to get down. I don't want to think about how long it will take for you to climb up it."

"I didn't take forever," I muttered, pushing past him. "I nearly free-fell the entire way down; only using the cliff face every once in a while to prevent myself from splatting on the ground. So, sorry I can't sprout wings and fly, instead of taking a whole extra few seconds to jump down to reach the ground."

Raikidan sighed and muttered to himself in his own tongue before following me. Once inside, I lit a fire in my hand and led the way. His lack of protests on me leading confused me, but it wasn't long into the walk before we came to a fork in the tunnel and everything became clear. He knew I was going to have to follow him in the end.

"This way," he said as he chose to walk down the left tunnel.

"Don't follow," the voice in my head said. *"Don't trust him."*

He didn't look back to make sure I followed, unfazed by the darkness that began to surround him as he walked out of the range of my firelight. Not wanting to be left behind and get lost trying to find my way out on my own, I sighed and caught up with him. Raikidan led me through the maze of tunnels without second guessing himself. It was as if he had come through here several times, to remember the way so well.

I held the fire up high to get a better look at the small tunnel. The walls were smooth, carved from years of flooding and rainwater rushing through them. *This tunnel is familiar… but why?* Whatever the reason, it intensified the unsettling sensation gnawing at my nerves.

Raikidan looked back at me. "You okay?"

"I'm fine," I muttered.

"You don't look fine. Don't tell me you're scared."

I snorted. "As if. I'm just getting a bad feeling about this weird cave."

Raikidan stopped walking and faced me. "You act like you've been here before."

My eyes flicked around some more. "It feels like it. I know, I know, it sounds stupid."

"No, it doesn't." I looked at him, but he was already continuing on. "Sometimes we see things that remind us of events that have happened in the past, or dreams we've had. Maybe you have been here before. Or maybe you're remembering tiny bits of something else that is making this place seem familiar."

I tilted my head, my forehead creasing. He continued on without me again, and at this point, if I let him out of my sight, I'd struggle to get out of here on my own.

I had hoped that weird feeling would go away as we walked, but it had only gotten worse. Eventually the feeling became so intense I stopped following Raikidan again.

"Eira?" Raikidan stopped and gazed back at me. I gazed around the tunnel with growing suspicion instead of responding. "C'mon." I stared at him when he grabbed my hand. "It's only a little farther."

I tried to pull my arm from his. "What is a little farther?"

Raikidan smiled and pulled me forward. "You'll see."

"See, he's not to be trusted."

"Raikidan, seriously." I tugged away from him again. "What are you keeping from me?"

His grip tightened and his intense blue eyes snared me. "Trust me."

His gaze fuzzed up my head, and the words that came out of my mouth weren't the ones I originally wanted to say. "All right."

"Fool."

Still holding my hand, he led me up the seemingly endless tunnel. I watched as the tunnel grew wider and less dark. I checked my flame to make sure I wasn't accidentally putting more power into it, but found it to be same size. We were getting close to the exit, and that sudden realization made me uneasy again.

I noticed Raikidan glance back at me, but he didn't utter a word. The fire in my hand began to die, and I was getting too worked up about the current situation to care. Moments later it died, plunging us into partial darkness. I tripped over small rocks and my own feet with my lack of dark-cave vision. I found myself moving closer to Raikidan, until I clung to him.

"We're almost there," Raikidan whispered.

"You said that a while ago," I muttered.

He chuckled. "That was no more than ten minutes ago, but I do mean it. Look ahead of us."

I did as asked and noticed a large light source. That's when I realized I could make out his features and more of what was around me. Raikidan picked up his pace, forcing me to keep up, and pulled me into the light. I blinked violently to get my eyes to adjust better. Raikidan let go of my hand and his presence disappeared, confusing me, and then reappearing behind me, sending me into a slight panic.

"I told you not to trust him!"

"Keep your eyes open and take a look," Raikidan whispered in my ear.

I swallowed hard but stepped closer to the mouth of the cave exit and peered out. My breath caught. The sun was setting casting red and orange rays across the land and sky, and had turned the clouds pink. It was like that dream I had, but even more beautiful. A sense of dread set in. That dream didn't end well for me, and everything about this situation reminded me of that moment.

I turned to look at Raikidan to find him still hanging back where I had left him. "I thought you said this was a short cut."

He chuckled and moved closer to me. "It is." I watched him warily as he walked past me and leaned against the mouth of the cave. He pointed to the right. "There's a small path right here leading up the rest of the cliff."

"But there's more to coming here."

Raikidan grinned and peered out at the landscape. "Beautiful isn't it? I thought you'd like to see it at this time of day. I'm just glad it's as nice as I thought it would be. You do like it, right?"

I half smiled and started to relax. "Yeah, I do." I didn't feel as uncomfortable now. There was something different about this situation. It wasn't like the dream.

"Don't be fooled."

Raikidan continued to grin. "Good. We should stay here for the night. The sun won't last much longer, and walking on the path in the dark wouldn't be smart. This part of the cave is also drier, so it won't be so uncomfortable to rest here."

Before I had a chance to think this option over, Raikidan shifted to his natural state and lay down close to the cave wall, giving me plenty of room. His space made me feel even more at ease. It was as if he knew exactly what had been bothering me all this time, and knew how to fix it.

Reaching into my bag, I pulled out a few large animal skins and laid them down on the ground for a soft, dry bed. Sitting down on my new bed, I reached into my pack once again and pulled out a blanket made from bear hide. Folding it into a makeshift pillow, I lay dawn and curled my body into myself.

"Good night, Raikidan. Thank you for bringing me here. It was nice of you. And so you know, eventually you're going to have to tell me why we're really here."

Raikidan grunted and I smiled a little as I closed my eyes. They snapped open a moment later when I sensed his presence around me all of a sudden. I propped myself up to see him curled around me. He had done this last night when I insisted on sleeping outside, much to Tla'lli's dismay. I didn't understand the meaning, but I wanted to know.

"Raikidan—" I looked at him but his eyes were closed and his breath was slow as if he were already asleep.

I let out a breath. "Guess I won't find out…"

I lay back down and closed my eyes. It didn't matter. What mattered was getting rest so I wouldn't be tired for our journey. We had a long way to go, and I had a feeling we'd be traveling much slower than before since there was no rush.

The air was cool and the leaves on the trees around me showed the change of the seasons. The stone bench I sat on was uncomfortable but I was too busy playing with my newly-cut hair to care much. The quiet gossiping whispers of the other soldiers in the courtyard crossed my ears. They spoke about my change, but I ignored them. I didn't care what they thought. I was already different from them as it was, so why did it matter that I showed how much I didn't fit in with them?

Metal footsteps headed my way, but I didn't pay them any mind. I already knew who it was, and I knew I'd be reprimanded for my actions, so there was no point in acknowledging her. I continued to pay attention to my hair, even when she sat down next to me, but I didn't refrain from passing her a glance.

Her long, aqua hair flowed over her shoulders and her bangs hid her eyes. Her armor shone and her crystal earring sparkled in the soft autumn sun.

"The change looks nice on you," she complimented.

My back straightened, surprise rippling through me. "You mean it?"

She smiled and ran her fingers through my hair. "Of course I do."

I gazed down at the ground. "I thought you'd be disappointed in me."

She laughed. "You're my daughter. You could never disappoint me. It took great courage to do what you did, and for that I couldn't be prouder."

"Yeah, courage…" My gaze drifted over the ground, and my hands reached for my side that still ached with pain.

"How bad is it?" my mother asked.

I sighed and pulled my hands back to my lap. "Pretty bad. The worse punishment I'll probably ever give myself."

"Deep?"

I nodded. "And on both sides."

She frowned. "I'm sorry."

I shook my head. "Don't be. It was my choice, and not one I made lightly."

"Well at least you don't pity yourself."

I snorted. "This is me we're talking about."

My mother laughed. "True. Oh, I have something for you."

I cocked my head. She had something for me? I watched her as she rummaged through a bag tied to her belt and pulled out a plain white box. She handed it to me.

"Well, a gift really," she corrected. "Sorry for the plain box. It was all I could find."

A gift? It wasn't every day she gave me something. In truth she rarely gave me anything, but that was because no one ever had anything to give.

Slowly, I opened the box. My eyes lit up at the sight inside. "Mother, it's beautiful."

"You like it?"

I pulled out the hair clip and held it up to the sun. Its green surface sparked brilliantly and brought a smile to my face.

"I love it." I looked at her. "But where did you get it?"

She half-smiled and pulled a red hair clip out of the same pouch she had pulled my gift from. "Well, in all honesty, I've had it for a while, but I misplaced it and only found it recently." She smiled. "Perfect timing, really. It's part of a matching set, from your father. He had them made for us. I didn't like how mine looked with my long hair, so I never wore it, only carried it with me."

My gaze on the beautiful emerald hair clip darkened, and I put it back in the box. "I don't want it."

My mother stared at me with surprise when I handed it back to her. "But, Eira—"

"I said I don't want it! I don't want anything from that liar."

She flinched from the harshness of my words. "He's not a liar, Eira. He really did care. He promised—"

"Stop it, mother!" I let out a tight breath through my lips, my hands clenching. "When are you going to stop believing in fairytales? When are you going to see the truth? He lied for the political gain of his clan, or whatever he calls it. He never cared, and never will. I want nothing to do with that."

My mother pushed the box back to me. "Eira, he loved me, and I loved him. That was no lie, and what he promised is no lie either. One of these days you'll understand. You'll see some day."

I snorted. "Love is a fairytale. The only thing I'll see is death. It's the fate of us all."

She shook her head. "One of these days, Eira, you'll be free and you'll find someone who will prove to you that love is something to believe in."

I rolled my eyes. "I'll believe that when I can fly."

My mother chuckled. "And he will teach you. That is how you'll know it's not a lie."

I sighed and walked off. "You need to open your eyes, mother. No one can love a monster, not that there is any love in this world that can be given."

She exhaled and spoke quietly. "You're so wrong in so many ways, my dear. You're so misguided. You will come to the realization of the truth I speak in time but... I fear I won't be around to see that day..."

I halted by the tree and clenched the box in my hand. "Don't say things like that, mom. I can't bear the thought of losing you."

My mother exhaled. "You said it yourself. All things die, Eira. It's just a matter of when."

I sighed. "I will wear it, but not because of him. You gave it to me, therefore it is from you and not him. I will wear this for you."

"Thank you."

CHAPTER 2

My hair clip sparkled in the low morning light as I held it up in the air. The light summer breeze tousled my free hair, and I tried from time to time to tame it behind my ears.

"Did you really care, Father, or am I right and it was all just political gain to save your clan?" I leaned back on one hand. Why did it matter? Mom was dead and he was nowhere to be found. All his promises had been lies, and for all it was worth, he was dead to me.

The sound of crumbling stone caught my attention. I looked over at the ledge where the path led up, and watched Raikidan climb his way up.

"You're still here," he said.

I snickered. "Don't tell me you thought I left. I left my bag with you."

"This is you we're talking about," he said. "You'd leave your bag here to make me think you were coming back so I'd wait all day for nothing."

"All right, you win that one." I grinned. "Though I have to admit I didn't think of that, so thanks for the idea."

Raikidan sighed. "Great."

I laughed and held up two recently-killed rabbits. "Come and eat so we can head out. We have a long way to go, and I have a feeling we're not going to have a friendly welcome-home party."

Raikidan nodded and sat down next to me, placing my bag between us. He took the rabbit and ripped into its fur to get to the flesh underneath. Pulling the other rabbit into my lap, I reached for my hair to pull it back, but Raikidan stopped eating just long enough to make me pause. I gave him a funny look.

"Don't put it up yet," he said. "It looks nice down." I pulled away and went back to putting my hair up. "Eira, did I say something wrong?"

I shook my head. "Don't worry about it. It's a personal thing. Just… don't ask me to keep my hair down, please."

"All right." He pointed to my rabbit. "You might want to eat that, though, before I take it from you as my own."

"You wouldn't dare."

Raikidan chuckled. "Eat it and you won't have to find out."

I grunted and tore into the rabbit.

"Hey, Eira?" Raikidan asked.

"Hmm?" I asked through a mouthful of meat.

"I asked you this once before, but you didn't answer the question fully, or at least I don't feel like you did, so I'm going to ask again. How did you get that hair clip?"

I put the rabbit down. "Yeah, I remember you asking that and you're right, I didn't answer it completely. I just told you it was a gift, which it was, but the full truth is that it was a gift from my mom."

He chuckled. "So you really were special to someone."

I looked down at the rabbit in my hands and grunted. "Yeah, I guess you're right."

"See, you're not a monster."

I snorted. "Don't start with that. You're not going to win."

Raikidan rolled his eyes. "Fine, but answer me this, will you? You told me you guys didn't have much to give each other, so how was she able to give you something so nice?"

"She had it made for me," I lied. "Someone in the North owed her a favor so she had him get a jewelcrafter to make this and a matching ruby one. She gave this one to me and kept the ruby one for herself to carry around, instead of to wear, since she thought her hair was too long to have it look good in her hair."

"Why didn't she just cut her hair?" he asked. "You did tell me human hair grows all the time."

I shrugged. "She liked having it long, not that it was overly long in the first place. It was shorter than mine, at least."

Raikidan's eyebrow lifted. "You had long hair once?"

I laughed. "What, can't picture it?"

"No."

"Do you remember that picture of me and her that I have?" He nodded. "Well that was taken a few weeks after I cut it. My hair used to flow past my waist."

Raikidan shook his head. "I still can't picture that."

I chuckled. "Don't try too hard. I hated having my hair so long. It was a pain putting up to keep it out of the way, so I'm sure I'll never have it much longer than it is now."

"It looks good at the length it is."

My gaze lowered to the rabbit again and I tried furiously to hide the small blush that had crept onto my face. Only my mother had ever told me my hair looked nice at this length. Everyone had always told me I should grow it back out. Even Rylan had the same opinion. I could never win anyone's approval with anything I did.

Raikidan's fingers grazed the tips of my hair. "It might even look better a little shorter, but what do I know? Not like my opinion matters much. It's your hair. You do what you want with it."

A teasing smirk slipped up my face. "Except color it?"

My jest caught Raikidan off-guard, but he recovered quickly and grunted. "That dye just makes you smell awful, that's all. If it didn't stink, I wouldn't care."

I shot him a dubious expression and voiced it slightly. For some reason, I couldn't find it in me to believe him on that.

Raikidan focused on his meal. "Let's just finish eating so we can leave."

I eyed him for a few moments before digging back into my breakfast. He was hiding something, but whatever it was would have to wait until later. First we'd have to get back to camp and face the wrath of one temperamental lightning shaman.

I gulped. The scary, blue-haired elven woman before us stared

Raikidan and me down with livid crystal-blue eyes. The sun peeking through the forest canopy, cast scattered light, shadowing her gaze, enhancing her silent anger.

Ryoko chewed on a fingernail and resisted twirling a strand of her brunette hair, as her golden eyes darted from Shva'sika to Raikidan and me. Rylan ran his fingers through his white hair in an effort to stay calm, but his blue and gold heterochromic eyes gave away his fear.

"I can't believe you two!" Shva'sika exploded. "Do you know how worried I was? The two of you leave in the middle of the night, leave no note explaining where you're going or how long you'll be gone, and I'm stuck here worried you've been captured…"

"Elarinya." I said, hoping her elven name would grab her attention better than her shaman one.

"…or injured…"

"Elarinya."

"…or maybe even gotten yourself into trouble—"

"Shva'sika!" I shouted, giving up on my calm attempt.

She stared at me with slight shock. "What?"

"Shut up so I can explain." Her eyes narrowed into a glare but she stayed quiet. I let out a breath, a small bit of relief washing over me. "One, I'm sorry we upset you, but we didn't know it would take so long. Two, you can blame this mostly on Raikidan since this was his idea, and I had no idea what we were doing, or where we were going, for that matter. It was also his fault there wasn't a note, and he's the one who made us leave in the middle of the night."

Raikidan's eyes snapped to me. "Hey!"

I glared at him and he lowered his gaze. He knew it was his fault and he couldn't deny it.

"And three, you're not going to be as mad when you hear about the alliance we made," I finished.

Shva'sika blinked. "Alliance? What are you talking about?"

I walked past her and sat down by the fire pit. "Sit down and I'll tell you."

Everyone gathered around the empty fire pit to listen to what I had to say. Shva'sika showed her impatience when I didn't speak immediately. "Well?"

I chuckled. "Raikidan and I had business in the South, and in the end came out with two more allies than anticipated to aid us in our rebellion."

"Allies?" Ryoko mused. "You can't be serious."

"Ryoko's right. Who in their right mind would want to help us?"

Rylan asked.

"Anyone who is sick of living in fear of Zarda," I said.

Shva'sika gasped. "It can't be. You didn't… I can't believe you did!"

Ryoko cocked her head to the side, her hair jostling. "Danika, what are you talking about?"

"Before I left the West Tribe, I had heard rumors the other tribes were planning on breaking from the pact they had with Zarda, and were going to fight back, even if it killed them all," Shva'sika explained. "Rumor said they had found someone in the home city who they were going to convince to allow them to help. I never thought it was true."

I nodded. "It is. They came to me with hopes I would say yes immediately, but I turned them down. At the time, I figured the less involved they were, the safer it would be for them. But while we were gone, I found out that wasn't the case, and chose to take the offer. But there was a catch to it. They already had an alliance, and if I was to ally with the South Tribe, I was also to ally with a red dragon clan as well."

Shva'sika's eyes widened. "You can't be serious."

"Quite."

"I was expecting you to say the druid clan that lived close to the South Tribe." She laughed. "A dragon clan was the last thing I thought you'd say."

I grunted. "They were the last thing I expected to run into on our little adventure."

Rylan scratched his head. "Can we back up a moment? Why would the shamans come to you in the city? Why not someone else?"

"Why not choose her?" Shva'sika countered. "She is a shaman, after all, and with her connection to the rebellion she was the best choice."

Rylan nodded. "I can see that."

Shva'sika focused on me again. "I'm impressed with what you've done, Laz, but you do know the other tribes will expect to be given that same chance, right?"

I nodded. "I know, and I'm fine with that. We need help. I won't deny that, and any assistance will get us closer to our goal. I don't know what the dragons can do for us, but the shamans will be a great asset."

Shva'sika smiled. "This is a good day. I'll forgive you for leaving without a word. Although, I'd like to know what you two were doing down there initially."

I glanced at Raikidan who was more occupied with the sky. "I don't know. Ask Raikidan. As far as I can tell, we never ended up making it to the destination."

Shva'sika looked at Raikidan expectantly, but he continued to scan the sky, completely oblivious of the current topic. She sighed in defeat.

Ryoko clapped her hands together and stood. "I'm bored. Let's go hiking."

"I think it would be best to let Laz and Raikidan rest," Shva'sika said.

I shook my head and rose to my feet. "I'm up for a walk."

"Are you sure? The South Tribe is a long ways from here."

I nodded. "Yeah, I'm fine. Besides, walking is good for you."

Ryoko squealed happily and ran off in a random direction. Chuckling, I followed, but turned around when Raikidan was the only one left not following.

"C'mon." I grabbed him by the arm. "What are you looking at anyway?"

Raikidan shook his head. "It's nothing. Where are we going?"

I snickered. "Well if you were paying attention, you would know we're going on a hike."

"Shouldn't we be resting?"

I grinned. "What, tired?"

Raikidan snorted. "I was thinking more about your energy level."

I rolled my eyes. "Sure you were. But if you must know, I'm fine. I'm accustomed to long walks like that."

"Right."

I let out an exasperated breath when he went back to gazing at the sky. "Seriously, Raikidan, what is so interesting about the sky? There are no clouds, no birds, nothing. It's just big and blue."

"I thought I heard something," he said. "But every time I go to look, nothing."

"You're going crazy," I muttered. "Maybe you should stay behind and rest. You might get some of your sanity back."

Raikidan snorted. "Even if I wanted to stay behind, I don't think you'd let me."

I glanced down to find I still held a firm grip on him. I let go and put a little space between us. *That was embarrassing.*

"C'mon, slow pokes!" Ryoko yelled. "We're going to race to the top of this little waterfall!"

"Not much of a race if Laz just scales the thing," Rylan muttered.

"And don't say she won't, because you know she will."

Ryoko huffed and I laughed. Picking up my pace, I joined the three and gazed up at the small cliff face. It wasn't at all impressive, but I knew it was because I had already seen bigger on my little journey with Raikidan.

"Any rules?" Raikidan asked.

"No cheating, no cheating, and no cheating," Ryoko said. "Oh, and no shapeshifting."

Raikidan muttered to himself as if he were hoping she'd forget that.

"Define cheating," I said.

"Um…" She thought for a moment. "…no killing?"

"Since that was a given, anything goes, right?"

"Um, yeah I guess," she mused.

"Then I'll see you ladies at the top," I challenged, taking off.

"Hey, that's cheating!" Ryoko called.

"You only said killing was. All is fair in love and war."

My eyes widened when a shadow blocked the sun over head. I looked up and yelped. Jumping to the ground, I nearly missed being crushed by a giant bolder.

"Taking a nap, Laz?" Ryoko teased as she jumped over the boulder. "You'll never win that way."

"Cheater," I growled as I scrambled to my feet.

Ryoko laughed and continued on. "I knew you'd dodge, so it's not cheating."

"Not yet at least," Rylan muttered.

Ryoko shot him a deadly glare and he fell back into place with Shva'sika.

"Don't tell me you're afraid of her," she teased.

"I value my life over a dumb race."

I rolled my eyes over his cowardliness and continued my race against Ryoko. She attempted to trip me, but I jumped. I tried to push her just enough to get her to falter and slow, but I also missed. Gazing at the cliff face, I grinned and scaled up to the next ledge, losing some ground in the process, but I knew I'd regain it back shortly.

Ryoko, thinking she would win this now with her small lead on me, picked up her pace. Not wanting her to get too confident, I matched her pace, but when a dark shadow flew over me, I slid to a screeching halt. My eyes widened by what I saw. "Ryoko, stop!"

Ryoko ignored my call, assuming it was a trick of some sort, but soon found herself attempting to slide to a halt when the massive red dragons flying above us tried to land right in front of her. Ryoko, lost her balance, and fell back on her butt, sliding a few more inches before she finally stopped moving.

Ryoko tipped her head back to stare up at the massive dragon with awe and curiosity, and then shifted her focus at me. "Please tell me he's a friend of yours and not here to eat me."

I wanted to laugh at her silly comment, but ended up snorting instead. "I wouldn't call him a friend, but yes, I know him."

I jumped down from my vantage point and strolled over to the two. I could hear Raikidan behind me growling quietly, and it made me wonder if he had known Zaith was around but didn't tell me. It would explain his bizarre sky-watching earlier.

"What do you want, Zaith?" I asked him. "Don't tell me you need directions to the city."

Zaith didn't shift to speak to me, much to my surprise, nor did he attempt to speak to me in his tongue. Instead, he lifted up his front claw, and my eyes widened with awe. Dangling from his only large, black claw was a gold, ruby-set necklace. Zaith moved his claws over me and let go of the piece of jewelry. I caught it and examined the item.

Ryoko moved from where she sat to look at it as well. "Wow, that's pretty."

I flicked to Zaith, skepticism clinging to me. "Is this really for me?"

Zaith exhaled and kept eye contact. Taking that as a yes, I looked back down at the magnificent necklace in my hands. But as I did, an unsettling sensation crept over me, and I knew it wasn't because of Raikidan's increasing aggression. Something didn't feel right about this gift. Zaith finally made a noise, but it was so quick at first that I thought I'd imagined it. It wasn't until Raikidan shifted and positioned himself over Ryoko and me that I knew for sure he really had done something.

The two dragons' chests rumbled as they spoke with each other, and Ryoko moved behind me. My unease grew. I nudged her back and tried to move us away from the two dragons. I blinked when Zaith only moved a slight muscle in his jaw and the two took flight.

I watched the two dragon grapple mid-flight and snapped viciously at each other. Their airborne fight didn't last long before Raikidan came crashing down to the ground. Ryoko and I jumped out of the way and scrambled to safety. Zaith quickly descended from the sky but Raikidan was ready for him, and he was thrown back into the woods, plowing over trees and other plant life in the process.

"What in Lumaraeon is up with these two?" Rylan shouted.

"Hell if I know," I said.

"It all started because of that stupid necklace," Ryoko muttered.

I looked down at the necklace. *She's right.* It had started because of it. What did it mean for Zaith to give this to me? A political offering I could see and would have guessed, but Raikidan's reaction indicated it wasn't that cut and dry, which might explain the bad feeling I had. I sighed and rubbed my temples. Dragons were so confusing.

"Laz, lookout!" Rylan shouted.

Raikidan's large body came flying at me. Reacting as quickly as possible, I dashed out of the way and climbed up the cliff face to get out of harm's way, narrowly avoiding Raikidan's long tail as it crashed into the rock bed. I watched Raikidan as he breathed heavily and went to see if he was all right, but Zaith moved between us and stared me down. I held his gaze and moved to my right but he followed, preventing me from seeing Raikidan's condition, and moved his head closer to me in the process.

Narrowing my eyes, I stepped back to my original position and again Zaith followed. My lip curled. He was trying to corner me. I despised being cornered—hated feeling like a toy. Knowing I'd have to fake him out, my eyes flicked to one side and positioned myself as if I was going to move that way and just as I noticed Zaith flexed to follow, I changed direction and escaped.

Zaith growled, but I ignored him as I raced over to Raikidan. Touching his face, I looked him over. "Hey, you okay?"

Raikidan exhaled through his nose, showing that the only thing damaged was his pride, but I looked him over some more to make sure.

I noticed a gash above his eye. "Let me clean this up. We don't need you going blind."

Removing my arm sleeve, I dabbed the wound and soaked up as much blood as I could. Raikidan tilted his head, giving me better access to the wound, but he didn't stay like that for long. Zaith snarled, and

Raikidan perked up and replied with similar intensity. These two bull-headed dragons were really testing my patience. *This nonsense stops now.*

The others had already taken safety in the trees by the path heading back to camp, so the only thing I had to worry about was getting Zaith away and Raikidan out of here.

I rubbed Raikidan's neck, feeling the texture of his hard scales. "C'mon, Raikidan, let's go. I don't want to be around him anymore."

Raikidan's focus drifted from Zaith and onto me. I held his gaze, and he responded by moving backward while keeping his head low, allowing me to continue to keep contact on his neck. We didn't get far before Zaith spoke to him again, and this time I could tell what he was doing. Zaith was taunting him and it was working.

Raikidan snapped his gaze on Zaith and started to stalk toward him. This pissed me off. I was sick of these two meatheads going at it. With as much strength as I could muster, I jumped up to grab onto Raikidan's horn, and yanked on him to get him to move back. Raikidan growled, but this time it wasn't at Zaith. Ignoring his protest, I yanked on him again.

This time, instead of growling, Raikidan shifted to his nu-human form, forcing me to let go of his now-nonexistent horn. "Let go, Eira."

Glaring at him, I grabbed him by the ear and pulled him away. His shifting ended up only making my job easier.

"Ow. Eira, stop, that hurts. Ow!" I ignored his protest and continued to pull him away. "Please, Eira, stop."

I continued to ignore him. He didn't fight hard beyond verbal protesting, as if this were all an act. He'd only tug on occasion to test if I would actually let him go.

Once we were out of sight of everyone, I released him. "What the hell what that?"

Raikidan rubbed his ear. "I don't know, you tell me. You're the one doing the yanking."

I punched him in the chest. "That's not what I'm talking about and you know it."

Raikidan sighed and scratched his head. He stopped when his eyes landed on the necklace I was still holding. Before I could react, he snatched it from me and tossed it. "Don't go after that."

I waited for an explanation, but when he just held eye contact, I became annoyed. I hated not getting an answer to my questions. I especially didn't like being told what to do, and I wasn't going to listen. I retrieved the necklace.

"Eira," Raikidan growled.

I whirled on him. "Don't tell me what to do!" He flinched and stepped back. I stalked over to him. "Unless you can back up your reason, don't you ever attempt to tell me what to do. Do you understand?"

Raikidan exhaled slowly. "It has to do with that stupid legend we talked about before."

I stopped advancing and furrowed my brow in confusion. "What? What legend?"

With great speed, Raikidan slipped behind me and held the necklace up to my neck. "Eira." A shiver ran up my spine when he spoke, and I didn't like that. "Eira, I can get you something nicer. Something better suited for you, and it won't mean the same thing. Just don't accept his proposal."

I froze. *It can't mean that.*

"Don't become his mate, Eira."

I gulped. *It does.*

"No!" I snatched the necklace from him and threw it. "Not human. Not dragon. Not a chance!"

I stormed off in a random direction. I couldn't believe this was happening. I couldn't believe that dragon asked that of me. I did my best to shut out the idea, but I was too angry and flustered for much to happen in my favor.

I was so busy being angry, I didn't notice we were being watched. And I barely noticed Raikidan mumble something in his tongue in a direction that wasn't mine.

3
CHAPTER

The cold, refreshing water from the river rushed around me as I emerged. My hair flipped over me as I gasped for breath, dragging a stream of water with it. I waded through the water to the rock formation that rested under the waterfall, and climbed up next to Ryoko. I ran my fingers through my hair and massaged my scalp.

The warm wind of the summer afternoon rushed over my cool skin, sending shivers all over my body. Ryoko, being self-conscious and paranoid as ever, held her arms protectively over her chest. She scanned our surroundings as if she expected someone to be watching in the shadows of the trees.

I shook my head. "Will you just relax, Ryoko? There's no one around here except us and the boys, and they're back at the campsite."

She continued to look around. "Yeah, and the guys are the problem."

I sighed. "Ryoko, we told them where we were going. They'd be stupid to come this way."

Shva'sika chuckled as she waded through the water over to us. "Laz, I wouldn't be scolding her if I were you. If they showed up you'd freak out."

"But they won't show up," I said. "I'm not paranoid like Ryoko."

"I'm not paranoid!" Ryoko shrieked.

"She's right," Shva'sika sided. "Just because you told them not to come this way doesn't mean they won't. It's a large forest, and it's pretty easy to end up somewhere you didn't intend."

Ryoko whimpered and looked around.

I set livid eyes on the elf woman. "Look at what you've done, Shva'sika! You've gone and made it worse with that comment."

Shva'sika shook her head. "I don't understand you two. Why are you so ashamed of your bodies?"

I snorted. "We're not ashamed." Ryoko's gazed lowered. I pinched my nose and let out an exasperated sigh. "Ryoko…"

"Don't talk to me with so much pity!" she snapped. "It's not like you have anything to be ashamed of…"

Shva'sika shook her head. "What is this nonsense you're babbling?"

Ryoko blinked. "Huh?"

Shva'sika lifted Ryoko's chin. "You're beautiful, Ryoko, and you shouldn't be ashamed of how you look. There is nothing wrong with your figure. You both need to learn to love your bodies as they are and not hide them. The female body may be fragile, but it's also powerful."

I snorted. "Elves may find them powerful, but they're utterly useless to humans."

"Oh don't be—"

"Laz is right," Ryoko interrupted. "It may be okay with your race for women to be seductive, but for humans it just makes you a slut. The only thing a woman's body is good for is to be something to look at, and to have a good time. Take it from me. No man cares that I have feelings. No man cares that I'm not completely useless. Sure, I'm not the smartest woman out there. Frankly, I'm spacey and quite dumb. But there is something going on in my head and I do have feelings, but it doesn't matter. I'm just something to look and grab at."

Ryoko sighed and rested her cheek in her hand. Her gaze never left the flowing water that went down stream. *Ryoko…* Shva'sika mouthed me an apology. I shook my head and went back to washing my hair.

Ryoko had it rough. She could knock down buildings and do something that should be inhumanly impossible, but getting a lick of respect to save her life, outside the circle of our group, was difficult for her. Though, she did exaggerate a bit in her emotional fit, not that I could fault her. That kind of pain would skew anyone's perspective at the best of times.

"Chin up, Ryoko," Shva'sika said as she began washing her face. "I bet there's someone who doesn't see you that way. Heck, I'm pretty sure I could easily find a nice elven man who would be genuinely interested in you."

"Doubt it," Ryoko muttered without taking her gaze off the water. "It's been decades since someone saw me as worthwhile. Now, I'm just a hopeless romantic."

Shva'sika shook her head and went about shaving. "I'll build up your confidence, even if it kills me, dear."

I snickered. "Careful, Ryo, she will."

"Not going to happen." Ryoko then shuddered she noticed Shva'sika's beauty routine. "How can you stand doing that? Doesn't it get annoying?"

Shva'sika's brow rose. "What, shave? Well I do prefer to wax because it's less time consuming, and I only have to do it once every few weeks, but I can't exactly do that out here."

I chuckled. "That's right, you don't know."

"Know what?"

"We experiments don't have to shave," Ryoko explained. "At least not our legs, arms, or underarms."

Shva'sika's cocked her head. "That's rather interesting. Why is that?"

I shrugged. "Like you said, shaving is time consuming. Even waxing takes time out of our day. And since we're soldiers, we don't have that kind of time to spend. But at the same time, women were still expected to live up to society's standards, so it was decided that was something we wouldn't have to deal with."

Ryoko nodded. "Yeah, though it doesn't mean our bodies aren't completely hairless. Well not all of us. Some are. It's kinda like a random grab bag as far as whether you are or aren't."

Shva'sika giggled. "I can see that."

Ryoko went to reply, but then stopped and grabbed Shva'sika by the face instead.

Shva'sika yipped in surprise. "Ryoko, what are you doing?"

"You have a scar on your face." She lightly traced it with her finger. It was a tiny scar and appeared quite old. It ran from just above her upper lip down to her chin.

"Yeah, I do…" Shva'sika replied quietly before trying to finish her washing.

"I didn't know you had one there before," Ryoko said. "It's faded, but I know I would have seen it before."

My eyes narrowed. "You wouldn't have, since she hides it." Ryoko looked at me. Shva'sika avoided my gaze. "Here she is, telling us to love how we look, when she can't even do it herself. Hypocrite."

Shva'sika rested her hand on her scar, covering it. "I know I'm a hypocrite and I'm sorry. I just can't stand looking at it."

"It doesn't look bad," Ryoko said. "If anything, it shows your personality."

Shva'sika shook her head. "No, it makes my face ugly."

I pinched my nose. "Now you're sounding like Ryoko. Knock it off, Shva'sika."

"You don't understand." I gave her a stern stare, but she held her ground. "You have scars on your body, yes, but not on your face. You don't get the same looks when it's a scar on the face."

"Danika, it doesn't make you look ugly," Ryoko insisted.

"It may not make me ugly, but it doesn't make me beautiful, either."

Ryoko sighed and flicked her gaze to me. "She doesn't listen well."

I thought for a moment and then snapped my fingers. "Let's try something. You can keep covering it while we're out here, but once we get to the city, you can't cover that scar for an entire week. If we're wrong, you can cover it after, and if we're right, you won't want to cover it."

Shva'sika's brow quirked up. "And what's in it for me?"

"Ryoko and I have to practice not being ashamed of our bodies, as you put it."

"Laz!" Ryoko hissed.

"For the whole week?" Shva'sika insisted on clarifying.

I nodded. "The entire week."

Shva'sika grinned. "I accept."

Ryoko groaned. "Why did you have to drag me into this?"

"Because it's the only way she'd accept," I said.

"But you know I can't do this!" she argued. "You both know I can't do this."

"You can and you will," I said. "Shva'sika agreed to the terms, and therefore you have to, too…"

I trailed off when I noticed movement in the trees. It hadn't been the first time in the past few minutes, but I had thought I had only been seeing things. Now, I wasn't so sure.

Ryoko turned to look as well. "Did you see something?"

I shook my head. "Just a squirrel."

Ryoko shrugged and resumed washing up. I went to splash water over my legs when I noticed the movement again. This time I knew there was something over there. I hopped off my perch. "I'll be right back."

"Don't get lost," Shva'sika teased.

I snorted and left the water to grab my clothes. I muttered as it took me a while to pull my clothes over my wet body. I should have worn the armor. I wasn't even sure what the reason was for me to be wearing regular clothes. Sighing with frustration, I barely managed to get my shorts buttoned before I was throwing on my long shirt and buttoning the three snaps, without worrying about anything underneath.

Crouching low, I snuck into the shadows of the trees and made my way around to the spot I was suspicious about. I ground my teeth when I reach the location and spotted the one thing I hadn't wanted to see.

"Rylan, we really shouldn't be here," Raikidan hissed.

Rylan sighed. "I know, I know, but—wait, where did Laz go?"

"Don't say stuff like that," Raikidan muttered as he peered around the tree he hid behind. "Shit, where *did* she go?"

"Murder them."

Standing up from my hiding spot and making as much noise as I could, I advanced toward them. "Looking for someone?"

The two men spun around, their eyes wide with fear, and fell out into the open, causing Ryoko to scream.

"E–Eira…" Raikidan managed.

"L–Laz, it's not as bad as you t–think," Rylan tried to defend.

"It's not bad?" I bared my teeth. "You're spying on us while we're bathing, you ass-hat! You shouldn't even be breathing at this point. Give me one good reason I shouldn't burn you both to a bloody crisp!"

The two backed up as I continued my advance, but were forced to stop when Ryoko blocked their retreat. She had dressed quickly and was now ready to give them their justified beating.

Rylan gazed up at her with fear-stricken eyes. "Ryoko, please listen. It's not what you think."

"Which one of you wants to die first?" she growled, cracking her knuckles and ignoring his please.

"Don't let her have all the fun."

Rylan gulped, his gaze flicking to Raikidan. "Every man for himself!"

Without missing a beat, the two scrambled to their feet and dashed off in different directions.

I counted down. "Three. Two. One."

Ryoko was already pursuing Rylan before I finished. I followed Raikidan's trail, but didn't try to catch up immediately. I wanted him to suffer, and the longer he ran, the longer he suffered. The voice in my head laughed with glee.

My pursuit came to a halt when his scent starting doubling over. *Smart.* I called out to him, my tone too sweet for the situation. "Raikidan, c'mon out." Silence. "Please, Raikidan." Silence still for too long. I forced a sigh. "Raikidan, I'll hear you out, if you come out."

Movement in my periphery caught my eye and I turned. Raikidan eyed me warily and I grinned. My reaction sent him running, but I didn't care. I knew he'd bolt when he realized he had been tricked.

"Hunt him."

"Raikidan," I cooed.

Raikidan picked up his pace in response to my call. I could smell his fear. The scent was intoxicating, driving my senses mad. I could hear the voice in my head craving his blood to be spilled, but I ignored it. I didn't want him dead, at least, not yet. I'd make him suffer first.

"Raikidan," I called again.

"Will you stop calling my name like that? It makes you sound insane."

"Please stop running from me, Raikidan. I promise I won't hurt you."

"We both know that's a lie."

"You sound guilty."

"You think I am."

"I caught you red-handed."

"You won't give me the chance to explain."

I snickered when Raikidan stopped running as a tall cliff blocked his path and left little options to get around it.

"Nowhere to run now, Raikidan. You can't climb as well as I can."

Raikidan turned to face me. I held his gaze and grinned. He did have options. There was enough room between us for him to make a run for it, and he could also fly away, so his decision to stand his ground piqued my interest.

"Let me explain," he demanded.

"Kill him and get it over with."

"I don't see what there is to explain," I replied. "You were spying on us, and that's not okay."

"We weren't spying on you! Or, at least, I wasn't. Rylan thought you guys went the other way to bathe, so he convinced me to follow. We ended up running into you guys, but before I could get Rylan leave, he saw Ryoko, and it was all over."

A muscle in the back of my neck twitched. "I don't believe you."

Raikidan stepped closer, all traces of fear disappearing. "I'm telling you the truth. I didn't watch you."

I shook my head. My fist clenched, my emotions twisting and pulsing. All sense of logic and reason disappeared as the confusion took over. "You're lying."

Raikidan tilted his head. "Why do you say that? I'm a dragon, remember? I'm different than humans."

"It makes no difference!" I shouted, startling him. "You're all the fucking same."

Raikidan placed his hands on my shoulders. "Eira, listen to me. I know you're upset, but you know how I am."

My shoulders tensed, conflict raging in me. Was he telling the truth? He acted sincere when topics like this came up in the past. *But he was there… He was looking…* My hand flew up and struck him in the face. Raikidan took a moment to react. Slowly he reached up and touched the red mark I left.

"Finish the job."

My fingers curled. I gnashed my teeth and then spun on my heels, stalking back to camp. I should have done more. Should have punched him—made him really see how angry I was. Or maybe it wasn't anger. Pain, or sadness maybe? I couldn't tell. There was so much chaos inside, I didn't know what I was feeling. I just knew I didn't want to be around him. He was just as guilty as Rylan in my eyes. He could have left and let Rylan get caught alone, but he chose to stay, and that made his words unbelievable.

I stormed into the campsite. Ryoko was already there sitting at the empty campfire. She had a nastier scowl than me. "Didn't catch him?"

"No," she muttered as she stared at the blackened dirt of the empty campfire pit. "Stupid mutt took off on all fours, and I lost him. How about you?"

"I did. I hurt him. I don't feel any better."

Ryoko huffed. "Figures it would be like that."

Shva'sika exited her tent and laughed. "Laz, dear, you may want to change your shirt. You look like you're about to fall out of it."

I tilted my chin down and heat rushed through my face. "By the goddess, did I really confront him like this?"

I rushed to my tent and changed into my armor clothes. I was so flustered it took longer than it really should have. *Get a hold of yourself, Eira.* When I came back out, Rylan was hesitantly making his way into the campsite. He carried a small lily in his hands. It wasn't difficult to figure out who he was being cautious of.

When he noticed me, he gave an apologetic smile but I turned away, sticking up my nose. He wasn't going to be on my good side for a while. Rylan sighed and looked to where Ryoko sat.

At first glance, it appeared as though she had no idea he was advancing toward her, but the slight twitching of her ears told me otherwise. Rylan knelt next to her and offered his peace offering, but she turned her body away from him. He attempted to talk with her, but she continued to ignore him. He looked at me for help, but I turned away.

I glanced back at the two when a hand smacked against skin, to find Rylan now sitting on the ground and rubbing his cheek. Ryoko, on the other hand, was moving to a different spot on the other side of the empty pit. Her control in her irritated state impressed me. A slap from me could easily break bone. For Ryoko, it took strenuous mental and physical prowess to control her kind of strength for such an action in a way that wouldn't outright kill someone.

It didn't take Rylan long to get back up and try to regain her favor. I had to give him credit. He was persistent.

Ryoko, finally fed up with him, hit him again and walked away, but that didn't stop him from following her. Rylan stopped his attempt when we heard someone approaching from the direction where I had entered the campsite. Slowly, Raikidan made his way into the campsite, rubbing his red cheek.

"What happened to your face?" Rylan asked him.

Raikidan jerked his head at me and muttered, "Ask her."

I glared at Raikidan. "You got off easy, remember that."

Shva'sika let out an exaggerated sigh. "You know what, I'm a little sick of this. Laz, Ryoko, go hunting or collect firewood or something. I think it's best if you're separated from the boys a little longer, until things cool down."

"Fine by me." I disappeared into my tent. When I came back out, I had my bow and quiver in hand.

Ryoko pushed past Rylan to join me. Rylan sighed quietly, as if he had given up. I was starting to feel bad, but I wished I didn't. He put this on himself, and now he was going to have to deal with the consequence.

The campfire snapped and popped as we ate in silence around the campfire, the only sounds to accompany the occasional clank and scrape of utensils were the nightly songs of insects and a lone hooting owl. Ryoko and I sat on one side of the fire, while Raikidan and Rylan sat across from us. Shva'sika resided between us, and from time to time I caught her glancing at us and then the guys.

Ryoko and I still hadn't spoken a word to them, much to both the boys' and Shva'sika's dismay. Shva'sika had hoped that by the time we returned with something to eat, we would have been more willing to hear the men out, but we had ignored them completely.

I looked up from my food when Shva'sika gasped, to find her staring up at the sky. Ryoko and I gave each other funny looks, and then gazed up.

"I saw a shooting star," Shva'sika whispered.

"Make a wish," Ryoko said.

I continued to stare at the sky, hoping to see another, but the sky remained dark. Sighing quietly, I went back to eating.

Ryoko gasped. "Another one!"

I glanced up again, and this time I saw one as well. And then another. "I don't think they're just shooting stars."

Ryoko's eyes sparkled and took off into the woods, her plate of food clattering to the ground. Shva'sika's brow twisted, her eyes flicking to me, and I motioned for her to follow as I put my plate down.

I trailed Ryoko's heavy scent as she bee-lined it to a large meadow just west of the campsite. The four of us finally caught up with her at the edge of the meadow, and arrived just in time to watch the meteor shower. Ryoko bounced around unable to contain her excitement, and Shva'sika was watching with awe.

Ryoko giggled. "Make a big wish!"

I watched as she closed her eyes to wish for something. I was curious what the wish would be. She never told anyone about her wishes, for fear they would never come true, even long after she had made it.

When she opened her eyes, she looked at me. "Aren't you going to make a wish, Laz?"

I shook my head and ventured out into the meadow. "My one wish will never come true."

A sorrowful sigh came from her as I continued to walk away. My eyes were taken off the sky when small flashing lights caught in my periphery. Shva'sika giggled and ran around like crazy, like some small child. It wasn't long until Ryoko joined her, the two of them stirring up hundreds of fireflies. The two women giggled and continued to have their fun. Watching them brought a small smile to my lips.

"Can this night get any cooler?" Ryoko asked.

"Looks like it's about to," Raikidan said.

I glanced at him, and then in the direction he was looking. My eyes grew wide at what I saw. Large Luna Moths fluttered out of the dark forest and into the night sky. Both Shva'sika and Ryoko stopped running around and watched as the eclipse of moths flew over and around us. The fireflies continued to fly around and seemed to make a light trail behind the moths, giving a magical feel to them.

"It's so beautiful…" Ryoko whispered. "And they're so huge!"

"Unusually huge," I said. "They shouldn't be more than a few inches long."

"In certain years, they grow larger than normal," Raikidan explained as he attempted to stand next to me. I turned away from him and he let out a heavy breath.

"But that's only a select few," Shva'sika protested. "The likelihood of a whole group of moths growing to these sizes is almost impossible."

"Almost, but not completely," Raikidan said. "There is a chance large numbers can, especially if the season is good."

"I suppose you're right," Shva'sika mused as she watched the eclipse of moths break up, ruining their mystical line.

"Why are there so many?" Ryoko asked.

"It's the end of their mating season," Raikidan said. "Though, I've never heard of so many clustering in an area during this time."

As I gazed around, tiny legs touched my shoulder. Looking, I found a large moth perched there.

"You must be really special to be graced by these creatures twice," Raikidan said, half smiling.

I only glared at him in response and put my focus back on the moth. Lifting my finger, I encouraged the moth to move so I could get a better look at it. I studied the moth until I heard Ryoko giggling. A smile appeared on my face. Ryoko had three moths perched on her, and Shva'sika received the same treatment.

I gave Raikidan a sidelong glance. "Guess I'm not as special as you thought, not that it's surprising."

Raikidan shoved his hands into his pockets and looked elsewhere. The moth flapped its wings and fluttered off, pulling my attention away from him. I watched as the eclipse of moths spread out across the meadow and disappeared into the night. The meteor shower was now long gone, and even the fireflies had nestled down into the blades of grass.

The moon and scattered stars were the only things left in the night, and they didn't hold my attention for long. I turned and headed back to the campsite, the excitement of the event quickly fading.

The thick canopy above me rustled in the light breeze. I lay on my back, exposed to the elements, and stared into the darkness of the night. Everyone had gone to bed hours ago, but I still remained awake. I didn't feel the least bit tired, and I was bored. There was no reason for me to be awake.

Sighing, I sat up. There was no point in lying down anymore. I surveyed the campsite. Only Raikidan and I ever chose to sleep outside the tents, and Raikidan didn't really have much of a choice. Why did I always have to be different? It's not like I couldn't sleep in the tent. I just chose not to.

Letting out a heavy breath, I stood and headed out of the campsite. I didn't know where I was going, and frankly I could barely see in front of me to know for sure, but I still stumbled my way through the forest. I continued to pick my way through until my feet brought me to the edge of the meadow.

I gazed around before I cautiously ventured in. There was nothing special about this place, so I wasn't sure why I came here. There was no unusual landmarks, no activity; just the chirring of crickets and peaceful stillness. I sat down and stared up at the starry sky, watching as they twinkled. A strange sensation fell over me. Then I did something I never thought I'd do at a time like this.

"I wish you were here, mother," I whispered. "I really need your guidance. I need help. You were the only one who ever understood. You were the only one who could help me when I was lost and uncertain... When feelings I didn't understand put me in states of confusion, you knew what to do. Why did you have to go? I wasn't ready to lose the only normal thing in my life. Why can't you come back and help me? Why am I not deemed ready to see you?" My lip trembled. "What am I doing wrong?"

The stars' twinkling was the only response I received. I sighed and pulled my legs up to my chest. I was on my own, again. Not even the one person who had ever truly understood me could help anymore. I felt... alone.

Surprise shot through me when Raikidan plopped down beside me. He didn't speak. He didn't even acknowledge me. I didn't know how to react to him being here. It would be stupid of me to think he didn't hear what I had just said, but why wasn't he saying anything?

"Eira, I'm sorry for upsetting you," he didn't look at me as he spoke quietly.

I stared at the ground. Could I forgive him? I swallowed. Of course I could. It wasn't like it was him I was actually mad at. He just made a good scapegoat, and that wasn't fair.

"Don't be, Rai. I'm the one who's sorry." He looked at me this time but I averted my gaze. "I shouldn't have hurt you. I should have heard you out. You're right. You'd have no reason to spy."

"Eira, don't take it like that. You're a beautiful woman. I didn't mean for it to sound otherwise."

I shook my head. "What would you know, Raikidan? You're a dragon. You don't think like us humans."

"Just because I don't think exactly like you, doesn't make it any less true. You see how the men react to you at work."

"They treat me like an object. I'm hard to get, and that makes it some exciting game to them. What more do they have to see?" I turned my gaze to the sky. "Not that it matters. I don't even care anyway."

Raikidan didn't respond this time, and I was okay with that. I didn't like talking about me. I didn't see a point in it. Lying back, I closed my eyes. I'd sleep here tonight. I doubted anything bad would happen, and Raikidan would more than likely leave to sleep elsewhere.

My eyes snapped opened when he proved me wrong, like always. I watched as he moved his large scaly body around me and laid his head next to me. It was that strange circle he was doing again. I watched as he readjusted himself until he was comfortable and closer to me, much closer to me than I would have thought he'd try. I could feel the muscles in his neck move as he breathed, and his hot breath on my skin. The feeling was soothing, not uncomfortable in the least. I didn't even feel confined, although I knew I should have.

Reaching up, I rested my hand on his warm scales and closed my eyes. A low, growling purr rumbled through his chest, soothing and helping me drift into unconsciousness.

CHAPTER 4

The breeze was light as it blew through the forest. The afternoon sun filtered through the canopy casting scattered light throughout the forest floor. The sounds of birds chirping filled my ears as I strolled through the thicket.

Rylan had managed to patch things up a little bit with Ryoko, and in an attempt to fix everything between them, he insisted on going on a hike with just her. Shva'sika of course chose to follow in secret so nothing bad would happen. This left Raikidan and me to figure out what to do with ourselves. Not that our time together lasted long.

At some point, he had gone off to do his own thing without saying a word, and I went on a walk of my own. I liked having this time alone; it allowed me to clear my head.

Above me, a bird called out to the forest with a small tune but didn't get a response. It sang again, and I frowned when it received no reply. It continued to try to find another bird of its kind, to no avail, and I felt bad. To be that alone… I knew how that felt.

My ears pricked when a bird called out in response to the one above me and I smiled. At least the bird wasn't alone. More than I could say for myself. It was hard being different. *It is what it is. No use moping over what can't be changed.*

I looked down at the ground when I kicked something. Spotting the stick, I picked it up to inspect. It was rather large for one you'd find randomly laying around on the ground. But based on one of the jagged ends I could only assume something large broke it off a tree.

I continued to look the stick over and wondered if I could make it into something. It had been quite a while since I had whittled. I doubted I'd make anything spectacular, but it wouldn't hurt to brush up.

Finding a spot under a large tree I drew a dagger. It wasn't the perfect tool, but it'd do. The songs of the forest surrounded me, and I found myself singing along as I whittled. My tune changed to one an old friend, Lakon, had made in the past and it had me thinking about him and what he was up to. Like Rylan, Lakon's passion had always been music, not fighting. His wife, Alyra, and his best friend, Devon, also former soldiers, shared his passion, and they created a band to pass the time. When they escaped Zarda's grasp and changed their records, they used their band to their advantage and became rather successful, the last I had heard. How they'd managed it was beyond me.

My singing and reminiscing stopped when footsteps approached. It appeared my time alone was now done.

"Why did you stop singing?"

I gazed up at Raikidan as he stood over me. In his hands were two dead rabbits. "I don't sing around others."

He sat down. "How come? Your voice is nice."

"Because it's a personal thing for me."

"Why?"

"Why does it matter?"

"Because there's usually a purpose to what you do, or why you think a certain way. Most are fairly open with their ability to sing if they have it, but you're the exact opposite. Why is that?"

I shrugged. "I've just never liked singing in front of others, so it just became something I only do alone."

"All right. What are you making there?"

I looked at the stick in my hand that wasn't becoming much of anything and shrugged. "Nothing."

He chuckled. "Was it supposed to be something?"

"No, not really. Just something to pass the time while I think."

"Fair enough." He held out a rabbit for me. "Hungry?"

I smiled and took the offering.

"So, can I ask you something?"

I chuckled. "You mean you weren't asking questions before?"

He pushed me. "Don't start."

"All right, all right, what's your question?"

"How come you follow the Council?" he asked. "It's obvious by the way you think and act and got all upset weeks ago that we weren't getting enough done, that you and they don't work well together."

I cocked my head. "What brought this up?"

He shrugged. "Just something I've been thinking about."

"Okay…"

"So, you're not going to tell me?"

"No, I didn't say that. I'm just confused."

Raikidan chuckled. "That's because you're overthinking. It doesn't matter why I'm asking."

"Yeah it does."

"You're suspicious."

"When your motives and the motives of the ones you follow are questioned, wouldn't you be suspicious?" I asked.

He looked at me funny. "I'm not really questioning your motives. I just want to know why you follow someone you don't get along with. It seems like a similar situation with Zarda, just they're not cruel."

I snorted. "They're a whole lot different than Zarda."

"Tell me why that is. Why do you follow them even when you're angry? Why don't you go rogue, or elect someone else to run things?"

I sighed. "Well, one, going rogue is a bad idea. I told you, attempting to take Zarda down on your own is a suicide mission. So we need to work as a group, even if we don't agree or if things don't go as we hope."

"So why not replace the Council?" he asked.

"Because it's not that easy. The Council has experience others could only wish they could obtain. They know how to keep such a large organization together when others would fail and destroy us unintentionally. I may not agree with some of the Council's decisions, or the pace we take, but that doesn't mean I think they should be replaced. I'd never want to be in their shoes. I wouldn't want to have to do all that managing. It's hard enough managing a small squad, let alone a platoon, or larger." My gaze lowered and a small smile spread across my face. "I don't even know how my mother did it. It's just not something I've ever been good at."

"I'm sure you did fine," Raikidan encouraged. "You do great with keeping your friends' heads on straight."

I chuckled. "Barely."

He patted me on the shoulder. "I'm confident you could put the Council to shame."

I grunted and ate more of my rabbit.

"So, what does the Council gain from all this?" Raikidan asked.

I raised an eyebrow. "Huh?"

"Everyone has a motive. Everyone wants to gain something from this. You want your freedom, as do the others. But the Council puts in all this effort to keep the rebellion going. They took up the position as leaders. So when Zarda falls, what happens to them? I'm not convinced they'd just up and hand over power to someone."

I chuckled. "You're probably right. While I don't know their true motives, just like I don't know the underlying motives of anyone who participates in the rebellion, I can't disagree that they wouldn't want to give up what they have. But, they also won't just up and take power. That would make them no better than Zarda, and no one would back them if they did."

"So, what do you think they'll do?" Raikidan asked.

"My guess, they'll propose an offer to the citizens that would allow them all to keep the power. I doubt after this is over, anyone will be willing to trust a single person in charge, or at the very least, allow them to stay in power for a long period of time. We'll want to have a choice on who rules us. Vote on it maybe. I'm not really sure. As organized as our cause is, that's not something that's ever been discussed."

"How would you like to see it go?" he asked.

I went back to eating the rest of my rabbit as I thought his question over. "Honestly, I don't care what type of ruling we have, as long as whoever in charge is fair to both ordinary citizens and experiments. I want to see everyone, including ordinary humans, treated fairly and with respect."

Raikidan nodded. "You want a center of peace then."

I gazed down at my hands. "I know it won't be easy to get others to see past the differences, but that doesn't mean things should stay the way they are. No one should be ostracized for being different."

Raikidan watched me and I didn't like it. I should have worded that differently so this wouldn't have happened. *That was really dumb of me.*

Raikidan stood suddenly. "Let's go for walk."

I cocked my head. "Huh?"

"Earlier I found a few places you might like to see before we head back to the city. I want to show you them. What do you say?"

I smiled and stood. "I'd love to."

CHAPTER 5

Shva'sika led the way down a narrow path in the woods. After doing our own things yesterday, we had decided today to take a group hike, but agreed to stay away from the river. We ended up choosing a random direction and found this overgrown path as a result. Now our curiosity was getting the better of us.

We stopped when we came to a small clearing. A strange, but familiar sensation ran through my body, though I wasn't sure why. Nothing in particular jumped out as out of the ordinary.

Shva'sika ventured into the clearing with her hand held up, making me wonder. "Laz, are you also feeling something?"

I nodded as I picked my way through the rest of the underbrush and entered the clearing. "You don't think…"

She turned and smiled at me with the biggest grin I'd seen from her in a long time. "Yeah, I think it is."

I found myself smiling just as wide. If it was true, then this was a huge find.

"Uh, guys, either of you going to tell us what it is that's been found?" Ryoko said.

Shva'sika smiled at her. "A Library entrance."

Ryoko tilted her head. "A what?"

Raikidan looked at me funny as he also wandered into the clearing. "But, there's no building."

I chuckled. "There doesn't have to be. The Library is an entity all on its own. It doesn't exist in just one place. Remember, I told you there were multiple entrances. Buildings are usually constructed around the entrances to protect them, but they're not necessary."

"Why isn't it necessary?" Rylan asked.

"The Library is a living essence," Shva'sika explained. "No one knows how it came to be or how it exists, but it does, and it's quite capable of thinking and protecting itself."

"How does it know how to protect itself?" Ryoko asked.

I went to respond, but instead drew a dagger and managed to turn in time to block a translucent sword swinging down on me. A translucent half-elven man clad in ancient armor held the sword, and he didn't look too thrilled to see us. Ryoko and Rylan backed up a little, and Raikidan went to advance but Shva'sika rushed over to hold him back.

"Trespassers, identify yourselves," the armored man ordered. "Or meet an untimely end."

I used a great deal of strength to push him away. "Usually it's best to say that before attacking."

"Identify yourselves," he repeated.

Shva'sika stepped forward. "My name is Elarinya. We're not your enemies, Guardian."

The armored man lowered his guard as he regarded her. "You are a member of the Lightshine family, are you not?"

Shva'sika nodded with a smile. "Yes."

The man sheathed his sword away. "I apologize. I meant no disrespect toward a fellow Guardian."

"It's quite all right. You're just doing your job."

"Can someone tell me what's going on?" Ryoko begged.

I hushed her. "Not now, Ryoko."

The translucent man gazed at me and his eyes widened. Before I knew it he collapsed to one knee. "My lady, please forgive me for attacking you. Had I realized, I wouldn't have. I meant no disrespect."

My brow rose. "Uh, it's okay. No harm done."

Raikidan snorted. "He tried to kill you. You shouldn't just forgive him so easily."

"It's not a big deal, Raikidan, really."

The man chuckled. "Your champion is far less forgiving than you. I thank you."

"Champion?" I looked at Shva'sika for answers but she shrugged in response.

The man stood. "I shouldn't block your way any longer. You must have important things to do in the Library."

"Actually, we didn't know it was here," I said. "We just stumbled upon it."

"Ryoko, don't touch that!" Shva'sika shrieked.

I turned to see Ryoko halting her reach toward a tiny crystal sticking out of the ground. "What? Why?"

I exhaled and walked over to her. "Because that's a Spiritual Crystal. Anyone who isn't experienced with the spiritual plane can be seriously harmed by one if they touch it." I knelt to get a closer look. "Although, I have to admit, this is a rather tiny crystal."

"The ones at each shaman village are the only large ones left," Shva'sika explained.

"But why is it here?" Ryoko asked. Shva'sika and I looked pointedly. She blinked and then gazed at the translucent Guardian before nodding with understanding. "Ooh, he's dead."

I rolled my eyes and the Guardian laughed.

"So what do Spiritual Crystals do?" Rylan asked.

"They can be used as anchors for spirits to access the living plane in a physical manner, or to allow those with spirit-walking abilities to access knowledge from the spiritual world without having to walk the plane," Shva'sika explained.

I pursed my lips. "But Maka'shi was using the Spiritual Crystal in the village when I was there last, and she looked to be walking the plane."

Shva'sika smiled. "Are you sure?"

"Her eyes were unfocused."

"Just unfocused, though?"

I nodded slowly, understanding. "All right, I get it."

"So, Mr. Dead Guy," Ryoko began, "do you use this crystal to protect this Library entrance?"

The translucent man chuckled at the name she'd given him. "My name is Lazei, and yes, I use it to protect the entrance. I swore to protect this entrance with my life, and was granted the ability to protect it in death as well."

"Who gave you that ability?" Ryoko inquired.

"I'm afraid I can't share that with you."

Ryoko pouted, and Lazei chuckled.

"So, is he the protection for the Library you were talking about, Shva'sika?" Rylan asked.

She shook her head. "No. Guardians help, but not all entrances have them. The Library is capable of protecting itself if it needs to."

"Just like that?" he sounded skeptical, unsurprisingly.

Shva'sika chuckled. "You really don't want to know what the Library would do to someone who was trying to get in to destroy its contents."

Ryoko gestured toward me. "Worse than what Laz would do?"

Shva'sika nodded. "Laz's treatment would seem like a snuggly kitty."

"Damn."

"Can we see this Library?" Rylan asked. "I know it was our plan to hike, but it sounds interesting."

Ryoko nodded enthusiastically. "I agree, and I don't like libraries."

I grinned. "You'll like this one."

"I'll show you in," Lazei announced.

We voiced our thanks, and followed him to the other side of the tiny clearing. He walked right for a large oak tree, but before he reached it, the space around him distorted. It was as if he was walking into vertical standing water. He then disappeared. Ryoko, Rylan and Raikidan halted for a moment, out of shock, but when Shva'sika and I walked through, they were sure to quickly follow. I glanced around once we were inside the Library. We were in a room, which surprised me. In my times coming in here, I had never come across a room.

The room had the typical crystalline floors, and the ceiling was also made of crystal. I couldn't identify the material the walls were made of, as they were filled wall-to-wall with bookcases. The shelves of the bookcases contained various books and scrolls, and in the center of the room was a large table with a map painted on it.

Curious about the table, I ventured over. I ran my fingers over the lacquer as I admired the map. It didn't look like Lumaraeon, but it'd be illogical for it not to be, making it quite old.

"Laz." I looked at Shva'sika when she called my name to find her pulling out large, rolled-up papers that appeared weathered and old. "Look what I found."

My eyes lit up. "Maps!"

Raikidan's brow knitted together and Ryoko giggled. "Laz loves her maps."

I took the maps from Shva'sika and laid them out on the table. Raikidan joined me, and I compared the diagrams with him while Lazei watched. I wasn't sure why he was sticking around, but I only cared about the maps at the moment.

With Raikidan's help, I was able to lay the maps out in what appeared to be chronological order. Some of the maps had writing in Elvish, and Raikidan thankfully was able to read what I couldn't translate myself, since Shva'sika was now engrossed in her own findings. Some others were in Dwarvish, which Raikidan was also capable of translating. But most of the maps had writing in Old Tongue, so it was impossible to know for certain if we had the order right.

Raikidan and I traced the maps and compared them. I was having fun, and from what I could tell, Raikidan found it fun too. It was nice seeing at least one person enjoy looking at maps, even if it wasn't as much as me. I wasn't sure why I liked them. I wasn't sure why I liked paper ones more than digital ones either. *It's probably because I'm weird.*

I glanced up when Ryoko gasped. She had a large book in her hands and her eyes shone with joy. Her ears also twitched, indicating the level of her excitement.

Lazei appeared behind her and peered over her shoulder before looking at me. "Entry about wogrons."

I chuckled. "I'm not surprised. Her ears are twitching. That only happens when she's excited, and wogron entries excite her the most these days."

"She hasn't been exposed to all the grand things in life," Shva'sika remarked slyly. "I'm thinking there's going to be at least one other thing to get her ears twitching."

I belted out a hearty laugh, understanding what she was insinuating, though Ryoko was too engrossed with her find to hear the sexual tease, disappointing Shva'sika a little. Rylan, on the other hand, had heard, and his face reddened a bit as he stared at Shva'sika, keeping her from being completely disappointed.

Raikidan began carefully rolling the maps up when there wasn't any reason to continue looking at them and I helped. When we had them put away I searched through the books on the shelves of the bookcase until one in particular caught my eye. It looked so old—far older than any book I had ever laid eyes on.

I dusted the book off and set on the table as Raikidan pulled up a chair for himself and me. He seemed just as interested.

"What do you have there?" Shva'sika asked.

"I'm not sure yet." I ran my hand over the leather cover. "The title is in Old Tongue."

This made her curious, and she abandoned her find to sit with us. Even Lazei appeared a bit curious. I opened the book and my eyes lit up. The contents were written in Old Tongue and, after making an attempt, I found out rather quickly the Library wasn't capable of reading it out to me.

"You're flipping pages. Can the Library not read it to you?" Shva'sika asked.

I shook my head. "This book was handwritten."

"That's rare," Shva'sika said. "Even for Old Tongue entries."

I nodded. "I don't think any scholars have seen this book before."

"I don't think anyone has been in this room in forever," Ryoko voiced as she put her book away to come over and investigate our find. "All these books and scrolls are covered in an even layer of dust that's so thick, I don't want to think how long they've been here."

I nodded as I flipped another page. "That would make sense. I didn't even know the Library had rooms."

Rylan's brow twisted. "Room? You mean there's more connected parts?"

I pointed to the doorway that led to the rest of the Library. "Go take a look out there."

He and Ryoko did as I asked, and Ryoko gasped. "Whoa…"

I chuckled and desperately searched for some sort of translation in here.

"Any words you recognize?" Shva'sika whispered.

I shook my head. "No not—wait, this here." I pointed to a particular word.

"What does it say?"

"*Mukarna.* 'Makers.'"

Raikidan's brow rose. "Makers? What's that?"

"We're not fully sure," Shva'sika admitted. "There are few texts on them, and all of them are in Old Tongue, so only Scholars are capable of deciphering them. What we do know, is none are around anymore and they had amazing craftsman skills. Some say they had the ability to craft anything from a god's weapon, and some even believe they were the ones to create the Dragon's Eye gems."

Ryoko looked at me. "Isn't that the gem you have?"

I nodded. "Yes. They have incredible power, if you know how to use them. But once they're used, they're gone. They've become extremely rare over the millennia, due to the lack of knowledge on how to make them."

Lazei took great interest in my words. "You have one of the legendary Dragon's eye gems?"

I nodded. "I guess they were around when you were alive then?"

"Yes. They were rare in my time, too. Can I see it?"

I hesitated, but didn't see how it could hurt to fulfill his request, and pulled out the one that was left from my bag. Lazei's eyes lit up at the sight.

"Laz, where's the other one?" Shva'sika asked.

"You had two?" Lazei appeared unable to believe that.

"I… used it," I admitted quietly.

Shva'sika tilted her head. "You used it? On what?"

I wasn't sure if I should tell her. I wasn't ashamed of what I had done, but I wasn't sure if Raikidan—

"She used it as a tribute," Raikidan said.

Shva'sika's brow rose. "Tribute? You mean for the alliance with the shamans?"

I went to respond, but Raikidan spoke for me. "No, for Pyralis. That's why we went to the South."

"Pyralis? You're joking, right?" Ryoko couldn't believe us. "No one knows where his grave is."

"The dragons do," Raikidan said.

"But, if that was the reason you left, why didn't you just tell me when you came back, instead of saying you never reached your initial destination?" Shva'sika questioned.

"Because I promised I wouldn't." I went back to looking at the book. Everyone took that as a sign to drop the topic.

"It's a shame we can't take this out," Shva'sika murmured. "We know quite a few scholars who would love to see this."

I nodded. "I really want to know what this book says myself."

"Laz has a bit of an obsession with the Makers," Shva'sika whispered to Ryoko.

Heat rushed to my face. "I do not!"

Ryoko giggled and whispered back, "It's probably 'cause Ryder shows signs of being one."

I gave her a stern look. "He's not a Maker. At least not this kind."

"Then tell me, how did he make that special weapon of yours?" Ryoko challenged.

I shrugged. "I don't know. He won't tell me."

"Won't?"

I nodded. "I've asked several times, since it's so unique, but he says it's a secret." I rubbed my chin with my thumb. "Now that I think about it, he never tells me how he's done any of his projects."

"That's strange," Ryoko said. "He's usually open with you."

I nodded as I thought about this.

"What are his limitations?" Lazei asked.

I shrugged. "I don't know. For all I know, he could make the first flawlessly-working plasma gun."

"Since he was able to make a shifting weapon that has the ability to become more than one, I can't disagree with that possibility," Rylan agreed.

"Sounds like a Maker to me," Lazei said.

Ryoko held out her hands to him. "Thank you."

I shook my head and put the book away. There hadn't been Makers in forever. There was no way Ryder was one. Besides, wouldn't that mean Rylan or I would be a Maker as well? I shook those ludicrous ideas away and ventured out into the Library. Today would be a good day to read. No one else protested.

6

CHAPTER

I plopped down on the couch with a sigh. We had only just gotten back from our vacation, and I had a lot of planning and catching up to do. Genesis had informed me she might have something for us to do later in the evening, while at the same time managing to avoid my question about the pace of the rebellion. That type of reaction had me assuming the Council was either still "talking" about it, or not listening to the concern, which was irritating to think about. But at the moment, I didn't have as much of a care about it as I normally would. I only cared about curling up and going to bed.

We had come back in a rush, and I wasn't even sure why. One moment, I had been sleeping peacefully by the dead fire, and the next moment I was shaken awake and pushed to pack so we could get back to the city. No one had told me why, but I knew by the quickness of the pace Ryoko set, something was up. We had made it back here in record time, but nothing was amiss when we made it home, so I couldn't understand what the rush had been about. Now I had no energy and couldn't think about important things.

My heavy lids closed, but before I had to force myself to wake up, the sound of footsteps on the basement floor did it for me. The door creaked open and, to my surprise, a lean woman with mocha skin, crimson eyes, and shoulder-length black-and-red hair strolled into the living room.

"Hey, Aurora," Rylan greeted from his spot at the bar.

"Hey, babe."

I flicked my gaze to the window to find the sun still casting orange and purple hues across the skyline. "It's not like you to leave the underground before dark."

Aurora shrugged. "It's close enough. Where's Ryoko? I have something for her."

I went to respond, but Ryoko poked her head out of her room before I could. "I heard someone was looking for me?"

Aurora reached into the messenger bag she carried, and pulled out a white bottle with no label. "I brought what you asked for."

Ryoko's eyes lit up, and she went over to Aurora to take the bottle. "Thanks. I was in dire need of those."

I eyed the bottle suspiciously. Something didn't feel right about this bottle. "Ryoko what is that?"

Ryoko waved me off. "It's nothing, don't worry about it."

I stood. "Ryoko, tell me what is in that bottle."

"Seriously, Laz, it's nothing."

"Tell me."

"Why should I? It's none of your business."

I stepped forward. "Don't make me turn that into an order."

Ryoko gasped. "You promised you'd never do that!"

"You never gave me a reason to. You've never done anything suspicious."

"I told you it's nothing to worry about! What's your problem?"

I ignored her question and switched my attention to Aurora. I didn't want to have to order Ryoko to tell me. It wasn't fair. But asking Aurora, while not fair of me either, wasn't off limits. "Aurora?"

"Don't you say a word, Aurora," Ryoko ordered.

I narrowed my eyes. Now I knew something was up. Aurora's eyes flicked between us. She looked torn, and I felt sorry for her. This situation wasn't fair for her, but I needed to know what Ryoko was hiding. "Aurora, what's going on?"

Aurora bit her lip.

"You promised," Ryoko pleaded.

I was getting sick of this. "Now, Aurora!"

"They're anti-transformation pills!" She gasped and held her hands up to her mouth.

"Aurora!" Ryoko shrieked.

"I'm sorry. I can't ignore her order over yours. You know that."

I stared at the two of them in disbelief. "A—anti-transformation pills? Tell me you're joking." Aurora's gaze fell to the floor and shook her head. I exhaled slowly and glared at Ryoko. "What are you doing with anti-transformation pills?"

Ryoko backed up toward her room. "It's none of your business."

I advanced with my hand held out. "Give them to me."

"No."

I narrowed my eyes and rushed over the couch. "Now, Ryoko!"

"Screw you. What I'm using them for is none of your business."

"You have no need for them, unless you're hiding something from me. Like a particular promise you made me."

"Screw off and leave me alone!"

I scowled. "Give it to me, now."

"Go to hell."

"That's enough!" Ryoko and I looked down the hall to see Genesis standing in the middle of it, her black hair hanging freely around her tiny form, and her livid eyes bearing into all of us. "I'm ending this right now. Ryoko keeps the pills." Ryoko stuck her tongue out at me, but sucked it back in when Genesis continued. "But it will be the last she gets. Aurora, you are not to give her any more. I don't care the reason for her having them. Those must be obtained from active scientists, and they are much too dangerous to continue to get. There will be no negotiating this. Now, I'm sending you all out on weapons pick-up duty, and Laz and Ryoko will be split up."

"Fine by me," I snarled.

I headed for the basement door, but Genesis stopped me. "Raikidan will go with you. Rylan will go with Ryoko. Seda will tell you where to find the weapons, and where to drop them off."

"Whatever."

I thundered down the stairs and headed for the secret passage. The sooner I got this done, the sooner I could get to bed and forget all about this.

A thick fog obscured my vision. I wandered around in hopes to find something,

even if it was just a rock or a shrub, but I found nothing. I didn't know where I was, or how I ended up here. It didn't feel like a place I should be. It felt... forbidden.

"What are you doing here?" I spun around but didn't see anyone. "What are you doing here?"

I spun back around when the voice came from behind me, but again I was only met by fog. "Who's there?"

In the fog, a black form appeared, and as it ventured closer, I was able to make out the shape of a man. My brow furrowed when the shape came into full view. It was Raikidan, but it also wasn't. There was something weird about him. His eyes were emotionless and dull, and his hair had no red in it anywhere. He looked guarded and cold.

"How did you get here?" Raikidan asked. "You are no Dreamwalker."

Dreamwalker? I had no idea what he was talking about. "Raikidan, where am I?"

"I see." I blinked with confusion at his strange reply. "He pulled you here."

I tilted my head. "Raikidan, what are you talking about?"

"If he brought you here, then you are welcome. I will not bother you anymore."

"Raikidan, no—wait!" My plea came too late. He disappeared back into the fog, and I was alone again. "Great. Now what do I do?"

Letting out a quiet breath, I continued to wonder around. It wasn't long before I noticed the fog dispersing and I heard quiet voices. I came to a halt when two people came into view. One person was Raikidan, and the other was me, but there was something strange about this Eira. Something... not human about her. Curious about what was going on, I stayed quiet and watched.

"Eira, what is it?" Raikidan asked. "What did you want to talk to me about?"

The Eira he talked to smiled. "Not talk to you about. Show you."

Raikidan shook his head with a chuckle. "All right then, what did you want to show me?"

Eira pulled out a small white bottle from a pouch that hung from her belt loop. "I've been keeping something from you. Something I don't think it necessary to keep anymore."

"Eira?"

Eira stepped back and let the white bottle drop to the ground. The bottle broke open and blue and red pills spilled out everywhere.

"I stopped taking these a while ago. They no longer affect me. They no longer hide the truth."

Raikidan took a small step forward, taking a great interest in what this Eira was doing. Eira closed her eyes, and her body morphed. I watched as she became a magnificent purple-and-blue-scaled creature, and noticed a small, delighted smile spread across Raikidan's face as he gazed upon the dragon before him. Pain flared in my chest. The pain grew when he, too, shifted to his dragon form and touched noses with her, while moving his body closer. This affection increased to playful behavior Raikidan had never shown toward the human version of me. Deep down, something told me this was more than a nightmare—it was a little more real than that.

All Raikidan wanted was for me to be a dragon, even if I was a different color. He wanted me to be something I'm not. He couldn't accept that I was human. He couldn't accept me as me, like everyone else. My chest felt like it was being squeezed. What I was, what everyone saw me as, was never good enough for anyone. No matter what I did was never good enough. Why could I never please anyone?

I had to get away from this. I couldn't handle it. Spinning on my heels, I made a hasty retreat. I didn't know where I was going, but I also didn't care. I just wanted the fog to come back and hide what I had seen. The fog did return, but the memory remained.

"You want to leave," a familiar masculine voice stated.

I glanced back to see Raikidan casually strolling next to me, except it wasn't the Raikidan I had just been watching. This was the Raikidan I had met in the fog.

My lip curled. "I walk my nightmares alone. Leave me."

This Raikidan tilted his head. "You think this is a nightmare?"

"I live a nightmare. I know when I am not accepted as I am. I know when I am not wanted. I will remain alone and go where no one can follow."

"I can show you the way out."

"I require no help, especially not from the likes of you."

Raikidan stopped following at my words, but I continued on. The fog thinned and a bright light began to shine through the gray. When the fog dispersed, I was left standing at the edge of a lake. I gazed around at the familiar setting.

The grass was green and the sand was soft. The dark water lapped on the shore before me, and also washed on the shore of a large island in the center. On the island was a large, stone building that resembled a temple, but I didn't know for sure. I never went there.

I came here a lot lately. Whenever a nightmare ended, I found myself here. And when one was about to start it'd disappear. But this time my nightmare didn't end. My mind remained on the event that I had witnessed.

Raikidan made it seem that he wanted to be my friend. He made it seem he actually liked me for me. But the truth always came out eventually. The truth was, I was alone in this world. Alone. It's what I was meant to be. There were no lies here. No betrayal. No pain. It was safe.

Footsteps crunched on the ground behind me, and a voice I didn't want to hear spoke, "Eira?"

I scowled. "Go away."

"Eira, please don't say that," Raikidan begged.

"I want to be alone."

"No you don't."

"What would you know? You're too caught up with your hopes and dreams."

"Eira, let me explain."

I threw my arm out to push him away when he touched my shoulder. I bared my teeth at him. "There is nothing to say! I'm not what you want me to be, and I never will be. I'm never what anyone wants me to be..."

"Eira, I—"

I walked away from him. "Leave me alone. I don't need you or your wishes of lies. I don't need anyone. I can be me when I'm alone. There is no pain when I'm alone..."

"Eira," a female voice whispered.

A dark mass formed a little ways before me. A small smile crept onto my face. I knew this darkness. Normally I ran from it, but this time I walked toward it.

"Eira," the voice called again.

"Eira, don't!" Raikidan cried.

I ignored him and entered the darkness.

"You're safe here," the voice whispered as it embraced me. "There is no pain here."

Emptiness crept into my chest, and my feelings melted away. Darkness was my only comfort, the only place I felt at peace. The light had forsaken me, so I embraced the darkness and smiled as the light slipped away.

7
CHAPTER

I sighed as I flipped the page of my book. Normally I would have let it turn on its own, but I needed something to do. That strange dream I had last night controlled my thoughts, and Ryoko and I were still on bad terms. I had kept to myself all day, but the lonely sensation clinging to my chest bothered me. And for once, I couldn't explain it.

I rarely sought out the company of others, always preferring to be alone, and last night's dream reminded me why. So why was I not okay with being alone now? Why, after what I had dreamt, would I want someone around? It didn't make sense.

The muffled sound of something large falling brought my attention back to reality. I looked at everyone else in the room, but they appeared just as confused.

"I think it came from Genesis' and my room," Seda said.

I leaned over the couch. "Gen, everything all right?"

The only response I received was another thumping sound. Ryoko slid off the barstool and took a few steps into the hallway, but stopped when something hit Seda and Genesis' room door. Ryoko and I passed each other a glance and then peered back down the hall.

Suddenly, the door flew open, and a tall, ebony-haired woman came stumbling out of the room. I was about to get up to walk over to the stranger to figure out what she was doing here, when I noticed the long pigtails and red ribbons. "Genesis?"

Ryoko looked at me funny. "Something wrong with your eyes? That can't be her."

Slowly, Genesis lifted her gaze from her wobbly feet, a large grin plastered on her face. "I did it! I figured it out!" She went to take a step forward, but she fell over and the two of us laughed at her. "Though, getting used to walking with these new legs isn't easy."

"Well you did skip the slow, growing-up stage to get used to it," Ryoko said.

"And the clothes," I teased, looking at her appearance.

She was still wearing her little-girl nightshirt and pants, and they were much too small for her now.

Genesis rubbed her arm. "Yeah, about that. Do you guys mind if I borrow some clothes? Seda's aren't going to fit me."

"Sure," Ryoko said, making her way to her room. "I'll get you some pants and shorts."

"I'll grab you some shirts," I said. "We can get you your own wardrobe later when you learn to walk right."

"And I'll help her up and teach her how to walk properly," Seda offered.

Genesis laughed. "All right. Thanks, you three. Eira, let me know when Ryder stops by, so I can thank him. You have no idea how much I hated being stuck in a child's body."

I chuckled. "I think I do, but you giving him thanks for smuggling that out would be nice."

I slipped into my room and headed straight for my closet. There was bound to be something for her in there, if I could find it through the trove of unnecessary dresses and other clothes I'd never wear.

"What's bothering you, Eira?"

I turned my head over my shoulder, finding Raikidan watching me from the entrance of my closet. "Nothing is bothering me."

"Then why are you avoiding me?"

I went back to my searching. "I'm not avoiding you, Raikidan. I've just wanted to keep to myself today."

"You're lying to me."

I paused for a moment. "Huh?"

"You heard me. I can tell because you act differently when you just want to be alone, versus when you make it your goal to avoid me."

I turned to face him. "Raikidan—"

My words caught when I almost crashed into him. Within seconds, he had moved so close to me that it went against all my personal space rules, and he hadn't even made a sound doing it.

I exhaled and pushed him away. "You know not to get that close to me."

Raikidan grabbed my hand and closed the space between us again. "And why don't you? What is so wrong about me standing near you? It can't be because you think you'll hurt me. You're fine right now. So what are you afraid of? Why are you avoiding me? What did I do? What am I missing? Help me piece something together here."

I yanked my hand away. "Knock it off, Rai. I've got important things to deal with."

Raikidan remained silent as I rummaged through my clothes. The silence didn't last long, however. "What's so important about you going through your clothes? Seems like you're just avoiding my questions."

I sighed. "Well if you had been out in the living room like everyone else, you would know I'm getting them for Genesis."

"Why would she need them?"

"Because she figured out the plans my son gave her."

"Plans? You mean the ones to make her age?"

"Yes, those ones. She now has the body of an early twenty-something-year-old and has no clothes to fit it."

"How did she figure it out without any of your modern technologies?"

I shrugged. "I don't know. Didn't feel like asking."

"You mean you were avoiding the answer."

I let out a tight breath. "No, I wasn't avoiding it. I just didn't care to ask. Now will you leave me alone?"

Raikidan grabbed the shirts I held and pulled me closer, spinning me around to face him in the process. His hand rested on my hip to prevent me from moving away.

"Raikidan, knock it off," I growled.

"Why are you afraid of this?"

"I'm not afraid. I just like my space."

"You can't lie to me, Eira."

My lip curled. "I'm not lying!"

"You have to have a reason for wanting your space."

"That doesn't mean I'm afraid of something. Fear doesn't have to be a drive."

"But it's what drives you."

I shoved him away as hard as I could, almost losing the clothes I had gathered. "I don't know what you're problem is today, Raikidan, but I'll only say this once more. Knock it off and leave me be!"

I stormed out of the closet and into the living room. Seda was waiting and took the clothes from me without a word, but I knew she was staying quiet on purpose. I didn't doubt everyone had heard our little fight. I had left the door open, after all.

I sat back on the couch with a grunt and flipped aimlessly through the channels on the TV. Ten channels later, I was already bored and I sighed. Today was just a bad day.

Someone knocked on the doorframe of the staircase that led down to the front door, but I wasn't interested in who was visiting until Shva'sika spoke. "Laz, I think you have a visitor."

I turned to see a young man with crew-cut white hair and blue and green heterochromic eyes standing in the doorway. I smiled. "Hey, Ryder."

"Hey, mom," he greeted back.

He looked older, a little younger than me, maybe twenty-five or so. "I see they advanced your age again."

Ryder nodded. "Yeah, but what you see is what you get. My body started reacting negatively, so I'm done aging unless it happens naturally somehow."

I chuckled. "Good. I don't think I could handle it if you looked older than me."

Ryder laughed and then held up a small satchel. "I brought the items you wanted."

"And?"

He exhaled playfully and pulled a sheathed dagger from a leather bag. "And I have your dagger."

I grinned and slid over the back of the couch. Ryder gave me a quick hug before handing over my weapon. The moment it landed in my hand, the weight I expected wasn't there.

"I upgraded it," Ryder said. "It's lighter and should be easier to use. The response time should be much faster."

"It was already fast."

"Well it's faster, trust me. And let me tell you, it was a bit harder than I thought it would be. I don't know why, but something was different about it when I was working on it."

I chuckled. "That's because the blacksmiths at the West Shaman Village took the liberty of trying to make it lighter. My guess, he did something to it to mess with your original design."

"That explains a lot. I also cleaned up the diamond coating on the blade and restored the appearance of the hilt."

I rubbed my hand over his hair. "You didn't have to do this, but thanks."

He pushed my hand away while smiling and handed me the satchel filled with the items I requested. "I got what I could, and then some. Figured the extra might come in handy at some point. What did you need all this for anyway?"

I sifted through the contents before speaking to him. "Come downstairs to help me make something, and you'll find out."

He nodded happily at the invitation and followed. I scattered the contents of the satchel on the oak table and went to a cabinet to grab a few tools.

"So what are we making?" Ryder asked.

"I promised to make something for Shva'sika."

"So you asked me to bring you gems and wire because?"

I laughed and set up a glass pane and sketched on it with a black erasable marker. When the overall design of a circlet was done, I used a green marker to make some final details and then looked at him. "That answer your question?"

Ryder grinned. "I knew I had to have gotten my skills from you. This will be a snap to make between the two of us."

I smiled. "I was hoping you'd say that. At least you don't find the idea dumb and plan to leave."

Ryder shook his head. "Why would I do that?"

I shrugged and picked up a silver wire and needle pliers.

"Mom." I gazed at him when he placed his hand on my shoulder. "I meant it. What reason would I have to think either of those things? I want to do this with you. This idea is great and I'm glad you're including me. I miss doing things with you. I miss having you around. I can't wait for this all to end so we can be together again like you promised."

I continued bending the metal wires into their desired individual shapes, the words I wanted to say lodging in my throat. When complete, I snatched a hammer and smacked a few areas, widening and shaping the metal. "I'm sorry for the choices I've made. If I had made better ones, maybe everything would have been different."

Ryder took a few of the shaped wires and began soldering them into place. "I tried to think of other ways that would have been better. I tried to make myself believe you made the wrong choice and would fix it. But never once could I find a better way. I couldn't find a better way because there wasn't one and I know that now. Now I just have to wait to make up for the time we've missed."

"I'll do my best to make up for it."

"Let me hang out more as a friend and you'll start to."

"Ryder, I don't think—"

"It'll be fine. Zo is my commanding officer. It won't be hard convincing him we're friends and met because of Zane or something like that. I'll think of some story that's believable, even to someone with some intelligence. Zo likes you too much not to believe that you made a friend who knows him."

I groaned. "Not that dummy. I can't stand him."

Ryder snorted. "And I can? I deal with him, and his thoughts that he feels all too inclined to share out loud."

"He won't get the hint."

"Zo is denser than a brick. Others in my company have noticed how you act around him, and can see you want nothing to do with him but that doesn't seem to stop him."

I shook my head. "What will it take for me to get him to leave me alone?"

"Start dating someone."

I snorted. "Like that's ever going to happen."

"Mom, why don't you try to find someone?"

I shook my head. "Please don't bring this up again, Ryder. I've told you, I don't want to talk about that. My reasons are my own."

Ryder sighed. "All right. I just want you to be happy."

"I don't need someone by my side to be happy."

"I hear that guy you spend all your time with is quite protective of you, why not him?"

I gave him a warning glance. "Ryder."

He held up his hands. "All right, all right. I just don't want you to be alone for your whole life."

"I have you and that's all that matters anymore."

Ryder grasped my shoulder briefly before continuing on with his soldering.

"Ryder, tell me something. When did Zo become your commanding officer? I thought you were under someone else."

Ryder halted his work and thought for a moment. "Not long after the first aging process happened. He said he could use my craftsman skills."

"Knowing him, he thinks you'll be able to do the impossible with the gun he's having the boys make down at the shop."

"You know I probably could."

"That's what I'm afraid of." I pressed my lips together. "You have talents no one can explain. You've made me a weapon that shouldn't function the way it does." My eyes flicked to him. "Speaking about that weapon, you still haven't told me how you made it."

He grinned. "It's my personal secret."

I snorted and sorted through the various gems on the table. Finding an emerald of the perfect shape, I wrapped and bent thin wires around it, creating an intricate and elegant design. Ryder took my new design and soldered the wires together to the two separate pieces he had put together. When he was done, I took the new object and gently bent it into its desired shape. While I did this, Ryder cleaned up the table and stuffed the extra materials into the leather bag they had come in.

"Done?" he asked me when he finished.

I shook my head. "Not just yet."

Pulling out a hand rotary tool, I attached a buffing wheel and shined the metal up. Once complete, I held the object up to my mouth, and with a deep breath, exhaled a weak flame to harden the metal. "Now it's done."

Ryder's eyes sparked. "Mom, that was amazing."

My brow knitted. "What was?"

"Breathing that fire. I didn't know you could do that."

Oh, right. I've never done that in front of him. Even though I kept it a secret from others, I never liked keeping secrets from Ryder. *Maybe I just didn't know how to bring it up… like his lineage…* "Not many do, and I intend to keep it that way."

His brow furrowed. "Why?"

"Because not everyone finds it acceptable."

"Mom, what happened to make you think the way you do?"

I shrugged. "I didn't fit in with anyone. Nothing more to say." I held the circlet up. "Now, what do you think of this?"

"It's perfect. And your friend will like it."

"I hope so."

"You won't know until you give it to her."

I headed for the stairs. "All right then, let's find out." I peered around the door when I made it to the top of the stairs. Shva'sika stood by the coffee table, and Ryoko sat at the bar again. "Shva'sika, come over here."

Her brow furrowed. "Why?"

"Because I have something for you. Now get over here," I said. Shva'sika sighed and maneuvered around the couch. "Now close your eyes and hold out your hands."

"Laz."

"Just do it," I ordered. Shva'sika let out an exasperated breath and did as I instructed. "And don't you peek."

Shva'sika's eyes shut tighter as if she'd been caught, and she waited impatiently, her fingers wiggling. I pulled her gift from behind my back, and Ryoko gasped at the sight of the circlet. Shva'sika's interest grew when I placed the gift in her hands.

"All right, you can look."

Shva'sika opened her eyes and her eyes grew wide and sparkled at the sight of the circlet in her hands. Slowly, she examined the head jewelry. "You really made this for me?"

I nodded. "I told you I'd replace your other one. Do you like it?"

"Like?" She threw my arms around me. "I love it!"

Ryder chuckled. "Told you."

"Well if you love it why don't you put it on for us all to see?" Ryoko teased.

Shva'sika let me go and put the circlet around her head. "Well, how do I look?"

"Amazing! You should go see for yourself!"

Shva'sika beamed with delight and dashed off to the bathroom to look at her new jewelry, but stopped when I called after her. "Shva'sika, don't forget to remove that cover-up. We have a deal this week."

Shva'sika chuckled. "Fine, fine."

"Eira, did you really make that?" Raikidan asked from his spot by my bedroom door once Shva'sika closed the door.

I nodded. "Ryder helped, but yes."

"Have you always been able to do stuff like that?"

I nodded, but before I could say anything, Ryoko spoke up. "She sure has. You should see her carvings!"

"Carvings?" Ryder and Raikidan both said.

Ryoko's eyes lit up. She dashed off into her room and came back moments later with two small carvings. One was made of wood and had been carved into the shape of a peacock with a fanned-out tail. The other was of a raging bull made from an ivory nut. Both figurines had un-carved, natural-looking bases, and the details of the carvings were made with great care and precision.

Ryder walked over to Ryoko and took one of the carvings to look over. "Did you really make this?"

I shrugged. "It's nothing. Just something I did in my spare time."

"Nothing? This is amazing!"

"Let me see that," Raikidan said as he strolled over to Ryder. He studied the statue for a few moments before looking at me. "Are you sure you're not from the North?"

I ducked my head, a wave of embarrassment rushing through me. "It's not that great, really."

"Don't be so modest." I peered past the two boys to see Shva'sika standing in the doorway of the bathroom. "One, I love this circlet. It's the most amazing one I've owned so far. And two, you really should think about making more and selling them. The caravans and traveling merchants would be more than happy to sell them for you and split the profits."

"I don't know…"

"Laz, it's a great idea," Ryoko encouraged. "It'd help us get a little more money, that's for sure."

"A little?" Shva'sika laughed. "She could make a fortune off of those carvings and circlets alone."

Ryoko's eyes lit up. "And Laz knows how to make other jewelry, so she'd be making bank!"

"I can get you the supplies," Ryder offered. "It's not that hard to do. Well, the wood and materials for jewelry, at least. Ivory nuts are a little harder to find."

"Guys, I haven't even agreed to this," I said.

My words fell on deaf ears like usual as Shva'sika continued the conversation. "I could find her those. Shamans usually have them stashed away somewhere, or know where the best places to source them."

Ryder nodded. "I'll do that then. I should go anyway. If I stay too long, I'll get in trouble."

I let out a defeated sigh. No one was going to listen to me. "All right, I'll walk you out."

"Wait!" a muffled feminine voice called out. Genesis' bedroom door flew open, and she burst into the hallway. She crashed into Ryder and gave him a tight hug. Ryder, taken by surprise, froze and his face reddened. "Thank you! Thank you, thank you, thank you."

"Uh, I um… uh… you're welcome?" I bit my lip at his loss of words.

Figuring it wasn't nice of me to allow him to stay in such a position, I extracted Genesis away from him and began taking her ribbons from her raven hair. "Gen, you're an adult now. You need to start wearing your hair like one."

"Oh, okay." She grabbed her other pigtail and released the hair from the ribbon.

"All right, now that you've been able to thank Ryder, he has to leave," I said.

"Okay, thanks again, Ryder!"

Ryder didn't respond verbally. He only blinked and stared at her. Shaking my head, I pushed him toward the door. As I ushered him away he took one more look back at Genesis before having to focus on walking down the stairs.

"She's too old for you," I whispered.

"Mother!" he hissed, his face reddening again.

I snickered. "I'm not blind, and neither am I stupid. She's too old for you. The body you've allowed her to finally have may be young, but after she gets used to it, she'll start to act more her age, and that's more than ten times mine, let alone yours."

"Mom, stop. I don't even know her."

I chuckled and opened the front door. "Just don't get any ideas, okay?"

"Just calm down, Eira, will you? I'm not going to be late."

I sighed. Now that we were outside, our normal conversations were going to have to be different. "I just don't want you to get into trouble because of me."

"You're my friend, Eira, I could care less if I got into trouble because of you."

I shook my head. "Well I'd rather you not, so get going."

Ryder smiled. "Sure. I'll stop by on my next time off and I'll bring those supplies you were interested in."

I smiled back. "I'd like that. Just don't go overboard. I can get them myself, too."

Ryder gave me a quick wave and ran off. I waved back, even though he couldn't see it, and watched him disappear into the city. As I turned to head inside, I noticed two soldiers observing me. *That would explain Ryder's sudden change in conversation.* Why they were here, I couldn't say, nor could I figure out why they were watching me. They weren't hiding the fact that they were, and there were several people on the street who could have distracted them at any point in time.

Not feeling comfortable with this, I slipped back into the house. Once I reached the living room, I noticed Argus standing in the hallway.

"Aren't you supposed to be at the shop?"

Argus nodded. "Normally yes, but Zane's been acting weird lately. He's been closing the shop early and today he hasn't left his room at all. He won't acknowledge anyone who's knocked on the door, so I came out to look for you to see if you can talk to him."

I shrugged. "I can try. Won't guarantee anything."

"Trying is all I ask."

I walked past him and headed down the long, twisted hallway. When I reached Zane's room, I rapped on the door. When I didn't receive an answer I rapped louder. "Uncle? Uncle?" I grunted when I didn't get an answer. "Uncle, I know you're in there. Now open up!"

"You can come in," came his quiet reply. "It's unlocked."

My brow furrowed. I opened the door slowly. Zane sat on his bed, fully clothed for a full day's work. He didn't acknowledge me when I came in. He didn't do more than stare at his hands.

I shut the door. "Zane, what's going on?"

"I don't know what you're talking about." He didn't look up from his hands as he spoke.

"Cut the shit. Argus says you've been acting weird, and now you won't even look at me."

Zane sucked air through his teeth. "Eira, can you tell me the color of my work clothes?"

I stared at him. Had he really asked me that? "Uncle?"

He worked his jaw. "And can you tell me if it's day or night?"

I was by his side, holding his face in seconds. I forced him to look at me. What I saw terrified me. His gaze was unfocused and dull. "U–uncle?"

Zane sighed and pulled my hands from his face. "I can't see anything anymore, Eira. My sight is all gone."

"How long?"

"Do you remember when your mother told you I had to retire because of an accident?"

"Of course. You still limp a little from it."

"Yes, well, I never told her the cause of the accident. I didn't tell anyone, for that matter. A few years before the incident, I came into contact with a strange chemical, and it got into my eyes. The scientists cleaned them out and found no permanent damage, so they sent me on my way. Unknown to any of us, there really was damage, and I started to have spells of blurry vision and momentary loss of sight. This is what caused the accident, and my need to retire early.

"Over time the spells have gotten worse, but I've been able to cope until these past few weeks. Last night was the worst, with me not being able to see for half the day, and now today is topping that with me not being able to see at all. It's not coming back this time. I can't work at the shop like this, and I can't get around on my own. I'm done."

"No, you're not done." I stood. "There might be someone who can help."

"Eira, don't tell anyone!" He tried to grab for me, but reached the wrong way.

"Zane, everyone is going to find out eventually if we don't try to fix it before it's too late. You should have said something sooner. This could have been avoided."

"There's no fixing this, Eira."

"You won't know until you try."

"Eira, please. For the love of the goddess, just listen to me this one time."

I ignored his plea and left his room. Setting a quick pace, I headed for the living room to look for a certain tall elf. Once there, I found her sitting on the couch, touching her new circlet a little more than needed.

"Laz, I can't thank you—whoa, what are you doing?" she yelped as I grabbed her by the arm and pulled her down the hall.

"No time. Shaman thing. Come now."

"You sound like a Neanderthal. Do you mind speaking in a proper sentence?"

I ignored her comment. "Can you cure blindness?"

"Excuse me?"

"Can you cure the blind?"

"Um, well it would depend."

"On what?"

"If the person was born blind for one, and if not, the reason for the person in question to have gone blind in the first place."

"Say this person's eyes were affected by some sort of chemical or toxin. And this toxin has been affecting them for years until finally going blind only recently. Can it be fixed?"

"It's a possibility. It would really depend on the toxin. But why are you asking all this? What is going on?"

Instead of answering, I opened Zane's bedroom door and pulled her in.

"Eira?" Zane waited a few moments before speaking again. "Eira, who did you bring with you?"

"Laz, what is going on?" Shva'sika questioned.

Zane froze at the sound of Shva'sika's voice. "Eira, I told you not to tell anyone!"

"Shut up, Zane." I spoke to Shva'sika next, but in a much kinder tone. "Can you help him?"

Shva'sika looked at me sympathetically, understanding why I was being so secretive. "I can try, but I won't promise anything."

"Trying is all I ask."

Shva'sika knelt in front of Zane and held his hands. "Zane, I can try to help you if you let me."

Zane didn't look at her. He stared at his lap, but I could see his eyes wandering as if he were desperately trying to see something in the room.

"It won't hurt, I promise," she told him.

Zane still didn't respond, and I couldn't understand why. It wasn't like him to be this prideful. Shva'sika was just trying to give him a chance.

"Please, let me try to help you."

Zane sighed and did his best to look at her. Shva'sika lifted up her hands up to his face, and after a few moments, they began to glow with a greenish-blue aura. I watched with bated breath as she attempted to heal him.

When Shva'sika's hands stopped glowing, Zane's eyes fluttered for several moments. When they finally stayed opened, he gazed around the room. His eyes shone with delight, and I knew my choice had been right.

"I've never seen this well in my life," he breathed. "Everything is so clear."

"Or you forgot what it was like to see so clearly," I muttered under my breath.

When he was done looking around, he placed his attention on Shva'sika and stared. The intensity made her swallow, hard, her tongue darting out to wet her lower lip.

Zane reached up and touched her face. I could only guess he had noticed the scar. "My sight must have been real bad if I didn't see that cute mark on your pretty face." He released her and patted her shoulder as he stood. "Thanks again, Elarinya. Now if you two will excuse me, I have somewhere to be, and some important things to catch up on."

I watched Zane leave the room with great interest. He had said her name so well this time. It was as if he were practicing it in secret.

"Boys, let's go!" he shouted. "We're days behind on projects."

Shva'sika remained crouched by Zane's bed, holding her face. Smirking, I headed for the door. "Told you so."

She gasped and I left before she could snap off a reply. I strolled to the living room and headed for my room. Just as I shut my bedroom door, a small log of wood was handed to me. I looked at Raikidan with a raised brow.

"Ryoko asked me to give it to you." He didn't look at me as he spoke. "She didn't say why, but it did come with this piece of paper."

I eyed him before looking over the wood. It was aged red oak and had a good density. *This will work well for carving.* I then read the note.

"Sorry for being a bitch yesterday."

"Yeah, I'm sure it's all her." I teased. Raikidan continued to avoid eye contact as I walked past him. "You don't believe I made those carvings."

"I've never seen you take interest in anything close to what I've seen today."

"I know it may be hard to believe, but killing isn't the only thing I know how to do."

"Eira, don't—"

"But, I do it at leisure. It's not like I can make a living off of this. It's not what I'm designed to do."

"Eira—"

"I'll make another statue to prove to you I did make the others. I don't know why everyone thinks they're so great, when there are better craftsmen out there, but I'll make it nonetheless."

Placing the log on my dresser, I strode into my closet and changed my clothes while thinking hard about what to carve into the wood. I wanted to make sure I didn't waste it.

When I was done, I left and searched for Ryoko. She wasn't in the living room or kitchen, so I went to her room to find the door closed, but still partially ajar. I knocked. "Ryoko?"

"Yeah?" came her reply.

"Want to go for a walk with me?" I asked.

She was quiet for a moment and then opened the door, her eyes uncertain. "You sure?"

I smiled. "I wouldn't be asking if I wasn't."

Her expression changed to one of excitement. "Okay, let's go!"

She linked arms with me and we headed out. I didn't have a destination in mind, so we took turns at random while holding conversation.

I laughed as she made some jokes and failed to make my own, but that had her laughing so I didn't care.

"So, you're not mad at me anymore?" Ryoko asked as we made our way through the Sector Three.

I let out an exasperated sigh. "Ryoko, how many times do I have to tell you, I'm not mad at you. Irritated you broke your promise, but I get it. You were scared you wouldn't be able to control it, even with time and practice."

"I feel bad for lying, but worse for acting so horrible when you asked. I didn't want you to be disappointed in me."

"Don't get so down on yourself. I didn't handle that well at all myself. I shouldn't even have pried. It was your business, not mine."

Ryoko grabbed my hand and smiled. I smiled back, but only briefly. The sight of a dilapidated building caught my eye. An older woman stood on the porch while a few children ran around yelling and screaming with joy.

"Wait, isn't that the orphanage?" Ryoko asked.

"I hope not. The state of that house looks terrible."

"I'm pretty sure it is," Ryoko insisted. "That's Matron Lyra. I've seen her at the store."

I went into deep thought as we continued on. "How often do you think they receive supplies?"

"Judging by the state of the building, I'm guessing not often. Why?"

"What if we did something about it?"

Ryoko's face lit up. "That's a great idea, Laz! We could even see if anyone else wants to help out. I'm sure we could get a lot of for them. If not building materials, at least other things they probably need."

"Let's loop around and head home to plan."

"Race ya!" Ryoko took off, and I yelled after her before picking up my pace. I was glad Ryoko and I had patched things up. And I hoped we'd be able to get something good thought up for those kids. They deserved it.

8
CHAPTER

Shva'sika pleaded with her eyes but my only response back was a glare. There was no way I'd give in on this. I didn't care if it was my responsibility or not, I wasn't working on my spirit walking. I didn't choose to be a shaman anyway. Someone with my past shouldn't have been picked.

"You need to do this, Laz," Shva'sika told me. "It's your duty."

"I don't care," I growled. "I'm not doing it."

"Why are you so reluctant to do this?"

"You don't need to know that."

"Laz, yes I do. As your mentor, I need to know so I can help."

"Why are you pushing me so hard this time? You've never pushed me to do this in the past."

"I just figured you weren't ready. Had I known you just didn't want to do this, it would have been different."

My lips pressed into a thin line. "You don't understand what you're asking me to do."

"Then tell me."

My eyes darted away. "You wouldn't understand."

"I think I would."

"You're wrong."

"Well unless you tell me, I'm confident this will be easy for you, and then I can get out of your hair once we're done with this session."

I let out a strained breath and stood. Without speaking to her, I walked over to where I had been working out before she had disturbed me, and started my routine up again. She wouldn't give up, so I needed to remove myself from the situation in order for her to understand.

"Laz, that is enough!" Shva'sika shouted. "You will do this instead of ignore it. This is your destiny."

"What do you know about destiny?" My eyes snapped to her. "What do you know about my fate?"

"There you go, acting all weird on me again. What is going on with you? Why won't you talk to me?"

"Because you wouldn't understand!" I shouted. "You'd just think I'd be so easy to fix, like everyone else. I can't be fixed!"

Shva'sika took a deep breath. "I don't know what's gotten into you, but maybe you should prove me wrong. I'll only make you do this one session if you can."

I let out a breath and stood still. She didn't understand what she was asking me to do, even if it was for one time. She didn't know what darkness she was telling me to walk into. "Fine. But you won't like what happens."

"We'll see."

I sighed and sat back down in front of her. Pulling myself into a meditative position, I took a deep breath. Shva'sika held her hands out in front of her and I rested mine on top of them. She'd guide me through the threshold to make it easier on me, not that it was possible to make this ordeal any easier. I went to close my eyes, but I became distracted when the living room door opened. I watched as Raikidan and Ryoko came down the stairs.

"We're about to start a training session," Shva'sika informed them. "If you need Laz, you'll have to wait."

Ryoko shook her head. "We don't need her. We were just curious about what you two were doing down here."

"Well if you're going to be here you'll have to be silent," Shva'sika said. "We need to be able to concentrate, and any sound could be problematic."

Ryoko nodded and came down the rest of the stairs. She sat down on the worktable to watch, and Raikidan sat down on the floor near Shva'sika and me. I took a deep breath and closed my eyes. Centering myself, I waited a few moments before opening my eyes. With Shva'sika helping me, I wouldn't feel my spirit split from my body, so I wanted to make sure I was fully crossed over before opening them.

I looked around. I couldn't see Shva'sika anywhere, and the dense fog that surrounded me was unsettling. Something wasn't right. I continued to stand still and look around. I didn't want to wander and get myself lost. That wouldn't be a good idea on this plane.

I tilted my head when I noticed a figure slowly walking through the fog toward me. I blinked to make sure I wasn't seeing things, and when I opened them again, several more figures were advancing. My head snapped in several directions. I was surrounded. My heart raced as the fog began to disperse. These spirits were angry. I didn't have to see their faces to feel it.

I jumped when I turned around and found a little girl staring up at me. Her eyes held unrestrained rage. She was bruised and bloodied, like many of the other spirits. My blood ran cold. *Her face.* So deeply embedded into my brain, I'd never be able to forget that face.

The girl pointed at me. "Your fault." I stepped back. "Your fault."

The spirits around me chanted the same words. My heart pounded. My breath came in heavy gasps. *Where did the air go?* Their chanting continued, and I held my ears in hopes to block them out. "I'm sorry!"

My eyes snapped open, and I gasped for air when my spirit slipped back to my body. Shva'sika's eyes opened, too, but before she could say anything, I jumped to my feet and bolted for the stairs. I needed to get away. I needed to be by myself.

"Laz, wait," Shva'sika shouted as she tried to run after me. "I'm sorry. I didn't know. I'm sorry!"

I didn't care. I told her it would turn out bad but she wouldn't listen. I didn't want her apology.

Slamming my bedroom door behind me, I leaned against it and held myself as I tried to calm down. They were so angry, after all this time they were still just as angry. It wasn't my fault. I didn't choose to do it.

"Eira?" Raikidan asked as he opened the window and climbed in. "Eira, are you okay?"

"Go away."

"Eira, tell me what happened."

My eyes clamped shut. "I said go away!"

He grabbed my shoulders. "Let me help you."

I smacked his hands away. "You can't…" I held myself again and slid to the floor. "You can't help. No one can…"

He knelt. "Please, let me try."

I pulled myself in tighter and hid my face in my arms. My chest hurt, the pain constricting it tight. "Just go away…"

He sighed unhappily, but did as I asked, leaving me to deal with my pain on my own.

9

CHAPTER

Amber wood shavings fell to the floor as I sat on the living room couch and worked. The dark memory had jolted me awake, and I had been unable to fall back asleep. Not that I wanted to. I didn't want that memory to come back.

My figurine was coming out nicely. I had planned to think more about what to make with this log before actually starting it, but I had needed something to distract me. And since Raikidan claimed it had been Ryoko who had given him the log, I thought a wolf climbing down a rock face was a good enough idea.

I looked up from my work when a door opened, to find Raikidan standing in the doorway of the bedroom.

"It's barely sun-up. Shouldn't you be sleeping?" he said.

I shrugged. "Can't sleep. Shouldn't you be asleep?"

He chuckled and sat down on the couch near me. "You got me there. So you really do make these."

I nodded. "Why would I lie about that?"

"I suppose you're right, but why don't you make a living off that? You'd make a lot of money."

"Because they're not all that great. I don't know why everyone is so impressed by them."

"Eira, you need to give yourself a little more credit."

I exhaled while shaking my head and continued to work. There was no point in arguing with him. He saw something great out of it, so who was I to say he was wrong?

"Eira, if you don't mind, I'd like to watch you make this."

"Sure. Just don't make comments, okay?"

"Sure."

Picking up a strip of sand paper I smoothed some rough edges and then went back to carving. Raikidan watched me intently as I worked and eventually ended up closer to me to get a better look. I wasn't thrilled with his proximity, but he didn't utter a word, and for that I was grateful and more willing to put up with his presence.

Minutes turned to hours, and before I knew it I had a little larger audience than I would have liked. Everyone but Ryoko and Rylan were in here, and that was only because I had forbidden Ryoko to see the figurine until I was finished, so Rylan took the liberty of whisking her away to the music room to play for her.

But, thanks to Shva'sika and her interest, I ended up with new tools. She had left at some point to speak with some traveling merchants, and had snuck out one of my older figurines to show them, along with the circlet I made her. They apparently liked them, because before I knew it, she was back with new tools as a gift, and telling me I needed more supplies so they'd have enough to sell. I wasn't at all thrilled with her making this decision for me, but there was nothing I could do about it now. The merchants wanted my carvings and smithing works, and I'd get seventy percent of the profits.

I smiled when I finished. It had come out better than I had expected, but I knew if I had seen a real wolf recently, it would have come out better. My brow furrowed when the figurine went from my hand and into Raikidan's within seconds. I glared at him. I wasn't done admiring it. But he didn't notice my irritation; he was too transfixed on the wooden carving.

A quiet gasp brought my attention from him to Ryoko, who was standing in the hallway with Rylan. Snatching the figurine, and ignoring Raikidan's snort of annoyance, I tossed it to her. "Enjoy."

She blinked. "Really?"

"You gave me the wood, didn't you?"

"Yeah, but—"

"Then it's yours."

Ryoko smiled. "Thanks."

I nodded and stood. Shavings fell to the ground and I carefully stepped over them so I wouldn't slip. Grabbing a broom from the utility closet down the hall, I headed back into the living room, but stopped when I saw the others greeting four people. There were two men and two women.

The darkness kept me concealed as I snuck around. There were guards all about. One wrong move, and this place would be on full alert, and I'd probably be dead.

The taller of the two men had an athletic build and short blonde hair and blue eyes, while the other had a muscular build and short brown hair styled with hair gel, and brown eyes. The elder of the two women was slender with long black hair and blue eyes, while the younger girl, who was the youngest of all four, had long black and blonde hair, blue eyes, and an athletic build.

I whirled around and thrust my dagger out when I sensed a presence. The person behind me moved out of the way and placed a light, friendly hand on mine.

"Easy, Commander. We're here to help, not hurt."

The man with blonde hair stopped greeting everyone when he saw me. "Hey, stranger."

I smiled. "Hey to you too, Lakon. Been a long time."

He chuckled and walked over to me. I wrapped my hand around his arm, and he pulled me into a half hug. "Too long. Eyri is an adult now."

I peered past him, at the young woman with the blonde hair. "Yeah, I see that. She looks good."

"I'm sorry, who are you?" Eyri asked.

"Eyri, that's rude," the other woman scolded.

"It's all right, Alyra," I insisted. "Last time I saw her, she only came up to my knee, and Devon had black hair and used different colored contacts every day."

Alyra laughed. "That may be, but I won't allow my daughter to be rude to people. Right, Lakon?"

"Yeah, sure," Lakon replied absentmindedly.

Alyra let out an exasperated sigh and I chuckled. Lakon had never been good at the discipline side of parenting.

"So what are you guys doing here anyway?" Ryoko asked.

"Well, we figured it was time to pay you guys a visit," Lakon explained.

"It's been a while, and since we heard Eira was back in town, we fig-ured now was the best time."

"Does everyone one know I'm back or something?" I questioned as I went to clean up my mess.

"By now, probably," Lakon replied.

"Lakon, Devon, what the hell do you think you're doing here?"

"We're here to help. This place is crawling with more guards than we first thought."

"I don't need help."

"Everyone needs help sometimes, and we're going to help you, because that's what comrades do."

"We're also here to ask a favor," Eyri said. "Mom says you guys would be able to help design a new song for us for our upcoming concert."

"When is it?" Ryoko asked.

"In two days," Devon said.

I snorted. "There's no way you guys can learn a new song in just two days."

Lakon chuckled. "I'd beg to differ. But it would be nice if you guys could help us. We've become real big and need something new."

"How big?" Rylan asked.

"We've been able to get passes to travel to other cities," Eyri replied.

Rylan ran his fingers through his hair and let out a slow breath through parted lips. I felt bad for him. Music was his biggest passion, but he gave up what Lakon and the others had, so he could get real freedom.

"So what do ya say?" Lakon asked. "Will you help us?"

I looked at Rylan. He was their best bet for a song.

"Sure, why not?" he agreed.

Lakon smiled. "Thanks."

"Wait!" Ryoko said. "They'll only do it if you invite us to this concert."

Lakon laughed. "I thought that was a given."

Ryoko's eyes squinted as she smiled. "Just making sure."

Lakon focused on me. "I'd actually like it if it was you who made the song, Eira."

I shook my head. "Pick Rylan to do it. He's the expert. I've only written a few songs, and he had to improve them after."

Lakon grinned. "And I didn't say he couldn't help after you lay the ground work. I need a song that can be sung as a duet, or a solo if needed in a pinch, and we all know you're the best for duets."

I sighed and leaned on my broom. "Fine, but I won't promise it'll be any good."

Lakon laughed. "I have confidence in you."

I rested my broom on the couch and headed for the music room. I'd clean up my mess later. Once in the music room, I went about my business, looking for music sheets and something to write with. Sitting at the piano, I thought about what to write.

Minutes passed as I stared at a blank piece of paper. Nothing came to mind, but that didn't surprise me. The few songs I wrote were made on a whim after something happened. This new way of developing a song was too alien to me.

Soft strumming started to fill the room. I glanced up to see Rylan playing his acoustic guitar on the other side of the room. It was a simple, light melody, but powerful. As he played, ideas stirred in my head. My hand began scribbling down lyrics before I had much time to mull the ideas over.

Before I knew it, I had the lyrics completed, and had asked Rylan to look it over to do the instrumental aspect since I was never good at that. And to also translate my work over to common. Rylan shot me a strange look when he was only halfway through reading the lyrics.

"What?" My eyes narrowed. "If it's that bad, just tell me."

Rylan laughed. "No, it's not bad. It's the meaning behind the lyrics. I've only seen you write one other song that's been this meaningful before."

I shrugged. "It's nothing, really."

"To you it is," he muttered.

I looked at him seriously, and he held my gaze.

"So, how's it coming in here?" Lakon questioned as he strolled into the room.

I held Rylan's gaze for a brief second longer before refocusing on Lakon. "It's not a duet like you wanted, but it could be turned into one with some work."

"Shouldn't be too hard," Rylan said. "There are plenty of areas that can be split for a second vocalist."

Lakon took the sheets of paper and mulled them over. Alyra came in and read over his shoulder.

"I like it," Alyra said. "I think it'll work well."

Lakon nodded. "I agree. Eira, would you mind helping Alyra learn the lyrics? I'll learn them later."

"Um, sure," I said, a bit hesitant.

Rylan took the sheets of paper and made a few copies before allowing Alyra and me to retreat into a sound booth with a copy of our own. No one would be able to hear us, so there wouldn't be any distractions. I strummed the guitar I had grabbed on my way in, and practiced the instrumentals before focusing my attention on Alyra.

She smiled at me. "You know I won't comment on your voice."

I sighed. "I know. I just don't do this often."

"I'll make the attempt when you're ready."

I nodded and took a deep breath. Exhaling slowly, I began her lesson.

I gazed around at the tall, temporary structure we stood under. It housed a great deal of sound and lighting equipment. I watched as dozens of stage crewmembers scrambled around to get everything ready. The warm-up band was already playing, but Lakon's band was the main act on this tour, and the stage crew still had a lot to do in such little time. It also didn't help that Lakon's band was missing, and no one knew where they were.

I watched as several people tried to figure out how to contact Lakon or the others. Ryder shifted his weight next to me. He had conveniently been assigned as a security guard, along with two other soldiers I didn't know.

I watched a man with a headset and clipboard pace back and forth near the stairs leading to the stage. "Where could they be? It's not like them to be late. The opening act is on their last song."

Just as he finished speaking those words, someone ran over to him and spoke with him urgently. The man exhaled with relief. I turned around when I heard rushed footsteps. Bolting into the back stage was Lakon and the others.

"Sorry we're late." Lakon gasped for breath. "We ran into a situation that we hoped to have had fixed before we got here."

"What type of situation?" Ryoko asked.

"Alyra lost her voice this morning," he said.

"No, don't tell me that." They guy with the clipboard held it up to Lakon. "You're on in ten minutes and she's needed for half these songs."

Lakon moved his hands in a motion to get the guy to calm down. "Don't worry. Eyri is going to take her place for those songs. She double-checked this morning to make sure she knew them all."

"Yeah but, dad, I still don't know the new song," Eyri said.

Lakon sighed. "I know. I'll just have to do it as a solo."

Ryoko frowned. "Aw man, that sucks. You guys were really hoping to do a duet for its big release too."

Lakon nodded. "Yeah, but it can't be helped."

"Maybe it can be." Ryder looked at me. "Eira, you know the song since you wrote it, and you can sing. You could help them out."

I grunted, crossing my arms. "Yeah, funny, real funny."

"That wouldn't be a good idea," Ryoko voiced. "Eira doesn't do well in front of crowds and cameras. And we don't want any of your rabid fans showing up at our house."

Lakon's eyes lit up. "We're not broadcasting this concert. We want to create a bunch of hype with the people here to start off our new tour, so we banned all communicators and other forms of tech that allow photography and filming."

Ryoko shook her head. "That won't stop people from seeing her identity. We can't do that, Lakon."

"Get her a wig," Blaze suggested. "Not that hard to find one."

"The band goes on in five minutes," the man with the clipboard said. "No way we can get her one in time."

"The soldiers are the only ones who know her," Ryder pointed out. "If we use a stage name and I tell the others to keep their mouths shut, we could pull it off."

Ryoko shook her head. "It's still not a good idea."

My eyes flicked between everyone as they planned. Ryoko was the only one who was trying to help me. "I love how everyone is making a plan for me without my consent."

Lakon's brow furrowed. "What do you mean?"

"I mean I'm not doing it," I said. "There's no negotiating that. You can sing this on your own."

"Eira, please help us out," he begged. "It'd mean a lot to us. We'll compensate you if you want."

"I don't want compensation, because I'm not doing it." I turned on my heels and found a bench to sit down on, far way from everyone else.

I couldn't believe they'd actually try to run with that idea. They all knew how I felt about singing in front of others. *The nerve of them...*

Ryder sat down next to me. "Hey, I think we need to talk about this."

"There's nothing to talk about."

"Yes there is," he insisted. "You didn't even give this any consideration before shooting them down. This is really important to them, and you're always being loyal to your friends, so what's stopping you this time?"

"Singing is a personal thing for me, Ryder. I don't sing in front anyone."

"You sang for me when I was a kid."

"That was different."

He sighed. "But it'll really help Lakon and the others out, and we can do a few things so people who don't know you won't be able to stalk you if they like you enough."

"Doesn't change how I feel about the matter, Ryder."

He let out a hard breath and then stood. "All right, fine. I can't make you do something you don't want to do."

He left me alone, but I didn't stay alone for long. Raikidan sat down next to me and I tried to ignore him.

He kept his voice low. "It'd mean a lot to him if you did it."

"I don't care if it means a lot to Lakon," I said.

"No, not Lakon. Ryder. I noticed his excitement at the thought of hearing you sing."

I shifted my gaze down to the ground. I knew where this was going. "As I told Ryder, and you before, singing is a personal thing for me."

"I understand that. I think you should be more open with your ability, however I understand your want for privacy with it. But even if you can't do this out of loyalty for your friends, could you do it for your son?"

He would play this card. Everyone knew I'd do just about anything to make Ryder happy.

"No one will say anything when it's over." He chuckled. "And if you obtain any rabid fans I'll get rid of them. Or get you away from them. Whatever works out better."

I stayed quiet to think about this.

Raikidan held out a few rolled up sheets of paper I assumed were the music sheets. "The others are making sure the concert goers didn't sneak in any technology that could film or take pictures and I even came up with a cover… stage… whatever it's called, name for you use."

I looked at the sheets of paper and then him. "You came up with my stage name?"

He smiled. "Yeah, I think you'll like it."

"What is it?"

"It's a surprise. But I know you'll like it."

I let out an annoyed sigh and he laughed.

We were quiet for a minute before I took the sheets of music from Raikidan. "Fine, I'll do it. But I'm not going to pretend I'm happy about it, or that I wasn't bullied into this decision."

Raikidan patted my leg and stood. "See it how you want. Just know the happiest person here will be Ryder."

"Yeah, yeah," I muttered, getting to my feet and climbing a nearby scaffolding to get a good view of Lakon's band performance before my unfortunate stage entrance.

I listened in when Raikidan went to tell the others of my decision. "She'll do it."

"Really?" Ryoko said. "You sure? Cause I'm pretty sure she would have said no."

"She just needed the right motivation," Raikidan said.

Eyri snorted. "What, us needing help wasn't enough motivation? My dad has had her back multiple times, so you'd think she'd show some—"

"Eyri, stop," Lakon said. "Don't you dare start challenging Eira's loyalty. If any of us were in trouble, she'd be the first to come save us, no matter the odds. But this isn't one of those situations. This is about my own pride, and I let it get the better of me. I knew she didn't like to sing in front of others, but I had it stuck in my mind to have this song sung the way I wanted it, so I didn't stop to think about that. Eira had every right to say no, and has every right to find some other type of motivation to help us. I'm just grateful she is."

Eyri sighed. "All right, all right, sorry."

I tuned them out and watched as the opening act finished and the stage crew went to work getting everything set up for Lakon's band. Once the crew was done, Lakon and the others entered the stage. The crowd went wild as Lakon spoke to them.

With the energy he was able to give this crowd, you could tell he was going to enjoy this concert. Especially when they showed a positive reaction when he apologized for Alyra's inability to sing today, and told them about his little surprise I was dreading to make up for it.

The energy of the crowd was high. Lakon and the others really knew how to give them what they wanted. I was happy for them. They were able to get forged identification cards so they could do this. Though, that happiness wasn't as high as it should have been, thanks to the dread hanging over me. I did not have a good feeling about my part in this concert.

Raikidan had climbed up here with me at some point and occasionally would watch me while I studied the song. Lakon and the others had marked it up so I could see where they had made the duet work, and they had even changed up some of the instrumentals. Raikidan let me know Lakon had requested I play the guitar while I sang as well. Normally I'd have declined, but having the instrument would make it easier for me to be on stage. *It's a good thing I had practiced the first draft, or this would be difficult to memorize.* Ryder joined us a little later and acted completely casual about it.

He was good at pretending to only know me as a friend. He hadn't slipped up, even a little, while we chatted occasionally during the breaks in songs. The music was loud, making conversation pretty much impossible, so whenever the band took a quick break, that was when we spoke, and that opportunity was coming up after the current song they were playing.

"Hey, Eira, thanks for being a good friend to me," Ryder said once the music ended.

I blinked. "Why wouldn't I be?"

He shrugged. "Well, to be honest, I don't have many friends. I'm not like the others."

"Because you make things?"

Ryder nodded. "Soldiers are meant to fight and protect. I can't do some of the most basic fighting maneuvers. Everything I do is geared around my building skills. My building skills got me my tactician position. It gave me the brain power to think the way I do."

"So what's the big deal?" I asked. Ryder looked at me quizzically. "So you don't like to do what everyone else does. Who cares? It just makes you unique."

Ryder chuckled. "Eira, don't take this the wrong way, but you remind me a lot of my mom." I tilted my head. "She always knew what to say to make me feel better or smile. She was there for me whenever she could be, and I rarely ever saw her without a smile, even though everyone else said they couldn't see it. It was like a special smile only I could see." Tightness gripped my heart. "Your smile reminds me of hers. It's light and warm, like the burdens of the world are all just lifted for a moment."

Ryder unzipped his vest and pulled out a small photograph. I examined it when he handed it to me. It was of the two of us. I was in my assassin uniform, kneeling down with him as he stood there with a huge smile.

"She was an assassin. The only assassin that I knew who could do her job flawlessly and still command a company of foot soldiers like there was nothing to it. She wasn't like the other assassins, though. She didn't enjoy killing. She just did it because that was her job. I think that's where I got my biggest trait from."

I remembered that day. My men and I had been assigned to go off to a battle that wasn't important enough to remember now. Ryder was so insistent that I didn't leave him, but I had to remind him of my job.

Jasmine took this picture for us. It was a promise that I'd come back, and it gave him something to look at while I was gone, since I didn't know how long I'd be away. I ended up being away for four months.

"What happened to her?" I asked as I handed the photograph back.

Ryder shook his head. "She just disappeared one day. Some think she turned traitor, and others believe she died somewhere on some secret assignment."

"But you don't believe either."

Ryder shook his head. "She always did what she thought was right and never believed blindly. She wasn't a traitor."

"But she's also not dead."

"I can't explain it. It's just a feeling that tells me she's out there."

"That's the bond of a mother and child. You know they're there. Even if it doesn't make sense, you just know she's alive." I looked down at my hands. "Or not…"

I could feel both Raikidan's and Ryder's gazes on me. I wished they'd stop looking at me. I didn't want to be the center of their attention. Not when I was like this. Especially when I was like this.

I sighed when Lakon spoke to the crowd about his big surprise. I knew it was coming, but I still didn't want it to.

"You'll do fine, Eira," Ryder encouraged.

"Doubt it," I muttered before climbing down from my perch. There was no point in stalling. It would only make everything worse.

Two crewmembers helped set me up. I took a deep breath when I was good to go and just waiting on Lakon. *You can do this, Eira.*

I took a deep, slow breath when Lakon introduced me as Xephrya. *Xephrya.* It was the name Raikidan had chosen as my stage name. He was right, I liked it.

Lakon also told the crowd I was an old family friend, and called me out. This was it. Taking a step forward, my instincts screamed at me to turn back. But once the lights of the stage hit me, there was no going back.

"Xephrya, why don't you say hi to everyone?" Lakon said, a deliberate teasing smile on his face. I half smiled, and just plugged in my guitar. Lakon laughed. "Xephrya is one of few words, but she's happy to be here for us. Right, Xephrya?"

I strummed my guitar in response and Lakon chuckled. "And eager, so without any further delay, here's our new song that Xephrya was kind enough to help compose for us, and now fill in for Alyra last minute."

Alyra started up the song with the keyboard intro and then Eyri joined in on the drums. When it was time, the rest of us joined in. Lakon stepped up to his microphone and the lyrics flowed out of his mouth flawlessly.

My nerves screamed at me to leave. But with each stroke of my guitar and each beat of Eyri's drums, those screams slowly dissipated. The crowd disappeared. The thought of being seen for what I was about to do stopped crossing my mind. This song I'd written, my song, was too close to my dead heart to not be consumed by it. It controlled me, and the words flowed with meaning from my lips when it was time.

Lakon joined in on the chorus, and then took over the singing when the next verse came. I happily let him take it over and played my guitar, aware that I wasn't done. Lakon did most of the singing, but there were parts I was still supposed to join in on.

Lakon stopped singing and I went into my guitar solo. When it was time for me to fade out and allow Lakon's quiet strumming to be heard, I let it come, and Lakon sang a few words before I took over. I put more emotion into this one phrase then I even had thought possible for me to feel. It was hard for me to tell others about myself. It was hard for me to get them to understand with words. But when I wrote a song that had meaning, it wasn't hard anymore. Just like it wasn't hard for me to carve it permanently into wood or metal.

But no one ever realized this. No one saw it past the surface. They didn't look deep enough to understand.

Lakon sang the last words, and I faded out the song with a few strums of my guitar. I let out a slow breath and the sound of loud cheering brought me back to reality. I squinted a little when I came back. The lights were brighter than I remembered.

Lakon wrapped an arm around my shoulders and ate up the praise of the crowd. I felt weird again, and the need to get away from the hundreds of eyes gazing at us took hold. Lakon spoke to the crowd before quickly ushering me and the others off the stage. I assumed he would stop forcing me to move when we were out of sight, but his pace only quickened.

"What gives, Lakon?" I demanded.

"We need to get out of here ASAP," Lakon murmured. "I think you've acquired a few more rabid fans than we first anticipated."

"I what?" I shrieked.

Lakon scratched his head. "Sorry, Eira. I didn't think they'd react *this* well."

"Fix it!"

"I am." Lakon swiveled his head as if he were searching for the best exit. "It won't last long anyway. Once our tour gets underway and they notice you were a onetime deal, they'll forget about you. That's how it goes in this business."

I went to say something, but a strong hand grabbed mine and pull me away while Lakon and the others weren't looking.

"Follow me," Raikidan urged as he pulled me in another direction. I nodded and stayed quiet. He was up to something, and my curiosity was getting the better of me.

I nearly laughed when I hear Lakon speak in the distance. "Ok, Eira—Eira?"

"Raikidan, where are we going?" I whispered as he pulled me away from the back stage.

"I'm going to get you out of here. Your friends are being too slow. You'll get caught up in the mass that's forming."

"Mass? What mass?"

"The mass we have to pass in order to get out of here the fastest."

I gulped. I didn't like this idea anymore. But I didn't have time to protest. Raikidan pulled me out into the open, down a path with a small gate and soldiers acting as security guards. People were shouting and screaming and trying to get over the small fence and past the guards. Raikidan broke into a run and I gladly followed. As I did, a smile spread across my face and adrenaline rushed through me.

Then the feeling faded when a distinct voice called out from the crowd. "Eira!" *It can't be.* "Eira, wait."

I groaned. It was.

"Eira," Zo called again. "Get out of my way. Eira!"

I should have known he was here. Ryder was, after all, and Zo was his commanding officer. I just hated how I could pick out his dumb voice out of hundreds. Or maybe that meant he was close. Too close. I picked up my pace and resisted the urge to locate him.

Raikidan took a sharp corner, squeezed though a break in the path, and led me into a back alley. He then led me to a main road and then into another back alley with a dead end. My breath came heavy once I was allowed to catch it again. I held my breath when we heard heavy footsteps coming from the street we had just come from. Raikidan slipped closer to me and we both watched as squad of soldiers ran past our hiding spot, black-armor suited and shaven-headed Zo leading them.

I let out a slow breath of relief. *One person avoided.* Now the next issue was avoiding anyone else who would have seen me.

"Eira, don't freak out," Raikidan whispered low into my ear. "And keep your mind open so it makes it easier for me to get us out of here."

"What—"

He spun me around, stopping my words from coming out, and held me close. A lump formed in my throat and no amount of swallowing would push it away.

"Relax," Raikidan hushed. "You can't shift if you're tense."

I blinked. That's what he was doing? How would making us shift get us out of here?

"Just relax."

I exhaled and gave it a shot. If it meant I'd be safe from the curse Lakon put on me then I'd give it a shot. My eyes closed and my body relaxed, only to remember my clothes weren't ready for a shifting process. *Shit!* The last thing I needed was to lose my clothes.

I opened my mouth to stop him, when Seda's words penetrated my mind. *"It's okay, Laz. I foresaw a day you'd accept an offer like this, and worked with Shva'sika to enchant your more commonly worn articles of clothing, and your cloth armor."*

I let out a relieved breath and thanked her.

A tingling sensation fell over my body, threatening to disrupt my concentration. I squeezed my eyes tighter, not wanting to ruin Raikidan's forced shifting attempt. It wasn't until his large presence disappeared that I opened my eyes.

I tilted my head and looked around as best as I could. The world was much larger than me, and my head didn't turn like I was used to. A small chirp escaped my throat, startling me. A small bird next to me chirped in response and hopped around a little to get my attention. I stared at the bird for a moment, only to realize it was Raikidan. He had turned us into sparrows.

Raikidan hopped around some more, and then it dawned on me. I didn't know how to fly. An angry chirp escaped my beak as I thought this. How was this supposed to help us if I couldn't even get off the ground?

"Eira, Raikidan wants you to follow him," Seda said.

"Seda, how am I supposed to do that if I don't know how to fly?"

She chuckled. *"I'll help you. Now move those little feet of yours to get used to them, and then try to get off the ground. Also, I'll be sending someone to retrieve your hair clip for you. Seems the spell didn't take like we thought it would have. And don't worry, it didn't break from the fall."*

I sighed mentally and did as asked. I was wobbly on these skinny legs, but I got used to them quickly. Once that tiny ordeal was over, my bigger challenge was next. I jumped around some more to give me the time to figure out how to get my wings to do what I wanted.

My first attempt to get off the ground was a flop, and my next few attempts weren't much better, either. These wings were heavy and awkward, and wouldn't do what I wanted. I made another attempt, and this time my wings moved like they were supposed to. *"Thank you, Seda."*

She chuckled, but otherwise remained quiet. Raikidan took off after me and together we darted around the corner of the alley back into the main street. Raikidan's movements were sporadic and hard to keep up with, but I did my best. I didn't know where he was leading me, but I followed nonetheless.

When the park came into view, I would have laughed had it been possible. Of course he'd lead me here, and what better place to hide from rabid people?

"Eira, you're going to need to pick up your pace a little bit," Seda informed me. *"Raikidan is having a hard time keeping you both shifted."*

"Okay, let me just tell the wings I don't normally have to move faster," I replied. Seda laughed. *"Here's a push."*

A burst of energy rushed through my tiny body, allowing me to keep up with Raikidan. Though once he realized I had caught up to him, he picked up his pace too, irritating me. The two of us darted into the tree line of the forest and searched for a secluded place.

By the time we found a good area, I could feel my shifted state wearing off. My body was becoming heavier, and it was harder to use my wings. I dashed to the ground as best I could, but before I made it, my body shifted back and I was forced to land on my own two feet. Unfortunately, I didn't have time to prepare and when my feet hit the ground, I fell and rolled.

Raikidan rolled on top of me when I stopped moving, and the two of us laughed raucously. I wasn't sure what was so funny, but I couldn't stop.

"Aio eny suvy," Raikidan murmured.

My laughter ceased and I furrowed my brow. "What?"

Raikidan stopped laughing and gazed down at me. "Uh, nothing."

"No, what did you just say to me, Raikidan?"

Raikidan shook his head. "It was nothing. Don't worry about it."

"All right." Who was I to press?

Raikidan pulled away from me, allowing me to sit up. The light breeze played with my hair, and I leaned back on my arms to relax; the horrors of today's earlier events fading away.

"You did well today, Eira," Raikidan complimented. "You have a beautiful voice. You really should sing more often."

I shook my head. "I don't want to. I told you, it's a personal thing for me. It made me uncomfortable doing that."

"It made your friends happy."

"I made them happy at the expense of my own happiness, but sometimes, I don't want to make them happy."

"Eira…" He reached over, the back of his fingers grazing my cheek.

Zarda grabbed my face. "I made you. Everything you are is because of me. You're not as perfect as I had wanted, but you'll do. You will do everything I say, and you will give me everything I want."

My pulse picked up and I jerked away from his touch. "Please, don't do that."

"Why? What's wrong with what I just did?"

"I don't want others in my space."

"Eira, that's not the reason. What I did wouldn't have caused that kind of reaction if it were. You can't lie to me."

I looked away and pulled my legs up to my chest. "I don't want to talk about it."

He rested his free hand on the wall and leaned in. My eyes widened and my breath caught in my throat.

"Why not? How do you expect me to understand if you don't tell me?"

I clenched my hands into fists and tried to stop myself from shaking. "I… I don't want to think about it…"

Raikidan scooted closer and rested his hand on my shoulder. "Eira, what am I missing?"

I sucked in a slow breath through my teeth in an attempt to calm myself. He wasn't going to let up, but I didn't want to talk about it. It hurt far too much to think about it.

"You belong to me and I will have you."

"Eira…" he murmured.

"Just stop, Raikidan!" I pushed him away. "Just stop, please. It hurts too much…" I rested my chin on my folded arms and resisted the urge to hide my face. I didn't need to look any weaker than I felt. Raikidan brushed my cheek as he tucked some of my hair behind my ear, and I sighed. "I was created to kill, but… but I was created for another reason too."

Raikidan's hand slid back to my shoulder. "Eira?"

"Zarda was obsessed with my mother, but she denied him over and over. Then he created me. I… I was made to be his in every sense of the word. But I refused him, like my mother, and it pissed him off. He was determined to have me, and no action was beneath him to try."

Raikidan's grip on my shoulder tightened. "Eira, he didn't—"

"No." I shook my head, my eyes shut tight. "No, but he tried. If… if it hadn't been for my mother, he would have."

"You didn't fight back?"

"I couldn't. I told you, we all have weaknesses, and Zarda knows them all. I couldn't protect myself, and if it hadn't been for the soldier who had been forced to leave me in Zarda's hands, my mother wouldn't have saved me."

"I don't understand."

I took a deep breath. It was becoming harder to deal with this memory. "I had been ordered to be brought to his chambers and left there, against protocol. Because of this, one of the soldiers who had escorted me there had gone to find my mother to tell her. She and Rylan came in just in time to save me."

Instead of speaking, Raikidan pulled me into a hug so tight, I thought my body would be absorbed into him. I didn't fight it. I embraced it. The pain of remembering hurt, but the agony of keeping it all a secret ebbed. I had suppressed the anguish for so long, it felt good to tell someone. It felt right for someone to know so they could understand.

"He shouldn't have done that to you," Raikidan growled. "You shouldn't have had to go through that. You shouldn't have to feel his grasp on you anymore. I can help you, Eira, if you let me. I can help free you from him."

"How?"

Raikidan pulled me into his lap and continued to hold me close to him. A lump formed in my throat. I understood what he meant and I wasn't comfortable with it, but I knew it was the only logical way. I had to face the problem head on.

"I'll put you back together," he whispered.

The lump in my throat grew. *He understands.* He understood the song and understood how broken I really felt.

I nodded. "I don't want to be controlled by him anymore. I don't… I don't want to be a broken toy."

"You're no toy, Eira, and I'll prove it to you."

10
CHAPTER

I tossed the flying disk for Rylan to run after, and then peered over to where Raikidan and Laz hung out on a park bench. Laz sat on his lap while pretending to read a book. I grinned slyly and focused on Rylan as he came back with the toy. Seda told us about Raikidan and Laz's little deal, and specifically told me not to see their actions as more than him helping her with her personal issues, but I couldn't help but hope. Laz never let anyone help. She never let anyone get that close.

Rylan lowered his head and kept his voice low. "Ryoko, focus on the assignment, not Laz."

"I can't help it," I said. "Something feels different about what's going on with them."

"Or you're just hoping that it's something more."

I sat down. "Is that wrong of me? I want her to be happy." My gaze turned to the two of them when Laz started laughing. "I know he's not human, but maybe that's not what she needs."

Rylan lay down on my lap. "She needs time, Ryo. The things she's experienced have made her reluctant to trust."

"You referring to you, or Tannek?"

"I didn't cause her any pain. I only annoyed her. No, I was referring to the crap Zarda put her through, and what happened with Amara and how it affected Laz, and"—he sighed—"and Tannek, yes. And yes, before you ask, I did feel some hatred toward him when he died and she withdrew. And I hated that my advances were still being rebuffed long after he was out of the picture."

"What about now?"

He shook his head. "She's just a friend now, Ryoko, and I like it that way."

"That's nice, but that's not what I was asking. I want to know if you still hate him."

"No. I realized my hatred was irrational since he didn't intentionally get himself killed. I do still hate that she's so closed off, but I can't blame her for being so afraid."

"So, I'll go back to my original question. Is it wrong for me to hope something deeper is happening between Raikidan and Laz?"

Rylan sat up and licked my cheek, making my heart swell, yet it made me feel uncomfortable at the same time. "No, it makes you a good friend for wanting her to be happy. Just be careful not to meddle too much too quickly. You don't want to smother any possibilities just because you're desperate."

I smiled. "Thank you. And for the advice as well. I'll try to keep it in mind."

Rylan picked up the flying disk and wagged his tail. I chuckled and rose to my feet to throw it. We continued this exercise for some time, while keeping an eye out for activity pertaining to the mission. We didn't stop until Laz closed her book and called for us.

I took my time cleaning up the toys I had brought for Rylan, and watched Laz and Raikidan head for the car. Raikidan reached behind Laz and rested his hand on her hip. She tensed with discomfort and her cheeks tinted several shades, surprising me.

This gesture wasn't anything new for him in this last week of him working with her. Hand holding and holding her close while walking, whether it be by her shoulder or hips, were the first gestures he had started with. Then it had progressed to more personal space-invading actions like lap sitting and what should be cuddling, but was mostly Eira fighting Raikidan's strong death holds. I honestly found it funny when this went on, and secretly hoped it would continue when we got home.

Rylan, unhappy with my purposeful slowness, snatched my backpack the moment I zipped it up and ran off toward the car. "Hey, get back here!"

I sprinted after him and passed Laz and Raikidan on the way. "See you at the car."

"Oh, okay," Laz managed to say.

I sighed with relief when I reached Rylan and the car. "I did not need that extra workout, thank you."

"I thought you'd want to observe from this angle," he said.

My brow rose. "What, now you're in on this?"

"I never said I didn't want her to be happy. I'm just not getting my hopes up."

"Right." I smiled at Laz when she and Raikidan showed up. "Ready to leave?"

Laz pulled the car keys from her pocket and unlocked the car. "Hop in."

Once Rylan and I were in the back seat, Laz and Raikidan slipped into the front and Laz pulled out of the parking spot. Raikidan grabbed her hand when she rested her arm on the console, and I did my best not to smile or laugh when she glared at him. She agreed to this treatment, but she wasn't exactly going along with it as willingly as she should be. *Oh, typical Laz.* She didn't know a good thing when it landed in her lap… or she landed in his lap.

Laz glanced at me through the rearview mirror. "What?"

I shook my head. "Nothing."

She snorted and continued driving. When we arrived and parked, no one spoke as we all climbed out and headed for the stairs. Once in the living room, Laz went to see Genesis to give her a rundown of our lack of success, and I put my supplies away before finding something to eat. As I prepped to cook something on the stove, Laz came out into the living room and Raikidan invited her to watch some TV with him. She hesitated, but then accepted the invitation, and I kept an eye on the two as I cooked.

Just as I was finishing cooking the bacon in my skillet, I noticed Laz starting to nod off. She hadn't gotten the chance to sleep much last night, thanks to an assignment Genesis sent her out on, so it didn't surprise me that she was struggling to stay awake now.

I cracked eggs into my skillet and out of the corner of my eye I noticed her start getting a bit cuddly with Raikidan. He watched the action movie playing and absently moved his arm from the back of the couch to Laz's shoulder. At the same time, his eyes also grew heavy. I bit my lips to keep quiet and continued to cook. Danika came into the living room and one look at the two "fake" lovebirds on the couch she grinned and walked out.

"They are fake lovebirds, Ryoko," Seda messaged telepathically from wherever she was in the house. *"I've already told you not to get ahead of yourself."*

"I'm sure there's something there. Even something small. Why else would this be going on?" I said.

"Because he's the only one she would trust to help her like this?" Seda said. *"She's too wary of humans."*

I turned off the burner and slid the eggs onto my plate. *"Tell me, Seda, is there a possibility for them? Even a slim one? And if not with him, with someone who can make her happy?"*

She was quiet for a moment. *"If Laz can let go of the past and move on, then yes."*

"To which part of my question?"

"I can't tell you that."

"Seda!"

"I'm sorry, Ryoko. She has to make a few more choices before I know."

I sighed. *"Very well."*

"Don't meddle where you don't belong."

"It's my job to meddle. Not like she won't return the favor someday."

Seda chuckled. *"Just be careful. You don't want to be the reason it doesn't work out between them."*

"Don't worry about that."

I poured a glass of milk and then looked at Raikidan and Laz, who were now totally zonked out. Laz was curled up to him with her head nestled under his chin, while Raikidan remained sitting upright with an arm over her shoulder. Happy butterflies fluttered in my stomach, sending a tingling sensation to my fingertips. I had to meddle. This scene was just too perfect for me not to.

I unclipped my communicator from my belt loop and attached the device to my head. I played with a few settings and the digital visor wiped across my eyes. Looking at the two sleeping birds I played some different settings until I had the right composition and then pressed the *call* button that had been temporarily changed to an *action* button.

The communicator flashed and a small image appeared in the corner. Content with the image, I accepted it and then removed the communicator from my head and reattached it to my belt so I could develop the image later. I'd take more in time, as long as this kept up. I prayed it would. Laz needed someone—someone who truly cared about her. She needed to know she didn't have to be alone.

It didn't matter to me Raikidan wasn't human. I was created from someone who was the product of that missing barrier. It was Raikidan's non-human nature that allowed him to think in a different way than a human—a way that somehow allowed him to understand her when so many before him had failed.

Maybe, because he wasn't human, Laz would be able to let go of her fears and let him in.

CHAPTER 11

(EIRA)

The air smelled of blood and burning bodies. Men, women, and children screamed in fright as they were hunted down. I stalked down an alley, listening to anyone who may be hiding. I stopped and faced a broken door when quiet whimpering caught my ears. Knocking the door down to the dilapidated house, I went inside and looked around. Huddled in a corner were a woman and a small child. The woman held onto the girl tighter as I laid eyes on them and advanced.

"Please," the woman begged. "We've done nothing wrong. Please, don't hurt us."

I strode closer to them and drew a dagger. The little girl whimpered. Her hazel eyes pleaded for me to leave.

"Please..." the woman begged.

"We have been ordered to purge this city," I stated coldly. "No one is to survive. That is my order."

I raised my dagger into the air and the woman screamed as she held the little girl tighter.

My eyes snapped open and I sat up. My body dripped with sweat, and my breath came out in ragged gasps.

Raikidan, woken up by my startled state, shifted and jumped onto the bed. "Eira, are you all right?"

I stared at my hands as they shook. How could I have done such a thing? They had been so innocent, and I had killed them without hesitation, without question, based on an order I had been given.

"Eira, what's wrong?" Raikidan demanded. "Please tell me what happened."

I pulled my legs into myself and just stared at my knees. What had I done? What kind of monster was I? It was all my fault. I could have turned away. I could have ignored the order, or pretended I hadn't seen them. It was my fault. "All my fault…"

"What?" Raikidan questioned.

"It's all my fault," I muttered. "It's my fault. I did it. My fault…"

The bedroom door flew open and three people noisily rushed in.

"What's going on?" Shva'sika demanded.

"I don't know," Raikidan said. "She woke up in cold sweat, and now she's muttering about something being her fault."

"Let me see," she ordered. He moved away and she took his place. "Laz? Laz, dear, what's wrong? What's your fault?"

"My fault…" Images of what I had done to so many people flooded through my head. "My fault…"

"Laz, please, speak to me. Tell me what's wrong," she begged.

Their faces—their fear—their accusing fingers. The pain I put them through. Being forced to see them again. "Your fault… All your fault…"

"Excuse me?" She questioned.

"It's your fault…" The memories continue to flood through my mind.

"Rylan, what's wrong?" Ryoko asked. "A bad headache?"

"No," he muttered. "Shva'sika, Raikidan, get away from her."

"Why?" Shva'sika questioned.

"Just do it," he ordered.

"Tell me why!"

He stumbled over to the bed. "Something is wrong. It may not be safe for any of you to stay in this room. You need to leave. Laz, can you hear me? Laz, you need to come back to us."

Images continued to flood through my head.

"They deserved to die."

Did they? Did they deserve it?

"They were weak."

Are they? Are they weak, or am I the weak one?

"You did nothing wrong."

Didn't I? Didn't I kill them just because I was ordered to?

"Laz, please. Pull yourself together," Rylan pleaded. "Guys, please leave."

"Are you sure?" Ryoko asked.

"Yes. It's just a precaution," he assured her.

"C'mon," Shva'sika encouraged. "We should listen. That means you too, Raikidan."

"Don't blame yourself. You didn't do anything wrong."

Yes I did.

"They were weak. They didn't deserve to live."

I'm weak. Does that mean I should die?

Rylan cried out in pain and curled up on my bed. "Please, Laz. Fight it. You've done nothing wrong."

My vision began to blur and then fade. Before I knew it, darkness surrounded me and someone was walking toward me. I backed up and readied myself to run. I didn't want to go through that pain again. I didn't want to see them accuse me of the crimes I had been forced to commit. My eyes widened when the person came into view. "Jasmine?"

The slim, black-haired woman looked at me with sympathy. "Eira, you need to let this guilt go. You need to forgive yourself for what you were forced to do."

I shook my head. "I don't deserve forgiveness. Murderers… monsters… don't deserve forgiveness."

"Eira, stop," she said, her voice sickeningly kind. "That's not what you are. You were only ordered to do those things. You were built to be unable to deny an order. You couldn't go against that at the time. You're a good person."

"No I'm not. I only cause problems."

"No, you don't."

"You'd still be alive if it weren't for me! Mom, Xye… Tannek… all those people who died by my hands, they'd still be alive if I had never come along. It was wrong to choose me to be a shaman. I'm not worthy… I don't deserve forgiveness. I deserve to be punished…"

My eyes widened when a tiny hand grabbed onto mine. It wasn't an aggressive grab. It was a soft, gentle one. It was the type of grab Ryder would use when he wanted my attention but didn't want to be a bother, or when he was trying to pull me out of one of my moods. My gazed dropped to see the little girl who had pointed at me during my last spirit walk. She was the one who was bloodied and bruised and started placing blame on me. *I can't forget her face…* But she wasn't hurt this time. And she wasn't placing blame.

She smiled at me. "I don't hate you for what you did."

I looked away. "Yes you do. I took your life without a second thought. You do blame me."

"No, I don't. None of us do." I took in my surroundings as more spirits began to appear. They too were the spirits from my last spirit walk and none of them looked angry. Concern blanketed their faces, as if they were worried about the state of mind I was in. "We don't hate you, Eira. You just made yourself believe we did because you hate yourself so much. Because of all the guilt you suppressed. We don't hate you, Eira, and we chose you because you are worthy of this position. We believe you are the only one who can handle what lies ahead."

"Why me?" The words barely came out above a whisper.

The girl continued to smile. "You have the qualities needed."

"How can you be so sure?"

"We believe in you."

"I get that. But why?"

She giggled. "In time you'll understand. But now you must go back. Your friends are worried about you; one very special one in particular."

My brow furrowed, but before I could ask her to clarify, she let go and waved goodbye. My eyes fluttered involuntarily. The darkness disappeared, and so did the spirits. In their place was my room and my friends. My eyes were heavy and my senses dull, but someone held me close, and a particular dragon was missing from the group of friends I could see.

"Eira?" Raikidan asked quietly. My eyes fluttered. *He is the one holding me.* "Are you back with us?"

I nodded in response.

"How do you feel?" Ryoko asked.

I was too tired to reply.

Raikidan wiped my bangs out of my eyes. "She needs rest."

I nodded as my eyes grew heavier.

"Sleep well this time, Eira," he encouraged.

I felt a little bit more at peace as I slipped into unconsciousness, my burdens slowly becoming a thing of the past.

"Eira, forgive yourself, because if you don't, you'll never know what it means to be free."

CHAPTER 12

I listened to Genesis' briefing on our next assignment. Ryoko and I would be doing this and it was a bit complicated, but I knew we could handle it. Seda stood suddenly from her bed and I cocked my head.

She had a small smile on her face. "We have a guest."

My brow rose. "A guest?"

"Go out to the living room and you'll see."

With a shrug, I stood and left their room. Just as I entered the hallway I saw Ryoko disappear down the entryway hall of the front door. She squealed loud with delight. "Raid!"

A masculine voice chuckled. "It's good to see you too, Ryoko."

Two pairs of feet clomped up the stairs and I watched as Ryoko dragged a tall and athletically-built young man, no older-looking than Ryoko or Ryder, with black hair into the living room. He wore ordinary street clothes, had a backpack slung over his shoulder, and unlike a lot of our other associates, wasn't covered in tattoos or piercings.

"Look who's here!" she said.

Raid scratched his head, his amber eyes struggling to look at anything but Ryoko. "Hey, guys."

I nodded with a smile and the others waved. I looked around the room to find Rylan wasn't around. Turning, I called down the hall, "Rylan, get out here."

Rylan's room door opened in response and he poked his head out. "What's up?"

A grin spread across his face when he spotted Raid and he jogged into the living room. The two embraced in a strong hug, bringing a big smile to my face. I could tell Raid hadn't come by for a visit for some time and, since he was never in one place long, it was hard to track him down.

Raikidan, curious about the commotion, came out of my room. One look at Raid and he was looking at me for answers.

"This is Raid," I introduced. "Rylan's brother."

Raid gave Raikidan a lazy two finger salute. "Hey."

"Hey," Raikidan replied. I could tell he was trying to figure out the whole brother thing. He still struggled to grasp the concept of how we work in that way.

"And before you ask, yes he shifts into a dog as well," I explained.

"Can't control it as well, though," Raid admitted.

I chuckled. "I have a feeling there's a reason for you to be stopping by other than to just say hi."

Raid scratched his head and avoided my gaze. "You guys wouldn't mind if I crashed here for a little while, would you?"

I snickered and Rylan shook his head with a sigh. "You shifted in public again, didn't you?"

"Hey, it's not easy for me to stay like this," Raid defended. "You make it look easy. Besides, I wasn't seen. It happened in an alley."

"But you were kicked out anyway," Ryoko said.

Raid nodded. "They gave the same reason as everyone else."

Ryoko smiled and wrapped herself around his arm. "There's a free room next to the music room. It's yours."

Raid grinned. "Thanks."

There was a glint in Raid's eye I knew all too well, but I stayed quiet as Ryoko led him to his room. It wasn't a good idea for him to stay here, but Ryoko was too clueless to know that. Rylan and Raid may be brothers, and they may get along, but not all the time. In fact, when Ryoko was around, they didn't get along at all.

I tried not to sigh as I watched the two disappear around the corner and notice how Rylan reacted to her gesture. How could she not see what she did to these two? How could she not find the happiness she claimed existed when two men competed against each other to give her everything? *Especially after Zeek. He'd have given her Lumaraeon if she asked for it. She should know those signs. I don't get it.*

"*Do you not get it, or do you, and wish you could have it?*" Seda questioned.

"*Stay out of my head, Seda.*"

"*There's nothing wrong with wanting something like that.*"

"*Speak for yourself.*"

She sighed. "*It's different for me, Laz, and you know it.*"

"*No, it's different for me, not you. I can't have things like everyone else can.*"

"*You don't see everyone's thoughts, wishes, and deepest secrets.*"

"*You can understand those wishes. You can sympathize with other's emotions. I kill that. It doesn't matter if the dead have told me I'm not to blame for what happened. That doesn't change what I did—what I'm designed to do. You don't have to deal with things like that. You can have what Ryoko has, but you're too afraid.*"

"*Speak for yourself,*" she muttered. "*Oh, and Genesis wants to finish briefing you when you're done disagreeing with me.*"

I sighed and headed to their shared room. I was surprised when Ryoko sauntered around the corner and met me at the door.

"Looks like she wants to talk to both of us," Ryoko said.

I nodded without a word, not wanting to spoil her good mood with my sour one. She opened the door and we both entered. Genesis lounged on her bed while Seda meditated on hers.

"You wanted to see us, Genesis?" I asked.

"Yeah, I'm changing the assignment a bit," she said.

I let out an aggravated breath. "You briefed me for an hour and now you're changing it? I hope you have a good reason."

"Of course I do!" she snapped. "I just got a call from the rest of the Council and one of our moles has some information that's crucial we get our hands on. I'm having him meet with Ryoko and disguising it as work for her and the boys at the shop. I'm going to have you two meet this mole in the park and you're going to bring Rylan, Raikidan, and Raid with you. If Raid is going to stay, he's going to work, and I'm willing to work around his shifting issue. While you wait for the mole to show up, do some casual surveillance to see if you can over-hear anything."

I nodded. "Okay, sounds simple enough. How will that affect the other part of the assignment you had me learn?"

"I've instructed your counterpart to meet you in the park instead of the previous location. If he doesn't meet with you before the mole shows up, he'll do so after. Then you'll complete the assignment as planned, and you'll have the boys as back up if needed. We have this retrieval mission well planned out, but there can be snags."

"Naturally," I agreed. "My only issue with this is including the boys. More specifically Rylan. We all know how much he hates shifting."

"I don't think we're going to have a problem with that," Genesis assured.

I knew what she was thinking. If Raid was going to be okay with it, Rylan would make sure Raid didn't get a leg up on him around Ryoko.

"Um, what about Raikidan?" Ryoko questioned. "We've never required him to shift for an assignment before. When Gen sent you out to get lost, Laz, he shifted on his own."

I scratched my head. "That's a good point. Honestly, I have no idea what he'll do when I tell him. The biggest issue will be getting him to shift into something that looks domesticated. He's still learning that stuff."

Seda slid off her bed and pulled a large book off a large oak bookcase. She handed it to me and I looked it over. It was a book about domestic dogs.

I smiled my thanks to her. "This should work."

She nodded and went back to meditating on her bed. I gazed down at the book, pretending to be interested in the contents.

"I'm sorry, Seda. I shouldn't have been so rude."

"Don't be," she said. *"I shouldn't have said anything. They're your thoughts and feelings and should be private. It's just hard to not want you to be happy, especially when I can see how you think."*

"Seda, we both know, it doesn't matter if I want that life of not, I can't have it. It's not my fate."

She sighed. *"I wish you wouldn't let what I told you dictate what you choose to do."*

"Fate can be changed if you make the attempt to change it. That's why I must remain alone."

"Sometimes we seal our fate by trying to avoid it."

Ryoko poked my shoulder. "You know, you should probably go and talk to Raikidan instead of looking over that book. We won't know if he's okay with the idea until you do, and if he's not, your looking would be pointless."

I nodded. "Good point. Do you want me to talk with Rylan or do you want to do it?"

Ryoko shook her head. "No, I'll do it. You'll have your hands full with figuring out what to get Raikidan to shift into if he agrees."

I nodded and headed for the door. "All right. Good luck."

Ryoko grunted. "Thanks, I'll need it."

Doubt it. If anyone could convince Rylan to shift, it would be Ryoko.

I walked out into the living room and looked for Raikidan. When I couldn't find him there, my room was the next choice. To my surprise though, he wasn't there either. I scratched my head. With it being so hot out, he usually opted to stay inside where it was cooler.

Closing the door, I sat down on my bed to think. He wasn't sparring with Rylan. I would have heard them as I passed the basement. He had to be on the roof. It was the only other place I knew him to go, even if it didn't follow his logical patterns. Just as I slipped off my bed to go check, the door to the bath Shva'sika had installed for me opened.

I blinked when Raikidan strolled out with wet hair and a towel. Shva'sika had used the empty room on the other side of the house to act as a host for the bath. She had installed it the day after we had come back to the city, and I had no idea Raikidan used it.

"It is okay for me to use that, right?" he asked as he pointed back to the room.

I nodded. "I don't see why not. But could you wear your towel a little higher?"

His gaze flicked down. His towel looked as though it'd fall off at any moment. "You have a problem with the way I wear this?"

"Yes, I do."

Raikidan chuckled and strolled over to me. "Well that's too bad. I'll wear it however I please."

My eyes narrowed toward the floor. I hated it when he did this. He was doing it on purpose.

He sat down next to me and placed his hand on the bed behind me. "I have a feeling you're here to talk to me about something."

"Could you at least be decent enough to get dressed?" I muttered.

"Just tell me what you want, Eira."

I sighed and pulled the book Seda loaned me into my lap. Raikidan took great interest in it. "We have an assignment."

"All right, what does it have to do with this book?"

"It requires you, Rylan, and Raid to be shifted, and I know you still don't know much about domestic animals."

"So you want me to use my shifting ability to help in this assignment?" He asked. I nodded. "All right, fine."

That was easy. I chuckled. "And here I thought you'd get mad for me asking."

"I don't know where you got that stupid idea."

I handed him the book and then headed for the door. "I'll let you look through that then."

"Wait!" I stopped. "You're not going to help me choose?"

I turned to look at him. "I didn't think you'd want me to."

"I don't know anything about these dogs. I won't know if it's a good choice or not."

I chuckled. "If it's not a dog that's smaller than my ankle and bounces when it barks, you'll be fine."

He worked his jaw. "But I don't want to make a stupid choice."

"It can't be stupid if you choose it. Your choice is your choice."

"I don't know how these dogs act."

I half smiled. *He really does want me to help.* I walked back over to him and thumbed through the book with him. He took interest in the larger breeds, but none caught his eye until we flipped to a page with a large, black and brown, semi-long haired dog.

"What is this one?" Raikidan asked.

"That's the Alsatian," I said. "It's a popular shepherd breed. Do you like it?"

He nodded. "It looks strong. Why is it popular?"

"They're strong and highly intelligent for one, but their best quality is their loyal, loving, and protective nature. They're a versatile breed, used as herding dogs for those who own farms, and they're a great choice for a work dog for people like military personnel. But they're also great for families or individuals who like having a great companion or guard. To be honest, I'm not surprised you've taken a liking to it."

"Why?"

I shrugged. "You just share similar qualities, that's all."

"Then it's settled." He stood and loosened his towel. "I choose that one."

"Raikidan!" I shielded my eyes. "What the hell do you think you're doing? I'm still right here."

Raikidan chuckled. "You're really going to be like this?"

"Yes, I'm going to be like this. Removing your towel in front of me isn't appropriate."

"I still don't understand what your issue is. It's not like I'm human or anything."

I sighed. He really was clueless. "Either shift while your towel is still on, or go back into the bathroom and shift. Do not disrobe in front of me."

Raikidan sat back down and leaned close to me, cupping my cheek. "And if I do?"

I placed my hand on his warm, sculpted chest and tried to push him away, but he didn't budge. "Raikidan, not now."

He stroked my cheek. "Yes, now."

I tried to push him away again while fighting an uncomfortable, warm sensation building inside of me. "Raikidan, we have work to do. Don't start with this."

Raikidan let me go, his fingers dragging across my skin painfully slow. Unfortunately, he wasn't done, and forced me to keep my hand on his chest. "It's the best time to start this."

I pulled hard to release my hand from his grip and headed for the door. "Fine, I'll leave."

Raikidan sighed. "Eira, wait. You win. I'll keep it on. Just don't leave."

"Why shouldn't I?"

"I'm going to need your help. I haven't shifted into this breed before, so I'm going to need a little guidance."

I clenched and released my fist. "You give me your word that the towel will stay on?"

"Yes. Please, just don't leave."

"Fine." I turned around and was surprised to see his back to me and him tightening the towel. Walking back to my bed, I picked up the book and held it up so he could look at it.

"Hold it like that," he told me. "Once I shift, tell me if anything is wrong."

"You're not even facing me. How do you know I'm holding it right?"

"I just do."

I grinned and flipped the book upside down. Raikidan, sure his towel would stay up on his own, turned around and placed his hands on his hips while a scolding look appeared on his face. I snickered and flipped it back over. He took a deep breath and attempted to shift into the dog.

The process was slow. My eyes darted away when his towel fell off. *I should have known this was going to happen.* I looked at him again when he gave a short bark. Raikidan tilted his head and then barked again when I didn't move, making me jump slightly. It didn't startle me, I just wasn't expecting it.

Placing the book on the bed, I crouched down and scrutinized his new form. He had the coat pattern and face shape correct. I made him stand. Both his stance and body shape appeared correct as well.

"You've pretty much nailed it. Your tail needs to be slightly longer and have a little more hair, but that's it."

Raikidan looked at me but didn't fix his shifting. Figuring he wanted to see the book again, I grabbed it and held it up for him to look at. Raikidan tilted his head as he studied the picture, and then attempted to fix his tail. When he had it right I rubbed his head, but he pulled away.

I sighed. "Raikidan you need to act like a dog as much as possible, and dogs like to be pet. They also wag their tails when they're happy or excited and they like to play."

Raikidan looked back at his tail, but it didn't wag. It didn't move at all.

I shook my head and stood. "I can't teach you how to do that. You'll have to figure it out on your own. I'm going to change for this assignment, so while I do, you stay here and figure it out."

I unbuttoned the three snaps on my shirt and discarded it on the floor as I reached the threshold of my closet. My pants were next, and I stood in my unnecessarily large closet, hoping to find something to wear. As I filed through the clothes on hangers, my attention was pulled from my search by the sound of something thumping on the floor. My face burned when I spotted Raikidan sitting inside the closet watching me with his tail wagging and tongue lolling out. Here I was, half naked in my undergarments, and he was wagging his tail and panting.

"Raikidan, I told you I was changing! Do you mind?"

Raikidan barked and his tail continued to wag. *At least he's figuring out how to act like a real dog.*

I failed miserably to hide some part of me with one arm, as I pointed to the doorway of the closet with my other arm. "That means get out."

Raikidan's ears flattened and his head lowered, but he didn't leave. He was doing quite well, to be honest. I was getting the feeling he knew how a dog acted and only pretended to not know.

"Please leave, Raikidan. This isn't funny."

Instead of leaving, he trotted over to a shelf and pulled off some denim pants without any rips in the knees. He dropped the pants on a circular padded chair in the middle of my closet, and then nosed around my obnoxiously large collection of shoes. I tilted my head when he pulled out a knee-high boot and dropped it on my pants. He went back to my shoes and rummaged around for the partner boot.

I knelt by the chair and inspected the boot. They were brown leather, with a shorter-styled heel than the rest of the heeled shoes I owned, and was styled with belts and thick, layered leather that gave the boot an armored look. Ryoko had bought me so many things I never knew I had these.

Raikidan dropped the partner boot next to me and huffed. I pet him on the head and his tail began to wag again.

"Thanks, Raikidan. I'll pick out the rest." He gave me a quick lick on the cheek and I chuckled as I wiped his saliva off my face. "Now let me change alone."

Raikidan snorted, but left the closet like I asked. Pulling my pants on, I pulled on some socks and secured my feet into my boots before rummaging around some more to find a good shirt to go with what I was already wearing. I sighed when I realized I had been looking for ten minutes and still couldn't settle for something. I wasn't good at this fashion stuff.

I turned around to search the other side of my closet and stopped when I noticed Raikidan peeking around the doorway. "Raikidan."

He disappeared, but then peeked around the doorway again. I had to refrain from laughing. Had I not known it were him, I would have believed he was a real dog. For someone who claimed to not know anything about domesticated animals, he was doing a good job acting as one.

"Raikidan, don't tell me you've been taking lessons from Blaze."

Raikidan growled and then crept into the closet. I just watched him as he made it to some vests that hung on a rack and sat in front of them. He didn't touch them, nor did he look at me—only waited. Taking interest, I strolled over and looked at some of the vests.

Most I wouldn't be caught dead in, but a denim one with a collar and a two-snap clasp in the front caught my eye. Raikidan's tail thumped on the floor in approval as he panted.

"Well this will work, but I need to wear something under it." Raikidan shook his head and I nodded. "Yes I do, Raikidan. Are you saying I should go out in public with an outfit that could easily reveal my breasts if I move wrong?"

He tilted his head and I rolled my eyes. *He just doesn't learn.* Making my way over to a dresser, I pulled open the drawers until I found a navy blue sleeveless top. Pulling it over my head, I slipped on the vest and then faced Raikidan once the collar was snapped together.

"So, what do you think?"

Raikidan barked and wagged his tail in approval. Smiling, I gave him a quick pat on the head and then left my closet. Thinking of a color to change my hair to, I wandered out of my room and tripped over a beautiful, black Alsatian of the short coat variety, with amber eyes.

I sighed. "Raid, do you mind not sitting right in front of my door?"

His ears flattened. "Sorry. I'm just trying to stay calm and out of the way."

I gave him a quick pat on the head in understanding and headed for the bathroom to pick out some hair dye. Raid followed.

"Where are Ryoko and Rylan?" I asked.

"I think they're still arguing in his room," Raid said. "They've been quiet, but I don't doubt they're still fighting in some way."

I sighed and shook my head. I thought she would have been able to convince him by now. I didn't understand his problem. He didn't have an issue back in the day. He tended to prefer that form, from what I remembered.

Raikidan trotted over to us and sat down next to Raid, only looking at him briefly before focusing on me.

Raid sighed. "Why can't I have a normal coat like him?"

"Your coat is normal."

"Black isn't normal. You barely see them."

"It's in the breed standards. Hell, the panda coat pattern is now recognized for the breed, so there's nothing wrong with the way you look."

"He's still lucky."

"He didn't have to shift with that color, or coat length."

"What, really?"

"Raikidan is a real shapeshifter. He can choose what to transform into and alter his physical characteristics for certain species if he wants to. The book we had just had the tan and black pattern with the semi-long haired coat, so we didn't have much of a choice."

He turned his head toward Raikidan. "There are rumors real shifters can shift into the opposite sex. Is that true?"

Raikidan shook his body in response and Raid cocked his head, clearly confused by our dragon's response.

"Raikidan can't speak common in any other form but a humanoid shape," I explained.

"Wow, that sucks."

"It might for you, but not for others who can't shift, like me. I know he'll bark and not accidentally speak."

Raid huffed. "Why can't Rylan and I have it easy?"

A teasing smirk slipped onto my lips. "You and Rylan, or just you?"

"Don't make fun of me. I try my best. It's just not easy."

I finished lacing the multiple colors of dye into my hair and faced him. "Maybe it's because you don't have a strong desire or care to look human, like your brother."

"You think that's the reason?"

I shrugged. "It's the only thing I can think of. Rylan hates shifting now. That's why we can't win a losing battle with him for this assignment, no matter how much we like to make ourselves believe otherwise. He won't join us. You'll see."

"That's it, I've had enough, Rylan!" Ryoko screamed. "Be an asshole for all I care. Laz and I will do this assignment with Raid and Raikidan since they're more than willing to do this."

I refrained from cringing when she brought up Raid's name. Adding him into the equation changed everything every time. Ryoko slammed Rylan's door and stormed down the hall.

"I'll meet you in the car," she muttered.

I cringed again when she slammed the basement door so hard that the force broke it off its hinges and it fell to the floor. "You two go with her to make sure she's going to be okay. I'll finish getting everything ready and meet you down there."

"Okay," Raid agreed.

He headed down to follow her, but Raikidan stayed where he was. I gave him a stern look, but he still stubbornly stayed put.

"You're a terrible listener," I said as I rinsed my hair.

Once my hair was thoroughly rinsed, I dried and styled it before leaving the bathroom. As I walked down the hall to look through a closet, I noticed Rylan leaning against his doorway watching me as I passed. I ignored him and continued on my way. Rummaging around the closet, I found a backpack and a few toys we'd be able to use, along with some dog collars and leashes we kept on hand just in case.

Figuring that was all I needed, I headed back to the living room. Rylan hadn't moved but I still didn't say anything to him.

"What, you're not going to call me an asshole, too?" he taunted.

"Since you already know what I'm thinking, I didn't think it needed to be said," I said.

"Why is it that I'm an asshole when I say no to something I don't want to do?"

I stopped walking. "It's because you give us a hard time for trying to convince you, but you give us no reason for arguing against something so simple."

"I don't like feeling more beast than man."

I grunted. "That doesn't even make any sense. You had no problem taking that shape back in the military. Hell, you seemed to prefer it. Now? Now you want nothing to do with it. You're nothing but a puppy who is afraid of his own shadow."

Rylan snorted. "Coming from someone who hides behind a mask?"

"This isn't about me, Rylan, so leave me out of it."

"You can't be a hypocrite, Laz."

"I'm not being a hypocrite, because this is bigger than just one person. This is about more than just me or just you. This is about you hiding from something you never used to hide from, and this is about upsetting Ryoko in the process. You've changed, Rylan, and she and I both can see it. You're not the same person, and that upsets her. You used to be carefree and would do anything on a whim. You used to be more like Raid."

His eyes narrowed, and the corner of his lip curled. "Don't you dare bring him into this!"

"I will bring him into this!" I snapped. "I will because he does a better job at making Ryoko happy. He does a better job at accepting who he is and what he can and can't do, unlike you. I'm starting to think Raid is a better choice for her."

Rylan looked taken aback by my words. "How can you say that?"

"I don't know, maybe because Raid puts in a hundred and twenty percent to make her happy? Maybe because Raid jumps at every chance to make her smile? Maybe because Raid bends over backward for her? You on the other hand, you don't ever act like you care. You barely put in eighty percent for her. You're not a good choice for her. You won't keep her happy. Raid is better for her and I should have realized that before I told you to go after for her. Give her up. You haven't told her how you feel by now, why bother pretending you'll try at this point."

I stormed off before he could say anymore. I pretended to be mad until I was on the stairs going down to the basement. Maybe now he'd try. Raid was a good choice for Ryoko, but I didn't believe he was the best. Raid wasn't the most responsible person, and he wasn't known for making a good effort, especially when it came to shifting.

Ryoko needed a man, not a dog. Rylan had the potential to be that man, if he could get over his insecurities. Otherwise, he wasn't a good pick, either. She needed someone strong who could support her while she fought her own problems.

Or a woman. We could be barking up the wrong tree altogether. Of course, Ryoko had rejected everyone woman I'd pointed out to her when we were out and about, so I wasn't even sure about that angle either.

I stopped walking when teeth latched onto my pants leg. I turned around. "What's up, Rai?"

Raikidan let me go and jumped up, resting his front paws on my shoulders and rested his head in the crook of my neck. I rested my head against his and gave him a hug back.

"Thanks," I whispered. "I needed that."

I pulled away from him and he gave me a quick lick on the cheek before hopping down. I rubbed his slobber off my face before continuing to the garage. Strong arms snaked around me, stopping me.

My face flushed several shades of red and a lump formed in my throat. "Raikidan, what do you think you're doing?"

He chuckled in my ear. "You said you needed it."

I exhaled slowly. "Remove yourself from my person."

"You didn't have a problem when I was a dog."

"You're not wearing any clothes."

Raikidan chuckled again. "Dogs don't wear clothes."

"That's different! Now, let me go, or else."

"Or else what?" He challenged low in my ear. "You won't face me."

I made a blind attempt to grab his face. "I don't need to face you."

Raikidan chuckled and pulled away. When his overwhelming presence disappeared, I stole a glance to see him back in his canine shape.

"Now stay like that." I went to walk off when I remembered the dog collars. "I almost forgot to give this to you." Raikidan watched as I rummaged through my bag. "There's a leash and collar law. You'll need to wear the collar all the time and if we're not at the park you'll need to be on the leash."

Pulling out a leather collar with silver pyramids from the bag, I faced him and strapped it around his neck. Raikidan sat patiently as I made sure it was secure. I pulled away and smiled. Raikidan tilted his nose down in attempt to see it, but to his frustration his head wasn't the right shape to do so.

I scratched him behind the ear. "Don't worry, it looks good on you. Now, let's get going. I don't want to keep Ryoko waiting any more than necessary."

Raikidan and I wandered into the garage. A large blue four-door truck beeped at us before I could think to search for Ryoko and Raid. I opened the back door for Raikidan and then hopped into the front next to Ryoko.

"Ready?" she muttered, clearly still in a bad mood thanks to Rylan. I was starting to think she liked Rylan far too much and needed to look elsewhere.

"Yeah, I'm ready."

She went to start up the truck but stopped when we heard a loud bark outside the truck. Ryoko and I looked at each other before I opened my door. Sitting outside the truck was Rylan in his wolf-dog form. His head was low and he gazed up at me with apologetic eyes.

His lip ring was gone, along with his ear chain. It made him look a little more normal, but not completely. Not that it wouldn't be a problem. We had a story for him if anyone got nosey.

"Change your mind?" I teased. He blinked slowly in response. "All right, let's go."

I noticed a small smile form on the corner of his lips and he jumped in. He climbed up on my seat to get into the back and I grunted. I had forgotten how big he was. I should have just opened the back for him. Ryoko glanced away from him.

Rylan dipped his head and licked her on the cheek. "Sorry."

Ryoko froze and her face flushed. Rylan jumped into the back and settled himself between the other two shifters.

"Oh, I can't forget." I rummaged through my backpack and pulled out a studded leather collar. "Raid, you'll need to wear this."

Raid sighed. "Do I have to? I hate those things."

"It's the law. Now come here so I can put it on you."

"Rylan isn't wearing one."

"Rylan has one. It just can't be removed." I glance at Ryoko. "Isn't that right, Ryoko?"

Ryoko's face changed several more shades and she stared out her door window. I refrained from laughing. She had a secret thing for men who wore chokers, and Rylan's collar with its small chain was close enough.

Raid grumbled to himself and slid half of his body off the seat. Once the collar was secure, I sat back and waited for Ryoko to start the truck. When she didn't, I turned my head to find her still staring out the window with flushed cheeks.

I snapped my fingers in her face. "You going to start the rig so we can go, or what?"

Ryoko blinked and then shook head. "Yeah. I'm just waiting to make sure no one changes their mind last minute."

"I'm not changing my mind," Rylan muttered.

"That's what you said in your room earlier," Ryoko shot.

I covered my mouth and tried not to laugh, but a giggle came out of my lips. I couldn't help it.

Ryoko's face flushed again and she started up the truck. "Let's go."

I snickered but stayed silent otherwise as she pulled out of the parking spot and headed for the garage door.

13
CHAPTER

The wind tussled my hair as I sat in the shade of a large oak tree and watched Ryoko throw a flying disk for Raid and Rylan. Raikidan lounged next to me. No matter how much I tried, I couldn't get him to play like the others. It made it hard to pass him off as a young dog.

The park was busy, and soldiers crawled all over the place, making me glad the assignment wasn't a drop. It was a lot less conspicuous, but more complex to pull off. The person we needed to meet up with was nowhere to be found, so Ryoko and I decided to play the surveillance game as Genesis suggested before we left. Unfortunately that wasn't working out all that well either, since the soldiers weren't talking much and the civilians were behaving.

Raikidan stretched out and laid his head on my legs. I patted him gently and smiled. "You sure you don't want to play? I know you'll do better than they are."

Raikidan's eyes drifted over to Ryoko and the two boys. He huffed and stretched out on his side.

I rubbed his exposed chest. "All right, lazy butt."

He wagged his tail in response. I went back to watching Ryoko play with the brothers and noticed a soldier jogging over to her with something that looked like an envelope tucked under his arm. Ryoko tossed the flying disk for Rylan and Raid to chase after one last time and waved at the soldier.

Raikidan rolled onto his belly and became alert as he intently watched Ryoko react to the newcomer. Rylan and Raid ran back over to her. Raid had the flying disk in his mouth, but he abandoned it when he reached Ryoko's side and began sniffing the soldier's feet. Rylan also sniffed the soldier, but not for as long, and just sat and watched the interaction with his tongue lolling out.

The soldier handed Ryoko the envelope he carried and she peered inside before nodding and speaking with him for a bit longer. When they were done, she walked over to me. I glanced around and found there to be too many people to open the envelope, so I'd have to make sure the first half of the mission was completed tactfully.

"Whatcha got there?" I asked.

"Oh just some plans the military wants us to look at for some projects. Sandren was going to drop them off at the shop later but saw me, so figured he'd just give them to me to hand to Zane to look over."

I nodded. "Cool. Sounds like they make sure you guys have a lot to do."

She smiled. "Yeah, that's the one good thing about it. Hey, do you mind if I store these in your backpack for now?"

I shrugged. "Sure. Don't see why not."

"Thanks."

When she zipped the bag closed, that marked our first task as complete. While I wouldn't doubt there were some plans for Ryoko and the guys to work on at the shop in that envelope, most of those would contain intel for the Council to see and plan around.

"Hey, you interested in getting a bite to eat?" Ryoko asked. "I know a place that has outdoor seating and allows dogs and even have a few meals that can be made for them."

I nodded. "That sounds great."

Raid barked and wagged his tail, and Rylan's ears perked with interest at the idea of eating. I grunted. *Boys.*

Ryoko looked at Raikidan when he didn't react like the other boys. "What, don't tell me you're not happy about being fed."

Raikidan stretched out into the grass and gave no signs of wanting to go anywhere.

I laughed. "Guess he'd just rather sleep."

"You're such an old man," Ryoko teased.

Raikidan lifted his head and I laughed when, what looked like a glare, crossed his face.

Raid pawed Ryoko's leg and whined and she giggled. "Okay, okay, we'll get going."

She snatched two leashes and clipped them to Rylan's and Raid's collars. I attached Raikidan's leash to his collar and tugged. He huffed and reluctantly got up. I rolled my eyes. He really was acting like an old dog.

Ryoko stuffed the flying disk into my backpack before I slung it over my shoulder and we headed toward the west entrance of the park.

"Alaria!"

I stopped walking and turned around when someone called out my cover name. An older gentleman, with salt-and-peppered hair and light skin wearing a jogging suit was running down the path waving at me.

I waved back and waited for him to catch up. "Hey, Myron. Looks like you've been getting your exercise in."

He took a few minutes to catch his breath. "I'm glad I caught you. I stopped by your house earlier but you weren't there, and your dogs weren't barking, so I assumed you'd taken them to the park and changed my jogging route. My wife and I are done borrowing your unit and I wanted to give you back your key."

I smiled when he dug through a pocket and pulled out a small silver disc. "Thanks, Myron. I hope it worked out well for you while your receiving box was being fixed."

He nodded. "It did, and we really appreciate the help. The missus said she left a special gift in there for you after she let the company know it was being transferred back into your name."

"Oh, I hope it's her homemade gourmet chocolate."

He winked. "You'll have to go find out yourself."

I laughed. "Well I should go do that. If they are, I don't need them melting on me."

Myron nodded and started heading back in the direction he had come. "Say hello to your parents for me."

"I will," I called after him. "And don't push yourself too hard. I don't want to hear you were so healthy for your age you gave yourself a heart attack."

He laughed and continued on. I stuffed the silver disk into my back pocket and Ryoko and I headed for the truck.

"Do you mind if we head to my receiving box first?" I asked her. "The air-conditioning at the building isn't that great, so if there really are chocolates in my box, I don't want them to melt."

Ryoko grinned. "Only if you share them with me."

I smiled back. "Of course." Raid whimpered and I chuckled. "Dogs can't eat chocolate."

He whined again and I just shook my head. Myron and his wife, Lessa, were both civilians who believed in our cause and helped where they could. They couldn't do a lot, due to their age, but they were useful, and Lessa always insisted on making some sort of treat for those she was working with that day. If you were real lucky, you'd get her amazing chocolates. I'd seen rebels get into a fist fight over who got the last one in a batch, and I couldn't blame them. I'd had a lot of chocolate in my time, and nothing could beat hers. They were almost worth dying over.

It only took a few minutes to get to the public shipping building. Ryoko stayed in the car, as the plan needed, and I headed inside to retrieve whatever Lessa had left for me. I took in the room as I headed to my box. There were several people in here checking their boxes, most of them rebels grabbing supplies dropped off in these storage boxes. At the far end of the small building was a woman sitting at a desk. She, too, was a rebel, who had helped get the supplies into the shipping boxes by overlooking the contents, against protocol. But the company had become suspicious and she feared a sweep by the military, so the Council had ordered all packages to be recovered, and smuggling operations to cease in this particular shipping center, until warning levels went down. Now with everyone grabbing their parcels at once, there were bound to be issues, and that's where I came in.

I slid the silver disk into the slot of the numbered box matching the key, and watched as the digital display did its thing. The door popped open upon access approval, and the machine ejected my key. Slipping the disk into my back pocket, I fully opened the door of the box and pulled out a brown paper bag. I could smell the treat inside before even needing to see it. It was a bag of chocolates.

Smiling to myself, I reached in and popped a small chocolate in my mouth. A pleased sigh escaped my lips as my shoulders sagged. "Lessa, you are the queen of chocolate making."

My indulging was interrupted when I sensed the presence of a few people behind me. I glanced back mid-chew to find three rather intimidating soldiers standing behind me. Well, they would have been intimidating if I were an ordinary civilian.

"Um, can I help you?" I asked.

"Ma'am, we need to see that bag," one of them said.

My brow rose and I swallowed the chocolate in my mouth. "Um, okay. Why?"

"Your suspicious activity in the park today has indicated you as a security threat to this city. Show us the contents of the bag."

I could hear Raikidan barking from the truck, and knew Ryoko was aware things were going as planned.

I gave the soldiers a funny look. "Suspicious activity? I just hung out with a friend and my dogs, and I happened to run into another friend who I had loaned this box to. He was done with it, so he gave it back to me."

"That is the activity we're speaking of," another soldier said. "Your dealings with this other party are suspicious, and the loaning of boxes is strictly prohibited."

I pointed to the woman at the desk. "If you have a problem with me loaning my box to a friend, talk to the company. They got the okay to allow the temporary hand-over, because my friend's box had been destroyed by vandals at the East Street facility. I've done nothing wrong."

"Give us the bag," the last soldier ordered.

"Don't give it to him. They belong to you."

I stared at them defiantly. "No. It's just a bag of chocolates given to me as a thank you. I've done nothing wrong, now leave me be." One of the soldiers knocked the bag out of my hands and the chocolate spilled everywhere. "Are you kidding me? What the hell is your problem?"

"If you had just cooperated, that wouldn't have happened," the soldier said.

"Make them pay!"

My fists clenched and I went to spit out a retort, but Ryoko's voice stopped me. "What in Satria's name is going on here?"

The soldiers turned to look at her and I tried to use this opportunity to pick up my bag, but one of the soldiers shot me a warning glance to not move. I glared at him but didn't want to escalate the situation just yet, so I stayed put and let my eyes scan the room when the soldier's attention left me. The few civilians in here grabbed their box contents, and tried to leave without being caught up in the incident I had created. The rebels, on the other hand, were trying to remain calm and collect their supply drops so the situation wouldn't escalate too quickly, ruining my planned distraction.

"So, is someone going to tell me what's going on or not?" Ryoko demanded.

"Ma'am, this doesn't concern you," one of the soldiers said. "Please go about your business."

"Like hell it's not my business. This is my friend, and you're causing her issues for no reason. Seems to me like you're just abusing your power."

Just as we had hoped, one of the soldiers stalked over to her. "You will leave."

With typical Ryoko finesse, she smiled innocently at the man and then grabbed him by the arm and easily threw him right out the door, sending him crashing into the truck. The boys went berserk. Raikidan hit the window in the front seat a few times with his paws as he barked, and Raid and Rylan attempted to bark out of the same rear window.

The two remaining soldiers became wary of Ryoko, and she just pounded her fists together. "You're dealing with a former Brute class here, ladies, and you picked the wrong people to try to exercise your power against."

Just then, the sound of glass breaking echoed through the door and I could swear the boys' barking was louder. *Oh no.*

Raikidan came barreling into the building with teeth bared, and Rylan and Raid weren't too far behind, barking their heads off. The three of them placed themselves between me and the soldiers, and their hands instinctively went to their guns. This wasn't going well now. The guys had been instructed to stay in the truck so nothing would get out of hand. But of course, typical of him, Raikidan didn't listen, and Rylan and Raid followed. *They'd better be following their ringleader to exhibit the pack mentality, or they're so dead!*

I grabbed onto Raikidan's and Rylan's collars in hopes it would help the situation, but Raikidan took that as a cue to try to lunge at the soldiers. Luckily Rylan didn't do the same, and Raid calmed down a bit.

"Calm the dogs," one of the soldiers ordered while the other looked at the panicking people who were now making calls.

"Hey, we have a problem," the soldier informed.

"Yeah, no shit," the other retorted. "Ma'am, control those dogs now, or we'll take drastic measures."

"They would be under control if you hadn't decided to be an ass," I shot back.

"Control them!"

The raise in his voice made Raikidan react, and he broke out of my grip. I watched as he lunged at the soldier and bit down on his arm. The man yelled in pain and tried to pry Raikidan off, even resorting to hitting him, but Raikidan refused to let go. He didn't shake his head, so that was good, but he had a grip on this guy that I wished he didn't.

The other soldier drew his gun, but Raid took action and bit him in the arm. Unlike Raikidan, Raid did shake his head, and the soldier screamed in agony, dropping his weapon. This was getting way out of hand.

I watched as people ran from the building; most of them rebels taking advantage of the situation and getting their drop packages out without being questioned and caught.

My eyes shifted to Ryoko, only to find her leaning against the doorway with her arms crossed and a smug smile on her face. She was getting way too much enjoyment out of this. "You going to help me here?"

"No," she replied. "I'm waiting for the cavalry to arrive, for me to explain the situation to."

"Don't you think it'll look bad if they saw my dogs attacking soldiers?"

"They're doing their job and protecting you. We have their protection paperwork in the truck, so don't worry about it."

Protection paperwork? I suddenly had a feeling this whole attack situation with the boys had been set up by Ryoko. Protection paperwork was certification dogs were trained to be used as a form of self-defense. Due to the training, all owners with trained dogs were required to carry the paperwork on them at all times when they brought their dogs out in public. I hadn't grabbed any paperwork like that when we left to do this assignment, so either Ryoko had packed it, or it had been given to her during the information drop for some reason.

"Rage, Raid, let go!" I ordered.

Raid released the soldier and looked at me. He panted and wagged his tail as if he were proud of what he had done. The soldier tried to move away, but Raid growled at him and the man stayed put.

Raikidan didn't listen to my command, however, and I suspected it was because the soldier he had was still trying to force him to let go.

"Hey, moron, stop hitting him so I can get him to let go!" I said.

The soldier glared at me. "He should have let go on your command."

"Not if you're showing to be a threat he won't. Now stop hitting him."

The soldier didn't listen, triggering Raikidan to clamp down harder and start shaking his head. I sighed as the soldier cried out.

I peered out of the building when several vehicles came to screeching halt. I sighed again. *Great.* The vehicles that had arrived were military, and, while I knew they'd show up with all the calls from scared civilians, along with rebels pretending to be so, I didn't want to deal with this. This part of the assignment had really gotten out of hand.

I watched as a general and a psychic walked into the building, while several soldiers looked over the one Ryoko had tossed.

"What's going on in here?" the general demanded.

I recognized him. I didn't know him well enough to know his name, but he was one of the few high-ranking officers we had on our side. I started to feel more relaxed. Things might not be as out of hand as I thought.

Ryoko, still leaning against the wall, looked at her fingernails. "Your buddies decided to abuse their power."

The general stared her down. "So you used dogs on them?"

"No, the glass of my truck broke when I threw one of the men into it, and they got loose."

"Are they trained?"

"Paperwork is in the truck," I managed to say as Rylan started to get excited all of a sudden.

"Why is there still one attached to one of my men?" he asked.

"Your man keeps struggling and hitting my dog on the head," I said.

"Galos, stop struggling," the general ordered.

The soldier glared at me, but listened to the order. Raikidan remained latched on until the soldier ended his struggle. He let go and trotted over to me, with his tail wagging. I just shook my head and grabbed his collar.

"Well, now that we have that under control, anyone care to tell me how things got this out of hand?" the general asked.

The psychic next to the general turned his head toward the ranked officer. "I already have the answer. It seems Galos was told of a possible suspicious dealing between this woman with the dogs and a man while at the park, and followed these ladies when they left. Their approach was too aggressive, and the woman became defensive. Events escalated from there because Galos and the men didn't handle the situation well enough."

The general nodded and focused on me. "What were these supposed suspicious dealings?"

I let go of Rylan so I could grab my key, and he and Raid started playing as if they were totally unaware of the serious situation at hand. Raikidan luckily wanted nothing to do with it, allowing me to trust him enough to let him go as well.

I held up my box key. "My friend was returning my key."

"Did you have clearance to allow him to use it?" the general questioned.

I nodded. "I even told these men that, but they didn't care."

The general noticed the bag of spilled chocolates. "What's that?"

"That would be my thank you, from my friend and his wife for going through the trouble of loaning them the box. She makes her own sweets."

The general nodded and looked at the two soldiers in front of me. "Get up and get moving. We have a nice mess to clean up thanks to you three." The general glanced at Ryoko and then me. "Ladies, I do apologize for this."

I nodded. "It's fine. Do you want to see the paperwork for my dogs?"

The psychic smiled. "I've already had a discussion with your friend, and she showed me where they were. You're cleared."

I smiled back. "Thank you."

Raid barked and wagged his tail at the psychic as if to give his own kind of thanks.

The general's eyes appraised the guys. "Strange pack you have, but well trained. Nice job."

He then turned on his heels and marched out of the building to start barking orders.

The psychic looked over at the remaining civilians in the building. "You all might want to grab your things and go. We're going to have to shut this place down for a bit." When they went about grabbing their things from their boxes, the psychic turned to Ryoko. "I'll go fix your truck."

She smiled. "Thanks. I hadn't intended on throwing the guy into it."

He chuckled. "Yes, I know."

The psychic left with the two trouble-making soldiers close behind him. The one Raikidan had latched onto turned his head over his should and shot off an ugly glare at me that I could only assume was to tell me to watch my back. I stuck my tongue out at him, and Raikidan barked in warning. The soldier glowered and turned to face ahead again, just as Ryoko stuck out her foot and tripped him. "Oops."

He snarled as he stood back up and dusted himself off as if he were fixing his dignity and left the building. I bit my lip so I wouldn't laugh, and decided to pick up my dropped bag of chocolates. We needed to get out of here anyway. Ryoko and I were now the last ones in the building, and I was sure the general we were lucky enough to deal with, while on our side, wouldn't be pleased with us dawdling.

Once I had my treats all bagged up again, I headed out of the building and met Ryoko on the sidewalk, watching the psychic as he pulled out the dents with his ability. He was also able to clean up the glass all over the ground and inside the truck at the same time.

When he was done, he looked at us. "All set. There are a few mechanisms that are broken beyond what I can fix, so you'll need to take care of that, but none of them are major issues."

Ryoko smiled at him. "Thank you. This saved me a lot of work at my boss' shop."

He chuckled and nodded before going about his business. I opened the back door for the boys to pile in, and then jumped into the front seat. Ryoko climbed up into the driver side and started the truck up.

I let out a sigh of relief when we pulled away and were finally cruising down the street. "That was a bit more chaotic than I had expected."

Raid shifted and sat forward. "I'll say. Can I have one of those chocolates?"

I placed the bag on the floor. "No. None of you deserve any chocolate after that stunt you all pulled."

"We were just doing what Ryo told us," he defended.

I shot her a dirty look. "So you did have something to do with that."

She held up a hand defensively. "Hey, whoa, hold on a minute. I didn't have anything planned. While you were inside that building, I was going through the papers I was given for my end of the assignment, and noticed the protection paperwork. Around the same time, those soldiers followed you in and I didn't like their body posture, so I told the guys they may need to jump in. I didn't expect Raikidan to break down the window."

Rylan shifted. "So because it wasn't planned for us to keep you out of the loop, and we did our job right, we deserve some of the reward."

"Yeah, besides, if you want to be angry with someone, be angry with Raikidan," Raid said. "He's the one who broke the window, after all, and as dogs, we follow the leader."

"Suck up."

I froze when Raikidan spoke. *He did not just shift in this car.* I knew I should have just kept looking forward, but my curiosity got the better of me, and I definitely regretted it.

"Rai, seriously?" I shrieked, whipping my gaze away, heat rushing through me.

"Whoa, Raikidan, dude," Raid said.

"What? What's going on?" Ryoko asked.

"Don't look!" I said as she went to look behind her.

"What, why?"

"He's not wearing anything."

Ryoko's hand flew up to the rear-view mirror to cover it, and her face reddened a bit. "Seriously? Why?"

I noticed the way her hand was positioned on the mirror and it almost looked like she was peeking. *Of course…*

"I wasn't wearing any when I shifted," Raikidan said.

Ryoko shot me a questioning look and I shook my head. "He was wearing a towel."

"Okay, that makes more sense. Please tell me one of you guys is wearing some armor cloth to give him."

"Yeah, already on it," Rylan said. "Here, streaker."

I stared out the window while Raikidan changed into something. He was such an indecent creature. I glanced at his hand when he laid it over the console, with his palm facing up. "You're not getting anything."

"I did my job. Share the reward," Raikidan said.

No way was that happening, but that didn't mean the others couldn't have a chocolate or two. I reached into the bag and pulled out two and handed them to Rylan, far out of Raikidan's reach. "Share with your brother."

He sighed. "Yes, mom."

"Yeah, they're truffles!" Raid exclaimed when he popped his into his mouth.

"Oh, oh, I want one, please!" Ryoko begged.

I chuckled and handed one to her and then ate one myself. Raikidan continued to hold out his hand for one.

"You're not getting one," I said.

"I deserve one too," he said.

"Like hell you do. You caused the assignment to get out of hand."

Raikidan narrowed his eyes and lunged forward. I tried to push him back, and even Ryoko tried to protect me, but he managed to steal two chocolates and sit back roughly in his seat. I glared at him and then sourly stared out the window.

Ryoko looked at me funny. "Are you legit mad at him?" I glanced her way and she focused back on the road. "Okay…"

"Dude," Raid whispered to Raikidan. "If I were you, I'd sleep with one eye open for a while."

Raikidan snorted and Ryoko giggled. Rylan also found his brother's lack of knowledge amusing and I found myself smirking a little as the two's laugher filled the vehicle.

"What did I say that was so funny?" Raid asked.

Ryoko quieted herself down. "You'll find it rare for a day to go by and he hasn't upset Laz in some way."

"And he's still alive?" Raid asked.

"Laz hasn't seemed to want him dead yet," Ryoko said, a irksome sly tone to her voice. "So some of us think she secretly likes that he's a pain."

I snorted and she laughed.

Rylan tapped me on the shoulder. "So, are we still going to lunch? 'Cause I'm super hungry."

"Yeah, me too," Raid agreed.

I chuckled. "Yeah we can go out for lunch, but I need to change up my look if you guys are going to eat as humans."

"We can go to the shop," Ryoko said. "I need to change out the truck anyway."

I nodded. "Good idea."

My eyes drifted down to Raikidan's hand when he dropped it on the console again. I glared at him, but he held my stare until I sighed and gave in.

Ryoko giggled. "See. She likes it."

"Shut up, I do not," I muttered.

"Oh don't be like that, Laz. There's not a single woman out there that doesn't mind being the damsel in distress every now and then."

I snorted and stared out the window. "No woman but me. I have no desire to be weak and pathetic."

"That's not what—"

"Ryoko," Raikidan said in a stern tone. "Stop."

"But—"

"Drop the subject."

"I can see how he's still alive," Raid said.

I grunted but continued to stare out the window. That is, until Rylan tapped on my shoulder. I glanced back at him and the moment we made eye contact, I knew what he wanted. I chuckled and handed him a piece of chocolate before going back to watching the city pass by.

CHAPTER 14

I huffed and sprawled out on the couch. I hated summer. It was far too hot, and today was no exception. Not even shorts and a cropped tank top were helping. The urge to expel the rising heat in my body was great, but I was too hot to move, and I wouldn't let others see it come from my throat. "Summer can go to hell."

"You said it," Blaze muttered as he sprawled himself out in front of a small fan that kept shutting off. "Stupid piece of crap."

"At least you have the breeze from that fan," I shot. "Can't feel that over here."

"Dude, Raikidan, how can you sit there and act like you're not over-heating?" Blaze asked.

Raikidan grunted. "Your human bodies are weak, and easily affected by the smallest change. Ours are not."

I snorted. "Don't let him fool you, Blaze. He's just as hot as the rest of us. He's just trying to be Mr. Tough Guy."

Raikidan glared at me and Blaze chuckled. "You're good at reading him."

"Someone has to, or no one would understand him."

Raikidan tossed a couch pillow at me, but I didn't defend myself or retaliate after it bounced off me. I didn't have the energy.

Rylan stood over me and handed me an ice disk. "You look like you could use this."

I sighed with relief when I placed it on my forehead. "Thank you."

"Hey, where's mine?" Blaze said.

"What do I look like, an ice box?" Rylan retorted as he walked back to the kitchen.

"Yes," I teased with a smirk.

"Don't make me take that away. You know I will."

I snapped my teeth. "I'll bite you."

He shook his head in response. I chuckled and went back to cooling myself off. I brushed the water from the melting ice all along my neck and placed the disk on my stomach to melt a bit.

"Okay, I'm getting out of here," Blaze announced as he rolled off the couch.

"Pervert," I muttered.

Ryoko and Shva'sika sauntered out of the hall as Blaze disappeared down it.

"What's with him?" Shva'sika asked.

Ryoko pointed to me as I shoved what was left of my ice disk down my shirt. "That's what's up."

Shva'sika shook her head. "How do you deal with that all the time?"

"You just learn to," Rylan said. "Especially when you're stuck with him as long as we have been."

Ryoko nodded and then joined him by the bar. "Can you hand me an apple?"

Rylan reached for the bowl of fruit and meticulously searched for the right apple. When he found the right one, he handed it to her and waited.

Ryoko bit into the apple and squealed when she was overwhelmed with juice. "That was juicier than I expected."

Rylan chuckled. "You're welcome."

Shva'sika sat on the back of the couch. "Impressive. You can pick out water level in objects. I've seen few water or ice elementalists and shamans who were capable of doing that."

"I can only do it sometimes, and it's not all that special," Rylan muttered.

Shva'sika crossed her arms. "You sound ashamed of what you can do."

Rylan pushed away from the bar and left the kitchen. "I'd like to be normal for once."

He made an attempt to head down the hall, but Ryoko grabbed his arm, and from the quick tweak in his face, it was tight.

"You are normal," she murmured.

Rylan looked at her and she held his gaze. Shva'sika's eyes flicked to me and I gave my head a firm shake. She was to stay quiet and wait it out. I could tell by the bond's pull that this interaction was something they needed, but it was short-lived when Raid came bounding down the hall. He wore boxers and board shorts, piquing my interest on where he was planning on going.

"So, Ryoko, what did they say?" he asked.

Ryoko released Rylan and turned her gaze to Raid. "I haven't had the chance to ask."

I resisted the urge to sigh. Leave it to Raid to mess it up. I knew he had done it on purpose. Something deep within told me so. I looked at Ryoko. "What's he talking about?"

"Well, since it's so hot, we figured we'd do what everyone else is doing and hang out at the park by the lake."

I sat up quickly. "I'm game."

Ryoko blinked. "What? Just like that?"

"It's hot."

"You know I'll make you wear a bathing suit, right?"

"Yeah."

"And it's going to be a bikini."

"I figured as much."

"Who are you and what have you done with the real Laz?"

Shva'sika giggled. "Trust me, it's still her. After she started training, heat began to affect her in a new way. It's a common side effect for fire elementalists; it goes away as they train. Until that day, we used the prospect of cooling off as a reward for her if she did anything we asked."

A devious glint came to Ryoko's eye. "Anything?"

I rolled my eyes and got to my feet. "Not anything."

Ryoko crossed her arms and huffed. "Whatever. So is everyone game, or are we going to have to figure something else out?"

"Yes," I said.

"Sure," Rylan and Raikidan replied.

"No." I looked at Seda, who sat in the corner, acting as unaffected by the heat as Raikidan. "I'll be staying here."

I crossed my arms. "I'm not okay with that. Genesis will more than likely join us, leaving you here alone."

"I'm fine with that."

"And pigs fly."

Seda shrugged. "I'm unregistered. I can't leave this house to go into the city."

"You can with this," Argus announced as he strolled into the living room. In his hands he carried a black watch.

My right eyebrow arched high. "Care to explain how a watch will help her?"

Argus chuckled. "It's not a watch. It's a cloaking device. I've been working hard on this, and I just finish testing half the settings."

I walked over to the other side of the couch and took it from him. "So this is the ultra-secret project you've been working on?"

Argus smiled. "Yeah. I didn't want anyone knowing about it until I knew it was going to work."

"Well almost anyone," I glanced back at Seda as I spoke.

Seda crossed her arms. "I knew nothing about it, thank you." She got up from her spot and joined us. I handed it over to her so she could look at it. "You said you only have half of the settings tested?"

"The settings for men," he clarified.

"Didn't test the ones for women?" I teased.

"Course not!" he shot back.

I chuckled. "You're so weird."

Seda laughed. "Well, I'd be happy to test the rest of it for you, Argus."

Argus smiled and absentmindedly ran his fingers through his hair. "Thanks."

Seda strapped the watch onto her wrist and began messing with the settings. It was interesting to watch her features change within a blink of an eye. One thing that didn't change, though, was the watch. It was always visible. Unless Seda hadn't found a setting that would change it, that might pose a problem.

"Gah! I have to know, how does it work?" Ryoko asked.

"It creates an electromagnetic field around the user that is so thin it's unnoticeable to the naked eye," Argus explained. "This field distorts in specific ways to create the illusion of change, as directed by the watch. A sensor in the watch can detect environmental change to make the illusion look real. The only thing I haven't been able to get down is the tactile aspect of it, what a person feels. The long-sleeved shirt Seda is testing now won't feel like one when touched. You'll feel bare skin since she is wearing a T-shirt in reality."

Ryoko crossed her arms. "That sucks."

Seda smiled. "I might be able to help you fix that. I'll work with you to get this just right."

"Um, thanks." Argus scratched his head. "You don't have to, though. I'll figure it out and I don't need to be wasting your time."

"Wasting time?" Seda laughed. "I have more time than I know what to do with."

I shook my head. "Just take the help, Argus. With two of you working on it, you're bound to find the right answer faster. But I have a question for you. Does that have the ability to change voices?"

Argus shook his head. "No. It's too far away from the vocal cords for it to work. I plan on making a separate device to fix that issue once I get this device right."

"Very well."

Seda giggled quietly. "Argus, can you help me? I was hoping I'd figure it out on my own, but I've gone and confused myself more."

Argus chuckled and moved close to her. "Sure. Let's see here…"

I skirted around the two and headed for my room to look for something to change into but Ryoko grabbed me by the arm and pulled me back down the hall. "Oh, no you don't. I'm picking out what you wear."

I sighed. "Does it really matter that much?"

"Yes." Her tone told me there was no arguing. "You boys should go to the park before us. We'll catch up."

I dug in my heels and looked at her funny like everyone else.

"What?" she asked, her eyes innocent.

"You make it sound like we're going to be a while."

She rolled her eyes and grabbed onto me again. "Of course we are. Everything has to be perfect."

I sighed as she pulled me into Shva'sika's room. "What is with you? Why can't average be enough? It's just a bathing suit that's going to get wet."

Ryoko gasped. "How could you think about getting wet?"

My brow furrowed. "Because it's hot?"

Ryoko shook her head and sat me down on the bed. "No. You don't swim. You sit in the shade to keep cool and all the while look good."

"That makes no sense! If I wanted to be dry I'd stay at the house."

Shva'sika's quiet chuckle wisped into the room as she entered and shut the door behind her. "I'm siding with Laz on this one, Ryoko. We're going to have fun and to cool off. Now instead of trying to argue, let's get Laz into something before she comes to her senses and tries to escape."

I rolled my eyes. They didn't get it. I wasn't going to run. I honestly didn't mind the idea of wearing a bathing suit. I didn't know why. In the past even the smallest thought of me wearing one would have horrified me, but for some reason, now I was okay with the idea.

I watched as the two picked out bathing suit after bathing suit and bickered about which one would look good or not. It was amusing really. It also felt normal to do. Was that why I was okay with doing this? Because it felt normal?

It didn't matter. I was determined to have fun and make the most of the opportunity to cool off.

The three of us strolled down the stone path leading to the lake. I carried a white volleyball under my arm and a long beach towel over my shoulder. A small smile was planted on my face and I had no desire to get rid of it. I already felt a lot cooler in the shade of the trees and I couldn't wait to be able to cool off more in the water.

The scarlet red bikini with matching sarong Ryoko and Shva'sika had me wear was light and comfortable, and not in the least embarrassing to wear. Ryoko, who was carrying a large cooler over her shoulder, had decided to change the bikini she had been wearing for an orange one with gold circle print. Metal rings held the front of her top and the sides of her bottoms together. She still wore her shorts low over her bottoms and she had swapped out her boots for sandals.

Shva'sika, who carried a towel for both her and Ryoko, wore a sexy, silver monokini that connected in the front in four locations by a large metal semi-triangular shaped trapezoid. A matching colored sarong draped around her hips, and leather-wrapped sandals were strapped to her feet to complete her outfit.

We strayed from the stone path to go down a worn, dirt one and disappeared into the forest. After a few feet, we emerged from the shadows of the trees and set foot on a small beach. Small waves from the lake lapped the sandy shore as the breeze blew. Several yards away, the rest of our company was just finishing setting up.

Rylan, Raikidan, and Raid were finishing their job setting up the temporary volleyball net in a grassy spot while Argus made sure there were enough umbrellas set up to keep everyone in the shade if needed. Seda and Genesis lounged under separate umbrellas. The two of them looked incredibly pale compared to everyone else. It was a little too obvious they didn't go out much, but, then again, I didn't look much better.

Seda sat up as we approached, her look taking me by surprise. She had only changed her eyes. They were still blue, but the veins were gone, and her pupils appeared normal.

"I didn't see a need to change too much," she messaged. *"This thing is unstable anyway. It won't be able to do much more than a simple change for long periods of time. Argus has a lot of work to do before it's ready to be used regularly."* I glanced around, knowing it was dangerous for her to do that. *"There aren't any psychics around. I won't get caught."*

"All right, if you say so."

Everyone stopped what they were doing when we approached, and I wasn't oblivious to the different looks I was getting. "What?"

Everyone but Blaze and Raikidan muttered to themselves quietly and went back to what they were doing.

I narrowed my eyes at Blaze. "What?"

Blaze shook his head and leaned back. "Are you sure you're Eira? The Eira I know wouldn't be caught dead in something that sexy."

I ground my teeth together and chucked the volleyball at him. Blaze threw his arms over his head and ducked. The volleyball flew past him, bouncing on the ground a few times before rolling a few more feet, stopping only when it ran into Zane's foot.

Zane picked the ball up, chuckled, and tossed it back to me. "Your aim is a little off, Chickadee."

I caught the ball and grunted before heading over to the temporary court. Rylan and Raid were still testing the tension on the support ropes while Raikidan just stood there and stared at me.

My forehead creased. "What's your problem?"

"I'm trying to understand the point to the cloth you're wearing around your hips," he said.

I walked past him. "It's a sarong. It's a fashion statement."

"It doesn't look practical."

"It's not. Like I said, it's a fashion statement. It's worn over the bottom of the bathing suit to make it look better."

Raikidan shook his head. "Whatever. Your… thing… is done being set up."

I rolled my eyes. He wasn't even trying to understand at this point. I kicked off my sandals and stepped onto the court. I would have preferred being on the sand, but with this being a temporary court, the net wouldn't be able to stay up on sand.

"Get off the court, we're not done," Rylan scolded.

My lips pressed into a thin line. "How is it not done?"

"Just get off the court and you'll see."

I sighed with slight aggravation and stepped back off the court. Rylan continued to work with the ropes with Raid, and finally motioned for Raikidan to come over to help them when it wasn't going as planned. I suppressed a laugh when I noticed Rylan and Raikidan were wearing matching board shorts. *You two would be that dumb.*

When I grew bored of waiting, I dropped the volleyball and headed for the water. I hummed contently once my feet touched the cool water. I didn't need another invitation to sit down and stretch my legs farther into the water. It felt so good I was able to ignore the fact that the sun was beating down on me.

"Seda, do you mind if I sit next to you?" Argus asked.

"No, I'd prefer you didn't." Seda laughed when he didn't respond, and I could only assume his reaction was priceless. "I was kidding! Of course you can sit here."

"Eira, you should put on sunscreen!" Genesis called over to me. "You'll burn otherwise."

I waved her off. "I already got some on. I'll put more on later."

"Don't come crying to me if you get burned," she muttered.

I rolled my eyes and then leaned back on my hands to enjoy myself. Although the breeze was warm, it still felt nicer than the stuffy humid air back at the house. I stretched my toes and buried them into the sand.

"All right, you brat, you can come back over," Rylan called.

I turned to glare at him for calling me a brat, but I couldn't muster one up when I noticed the spread-out sand on the volleyball court. I watched as Raikidan finished dumping the last bag of sand onto the ground and discarded the empty bag carelessly. Ryoko was already digging her toes into the fresh sand and she waved me over to join her.

Not needing another invitation, I dashed over to her and picked up the volleyball. I held it up to show her I wanted her to play and she nodded enthusiastically. Ducking under the net, I mirrored where she stood, and set the ball up. Ryoko bumped the ball and sent it back over the net. I bumped the ball with my wrists and sent it back over to her.

The three boys sat down in the shade of some trees and watched us as we warmed up. It was hard to concentrate on what I was doing, knowing they were watching us, but I did my best. After a few passes, Ryoko messed up. I yawned with boredom as I picked up the volleyball after it stopped rolling from Ryoko's wayward pass. It wasn't fun with just the two of us. As I turned to head back to the temporary court, a small smile spread over my face. Genesis and Shva'sika stood in the sand on either side of the net, turning our one on one to a two on two. This meant we could have a real match.

I stood next to Shva'sika and handed the ball over for her to serve. Ball in hand, she took a few steps and served it. Genesis made an attempt, but the volleyball hit the net and landed in the sand. We laughed and Genesis kicked the ball angrily, stubbing her toe on the firm surface, making us laugh more. Ryoko picked up the ball and served it to us, and Shva'sika didn't hesitate on sending it right back to them. This time the ball stayed off the ground for a few passes until Shva'sika and I crashed into each other. We only laughed at our miscommunication and went back to playing.

Blaze stretched and walked over to us. "I'm bored, so I'm going to join you ladies."

"Uh, you can't," Ryoko told him. "It would make the teams uneven."

"I'll join to make it even," Rylan and Raid offered in unison.

The two scowled at each other, and Shva'sika and I passed each other a glance. Raid being here was going to make things a little too interesting, it seemed.

"That still makes the teams uneven," Ryoko said. "Unless Raikidan joins, too."

"I don't know how to play," Raikidan said.

Ryoko huffed. "Well, that throws that idea out, so one of you is going to have to sit out and switch in at some point to make this all fair."

"Not really," Genesis objected. "I only know how to play because I've watched this game so much on TV and I'm hardly any good at this. If he gets a crash course he'd have equal skill as me."

I agreed with her and waved Raikidan over. "Raikidan, get your ass up. You're on our side. You are too, Blaze."

"Whoa, wait a second. He just said he couldn't play. No way in hell am I being on the same team as him. Take Genesis and I'll be on the other team."

"No, we're going to make the teams fair and have Gen on one side and Raikidan on another."

"I don't want to be on a team with a handicap."

"Then you can sit out!" I snapped.

Blaze flinched. "But I don't want to sit out."

"Well this team's issue is your fault, so either you're on this team or you sit out. Your choice."

The boys behind me found enjoyment in Blaze's scolding, but a quick glare from me stopped it.

Blaze sighed. "Fine, I just don't want to be bored anymore."

"Good. Everyone warm up if you need to, or just hang tight, I'm going to give Raikidan a crash course on how to play real quick."

Ryoko tossed the volleyball at Blaze. "Thanks a lot. Now you got her into her bossy mood, killing everyone's fun."

Blaze tossed the ball back at her. "Don't go pointing fingers at me. I just wanted to join in. It's not my fault the two dogs wanted in as well."

Rylan and Raid glared at him, and Ryoko chucked the ball at Blaze, nailing him in the head. "I vote he doesn't get to play now."

Shva'sika laughed. "If he didn't receive head trauma from that hit, I say he should."

I rolled my eyes and walked over to Raikidan, who hadn't really moved much except to stand. "This won't take long, it's real basic, although, I'm getting the feeling your understanding how to play more than you're letting on."

"I get the concept, if that's what you're asking, but I don't know how to play all that well. I'm still trying to understand how you hit the ball and figure out whose turn it is to hit it," he said.

I positioned his arms into the most basic pass position. "There isn't any turn-taking, per se. If the ball is closest to you then you take the shot. But it is advisable to call it out so you don't crash into someone with the same idea. The one rule you have to be aware of is that once you touch the ball, someone else must touch it before you touch it again.

"As for hitting, there are three moves that are used the most, besides serving. This one I'm about to teach you the most used by far. You use this stance to pass the ball to teammates or to get it over the net. You need to bump it off your wrists and, depending on how you angle your arm, will determine how the ball will fly. Got it?"

Raikidan nodded. "I get it. I'd like to practice, if that's okay."

I thought for a moment. The others had the volleyball and I hadn't thought to bring a spare.

"Heads up!" Ryoko yelled.

My eyes snapped to the volleyball sailing through the air at me. Getting myself into position, I bumped the ball into the air and looked at Raikidan. His eyes flicked to me briefly and then back at the ball as it came back down. Positioning his hands like I had shown him, he hit the ball off his wrists but his arms were angled too much and the ball came flying at me. Pulling back, I barely managed to escape and the ball hit the net.

"Yeah, he sucks," Blaze muttered.

I glared at him before looking at Rylan, who was picking up the volleyball. Without having to ask, he tossed it back to me. Catching it, I spun on my heels. I focused on Raikidan, who watched me with apprehension. My brow furrowed. He couldn't expect to get it right the first time, could he?

"That wasn't too bad," I said. "You just need to have your arms at a flatter angle. The angle is supposed to be just small enough to pass it to a teammate or get it over the net."

Raikidan nodded. "All right. I guess I'll try again."

I nodded and set the ball so it would come down just right for him. Raikidan, distracted by my alien move, barely managed to hit the ball this time and it flew off in a random direction. I laughed and ran after the ball. When I came back, I set the ball again, and Raikidan took the maneuver better and was able to get a better, but still not perfect, hit on the ball.

I retrieved the ball once again, but before I could set it up for him, Raikidan grabbed my hands and stared down at the ball. His brow was furrowed, so I waited for him to say what was on his mind.

"Eira." His voice was barely above a whisper, as if he didn't want anyone else to hear. "Would it please you more if I just didn't play?" My brow rose with slight confusion from his choice of words. "I'm not getting the hang of this fast enough, and I'm keeping you from your game. I know you said you need even teams, but I'd be more of a hindrance than help at this point. You'd be better off with an unevenly-teamed game."

I waited a moment to speak, making sure my words came out right. "It would please me more to see you play." He watched me intently. "It's just a game, Raikidan. It's supposed to be fun. It doesn't matter if you can do this perfectly or not. It doesn't matter which team wins in the end."

Raikidan took the ball from me. "Very well. Now, show me how to do that weird pass you did."

I chuckled. "It's called a set. It's used to set up a teammate to spike."

"What's a spike?"

I grinned. "Let me show you."

Taking the ball back from him and spinning on my heels, I tossed the ball to Blaze, who barely caught it.

"Hey watch it!"

"Set it for me," I said.

"Why?"

"Because I said so."

"You're too far away."

"No, I'm not, now set it or I'll have someone more competent do it."

Blaze grumbled and set the ball high, giving me the chance to run over there. My sarong untied and fluttered to the ground, but it didn't stop me. Pushing off the ground, I slammed my open palm down on the ascending volleyball as it came into reach and forced it into the sand on the other side of the net. Raid jumped out of the way before it could hit the spot he chose to stand in and grumbled. I landed gracefully on my feet and let out a quick breath from the extra effort I put into the spectacle.

Ryoko chuckled as she picked up the ball. "Hey, lady, mind putting some clothes on?"

I stuck out my tongue at her and she copied me. Turning away, I picked up my sarong and tied it back around my hips as I walked back over to Raikidan.

"That is a spike. Unlike normal passes, there aren't as many chances to set one of those up so there will be a slim likelihood of you actually being capable of trying for one."

"Was it necessary to run all that way?" he teased.

I shook my head. "Don't you start or I'll change my mind about you playing."

Raikidan chuckled. "So that move you called a spike looked simple enough, but how to do you do the set?"

My lip twitched. Spikes weren't always as easy as that one, but I was going to stay quiet. If I was lucky he'd find out for himself.

"The set position is actually pretty simple," I said as I started to place his hand in the right shape. "Your index fingers and thumbs come together into the shape of a triangle while you other fingers fan out and curve up so they can cradle the ball."

"Okay, that's simple enough, but how do I push it back into the air?"

"By using the ball's momentum against it. When the ball lands in your hands, you push it back up and then your teammate takes the chance to spike it, as long as you made the ball go up correctly."

"And what if I don't set it up right?"

"Well if you don't do it right, it could go over to the other side of the net and be an easy set up for the other team."

"Fair enough."

"So, are you ready to start playing?"

"No, but I might as well."

I laughed and motioned him to follow me. Everyone got into their positions, and Blaze was the first to serve the ball.

The ball sailed past me and landed hard in the sand. Blaze snickered, his inflated ego getting even bigger over his lucky point gain. My eyes flicked to Ryoko and she nodded. It was time to stop pretending.

At some point in our game, Blaze felt the need to tell us how bad we women were at this, so we decided to mix up the teams. It was now a battle of the sexes, and for the most part we had been letting them think Blaze was right. Not anymore. We were going to come back with a vengeance, and it was going to feel good. Or at least, that was the plan.

I pretended to not care and tossed Blaze the ball. "Guess it's your turn to serve again."

He had a wide grin plastered to his face. "Damn straight."

"Let them have a turn, Blaze," Rylan said. "It's no fun when you hog the ball."

"Well if they played better they'd get a fair chance," Blaze shot back at him.

Raid rolled his eyes and stole the ball from under Blaze's nose. He tossed it over to Ryoko with a sly grin, but Ryoko didn't react, which didn't set well with him. But contrary to what he was probably thinking, it wasn't Rylan who was stealing her focus. She stared intently at the ball, and I knew that look. She was plotting.

"Hey, Ryoko, any day now would be great," Blaze taunted.

Ryoko blinked and then shook her head as if she had been spacing out. She glanced at me before looking at Shva'sika and Genesis. The two nodded, signaling they knew what to do, and Ryoko took a deep breath before she served the ball. The volleyball soared over the net and came back seconds later when Rylan hit it. Genesis took the opening and bumped the ball back over, but Raid countered her pass. Unfortunately for him, his pass was too high and short, and Shva'sika took the opportunity to set the ball up for me. I made myself hesitate, so as to not give ourselves away yet, before rushing up to the net and spiking the ball. Blaze, caught off guard by our supposedly new skill, was unable to stop the ball from colliding with the sand.

His eyes went wide with disbelief. "What the hell?"

I shrugged and walked away from the net. "Lucky shot, I guess."

"You had to insult them, Blaze," Rylan muttered bitterly.

Raid ran his hands through his hair. "We're so screwed."

I chuckled before taking my position in the back of the court and bending over to stretch. Ryoko served the ball again, and the four of us worked together to rack up the points against the boys, to catch up with the score we'd let them make.

I stretched again when the boys demanded a break from our assault, and we kindly gave it to them. We all stayed on the court while the boys went into a huddle. Zane, Argus, and Seda were laughing from their shaded spots as they watched the boys try to figure out a way to make a comeback.

Argus and Seda shared an umbrella and sat rather close together, and I tried not to smile. It wasn't good to see things that weren't there. Seda and Argus were just friends, and with Seda's psychic nature, I wasn't sure if that would ever change. Few could handle what she was. Nioush was a prime example of that.

As I looked at Seda, pain plucked my still heart. She was only able to be here with everyone because of that stupid watch. She couldn't come out in public without it—not until things changed. So, why were we here having fun when there was work to be done? Without us helping to cause things to change, she would have to hide. It was only once we achieved our goal that she could truly be who she was. But I would never see that. It wasn't meant to be for me.

"Don't worry, Laz, that day will come, and you will be there to see it," Seda said.

"Don't start making things up on me, Seda. You and I both know that isn't my fate."

"Life has infinite timelines, created by every possible choice out there. Every choice changes our course in destiny."

"You've checked my fate many times. It's stayed the same."

"I don't have access to all the timeline branches. There is still a chance it will change."

"This is me we're talking about, Seda. Fate has never been kind to me."

She sighed. *"Try to have an open mind."*

"Laz, watch it!" Ryoko yelled, pulling me away from my conversation.

I ducked just in time to miss being hit by the ball.

"That was close," Genesis mumbled. "You okay, Eira?"

"Yeah I'm fine. It didn't touch me."

"That's not what I meant. You kinda went somewhere else on us all of a sudden."

"My fault!" Seda yelled over to us. "I was distracting her! Sorry!"

I stuck my tongue out at her as if going along with it, and the others knew to just accept it. I picked up the ball and threw it over the net so the boys could serve it again. As we continued to play, the sight of approaching soldiers caught my eye, but only because I recognized the one leading them. Zo walked over to the three sitting under the shade, and evidently found no reason to be courteous, because he went straight to being a thorn in everyone's side.

"So, Argus, looks like you've finally gone and gotten yourself a new girlfriend."

Argus' eye shut in embarrassed frustration, and his cheeks tinted pink. Seda's face also flushed. "She's not my girlfriend, Zo."

"Pity. She's cute," he teased. "Name's Zo, sweetheart."

"Uh, Seda," she introduced extending her hand. Her lack of a fake name surprised me, but then again, the real her was dead, according to records.

Zo took her offer and kissed her hand. That's when he noticed the watch. "Not common of women to wear men's watches."

Seda pulled her hand away and spoke quietly. "It was my father's…"

"Oh, uh, my apologies."

Ryoko and I looked at each other, and then at the others, who all nodded. It was time to either get rid of him or get to work.

Zane sighed. "Zo, is there a reason you're here, or are you here just to bother us?"

Zo opened his mouth to defend himself, but my shout stopped him. "Heads up!"

The volleyball flew right at them. Most of his lackeys had enough time to dodge the renegade ball, but the hard sphere ultimately pegged Zo in the head. *Wow, his reflexes suck.*

"Nice going, Eira," Blaze joked.

I stuck my tongue out at him and ran over to the umbrellas. Zo already had the ball in his hands by the time I made it to them. "Sorry about that. Ryoko didn't set that up right for me."

Ryoko gasped. "It was so not my fault!"

I rolled my eyes and made an attempt to focus my attention on Zo, even thought he was giving me a look I'd rather he not give. "So what are you doing here, Zo?"

Zo spun the volleyball on his finger. "Just patrolling to make sure the park stays safe with so many people around."

"Not that there are a lot of people on this end of the lake," Argus muttered.

Zo gave Argus a funny look, but Argus was looking elsewhere so he placed his focus back on me. But before any more conversation could transpire, a squeak escaped my lips when someone picked me up and threw me over their shoulder.

"C'mon, Butterfly, you're wasting time, and we have a game to finish," Raikidan scolded as he turned around.

"Rai, put me down!" I shrieked. "I haven't been gone long. I don't even have the ball!"

Raikidan turned and held his hand out to Zo. The two men stared each other down until Zo reluctantly handed over the volleyball. I let out a quiet sigh. I hated the tension between them. I didn't understand it.

"I think you do understand," Seda teased.

"Don't you start," I threatened. *"And you shouldn't be talking to me like this. There's a psychic in this patrol."*

"Calm down. He's on our side."

I could faintly hear his low chuckle, but I pushed him out of my head. I grunted when my body bounced on Raikidan's shoulder the moment he started walking away from Zo.

"Caveman," I muttered. Raikidan shook me a little while grinning, and I smacked him in the head, a small laugh giving away my lack of anger. "Asshole."

Raikidan chuckled and continued carrying me back to the volleyball court. I stopped struggling, knowing full well he wasn't going to let me walk on my own. He finally put me down once he set foot on the court, and I smacked him in the arm before ducking under the net and taking my position with the girls. Raikidan handed the ball over to Raid, who waited for the guys to get ready before serving the ball.

The game went smoothly—for a while—until Genesis and Shva'sika forgot to communicate. Their bodies collided, the ball went flying into the lake, and we were all left in stitches. The two argued about whose fault it was, which only made us laugh more. Ryoko and I were the first to get our laughter under control, and we looked at each other. Someone was going to have to go get the ball, and if it was going to be between Shva'sika and Genesis, we'd be waiting a while.

"Race ya!" she challenged as she took off toward the water.

"Hey, no fair!" I yelled. "Cheater!"

Ryoko laughed and continued running. I took off after her, and it didn't take much to catch up. Our feet touched the waterline at the same time, but Ryoko was the first to reach for the volleyball. Unfortunately for her, she fell and splashed into the shallow water. I picked up the ball and laughed at her.

Ryoko glared at me. "You pushed me!"

I continued to laugh. "Ryoko, I didn't push you."

"Yes you did! You knew I didn't want to get my hair wet, so you pushed me."

I stopped laughing and looked at her sincerely. "Ryoko, I didn't touch you."

"Felt like someone touched my back."

"You fell on your own."

Ryoko gazed down at the water and scratched her head. "Wow, I suck."

I laughed again, but my laughter was cut short when something crashed into my body and I fell into the water. I sat up and glared at Raikidan and Rylan, who stood near us laughing. It was a little obvious now, Ryoko's accusation was partially correct.

Ryoko roared with anger and snatched the floating volleyball between us and chucked it at them. "Assholes!"

Rylan stopped laughing and ducked just in time for the ball to miss him and hit Blaze, who was laughing back at the court. Everyone else laughed at his misfortune, but Ryoko and I were too pissed off to care who it hit.

Raikidan stopped laughing when he realized I didn't find what they did funny. "E–Eira?"

I narrowed my eyes and ground my teeth. "I'm going to skin you!"

"Dude, run!" Rylan said.

The two took off in opposite directions down the beach, and Ryoko and I jumped to our feet to pursue them. I lost track of how many times Raikidan whipped his head over his shoulder to gauge the distance between us, but every time he did, I gained a little bit of ground on him. Raikidan finally came into my reach, and I shoved him into the sand. I slid to a halt in the wet sand and kicked it up into his face in anger.

"Ass-hat," I spat before storming back down the shore.

I pulled my hair clip out of my hair and teased it roughly with my fingers to get as much water out as possible. Twisting my hair back up into the hair clip, I messed with my unruly bangs, but gave up. My bangs always curled up when they were wet, unlike the rest of my hair, and only a flat iron or heat on my fingers ever fixed it.

As I headed up to sit under the shade of an umbrella, Shva'sika grabbed me by the shoulders and spun me around. "Back to the water you go."

"What gives?" I complained.

"It's time you cooled off from this heat. You're already wet, so you might as well hang out in the water."

"But I need to get out of the sun. I'm going to burn, even with sunscreen."

"You'll be fine. Besides, you could use a little color."

"I don't need to be as red as my bathing suit!"

"Calm down. You're not going to burn. You still have a little while before you need to apply more sunscreen." Shva'sika lowered her voice. "Besides, I'm starting to understand why you can't stand that Zo guy. He's giving me the creeps and won't go away."

"You're just getting creeped out by him now?"

She hushed me. "Yes. It takes a lot bother me."

I pursed my lips. She had a point. Not wanting to be anywhere near Zo or his goons, I walked back down to the shore with Shva'sika. I dipped my feet into the water, enjoying the coolness. I looked up to see what Raikidan was doing, but I couldn't find him. He wasn't where I had left him, and there weren't any new foot prints to tell me had wandered back this way. It was for the best anyway. I'd probably try to drown him, given the chance right now.

I sat down and leaned back to relax. The water rushed over my legs, cooling me off, and I sighed happily. Seda and Genesis came down to join us and began splashing around. I shielded myself when they went after me and I made an attempt to ignore it so they'd leave me alone, but when Shva'sika joined in on the assault, I changed my mind. We all laughed and enjoyed the change of pace from competition to leisure. I stopped splashing around when Ryoko stomped through the water over to us.

"I guess it's safe to assume you didn't catch him," I said.

Ryoko held up her fingers to make a measurement. "I was this close. This close! Then he took off into the woods and I wasn't going to run after him with bare feet."

I splashed her a little and she squeaked. "Well, forget about it and have some fun. It's not worth it."

"He pushed me! Of course it's worth it."

I splashed her again, but this time with quite a bit more water. Ryoko huffed with annoyance and stared me down. I grinned and splashed her again.

"That's it!" Ryoko swung her arm and sprayed me with a wave of water. My retaliation consisted of laughter and a wave of my own sent her way.

Ryoko laughed this time, but instead of splashing me back, she hit Genesis with some water. The water then became a war zone until I had enough and backed out. I sat in the shallows, watching them continue on with their little game. The longer it lasted, the crazier their antics became.

I cocked my head, puzzled, when they stopped suddenly and observed something behind me. They had stopped laughing, and Ryoko had an ugly scowl marring her face.

I turned to see Rylan and Raikidan making their way down to us. In Rylan's hand was a small tray of snow cones. If they thought snow cones were going to make Ryoko or me feel better, they were dead wrong. I for one didn't even like snow cones.

Ryoko crossed her arms. "If you think a snow cone is going to get me to forgive you, you're sadly mistaken."

Rylan shook his head. "They're not for you. I only have three here, and they're for the ladies next to you."

Ryoko glared at him, not that I could blame her. He really did only have three snow cones on the tray, which meant neither she nor I was going to get one. What were they up to?

Rylan then pulled his other arm from behind his back, revealing an ice cream cone with green ice cream, a light brown liquid, multi-colored sprinkles, and some other weird candy on top. "But you can have this, Ryoko."

Ryoko gasped. "Is that mint ice cream with peanut butter sauce, sprinkles, and candied bacon?"

I choked on a breath of air. "Candied what?"

Genesis and Seda laughed and Ryoko glared at us. "Leave me alone! It tastes good."

I shook my head and laughed at her. She had some weird tastes.

"So is it really candied bacon, Ry?" Ryoko asked, her hands coming to her face, giving her an adorable pleading look.

Rylan chuckled. "Promise not to pulverize me, and you can find out."

Ryoko sighed and then held out her hands with a pout. Rylan snickered and walked over to them. The four of them accepted his peace offering and ate contently. I went back to washing water over my legs to keep me cool. I knew there wasn't any for me, so there would be no point in waiting for something that wasn't going to happen.

Raikidan chuckled in my ear. "We didn't forget about you."

I tilted my head when he offered me a wafer cone with chocolate soft serve ice cream topped with whipped cream, peanut butter and chocolate sauce, and rainbow colored sprinkles.

"I know how much you like chocolate."

"You really think chocolate ice cream would be a good peace offering for pushing me?"

He kept his voice low. "It's also a peace offering for what I did on that assignment the other day. I know I should have stayed in the car, but I thought it better to protect you instead. I know you can handle yourself, but I feel like you need to be willing to let someone else help. I let that get the better of me and I made the situation harder on you. And for that, I'm sorry."

I took his offering and then smiled wickedly. I turned and smooshed it a little in his face. "I forgive you."

Raikidan wiped his face as I ate the rest of my sweet snack. He smirked, and I grunted when he splattered my cheek with the ice cream on his hand. I tried to rub it away with my free hand, but it was a little difficult as it was sticky and the hot sun was making it dry fast.

"Jerk," I muttered as I dabbed some water on my face.

Raikidan chuckled and then touched my back. "Your skin is turning pink."

I glared at Shva'sika. "I told you I needed more sunscreen."

Shva'sika shook her head. "You burn way too easily."

How my elven friend didn't suffer the same issue was beyond me. I rose to my feet and headed for some shade. Raikidan followed me, after washing his face, and when I sat down on a towel under a large umbrella, he handed me a bottle of sunscreen. I gave him my ice cream and went about applying the cool liquid. I made an attempt to get my back, but failed miserably.

"I'll help," Raikidan offered, reaching for the bottle of sunscreen.

"No, I got it," I insisted.

Raikidan grunted, but sat back and waited anyway. I sighed and gazed at him with a pout when I gave up. He snickered and handed me my ice cream cone. I took my dairy treat and ate it while he applied the sun screen. His gentle, but firm hands pacified me, and I couldn't help but think about how good he might be at giving a back massage. *Not that I'd ever want one.*

I glared at Raikidan when he stole my ice cream from my hands and replaced it with the bottle of sunscreen after he finished with my back.

"I bought it," he said.

"You bought it for me."

"I gave it to you as a peace offering, and you seem pretty peaceful now."

"I can change that."

Raikidan stared at me for a moment and then reluctantly gave the treat back. I started eating my ice cream again, and eyed the soldiers who were still hanging around. Most of the soldiers were paying attention to everything going on in the park, but Zo didn't feel as inclined to work. He and Zane were talking about projects the boys had to do, and it bored me.

Handing the rest of my ice cream to Raikidan to finish off, I laid down to relax. I continued to listen to Zo and Zane's conversation, making me think about the paint job I still had to do on my motorcycle. I had finished my helmet some time ago, but I hadn't had the time between work, assignments, and that small vacation out of the city to get over to the shop.

Maybe I should do that soon. It sounded like a good idea. It wasn't going to get painted on its own, and my helmet looked dumb without something to match it. *Maybe I'll ask Azriel for some time off.* I needed a change of pace anyway. I could make it look like I was still working at the shop for Zane, and that would give me a nice break from the hell I had to endure to make Azriel happy.

I closed my eyes. *Good plan, Eira.*

CHAPTER 15

I held my breath to remain steady as I welded a new link to Rylan's neck shackle, and I was grateful that he was being patient and still. Even with a fire-resistant cloth protecting his neck, something could go wrong if I wasn't careful.

He had come to me earlier and asked to help him with his shackles. Apparently the ones on his wrists were getting in the way too much, and he needed a way to keep them from doing so but to also stay a bit fashionable as well. Even though I couldn't see how chains could ever be fashionable, I agreed to help him anyway. Or try to. The material these chains were made of made it difficult to add something to them, and taking the collar off was out of the question.

Rylan worked up a design that was removable and I proceeded to create it, even though I doubted it was going to be any less annoying than before. I was actually sure it'd be more so, but that was why it was a removable design, just in case.

I let out a breath when I finished and scrutinized the design to make sure it looked good. The chains on his wrist shackles had been extended and connected to a large silver ring. His neck shackle now had three chains hanging from it, and they also connected to the silver ring, positioning it in the center of his chest.

"Okay, we're done," I said. "What do you think?"

Rylan smiled. "I like it. It's light, and exactly to the design I was looking for."

I nodded. "Good."

We looked at the stairs when the door to the living room opened and Ryoko came jogging down into the basement.

"Hey, Ryo," I greeted.

"Hey," she said with a smile. "Just figured I'd come to see what you two are up to. You've been down here a while."

I pointed to Rylan. "Just finished up a fashion request for the diva."

Rylan snorted and Ryoko laughed. "What new fashion statement is trending now?"

I shrugged. "A new chain look."

She took notice of my work and appraised Rylan. She then nodded. "I like it."

Rylan smiled. "Thanks."

My gaze shifted to the stairs again when the door opened again, and raised a brow in slight confusion when Shva'sika made her way down. "What are you doing home? I thought you went to do some shaman-related things."

She nodded. "I did, but then I was called to do something else."

"That something requires you to come down here?" She was never directly involved with rebellion affairs, and she didn't know how to drive, so I couldn't think of what she'd need down here.

"No, I just came to get you."

The look she was giving me was making me uneasy. "Me? Why?"

"She's asking for you."

I blinked. "Who?"

"Arcadia."

Ryoko and Rylan looked at each other, but remained quiet.

I stared at Shva'sika for a moment and then shook my head. "Wait, what? Why? She never makes contact with anyone."

"Not true. She comes in contact with full-fledged shamans all the time.

"But I'm not a full-fledged shaman."

Shva'sika nodded. "That is why you are being summoned. She says you need to progress through this next step in your training. It's your turn to take a trip to Hell." My eyes opened wide in shock. "All shamans are brought through this process before they can be considered for full shaman status."

I held up my hands. "No. There's a mistake. I'm not ready for that kind of stuff."

"She thinks you are."

I shook my head. "Shva'sika, I just barely got through my issues with the spiritual plane. I'm not ready to go to Hell, even if it is temporarily."

"You don't have a choice." I glared at her. "You're willing to defy a summons from a god?"

I sighed. "This isn't a good idea."

She smiled a little. "It's not going to be that bad. I did it and came out in one piece, I'm sure you'll have no problem."

I thought this over for a moment. "What am I supposed to do?"

"You just need to go to the spiritual plane. She'll be waiting for you and then she'll tell you how to get in and out of Hell, and the rules you need to follow while there."

"I have to know, why do I need to know how to get in?"

"I think you already know the answer to that."

My lip twitched. "Do we really get information from such corrupt people?"

"As shamans, we do not pick sides. We collect the information needed from whoever can offer it. Whether it be from a spirit who was sent to move on, or sent to Hell, it doesn't matter. That is our way."

I took a deep breath. She had a valid point. Not picking a side was a weakness of mine. "Okay. Where do you want me to do this?"

"Wherever you feel most comfortable. You may be there for a while."

"So, my room."

She giggled. "I guess that makes sense. Do you want my help?"

I nodded. "I think I'm going to need it."

She motioned for me to follow. "All right, let's get started then.

I sighed and reluctantly followed, leaving Ryoko and Rylan to go about their own business. This wasn't a good idea. I may have felt better about going to the spiritual plane, but that didn't mean I was experienced enough yet.

I sat down on my bed while Shva'sika shooed Raikidan out, not that I wasn't expecting him to be back in here when I came back from my little trip. He didn't like being forced out of here, especially lately, and definitely not without a reason, and Shva'sika had done just that.

Taking a deep breath, I placed my hands over Shva'sika's when she situated herself, and closed my eyes. Once my spirit shifted from my body to the other plane, my eyes fluttered open. I got to my feet and peered around the dark area, which was covered with a thick fog. *Not what I was expecting.* Had Shva'sika not been standing beside me, I would have started to think something bad was going to happen again.

My attention was pulled to one direction when I heard the clopping of wooden shoes. Through the thick fog, I could see two lights of different heights approaching us.

"Looks like she's here," Shva'sika said. "Do you want me to stay here for when you're done?"

I shook my head. "I know how to come back."

She nodded. "Okay. If I feel like you need more spirit to keep your body from passing out, I'll feed it some while you're gone. Your body has become more accustomed to the transition, but it's still not where it can indefinitely continue on its own."

I grinned. "If I get a headache I'm blaming you."

She giggled and then disappeared as she went back to the physical plane. I then went back to waiting for the approaching lights. As they came closer, the fog thinned until it revealed a tall, fair-skinned, white-haired woman with plate crystal eyes. The woman wore ancient swordsman attire I had only seen in library books, and was adorned in magnificent jewelry. Several Katanas were tied to her hips, and in her hand she carried a bamboo pole with a lantern attached to the end.

By her side walked a magnificent white wolf with piercing amber eyes. The wolf carried a matching lantern in its mouth and, as they stopped advancing, it placed it down on the ground and waited.

I bent down on one knee respectfully. "Arcadia."

Her sullen expression twisted as she tried to smile. "It's good to finally meet you face to face, Eira." Her hollow voice took me by surprise. "Are you ready?"

"I suppose, though I don't really know what I'm doing," I admitted as I stood back up.

She chuckled. "Since those sentenced to Hell cannot leave, I'll be showing you how to enter and leave in case you need information from someone there. It is an important skill to have."

"Are there any rules for me to follow?" I wanted to make sure I didn't mess this up.

She nodded. "Don't make any deals. It will only cause you problems. If at any time I must leave you, stay with Maiyun. If she hands you her lantern take it. It will protect you from the most dangerous of souls. The last rule is to not show fear, but I don't have any doubts about you on that rule."

I chuckled and then nodded. "All right, then I'm ready.

She turned and walked back the way she came. I set a quick pace to catch up with her. I didn't want to lose her in this fog, although we didn't need to walk much farther. When she stopped walking, I looked around. There was nothing but fog surrounding us. Was this Hell? Was it really that easy to enter? No, that couldn't be right. If it were that easy, Arcadia wouldn't need to waste her time showing us how to get there.

Arcadia lifted her free hand and reached out into the fog, but as she did, the fog began to ripple as if it were a sheet of water. "This is the entrance to Hell. Touch it."

I lifted my hand and did as she instructed. The fog ripped when I touched it, but I didn't feel anything.

"Good. Take notice of how the fog rolls across the ground and through the air. Notice how around this door, it makes a subtle frame. The more you see it, the more you'll be able to recognize it when you approach."

"How do I find it anyway?" I questioned. "How will I know where to look?"

"I watch over this plane. I know when spirits come in to be guided, and I know when shamans enter to seek information. I can sense what the shaman needs, and I can either place their spirit in the location they need to be, or tell a spirit with the proper information to meet them. If you are looking to enter Hell, I will place you by the door. You just have to go to it."

"Sounds like a tough job."

"It used to be, when I was inexperienced and was just allowing the living to come here momentarily. But now it's a simple task, even when having to manage several tasks at once. Now, follow me."

I nodded and walked through the door after she passed through. Once on the other side, I took in our surroundings. Dark, ankle-deep water covered the rocky ground, and dead plants and trees were sprouting out of it. Ancient tombstones and rocks scattered about had eerie lights emitting from them, and a thin fog blanketed the area. It looked like a dark forest from some horror movie or bad dream. "This is Hell?"

Arcadia nodded and began to walk. "Yes, this is what it looks like. Dreary place, isn't it?"

"Well, it's fitting," I murmured as I followed and continued to look around. Arcadia giggled and I looked at her funny. "What?"

"I'm sorry, but I've watched you for some time, since you're a shaman, and your dry humor reminds me of my brother sometimes."

"Brother?"

"Yes, Phyre."

I tilted my head. "I'm going to be honest, I don't understand."

She nodded. "I apologize again. I nearly forgot you're from Dalatrend. Texts that have our histories in them are banned. You wouldn't know this because Zarda declared they be removed from public sight long before you were born. And many texts, besides those protected within the Eternal Library, have been destroyed over the millennia."

"Eternal Library?"

"You refer it to as just the *Library*."

I nodded. "Okay. This is making a bit of sense. Could you explain it to me, since I've never been allowed access to this information?"

She smiled a little. "Of course. This will come to a shock to you, but we gods were once mortal and had special abilities that led us down the path of immortality. My mother is Lunaria, and while she was mortal, she met my father, Solund, and later on they had Phyre and me."

"Lunaria is you mother?" I mused. "I guess that makes sense, for you at least."

Arcadia giggled. "Well, if you knew about the abilities of both my parents, you'd understand a little more, but then again, things are a bit different now than when I was mortal. When I was mortal, many millennia ago, Lumaraeon was still difficult to live on. We had spans of years where the earth moved and natural disasters were normal. Then they'd stop and it would be peaceful for a span of years.

"During this time, mortals were quite ordinary. They had no connections to the elements. No connections to animals. At this time very few had ascended to god status. This is the world I came from—a world that on a rare occasion produced a mortal with a special gift and, if used right, would send him down the path of immortality."

"So you and your family were these people?" I guessed.

"Yes. As family lines mixed, these abilities manifested more often, but it was still considered rare. Both my parents had particular abilities, and their blood was passed to my brother and me."

"Lunaria and Solund are considered the moon and sun gods to us. What do their abilities consist of?"

"An ability that is rare these days." She half smiled. "They were light benders."

"Light benders?" I echoed.

She nodded. "They were capable of bending light around them, with the help of objects such as weapons. My father could only bend sunlight, while my mother could only bend moonlight. Though, you're no stranger to this ability, are you?"

I nodded in thought. There was one person I knew who was capable of harnessing that ability. "Why is it so rare?"

"Because as time passed, the ability changed into what you call spirit energy."

I tilted my head in thought. That was interesting. "Did you have anything to do with that?"

She chuckled lightly. "No. Light bending changed on its own as bloodlines mixed. My ability wasn't light bending. I could see the dead. That's how my unique ability manifested. As a child, I thought it was normal to see the deceased. Though, when my gift was made known to others, I found out how wrong I was, and few believed I was capable of it until I predicted that a particular wealthy man at a party my parents were hosting would die soon. As I grew older, I set out and put the dead at ease, because back then, the spiritual plane didn't exist, and that path led to my ascendance."

"There was no spiritual plane?"

Arcadia shook her head "There wasn't one for some time." She halted and looked around. "It wasn't until Phyre, Valena, Kendaria, and some of the elemental gods ascended and pacified the land did we create this."

I gazed around. We now stood at the edge of a clearing of the dead forest, the perimeter marked with broken down iron gates and lights. The clearing was large, rocky, and still covered with a great deal of water. In the middle of the clearing was a tall tree that rested on a rock, surrounded by a pool of lava. The roots of the tree grew into the lava, and the bark of the tree was charred, though it was obvious it was alive, as the branches had violet flowers without leaves growing from them. The lava, as if acting as the tree's life source, like water would, fed into the tree, causing the ancient symbols carved into the bark to glow with life.

Talismans hung off the branches of the tree and tiny white lights suspended in the air twinkled, piquing my curiosity. I found myself moving closer to the tree, but Arcadia stopped me. "Hold on. Don't get too close."

"Sorry. I guess my curiosity got the better of me," I admitted.

"It was the memories."

"The what?"

"The lights. They get everyone."

"Those are memories?"

She nodded. "This tree was placed here as a reminder of what these souls gave up. It reminds them of life and beauty and, while you can't hear or see them that well since you're part of the living, the memories show them what they gave up."

"Fire and brimstone have nothing on this place," I murmured.

"That was Phyre's philosophy when he suggested making this place."

"Yeah, about that. Care to explain that better to me?"

"It's quite simple. The spiritual plane didn't exist until we created it, so spirits wandered on the living plane until we created a place for them pass over to, or to go to Hell."

"Okay, why does Hell have a name and the area spirits pass over to does not?"

"Because I didn't think it was needed," she admitted. "Hell wasn't meant to exist, but it was determined as a necessity because there were some souls that just weren't worthy enough to know peace. So we created and named Hell in hopes that less would end up here."

I nodded and stared at the tree. She had used the word *soul* several times now. It was an interesting word to use, and not one I was unfamiliar with. I heard a lot of old shamans using it. They always said spirits and souls were different, but I had always equated them as the same thing. But by the way Arcadia spoke, I knew I was wrong to think that. Souls were what resided in our bodies. They were our life essence that mixed with our life element. Spirits were just the form they took to resemble who they were in the life they had. To simple people, they'd just be called *ghosts*. A stupid word really.

As I thought about souls, a thought came to me, but it didn't feel related to my mission here, so I kept quiet. But Arcadia noticed the wheels turning in my head. "You have something on your mind."

I hesitated. "It doesn't have to do with this place so it's not important."

"You're welcome to ask," she encouraged. "Depending on the question, I might be able to give you an answer."

I nodded without looking at her. "It has to do with what you told me earlier; you and the other gods ascending to immortality and all. If that's true, then where do Genesis and Zoltan fit into that statement? They're the gods of life, right? How could they ascend if they made everything?"

Arcadia chuckled. "They're the exception. No one knows where they came from. Not even Genesis and Zoltan themselves know. The first thing they remember was waking up on an inhospitable Lumaraeon alone."

"So they had to find each other before creating the world?"

"Sort of. You mortals see Genesis and Zoltan as the gods of life, but that's only half of the truth. Genesis is the goddess of time and Zoltan the god of matter, so they were able to create small changes to the world without each other, and what they created became bigger, or more effective, if the other had been in that area some time before them. It wasn't until they found each other that they were able to combine their powers to create the start of the life you know now."

"So, it's possible their ascendance didn't happen until they met each other?"

She nodded. "It's possible, but because it's unknown how long they had been on Lumaraeon before finding each other, it's hard to say if they ascended before or after their meeting."

I eyed her slyly. "But in the end, it doesn't matter, right?"

To my surprise, she shook her head. "It does matter actually, because it's knowledge not even the gods have. We question why we came to be. Why we have abilities that others don't."

"Well, I can't explain why we exist, but I can take a guess why we have the skills we do," I offered.

"Go on."

"Because Genesis and Zoltan created everything, can't it be possible their power was passed through their creations? Could it be that passive transfer made it so only a few could physically manifest the power, where others just passed it through their genetic lines?"

Her eyes widened. "That could be it. I'll have to tell the others, for us to think over."

"I heard once, that if a god was no longer believed in, they disappear. Is this true?"

"It's half true," she admitted. "We lose our immortality and some of our power, but we don't disappear. We just become mortal again and either have to attempt to ascend back to our immortality, or we die from the aging process our new mortality gives back to us."

I nodded and then looked around when a loud, echoing roar pierced the air. It sounded like—

"An ancient dragon's soul," Arcadia explained. "Made a pact with Nazir for power, much like most of the souls here."

"Do all spirits that make pacts come here?" I was quite curious about this.

She took a deep breath, as if the question I asked was a loaded one. "All pacts are carefully evaluated and judged accordingly, or, at least, that was how it's supposed to be. Without Rashta, it's hard to pass judgment on corrupted souls."

"Rashta? As in the goddess of judgment and rebirth?"

She nodded. "Yes, that's her."

"Why isn't she helping with the corrupted souls? Isn't it her job to pass final judgment on certain matters?"

She nodded and appeared to be piecing out the right answer. "Yes, that is her job, but she's… missing."

"Missing? Don't you mean she lost her god-status?"

"No, she's well believed-in. She's just missing."

"How in Lumaraeon can a god go missing?"

Arcadia chuckled. "As gods, we watch over the mortal races. They need our attention. Because that is our job, we don't have the power to monitor each other. At least, not all of us. The few gods who travel across time are capable of it, though they are so busy with their jobs, they cannot help. Rashta herself could, but she was the *Judge*. She needed that power to keep us from getting too involved with you mortals, and to keep us from corrupting ourselves with power."

"Didn't seem to stop Nazir."

She chuckled again. "Nazir has his own interesting story. He became one of us because of his corruption. He was the embodiment of death and corruption. Rashta can't change that. Her power can't change what made us gods."

"I see." I thought for a moment. "Does this mean, with Rashta's disappearance, Zarda wouldn't be sent here if he was deemed corrupt for whatever reason?"

Arcadia frowned. "I cannot share the fates of other souls to you, especially for your own gain."

"I understand that, but I believe he is corrupt, even if none of you deem it so, so I'd like to understand the process."

She nodded slowly. "It's not impossible for us to make a judgment call. His soul would wait on the *Plane of Between* for some time while we evaluate him."

"Plane of Between?"

She nodded. "It's a plane you're quite familiar with. It's the plane a soul will meet you on so you don't have to fully cross over to the spiritual plane. This plane is where you can still see the living world around you."

"That's not the spiritual plane?"

She shook her head. "No. The Plane of Between is also experienced by just hearing the voice of a soul."

I nodded. "Okay, I get it. So what happens to a newly departed spirit once they reach that plane?"

"They wait for us to judge how corrupt they were in their life. If they made a Pact of Power with Nazir, then they don't need our full judgment. While mortals have free will to choose a path that we cannot change by force, it is against Cosmic Law to allow such a soul to continue on to a place of rest. If they are a pure soul, a soul that made a Pact of Selflessness, or were seen as corrupt by mortals but had no corrupt means behind their actions, they are allowed to pass on. This is the only way we can do it without Rashta.

"But without her, corrupt souls, with corrupt intentions and means behind their actions, are hard to judge, and sometimes her determinations for other souls were better than ours. Sometimes we make mistakes, but only she can fix them because she has the knowledge."

"So you could wrongly judge someone and only she'd be able to fix it when she reappears?"

"Yes. That's why this topic is a little difficult to speak about. We don't have the kind of powers Rashta does, so we can't judge as well as she can, and we don't like to know that we've sentenced someone incorrectly."

She looked in another direction with a furrowed brow. I pursed my lips. "Something the matter?"

"Not sure," she admitted. "Sometimes souls try to escape here, particularly when they notice I bring a new shaman in, or a shaman enters looking for a particular soul."

"You can go check," I said.

"Are you sure?" she asked. "Since it's your first time here in Hell, I'll be leaving you here. It's for your safety."

I nodded. "I'm confident I'll be able to handle it. You told me the rules to follow."

She half smiled. "Good, you'll need to remember that. Maiyun will stay with you, but she will need to feed off your fearlessness. As fearless as she was in life, Hell is not a place she is fond of, and at times she can give into her fears."

"I've been meaning to ask about her," I admitted as Maiyun sat next to me.

Arcadia chuckled. "I already know what you're going to ask, since everyone does. I had her while I was mortal, and when she died, I preserved her soul so she could help me."

"Didn't want to work alone, right?" I guessed as I pat Maiyun on the head.

"She helped me deal with my ability," Arcadia admitted. "As much as I told people I was okay with it, I lied so they wouldn't try to help with something they struggled to understand. Maiyun helped me in their place, and I couldn't just accept being alone once she died. I know, it sounds selfish…"

I smiled kindly. "Maybe it is, but I don't see Maiyun complaining. She seems pretty happy to be by your side still."

Arcadia smiled. "Thank you. I'll be back as soon as I can." She turned to leave but stopped. "Oh, and the reason you need to make sure you don't show fear here, Eira, is because if you do, the rules here allow the corrupted souls to touch you, and if they do, they will corrupt your pure soul. If you are corrupted, I can't allow you to leave."

I nodded. "I understand."

I watched her leave, and then gazed down at Maiyun, who looked a little unhappy to see Arcadia leave without her. I patted her on the head with a smile. "It's okay. She'll be back soon. I know I'm not as good company as her, but I won't bite at least."

Maiyun licked my hand as if to accept my friendly offer, and I pet her on the head some more. I scanned the area when I thought I heard something moving around in the woods. Maiyun began to whimper, and I hushed her softly as I continued to look around. Movement of a large shape caught my eye, so I knew we definitely weren't alone.

Maiyun nudged me. My eyes flicked down to find her holding her lantern and gazing up at me. I reached down and accepted the lantern from her. Lifting it over my head, I called out to show them I wasn't afraid. "Show yourself, soul. You can't scare me."

"Have you come here to mock us, *Ancient Soul?*" A deep voice hissed. "Have you come to point out what we've done wrong, so that we suffer more?"

I turned around when I sensed a large presence behind me. I was taken aback by the large black dragon towering over me, his hateful but pained eyes burning into me.

"Who are you?" I demanded.

"Wouldn't you like to know, Ancient Soul?" he sneered. I was rather surprised that I could understand him, but the rules around speech on this plane were far different than that of the living one.

My head tilted. "Why are you calling me that?"

"Don't mock me, Ancient Soul," he hissed. "You've been blessed with many lives, while we have to relive the pain of what we lost."

"You mean, what you gave up."

He roared in anger, scaring Maiyun, but I reassured her while I coughed. "Your breath smells like death. I'd appreciate it if you didn't do that again."

"Stop mocking me, Ancient Soul!"

My eyes narrowed. "Stop calling me 'Ancient Soul.'"

"I do not know the name you call yourself in this life."

"My name is Eira," I said. "Who are you?"

"Anir. Does it ring a bell?"

"No, should it?"

"Yes. You're the reason I'm here!" He bared his teeth. "You're the reason they judged me incorrectly upon my death."

My brow furrowed. "I think your memory has done a little melting while you've been here."

"It was your fault! I gave up everything, and in the life you lived then, you couldn't have cared less," he seethed. "I made a pact so you'd see you were wrong to walk away from me, but all you did was hate me."

"Because you're a coward." His eyes widened at my insult. "I don't know why you think I'm someone from your past, and frankly I don't care, but I can see why she wouldn't want you. No one wants a coward. No one wants to rely on someone who would be so foolish as to make a pact just to appear better than they really are."

Anir roared in anger, and this time I was unable to keep Maiyun calm. She panicked, and before I could do anything, she ran off into the dark woods. "Maiyun, no, come back! Maiyun!" When she didn't come back, I turned and glared at Anir. "Now look at what you've done."

"That look… it's the same. Lifetimes of rebirth, and you still are capable of that same look." He sounded almost sad. "That look broke me. It's the look that made me see how wrong I was, and how much I had hurt you."

"Well, if you're looking for a pity party, you're going to have to search for it from someone else," I spat. "I have to go find Maiyun now, thanks to you."

"Please don't leave me again," he begged as I walked away.

"I can't walk away 'again,' because this will be the first time I've ever walked away from you," I said. "A soul like mine, it could never be allowed to have more than one life."

He sighed. "Even in this life, you see yourself as some mere stone, instead of the gem you truly are."

I let out an aggravated breath and trudged through the water. I wasn't going to correct him again, and I wasn't going to get in that debate with a stranger, especially when I had something more important to do. I needed to find Maiyun. Arcadia said she was a preserved spirit, but I wasn't sure if she could be corrupted or not. I wasn't going to be the reason Acadia couldn't have her companion follow her around anymore.

I called for Maiyun over and over as I tried to find her. Due to the nature of this plane, she didn't have much of a scent to track. My heart started to feel heavy when I continued to receive no answer. I was starting to worry about her. I wanted to blame that dragon for showing up and scaring her, but I knew it was my fault. I wasn't able to keep her calm, after all…

I stopped walking when the sound of a child crying echoed into my ear. This perplexed me. Why would a child be here? Being too curious for my own good, I followed the sound until I came to a small girl with pale skin and dark hair sitting on a rock. Something didn't quite feel right about her as she cried, but I couldn't place what.

The girl's crying slowed to a sniffle when she noticed me approaching. "W—who are you?"

"My name is Eira," I told her with caution. "Who are you?"

"Dela," she sniffled.

"Hi, Dela, why are you crying?"

"'Cause… 'cause I'm lost and scared…" She started to cry again. "I don't know where I am. This place is scary! Mean people walk around here trying to scare me, and they talk about being dead. I want to go home! I want my mom…" She stopped crying when she noticed the lantern in my hand. "You're not one of those mean people who says they're dead. You can help me!"

"I'm not sure if I can, Dela."

"But you can bring me back to my mom!"

"Dela, this is going to be hard to understand, but you're dead." Something wasn't right about this girl. Even as a spirit, she would know she was dead. I had been told that time and time again, even when they'd try not to believe it happened, they'd still show signs of knowing the truth.

She blinked. "What? No, that's not true. That can't be true."

"Yes, Dela, it is true."

She shook her head. "No!"

"Then tell me, what were you doing before you ended up here?"

"I was going somewhere," she explained. "We were in the car. Dad was driving us somewhere when I fell asleep. Then I…"

Something in her eyes told me this wasn't right. Something wasn't right about her, but I continued to play along. "You woke up here, right?"

"No, I didn't wake up. This is a bad dream," she insisted. "Mom says when I've been bad I can dream about a place like this. It's a place where bad people go when they die. I thought she was saying it to scare me…"

"Dela, I'm sorry, but you're not dreaming." I needed to get through to this girl. I needed to find Maiyun, but my job as shaman was making that difficult now.

"No, I'm not!" she shouted. "Tell me how to wake up from this place!"

I sighed with aggravation. "Dela, stop this."

"Take me away from this awful place!"

"No, Dela, I can't take you anywhere, because you were sentenced here. You died and you were sent here."

"No I wasn't," she insisted "I'm just a kid. Why would a kid be sent to a place like this?"

There was the slip-up I was looking for. "You're not a child. You're just disguising yourself as one."

She looked at me with hurt eyes. "Why are you being so mean?"

"You can't fool me, corrupted spirit. You can't get me to believe your masquerade."

She scowled. "How? Tell me how you knew."

"It's in your eyes," I explained. "You can't hide your true nature, because your eyes give you away."

She glared at me. "You're one to talk."

I chuckled. "I never said I was trying to hide. You can't use me as a tool, because I refuse to be used like one again, even if that is my purpose. You can't possess my spirit, because you'll just wind up here again… because no matter how much good I try to do, no matter how much I try to make up for my past, I will end up here too."

"But you live now. You will give me life once again!" The little girl changed shape into a large, black, featureless sprit and came at me.

Staying calm, I closed my eyes and felt the spirit phase through me. I opened my eyes and turned to face it, to see it, trying to understand why it was unable to touch me. "I'm not afraid to die. It's what I deserve, after all, but I have a job to do, and until that job is completed, I can't die. Now, if you'll excuse me, I have someone to find."

The spirit snickered. "You'd better hurry before it's too late."

I narrowed my eyes. "You were just a distraction, weren't you?"

"Arcadia should know better than to leave that pup alone in this place." It chuckled and began to disappear. "It's so full of fear here, it's intoxicating."

Cursing, I took off into a full sprint. I didn't care how much noise I was making, or how much attention I'd draw to myself. I was not going to take that spirit's words as some sort of bluff.

My heart skipped when I heard Maiyun whimpering and growling. I didn't stop running until I found her, and was horrified by what was going on. Maiyun, sopping wet from her run, was crouched down as low as possible without submerging her face in water, while dark, featureless spirits surrounded her. Some occasionally reached out to grab at her.

I growled and threw the lantern at them, knowing full well I couldn't conjure up any fire from my chest. "Leave her alone!"

The spirits scattered in an attempt to avoid the light, and the lantern crashed to the ground just past Maiyun. Taking the opportunity before the spirits collected themselves, I rushed over and wrapped my arm around her protectively. She whimpered, and I hushed her quietly while keeping an eye on the spirits. There were getting closer again, and I thought I could hear them hissing out terrible things they wanted to do to the poor wolf. When a spirit tried to reach out, I retaliated, and it shrunk back but didn't leave.

I didn't understand what they wanted from Maiyun. I couldn't understand where Arcadia was for that matter. Shouldn't she be able to tell there was an issue, or was the problem she was dealing with a bigger one?

I held Maiyun tighter when the spirits closed in as a group. Whatever they wanted, they weren't waiting for it now. Pulling Maiyun into a more protective embrace, I closed my eyes. "It's going to be okay, Maiyun. I'll protect you."

Maiyun licked my elbow and just as she did, a warm sensation grew inside me, feeling as if it were projecting outwards. I assumed it had to be my courage as the spirits tried to harm us. Since I wasn't afraid, and they were howling in anger, or what I speculated to be anger, it was the only explanation.

The sloshing of feet running through the water toward us echoed through the area. I didn't open my eyes, even after the noise stopped, until a hand touched on my shoulder. "Eira?"

I opened my eyes and gazed up at Arcadia. "Hey."

"You two okay?" Worry filled her eyes.

I nodded and stood, making sure to retain contact with Maiyun, in case she was still a little scared. "Yeah, we're fine, thanks to you."

She tilted her head. "Me?"

I looked around. "Yeah, you got rid of those spirits, right?"

"Oh, that, yes." She pat Maiyun on the head gently. "Care to tell me what happened?"

"Shortly after you left, some dragon spirit started freaking out at me. It scared Maiyun to the point that she ran off, even as I tried to keep her calm. I chased after her and found her being attacked, and did my best to protect her. Then you showed up."

Arcadia pursed her lips. "What dragon soul?"

"He called himself Anir."

She nodded. "The ancient soul you heard prior to me leaving your side. He didn't give you much trouble aside from scaring Maiyun off, did he?"

"No, he was just bothersome. Kept calling me 'Ancient Soul' and tried to convince me I was someone from his past, just in a new body, as if I had been given a second life or something like that."

Arcadia started thinking. "Interesting…"

"Souls can be reincarnated, right?" I asked. She nodded. "How often does it happen?"

"Tricky question," she admitted. "There are no set rules as to when or why a soul should be given another life, especially now with Rashta missing. She used to say when and why, but now souls are just reborn at random. Some souls are never reborn, while others are reborn multiple times."

"I'm not an ancient soul, am I, Arcadia?" I questioned.

She shook her head. "I'm afraid I can't answer that."

"Why not?"

She chuckled. "Because I don't know."

"Oh, okay." I found that quite strange. She was the keeper of this plane. Shouldn't she know things like this? "Can gods be reborn?"

She looked at me funny. "Pardon?"

"Well, you said Rashta was missing, and she's the goddess of judgment and rebirth. Couldn't that mean she could have died, and been reborn into a new life with a new identity?"

Arcadia shook her head. "As long as a god is believed in, it's impossible for us to die. Since death is required for rebirth to happen to a soul, it would be impossible for Rashta to be reborn without losing her status as a goddess. Besides, if that were the reason for her disappearance, Genesis and Zoltan would know."

"I suppose…"

"You don't believe me."

"It's not that. I'm just thinking." Truth was, I wasn't sure what to believe. *Why does it feel like she's hiding something?*

"I should show you the way back now," Arcadia stated. "I've kept you longer than I had intended."

I nodded and followed her as she started to walk off. Maiyun picked up her lantern and then happily followed us. I patted her on the head as I mulled over everything that happened. Between the confrontation with Anir and the information Arcadia had given me, my mind was trying to piece together a puzzle I wasn't sure was solvable, or that didn't want to be solved at all.

16

CHAPTER

My pace was quick as I headed for Genesis' and Seda's room. Seda informed me of an assignment that needed special handling, and I wasn't going to say no. When I reached the door, I pressed my back against it when Argus appeared in the hall. These halls may be bigger than the ones in the back of the house, but it was still easier to just let one person pass at a time. But he surprised me when he stopped in front of the door as well.

"Are you going into their room, too?" he asked.

I nodded. "Yeah."

He grinned. "Well if they want both of us, then this should be interesting."

Want us both? That was a strange thing to happen. I couldn't remember, besides during a skirmish, when Argus and I had ever worked on an assignment together. Not that I was against the idea, I just wasn't sure how the two of us could accomplish an assignment together when we had vastly different skills.

I opened the door, and the two of us strolled in to find Genesis reading some papers, and Seda, like usual, was meditating. She told me once why she did it so often. It apparently not only helped with obtaining important pieces of information from the *Life Timeline,* but it helped with keeping her psychic ability in check. She said it wasn't uncommon for the average psychic to meditate up to ten hours a day. Although she seemed to be rather alert, so I had a feeling she wasn't meditating as hard as she should have been.

Genesis glanced up from her papers. "Oh, good you're both here. I have a very important assignment for the two of you to work together on."

Argus and I exchanged a look and then focused back to her.

"Okay, go on," I said.

She laid her papers out on the bed and I ventured closer to get a better look, even though I figured I wouldn't be able to read them. To my surprise, they were coded in the symbolic language I had created.

"The Council has been tasking the rest of our team with a great deal of surveillance assignments, and they uncovered something interesting. According to the reports, inside the military outpost in Quadrant Four, there is a research facility disguised as a supply house."

I scanned some pictures that had been printed out on the papers. The building looked as I would expect any supply warehouse. "You said this post was in Quadrant Four. This wouldn't happen to be the one at the end of Cypress Street, would it?"

Genesis nodded. "Yes, that's the exact one."

"That one has a lot of security."

"Yes, I know."

Argus chuckled. "I think I get what's going on here."

Genesis grinned. "Good. But I'll spell it out to make sure. The Council believes this research facility has some valuable information we could use. I've volunteered the two of you to infiltrate it and take whatever you can. Eira, you were an obvious choice, being able to slip in and out of a location without detection with relative ease. I've chosen you, Argus, because it's not soldiers we have to worry about protecting the place. It's the technology. Knowing this, I knew you'd be the optimal choice to help her get into the building." She grinned. "And I found some old paperwork on you, showing you had once been up for selection to be trained as an assassin."

My eyes widened at him, surprised. He looked away and rubbed his neck. "Yeah, but I didn't make it past the first round of selection."

"So?" I said. "The fact that you were up for selection, when you weren't designed to be an assassin, is impressive in its own right."

He smiled meekly. "Thanks."

Genesis looked between the two of us. "So, are you okay with him working with you, Eira?"

I nodded. "I have no issues with any part of this assignment. I trust Argus will be an excellent partner in crime."

Argus laughed. "I'll try not to let you down. But I do have a request."

"Go on," Genesis said.

"I think it would be wise to have at least two lookouts," he suggested. "That way we have eyes outside of the building."

I nodded. "Good thinking. We don't need any surprises."

Genesis nodded as well. "I agree. I'll assign Rylan and Raikidan to help. I believe they will be best suited for that task."

I agreed and then switched my focus to Seda. "Would you mind letting Rylan know? I'll fill Raikidan in after this."

She smiled. "Of course."

I set my eyes back at Genesis. "We'll leave at sundown to take the advantage of the cover of darkness."

"You know best." Genesis looked at Argus. "Bring whatever tools you think you'll need. While the rest of the Council believes what we're looking for will be creations laying around on a table or stored in a secure safe, I suspect the information we are really seeking will be blueprints or plans, stored on computers, and will need to be constructed later."

He nodded. "I understand. I'll bring the best, most lightweight equipment I can. Eira, is there anything you need me to bring?"

My brow furrowed in thought. "Uh… not that I can think of specifically. I'm not as tech-savvy as you, so as long as you bring what you think will help, I'm fine."

He nodded again. "I'll try not to let you down, then."

I placed the paperwork back down on the bed and headed out of the room to inform Raikidan of the plan.

I listened for the sound of guards before noting the coast clear and slipping out of the shadows. Argus was close behind and almost as quiet as I was, impressing me, what with all the gear he carried. I could see why he had been selected and, with a bit of training, would do quite well as an assassin. But I'm sure he was rather happy to have not been picked. I know I would have been.

We came up to the entrance of the building, and Argus went to work hacking the lock while I kept watch. At the sound of scattering pebbles, I activated my heat sense ability and scanned the area. No warm color signatures moved about, but I wasn't going to take any chances and let my guard down for a second.

We had expected this place to be lit up better, and had planned for such an experience, but we learned quickly that the military really wanted to make this place look like a simple storage house.

I cranked my neck over my shoulder when something *clicked* and Argus waved me to follow as he opened the door. With quick steps, I closed the distance between us and was careful to shut the door quietly behind me.

"You're moving around rather well in this dark environment," he complimented in a hushed voice.

"Heat sense," I replied. "Allows me to see heat signatures, making it a little easier to move around."

"That's handy. Wish I could see. This place is ridiculously dark."

I grabbed his hand. "Just follow me. When we get to a good room, I'll keep watch and you can use a flashlight."

"Okay."

I led him down the long hall, until we came to the first door on our left. I forced Argus to touch the door so he knew I was choosing this room, and he checked to make sure it wasn't a secured door. Discovering it wasn't, he opened it but found it to only be a utility closet. We moved on and tried the next door, only to find it to be a bathroom.

I blew out a breath and Argus chuckled. "Third time's the charm?"

I led on and we tried the next door, but it was an empty room.

"Guess not this time," I muttered.

"Something is weird about this place," Argus observed. "This hallway feels rather long, and there have only been three doors, with only one leading to a room that happens to be empty?"

"There are also no sounds of people, or any heat signatures indicating someone has walked or patrolled down here recently."

"Do you think it would be unwise to use a flashlight?"

"We should be extra cautious."

"All right."

We proceeded on until Argus stopped suddenly.

"What is it?" I asked.

"I hear the humming of a computer," he said.

I blinked. "I only hear a weird buzzing noise, but it's faint."

"Yeah, that's what I'm talking about," he said. "How long have you been hearing that?"

I shrugged. "Since we passed the utility closet."

I watched as he started inspecting the walls. I couldn't see how that was going to give us an answer, but I let him do his thing. He was the master genius here. To my surprise, he found something. A *click* behind the wall sounded and then a section of the wall slid away. *A hidden door?* We peered in and found a large, dark room. Argus turned on a flashlight, to find the room filled with computers and tables with projects in progress.

I nodded. "You actually found a room. Impressive."

He rubbed the back of his neck. "It wasn't much, really. I just figured because we hadn't found any rooms yet, and you said you had been hearing the computers pretty much this whole time, they had to be hidden. It's a smart move on their part."

I grinned. "But they didn't expect we'd have a genius on our side."

His face reddened a bit and he headed into the room. "I'm no genius. Just a little smart."

"Right."

Argus went about his job, and checked out the computers while I scanned the projects on the tables. There were several plans laid out that appeared to be weapons, or potential weapons, though I couldn't read what any of them were. I snatched them up anyway, knowing they'd either be useful to us, or, at the very least, could hinder Zarda's force a bit if they went missing. The last plan I grabbed caught my eye particularly. The papers depicted large gauntlets, and what looked to be elements spewing out of it.

I shifted my focus to Argus, finding him going to town on the giant computer. I smiled. He appeared amused, as if he were enjoying his job. *Cute.*

My communicator crackled, pulling my attention away. I adjusted my signal and connected with Rylan as he was finishing his sentence. "Come again? I had signal interference."

He sighed. "No wonder you hadn't heard me call in these last three times."

"Three? Wow, I just heard the tail end of this last one and it was rather fuzzy," I said.

He chuckled. "Right, right. I was just checking to make sure things were going smoothly in there. It's quiet out here. Raikidan decided to fly around the compound as an owl just because he's bored."

I chuckled. "Well things are a bit more exciting here. Took us a while, but our resident genius found a hidden room with a lot of good stuff." I watched as Argus started to become very excited. "And I'll have to signal you back. It looks like Argus found something of interest."

"How good?"

"Imagine Ryoko in a four-story candy store."

Rylan laughed and then cut the connection. I strolled over to Argus and peered over his shoulder. Numbers, symbols, and what I assumed were words ran over the device he was using to hack into the computer.

"You're awfully happy."

He chuckled. "I've found some nice information. I'm pretty sure I can singlehandedly create a few things from most of it."

I grinned. "I like the sound of that. Care to share what you found?"

"The only complete ideas are some new weapon styles that are far more powerful than anything in use now, which use a type of ammunition that would be easier to obtain, or even make. The incomplete ones are mostly weapons, but there's a plan about special communication devices I'm pretty sure I can work into our communicators."

"I'd definitely agree those are some promising finds. But are you sure the files are safe?"

Argus nodded. "I have a few trace killers running on this device. So if any sort of tracer is attached to any piece of information I'm taking, it'll be killed immediately."

Argus never ceased to impress me. "That's rather interesting. I had no idea that kind of thing existed."

He chuckled. "We *smart people* don't like to share the programs so I'm not surprised. The one I created can also destroy the original file if I want."

I grinned. "Would you be willing to do that? Not to everything, but anything that would really put a halt to some plans that could give us trouble."

He nodded. "As long as you're okay with these researchers getting into trouble."

"I can live with that."

Argus shook his head while smiling. "All right."

I watched him punch a few buttons on his portable device, and then observed as some of the files on the computer disappeared. The process fascinated me. Watching Aurora work did the same thing to me. I knew quite a bit about the technology we had, but not like Argus and Aurora. They were something else.

"Did you find anything?" Argus asked as he continued to punch away on buttons.

"A few plans," I replied. "One I think that would be a great idea to consider building from the looks of it, but I'll give it to you later to decide for yourself."

"I'm okay with that." He then removed his device from the computer. "I'm done. There was a lot of information, including a map of this place and a few other places that I'm sure will come in handy down the road."

"Really?"

He pulled up a map and showed me. "This one is of this building. We're in the largest room."

I nodded. "Makes this find that much more impressive. Do you want to go into these other rooms?"

He chuckled. "No need. The computers are networked together, so I was able to steal all worthwhile information without needing to leave the room."

I almost laughed. "Nice work. I guess we'll get out of here then."

"Might as well, while the odds are in our favor."

I nodded and led the way out, making sure I was still cautious and aware of any potential dangers.

CHAPTER 17

I clicked the power button to my communicator. That had gone well. I knew she'd be happy, but happy would be an understatement for what actually happened.

Ryoko held her hands close to her chest and her ears twitched, showing her eager impatience. "Well?"

"Everything is good," I said. "She's excited to have volunteers. Based on her reaction, I'm thinking she hasn't had any for a while."

Ryoko threw a fist into the air. "Woo! I'll go pack the car up with supplies."

I nodded. "Good idea. Grab Rylan and Raikidan to help. The faster we get things packed up, the sooner we'll get there. I'm going to go tell Genesis everything is good to go, and I'll grab Raid. I think he's still sleeping."

She nodded and headed for the basement to pull the boys from their little sparring practice. I poked my head into Genesis and Seda's room, but before I could say something Genesis spoke. "I heard. Glad it's going to work out. Those children need the help."

I nodded. "That's why I thought about it when Ryoko and I passed it the other day. I could hear she had a lot of kids to take care of, and it sounded as if she had very little to no help."

Genesis nodded. "It'll also be good face for our cause too."

"I'm more concerned about the children than our face," I stated. "Not like we're going to tell her who we are anyway. Now, I'm going to get Raid."

She huffed. "Okay."

I had been a bit rude, but I didn't like that she had been thinking about our cause at the moment, instead of what really mattered. This wasn't the time.

I headed down the hall, and when I came to Raid's room I listened. It was rather quiet but I knocked anyway.

"Yeah?" The reply surprised me. Even though I hadn't heard snoring, which he was known for, I didn't think he was awake.

"It's me," I said. "Need to ask something of you."

The door opened and Raid smiled at me. "What's up?"

"A couple of us are going to volunteer at the orphanage. You wanna come?"

Raid's eyes sparkled. "Yeah I do!"

I chuckled. "Glad you're excited about the idea. Ryoko, Rylan, and Raikidan are all loading up the car now with supplies."

He nodded. "Okay, great. I just have one request."

"What is it?"

He paused for a moment. "Do you think I can go in my dog shape? I'm having some difficulties controlling my ability today. I promise I won't talk."

"Was that why you were so quiet in here?" I asked.

He nodded. "I was trying to concentrate and keep things under control."

I chewed on my lip as I thought about his request for a moment. "Let me ask the Matron. Some of the children might be afraid of dogs. Or allergic."

He nodded and waited as I unclipped my communicator from my belt loop and searched for the right signal again.

"Hello?" came the answer when I found it.

"Matron Lyra?" I asked.

"Oh, Eira, hello again," she replied pleasantly. "What can I do you for?"

"My friend, Ryoko, had the idea of bringing our dog with us for the children to play with and I was wondering if that'd be okay. He has all his shots, is friendly, and gentle with small children."

"Oh, that would be wonderful!" Matron Lyra said. "The children have been asking for a pet for some time so I think this will be a nice treat for them since I can't get them one."

"All right. I'll get Raid prepped for the ride. Thank you, Matron Lyra."

"I look forward to seeing all of you." She laughed and I thought I could hear some quiet voices near her. "And the children are getting excited too."

I chuckled. "I'll try to get everyone out the door soon."

"See you then."

I turned my communicator off and smiled at Raid. "Looks like you're good to go."

Raid's eyes lit up, and he instantly shifted to his dog form. I laughed as he jumped around and barked with excitement.

"Careful, I might get the impression you like kids," I teased.

He held his head high. "And who says I don't?"

I smiled and went to go get him a collar and leash. Hearing that was actually rather nice. I didn't know many men who were so open about their opinion of children. At least, not in a positive way. As much as I knew I made a terrible parent, I liked children. They were innocent, and most of them were cute. But it was also expected of women to like children. It may be built into our DNA to care for and like them, but it was society that expected more from us. It was a harsh expectation I wasn't too thrilled about. So hearing men say they cared just as much, or more, about children without those expectations placed on them was a nice thing.

I grabbed a collar and leash from the closet, as well as a few toys for the kids to choose from. Just as I turned around, Raid jumped up and snatched the leash and collar from me and took off for the basement. I chuckled and shook my head before following. When I managed to catch up, we were in the garage and he was sitting patiently while the others were loading the last bit of supplies into a SUV. We had collected a lot from other groups, and I hadn't realized how much had been given until I watched Rylan struggle with shutting the trunk without bending the hatch. The back seat was full, and it appeared some of the items were threatening to spill into the front seats.

"Ready?" I asked.

Ryoko nodded. "Yeah that was the last of it. We're definitely going to have to take more than one car."

I snickered. "Yeah I can see that. Raid and Raikidan can come with me."

They nodded and I headed for my car while Ryoko and Rylan hopped into the packed SUV. Raid's tail thumped happily as he tried to sit still as I pulled out of our parking spot, but I wasn't paying attention to what he was doing. I was more interesting with Raikidan. He was quiet and almost looked upset.

"You okay, Rai?" I asked.

"Yeah, I'm fine. Just thinking."

"You know what we're doing, right?"

He nodded. "Yeah, Ryoko told me."

"Okay." I got the feeling he didn't want to talk. Whatever he was thinking about was making him a bit irritated, and I didn't want to make it worse. I laughed when Raid started pacing. "Raid, calm down. Your pacing won't speed up the time it takes to get there."

He huffed. "I know. I'm just excited."

"I think this is honestly the first time I've seen you so excited about something."

Raid ducked his head as if he were embarrassed. "Yeah, so what?"

"So nothing," I said with a small laugh. "It's just an observation."

Raid snorted and went back to his pacing, but Raikidan wasn't so okay with it. "Will you stop that? It's annoying!"

Raid immediately stopped at his outburst and I just stared at Raikidan. "What is your problem?"

"Nothing," he muttered. "It was just annoying."

"Don't you dare lie to my face."

"I'm not lying."

"Yeah, bullshit."

"Hey, Eira, it's okay. If the pacing is bothering him I'll stop," Raid defended.

"Except your pacing isn't bothering him. Something else is, and he's taking it out on you," I said as I glared at Raikidan before turning my eyes back to the road.

Raikidan crossed his arms and didn't say anything. I didn't know what his problem was, but he had no right to take it out on Raid.

I pulled up to the orphanage and parked the car. One look at the building and it had me upset. The condition was even worse close up than when I had seen in from afar while walking with Ryoko. We may be in the third quadrant, and the orphanage may look like a real house, but it looked as if a first quadrant house had been dumped into the third.

There was a broken window with plastic over it, and another window that was boarded up. The front porch was broken—frankly looked unsafe for anyone to step foot on—and the roof needed more than a bit of patching. This place needed work, and I couldn't believe these children had to live here.

"This place looks awful," Raid murmured, mirroring my thoughts. "I can't believe it could be allowed to get to this state."

I snorted. "You really think Zarda cares about orphans?"

"Well, no, he pretty much hates kids, but you'd think the citizens would help out every now and then. At the very least they wouldn't let this place get into such a state."

"Why would they? All they care about is themselves," I muttered as I climbed out of the car.

Raid hopped into my seat and waited while I fastened the collar around his furry neck and clipped the leash to him. Rylan walked over to us as Ryoko went about unloading the SUV.

"Looks like the supplies we brought weren't what they really needed," he said.

"If this place is in this condition, I'm pretty sure they're going to need the supplies we brought, and more," I said.

"Hey," Ryoko called. "You going to give me a hand or what, Rylan?"

"Sorry!" he called back.

Just as he ran over to help her, the door to the orphanage opened and a slim woman with blonde and gray hair, cerulean eyes, and alabaster skin stepped out. I figured she was Matron Lyra.

She smiled. "You must be Eira."

I nodded. "I am. This is Ray, and the two by the other car are Ryoko and Rylan." Raid barked and I laughed. "And this is Raid."

Two young children poked their heads around Matron Lyra when they heard Raid, and they squealed with joy. Before she could stop them, they ran out to us, and Raid started jumping around with excitement. But to my surprise, the two girls didn't start petting him right away. They stopped when they got to us and gazed up at me with pleading eyes.

I smiled. Their manners were impressive, and they were adorable. I guessed them both to be around four or five. "You can pet him."

They two girls smiled wide and then mauled Raid with love, who was all too eager to eat it up. More children poked their heads out the door, but they looked for Matron Lyra's permission first. Her eyes went to me and I unclipped Raid from the leash in response. Matron Lyra nodded at the children and they happily ran out to meet Raid. I kept an eye on them while going to the porch to officially meet with Matron Lyra.

I was expecting her to be rather formal and shake my hand in greeting but instead she pulled me into an affectionate hug.

"I'm very glad you've come. It's been a long time since we've had volunteers," she admitted. "But I must ask, what are your friends grabbing out of that car?"

"Supplies," I said.

Matron Lyra gasped. "You didn't need to do that!"

I looked around the porch and then gave her a long look. "Want to tell me that again?"

Matron Lyra laughed. "You have quite the attitude. You remind me of me when I was younger. You must have all the boys wrapped around your finger."

I snorted. "No."

Raikidan walked up on to porch and studied the outside before showing signs of wanting to enter the building. "She likes to scare them away. We think she secretly gets enjoyment out it."

My nose scrunched, but before I could spit out a retort he focused on Matron Lyra. "May I go in to look around? I'd like to get a good idea of the projects I'll need to do today."

Matron Lyra gasped. "No, please don't. You're here for the children, not to work."

"They need a safe place to live," Raikidan said. "That's how I help them."

She blinked and then stepped aside. Raikidan nodded his thanks, and disappeared into the house. Matron Lyra faced me. "He's a bit aloof around children, I can assume?"

I nodded. "He's always been a bit weird around them. He doesn't like to talk about it, and I don't press. But he did want to come and help out. Him doing physical labor is his way of doing that. It's best to just let him do his thing. Not even I can change his mind, and I'm exceptionally stubborn myself."

Matron Lyra giggled. "I sense a great deal of fondness toward him from you."

I shrugged. "He's a good friend."

There was a twinkle in her eye as she giggled again. "Right."

We gazed out to the children, and Matron Lyra shook her head when they started to get a little out of control and spread out everywhere. I observed as she attempted to round them up. I would have helped, but I wanted to see how she worked, and I was thinking about Raikidan. What I had said was made up on the spot, but as I thought about it, I wondered if his irritation earlier was because of this whole "dealing with children" thing. I had never talked to him about it before we had decided to do this. I never thought to find out if he liked being around kids.

He was pleasant with Matron Lyra, but that was to be expected. I never had to worry about him being nice to women, unless they were some sort of threat. And he was showing a desire to fix the building up on his own accord, so I wondered if he thought children were important but just didn't particularly enjoy being around them.

I nearly rubbed my temples. *I should just ask him later about it.* It was better than speculating and stopped the headaches.

"Hey, can you give us a hand?" Ryoko called. "There's a lot of stuff here and with Ray off doing whatever it is he's doing, we could use you."

I nodded. "Sure thing."

I jogged over to the car and helped unload, while Rylan brought things into the house to "put them anywhere there was room," per Matron Lyra's words. Come to find out after Rylan's first trip into the house, the inside looked worse than the outside. I instructed him to go help Raikidan figure out what needed to be done so we could get the supplies in and start working on the projects sooner rather than later.

When I brought supplies into the house and was able to get a good look at the mess myself, I had a feeling we'd break the bank with the costs for repairs, but I didn't care. None of us did. These children deserved better. It was a shame they were orphaned or abandoned in the first place, but for them to have to live in a home like this, they might as well live on the street. It might have been safer. No, I was certain it was safer.

As I put a box of food down in the kitchen, I noticed a little girl peeking around a doorway. She ducked away, and when she peered around again, she pulled back when she saw I was still looking her way. I found this rather strange—I would have thought Matron Lyra would have wanted all the children together, outside playing with Raid.

I walked outside to find her on the porch, watching the rest of the children. "Did you know there's still a child inside?"

Matron Lyra smiled. "That's Myra. She's shy and typically hides when we have visitors. It makes it hard to get potential parents to think about adopting her. She's the youngest here, and as much as I care for her, I don't want to see her growing up in this place."

"I doubt you want to see any of the children here for long."

She nodded. "I'd prefer this place to not have to exist."

I chuckled when Raid walked up the steps and plopped down by my feet with his tongue lolling out. The children ran up to us, and unlike Raid, were far from exhausted.

I placed my hands on my hips, a teasing smile spreading over my face. "Look at what you guys did. You actually managed to tire Raid out. It usually takes five of us and a whole hour of play time to do that."

The children giggled and one of the older girls came over to Matron Lyra. "Lyra, can we keep him?"

Matron Lyra smiled at her. "No, Elara, we can't. He belongs to Eira."

Elara gave me pleading eyes in hopes I'd say otherwise, but I shook my head. "He's going to have to come home with me. Raid is on a special diet that you guys wouldn't be able to afford."

Elara pouted, but stopped when Raid got back up on his feet and shook himself. He looked ready for another round.

Just then, Ryoko came up to us with a box. "This is the last of it."

I nodded. "Good."

Matron Lyra unhooked a communicator from the belt loop of her pants and looked at the time. "It looks like it's time for me to start making lunch. Eira, would you help me?"

I nodded. "Sure thing. I'll warn you though, I'm a pretty terrible cook."

She laughed. "That's fine. I'll make sure I give you tasks that are easy. And Ryoko, do you mind watching the children after you put that box down? I don't need them getting into any trouble."

Ryoko nodded enthusiastically. "Of course!"

Matron Lyra smile and I followed her inside. When we made it to the kitchen, Raikidan and Rylan were just walking out.

"We're going to go out to get more supplies," Rylan informed me. "We've figured out what needs the most work."

I nodded. "Great. If you need extra help, make some calls. The more hands, the better."

"Yeah, I'm going to agree with you on that. I'll give you a call if we find some extra hands."

I chuckled. "Okay. And we should have lunch ready by the time you get back."

"Good, I'm starving."

I snorted and pushed him toward the door. "Get out of here."

Rylan chuckled and headed for the door. Raikidan looked at me and I stared at him back.

"What?" I asked.

A teasing smirk tugged at his lips. "Not going to push me too?"

"I will if you don't get your butt moving," I said.

He chuckled and headed for the door, but just as he passed me I kicked him in the rear. He shot me a warning look but I just stuck my tongue out at him.

Matron Lyra giggled and then tugged on my arm. "C'mon, dear. We have a lot of mouths to feed. You can pick on your friend later."

"All right, all right."

Matron Lyra went about searching for ingredients but after watching her open bare cabinet after bare cabinet, I was glad we came when we did. I ended up opening one of the boxes next to me and found loaves of bread. "Matron Lyra, do any of the children have sensitivity to dairy or wheat?"

"No, why?"

I pulled out the loaves of bread, and then opened a cooler and retrieved some cheese and butter. "How about we make the children grilled cheese?"

Matron Lyra smiled. "That's a good idea. I'll make some soup as well."

I nodded and started setting up the bread and cheese while Matron Lyra got out the soup cans and cookware needed for us to get everything going. When we were all set up, I buttered the bread and handed her the slices and the cheese when she was ready.

"I want to thank you for helping today," Matron Lyra said. "It's been some time since someone has come by to help. And while I'd like to say what you're doing for us is overboard, I know this place needs to be fixed up, as much as I wish it didn't. The funds I get every month are so low, I can't focus on making this place better for the children."

I smiled. "You're welcome. We're glad to help. All of us believe you and the children deserve it. I really wish they didn't have to be here, but we don't live in a perfect world, so we have to make do with how the world is. Since we can't keep them out of here, I want this place to be a nice home for them to live in, until a family finally comes by and takes them away to a place where they can be loved unconditionally."

A somber expression fell over Matron Lyra. "Barely any of them will be adopted… Most will grow up here, and then when they're eighteen they'll struggle to make it in this city. People don't want to adopt, and it's sad. I was adopted. I was a blessing to my parents and I wish more people could see how much of a blessing these children would be to their lives."

"It's hard to change the minds of people," I said. "Zarda has the people of the city believing these children are worthless and a waste of space. He's wrong, and they're wrong to blindly believe him. But it's not impossible to change their minds. Maybe we can help. Getting them into the eyes of the public may help their chances. Maybe we can work up some time to take them out into the city."

Matron Lyra smiled. "That's a very kind thing for you to suggest. I don't know if it'll help, but it's worth a shot. For the sake of the children, I'm willing to give it a try."

I smiled and then turned my attention toward the dining room when I noticed movement. It was Myra. Her wavy, ebony hair curtained her eyes as she peered around the doorframe. When she realized I'd noticed her, she ducked away.

"Myra," I called. "It's okay. I'm not here to take you away."

I didn't receive a response right away. It took a few moments, but she finally peered around the doorframe again. I motioned for her to come over, but she stayed where she was. I grabbed a slice of cheese and knelt, holding it out to her in hopes she wanted it. She moved forward a little, but then moved back as if she were fighting herself.

I looked away when I heard heavy panting behind me, and smiled at Raid as he stood in the doorway to the living room. My eyes darted to Myra in hopes she'd find interest in Raid, but she was hiding again. *She really is timid.*

"You want water?" I asked Raid.

He barked and wagged his tail. I smiled and grabbed a bowl and filled it with water for him. As he lapped up the water, Myra became curious and peeked around the doorframe to watch him. He took great interest in her, and took a few steps closer to her. She ducked back, but that didn't deter him. Matron Lyra and I watched as he sat against the wall and peeked around the doorframe. I smiled when Myra giggled, and Raid pulled his head back. She then peeked around the doorframe and giggled when she spied him.

Raid's tongue lolled out. He then licked her in the face suddenly. Myra squealed and Raid ran to the other side of the kitchen. He went down into a play bow and wagged his tail to encourage Myra. She giggled and ran after him. Matron Lyra and I laughed as the two played.

"He's so good with the children," she observed.

I nodded and went back to getting bread ready for her. "Yeah, he is."

"Eira, you're part of the resistance, aren't you," she said boldly.

I blinked. "What?"

Matron Lyra smiled. "It's okay. I support the resistance. If I didn't have the children to worry about, I'd be actively supporting you."

I focused on the piece of cheese I had in my hand. "Is it that obvious?"

"Besides the fact that you blatantly insulted Zarda, it's because you're so willing to help," she admitted. "Not even the soldiers are this willing. They come by when a street residence makes a complaint or concern, but they don't help, if the state of this place wasn't proof enough. Most of them show obvious sign of not caring about the children in the least. You four aren't like that. You care for the children and the people of this city. That's how I know. The resistance wants the people of this city to be free and happy."

"Matron Lyra, I want you to understand, this is by no means a ploy to recruit you or anything. We made the choice to come and help because we wanted to. Many other members of our cause did help with donations, but this visit isn't sanctioned by those who lead us."

"I know. I can tell you're here because you want to be. But I also want you to be aware, I also knew where you stood in this city because you also show signs of being a former soldier. It's in the way you walk. And in your eyes. You're very guarded, even when you try not to appear to be. You show signs of being afraid of hurting the children when they're close to you, but you want to help them, so you try to be close without risking their safety."

I frowned and put a sandwich together to hand to her. My eyes flicked down when a small hand tugged on my pant leg. Standing next to me were Myra and Raid.

"Cheese?" she asked.

I smiled and handed her the slice of cheese I had set aside just in case. "Just be careful of Raid. He might take it from you."

She giggled and happily ate her snack. Raid gazed at me and whined. I chuckled before breaking up a cheese slice and tossing the pieces to him. He caught them and scarfed them down. His enthusiasm made Myra giggle.

"How is the soup coming?" I asked Matron Lyra in hopes to change the subject. I didn't mind that she'd figured out we were rebels, but I didn't like that she had mentioned how easy it was for her to see that I was a former soldier. *I thought I was good at hiding that…*

"Almost done," she said, taking the topic change in stride. "And this should be the last sandwich, so lunch should be ready very soon."

"Good, I'm hungry." Rylan's sudden appearance surprised me.

"That was a quick run to the store," I said.

"The stores barely had anything we needed. We were lucky to get windows and tarps," he said.

I shook my head. "That would figure."

"Ray gave Elarinya a call and she said she'd get us some help, so that's a plus."

I nodded. "She'll probably give her family a call and they'll get this place better than new."

"Now, none of you go overboard," Matron Lyra chided. "We don't need anything fancy."

I chuckled and started piling grilled cheese sandwiches on plates. "Our friend, Elarinya, is from a long line of craftsmen elves. They'll be the best to fix up this home. If they go overboard you can blame Elarinya. Simple isn't good enough for her."

Matron Lyra laughed. "All right. Soup is now ready. I'll go get the children inside so we can get lunch underway."

"They're already inside," Rylan said. "They're playing with Ryoko on the couch."

Matron Lyra smiled. "Well that makes this that much easier."

She went out into the living room and told the children to wash up for lunch. They cheered, and moments later it sounded like a herd of elephants were stampeding to the bathroom. While Matron Lyra was dealing with the children, Rylan helped me get the soup set up on the table. Just as we were done and going for the sandwiches, the children rushed into the dining room and took their seats.

Raikidan came into the dining room when I was giving the last child his sandwich. I jerked my head toward the kitchen as I walked over to him. "Your sandwich is on the count—hey, that one is mine!"

He bit into the grilled cheese sandwich I had put on a plate for myself and headed for the living room. "Mine now."

I stomped my foot. "Rai!"

"You can have the one on the counter," he called back.

I sighed with aggravation and headed into the kitchen to grab the last grilled cheese. Matron Lyra followed me and I looked at her funny as I bit into my sandwich. She was smiling in a strange way; it was weird. "What?"

She began scooping soup into a bowl. "The two of you are cute."

I rolled my eyes and continued eating. I knew where this was going.

"What, don't tell me you don't like him at least a little," she said. "He's helpful and seems to know how to keep you on your toes. He comes off as the protective type and, even though he's a bit aloof around the children, he could warm up to them in time. Not to mention he's quite handsome. Many women would kill for a man like that."

"I don't believe in love," I stated.

"Oh, you don't?" She, like many others, didn't sound as if she believed me.

"No."

"But you used to."

"Yeah, when I was young and stupid. Then I learned."

"One bad experience doesn't mean they'll all be that way."

I stared at my sandwich and frowned. "I never said it was just one…"

Ryoko poked her head into the kitchen. "Hey, Ray is looking for tools. The guys weren't exactly smart enough to go home and pick some up."

Matron Lyra glanced at me briefly before looking at Ryoko. "I don't have many, but they're locked away in a utility closet so the children don't get into them. I'll fetch them."

When she left, Ryoko focused on me. "You okay?"

I shrugged. "Yeah, why wouldn't I be?"

"I just thought you might have been on your way back to a time that you wouldn't want to be in," she said.

I shrugged again. "I'm good."

"Okay."

She left, and I went back to eating until Raikidan appeared in the doorway. "Can you give me a hand? Rylan is paying attention to the kids now and I want to make sure I get a little help when replacing these windows."

"Sure. Just let me finish my food."

He nodded and ducked back out. I ate my lunch a bit quicker, and then entered the living room. Matron Lyra was setting out tools for us, while Raikidan worked on prying off the wooden boards covering one of the broken windows. I inspected the new windows the boys had purchased, and then went about helping Raikidan with the boards and plastic that had covered the other windows.

The children became curious about the work we were doing, but Ryoko and Rylan managed to keep them away so they wouldn't get hurt. Raid, on the other hand, insisted on getting under my feet every now and then, and I had to shoo him away until Ryoko managed to get him under control. Of course with her giving him attention, he attempted to keep her concentration on him and not on Rylan, even if she just wanted to ask a simple question or request.

Matron Lyra laughed. "I'd watch that dog if I were you, Rylan. Contrary to popular belief, a dog is a woman's best friend, not diamonds. He'll steal your girlfriend from right under your nose if you're not careful."

Rylan's face reddened, as did Ryoko's. "She's not my girlfriend, Ma'am."

Matron Lyra stared at the two, dumbfounded. "You sure about that? You two act awfully close. Don't lie to me now. No shame in it."

Ryoko did her best to calm Raid down as he started jumping around. "No, really, we're just friends."

"Well, it seems I'm getting all these friendly pairings mixed up today." She shook her head. "Shame. How I pictured things in my mind, it all worked out so well."

I noticed the slight upturn of her lips and a nearly hidden twinkle in her eye. She wasn't convinced in the least, but she played her disappointed part well, I gave her that.

By the time we had the windows done, Rylan had jumped in to help, and many of the children had fallen asleep on the couch or floor while attempting to fight their naps. I wiped away a few beads of sweat that had formed on my brow, and then appraised our work. It was already looking better in here, and we had only done the living room and dining room. I would have liked to do more, but it was starting to get late.

"I think that'll do it for today," I told Matron Lyra when I handed her the tool box.

She smiled her thanks. "I really appreciate what you've all done today. I can sleep a bit sounder knowing this place is a little bit safer for the children."

I looked down when a small hand tugged on my pant leg. I smiled at Myra as she peered up at me with sleepy eyes. "What is it, Myra?"

"You come back," she said.

I knelt and smiled at her. "Of course we'll be back. And I'll make sure I bring Raid too."

She smiled and gave me a quick hug before latching onto Raid. Raid wagged his tail.

"She's taken quite a liking to you," Matron Lyra said as I rose to my feet.

"I think she likes Raid more."

Matron Lyra giggled. "This is true. I won't be surprised if one of these days you visit and he won't be coming home with you."

I laughed with her and then said my goodbyes to the children who were still awake. Ryoko and Rylan did the same, but Raikidan kept his distance, as I had expected. He really hadn't shown much interest in the children. I wanted to ask him about it, but I knew now wasn't the right time or place. I'd have to remember to ask him later.

I called for Raid, who was a little reluctant to leave, though that might have had something to do with Myra, since she really didn't want to let him go. Eventually, he slipped her grasp and followed us out of the orphanage. We said our goodbyes to Matron Lyra, and promised to be back another day with more help to fix the place.

As the group of us headed for the cars, Ryoko began teasing both Rylan and Raid on how good they were with the children. Rylan's face reddened as he tried to brush it off as nothing major, but Raid didn't back down, just as he hadn't with me, catching Ryoko off guard. I had to refrain from smirking when Rylan started sulking as Ryoko held a conversation on kids with Raid. *Gotta come up with something to top your brother now, Ry.* Ryoko had her mind set on having children one day. She loved them a lot. It was why she had volunteered to pose as Genesis' mother for cover stories.

Their conversation ended when we split up to jump into our vehicles. Raid chose to join Raikidan and me, instead of going with Ryoko, perplexing me. "You sure you want to come with us, Raid?"

He lay across the back seat so he'd be hidden, and shifted to his nu-human form. "I thought it'd be a good idea to leave in the same car I came in. The Matron doesn't know we all live together, so it could raise some suspicion."

"She knows," I said as I drove off. "It didn't take her long to figure me out."

Raid sat up. "Wow, really? I always thought you were one of the best at hiding that."

I chuckled. "Same here. She's a sharp lady."

"So, since she knows, are we really going to come back?"

"Don't worry, you don't have to give up your dream of being mauled by those children again. The Matron is safe."

Raid relaxed. "Good. I didn't want to have to show up as a stray one day."

I laughed and glanced at Raikidan, who had been quiet the whole time. I had to remember to talk to him when we got home. He was just acting too strange to let this go.

18

CHAPTER

Paint streaked behind my small detailing brush as I sat on my motorcycle and leaned over the gas tank, painting in the small details of my design. The way I sat was weird, but it allowed me to get these few details just right to line up with the rest of my paint work, so I wasn't about to change what I was doing. I tilted my head when I finished with the blue, and then slid off my motorcycle to grab the brush I used for detailing with reds.

Leaning over my motorcycle once more, I worked, becoming oblivious of the work the others were doing around the shop. I almost messed up when someone leaned on my bike, pissing me off. I had been working on this tirelessly to get it to look right. I snapped my gaze up in irritation, but my expression changed from anger to surprise when I saw that the person who had disturbed me was Zo. "Um, hey, Zo."

Zo grinned. "Eira."

I sat up. "Can I help you with something?"

Zo's eyes drifted from my eyes to somewhere lower than my chin, sending a wave of discomfort through me, and then snapped his gaze to my bike. "Just admiring your handy work. Please, don't let me distract you from what you're doing."

Liar. I bit my tongue and smiled instead. It was best to not create a bad situation. "I'd love to, Zo, but you're leaning on my bike."

Zo chuckled and stepped away, allowing me to go back to work. My painting didn't last long, however. His watching me made me too uncomfortable. Instead, I sat back up and looked over the work I had done. When Zo frowned, I knew it was time to keep this unfortunate conversation going. "Something the matter, Zo?"

"What? Oh, no nothing's the matter. Just trying to understand your choice in subject."

My brow furrowed and I slid off my motorcycle to look at the image I had painted in full. "What's wrong with a dragon?"

Zo shook his head. "Why would a nice girl like you want such a bloodthirsty, evil creature on her bike?"

I grunted and walked over to the bench with my paints. "You people of the city may see them that way, but the people of my village don't."

"And how's that, Sweetcheeks?"

"It's all in the words you just said." I picked up my helmet and looked it over to make sure the two would match in the end. "You all think dragons are these bloodthirsty, heartless killing machines, but the people of my village see something better. To us, dragons are a symbol of power, intelligence, balance, strength, courage, and even fortitude."

"You speak as if you believe they're still around."

I turned and smiled slyly at him. "Just because you can't see something doesn't mean it doesn't exist."

Zo strolled over to me and took my helmet to examine it. "The boys told me you were doing them a favor and testing a new style of helmet that would help us with communicating with each other."

"Yeah, but it's real glitchy right now," I lied. "Half the functions don't work properly, and the other half don't work at all, but the most frustrating part is that the communication function we really want to work cuts in and out. Of course, because it's more of a side project to everything else you have them doing, it doesn't get much time for fixing or testing."

"You sound disappointed."

"Only because I actually like this project. It's a lot of fun to work with Argus on, even if I don't get to do much more than testing."

Zo chuckled and handed the helmet back to me. "So, Eira." I gulped. I had a bad feeling about that beginning line. "I was thinking maybe you and I could grab a bite to eat and see a movie."

Oh great. It was only a matter of time before this came up. "You mean like… go out on a date?"

Zo grinned. "Yeah."

"Don't do it."

I rubbed my arm. "Well, um…"

"Don't go anywhere with this creep."

"She'd love to!" Ryoko chirped.

My brow furrowed at her sudden appearance. "Excuse me, are you Eira?"

Ryoko rolled her eyes. "I just said what you were about to say."

"Excellent. I'll pick you up at seven." Zo spun on his heels and headed out.

"Don't let them get away with this! Say something."

I stood there in a dumbfounded daze. *What the hell did I—* When the shop door closed behind him, I turned on Ryoko. "Why did you do that to me?"

"Because you were going to have to say yes, and I knew you were thinking of some way to say no."

I crossed my arms. "I don't have to say yes to anything."

"You do if you want to keep him thinking you find him a little interesting."

"I don't want him to think that! I can't stand him. It's because of this stupid place he even knows I exist."

Ryoko rolled her eyes. "You're being so dramatic. It's not going to kill you."

"What's not going to kill her?" I turned around to see Rylan and the boys walking over to us.

"Besides Zo. Unless you count him bothering Eira hazardous," Blaze said. "What was he doing here anyway? He didn't talk to anyone when he came in. Just went over to Eira."

A sly, teasing smile slipped up Ryoko's face, her eyes going to me. "That's because he was determined to get Laz to go out on a date with him."

I scowled. "Not like you let me put up much of a fight."

Rylan crossed him arms. "Laz, go on a date?"

"Ryoko made my choice," I muttered.

"It wasn't much a choice." She crossed her arms. "You were going to have to say yes and I knew you wouldn't't."

I sighed in defeat. She was right and I hated it. Genesis would have had a fit if I had turned him down. *First time ever on a date, and it has to be with a creep like Zo…*

Ryoko grabbed my wrist. "C'mon, we have to get you ready."

"What? Now?"

"Yes now. He's going to be at the house in two hours. You need to be ready."

I groaned as she dragged me to the door. "Someone shoot me now."

My shimmery, silver shirt clung to me like static, and my heeled shoes hurt my feet. The city lights lit up the streets as Zo and I walked them in silence. The silence was an awkward, uncomfortable one for me, but Zo, as usual, was oblivious. He thought this date had gone well, but I was of the opposite opinion. The moment he arrived, it had started off on the wrong foot.

Zo had no car, claiming it was in the shop, so we had to walk everywhere. Ryoko, thankfully, was sure to make a few snide comments about poor manners and timing for his proposed date without a car, which he hadn't missed. It went south from there, almost immediately, when he admitted to me on our way out of the house that he had left his money at the barracks.

I knew better, though. Zo spent a lot of time at Twilight or, from the talk I overheard from other soldiers while working, Midnight, so that meant the little allowance he got to appear normal was all but gone. Zo also liked to gamble, and to make money for this date, I guessed he had made a bet with his company on it somehow.

When we reached the barracks, which looked more like a house, Zo went inside while I waited out on the street. He had offered to let me come inside, but since I wasn't about to trust him, I declined and remained on the street. Once he had the money, he took to me to this nice restaurant, which had been the highlight of the evening. It hadn't been too fancy, but it was pricey. I had chosen a burger to eat, since it was one of the choices on the lower price end, and when they had brought it out for me I was surprised by its size.

I had expected the burger to be small, even smaller than most, since it was a fancier place, but instead, the burger was nearly the size of my head. The most surprised of us was Zo, who didn't think I was capable of finishing such a meal. But I did, and it had been easy. I even ordered some cake as a dessert. Zo wasn't sure how I stayed so thin with the way I was able to eat, and I had played it off as if my stomach was more of a bottomless pit than a stomach. During this time, I had made small attempts to extract information from him that would be of help to the rebellion, or even just me, but had no success.

The movie after dinner had been the worst event of the evening. Zo really didn't know a thing about me. He had prepared himself to have to sit through a boring chick-flick when I couldn't stomach those, either. It was also obvious he was new to this 'dating and not hooking up for a night' thing when, not even fifteen minutes into the movie, he was snaking his arm around my shoulders and making an attempt to get something I had no intention of ever giving him.

Although unplanned, the popcorn that had been in my lap had fallen onto the floor, saving me from that very uncomfortable situation. Zo, of course, didn't see a big deal in the loss of popcorn, but I had insisted on getting some more. It gave me a good excuse to get away from him for a short time, and made it so he couldn't continue his awful attempts until I came back, which he did.

Zo made several more attempts during the movie, but I used the movie to my advantage. Even though I found the film boring, I pretended to find it quite interesting. Zo, although upset by my lack of interest in him, continued to try. He couldn't get the hint. Before the movie, it had been the same deal, with him getting too close, or his hand wandering to areas it shouldn't.

Now that the movie was over, Zo walked me home, much to my relief. He was also, much to my surprise, giving me some breathing room, but that didn't last the moment we reached the front door.

I brushed my bangs away from my face as I faced him and was taken aback by how close he had moved to me. "Um, well, thanks for taking me out tonight, Zo. It was… interesting."

Zo smirked. "I'm glad you enjoyed it."

I wished I could just punch him. *How can someone be so dumb?* "Well, I guess this is good night then."

"I guess so."

He leaned into me and my eyes widened. Instinctively, my hand flew up at his face, but I caught myself in time to make sure my touch was light and it was only my fingers coming in contact with his lips instead of a solid fist.

I looked at him warily as he pulled away and rubbed his head while letting out a tense slow breath. "All right, sorry."

I continued to give him an apprehensive gaze as I opened the door. I let out a hard exhale and relaxed against the door once it was shut and separating us.

"Stupid!" I heard him say through the door as I collected myself. "I should have known that was going to happen. She had been avoiding that all night. Fuck!"

I had to bite my lip. Not only did he sound absolutely ridiculous, but he actually sounded like a normal man for once. I still felt as though he treated this date as more of a game than anything, though. The way he didn't want to listen to my obvious cues, hadn't made any good attempts at small talk to allow us to get to know each other, and thinking this had gone really well, it's as if we were on two completely different dates.

My conclusion wasn't that surprising. Zo was a soldier like me, and unlike civilians, we didn't have good pasts to speak of. You never knew when your last day was, so it was best not to make connections with others.

I sighed. Men and women would hook up with others for a night and then go on their way. I tended to rationalized men's behavior because that's what I had been surrounded by. It was all I had known. But I knew it was just me who had been filled with hate. I lived with men who weren't like that, except for Blaze of course. *Tannek wasn't like that…*

My hands tightened around my waist. *I'm just angry because of how unfair—*

"Laz, is that you down there?" Ryoko called. I thought I caught a small laugh in her voice. "I heard Zo's cursing outside."

Collecting myself, I stormed up the stairs. Zo didn't matter. None of that did. I had been forced to go out on date with him, although Satria knows why he even asked, and it had been just as awful as I had imagined it would be.

"So how was your date?" Ryoko teased.

"I don't want to talk about it," I muttered as I headed for my bedroom.

"Oh c'mon, it couldn't have been that bad."

"If you wanna find out, you go out with the ass-grabber next time." I slammed my door shut.

"Yikes, that is bad," Ryoko mumbled.

I sighed as I rested against the door. Why had Zo even asked? Soldiers hooked up for a night and then it was done. There were plenty of women who wouldn't mind being a one-night stand. Some even preferred it.

So why waste time chasing me? What made him think it was worth it? Not that the end result he wanted would ever happen, but still, why? Was I really worth it?

I kicked off my shoes haphazardly and then flopped down on my bed, uncaring that I was still in my date clothes. Minutes passed and I couldn't stop wondering, *why?* I didn't even want to continue the thought. The answer didn't matter, but my brain wouldn't let it go.

I sat up when someone knocked on my door. "Yeah?"

"It's me," Ryoko replied. "Can I come in?"

"Sure."

The door opened and Ryoko came in. "Hey, um, I know you just got back and all from your date, but Genesis wants us to go out and blow a few places up."

I sighed. "I can't get a break, can I?"

"Sorry, I know you'd like some time to relax."

"It's fine. We should be out on more assignments anyway."

"Well, I'll meet you upstairs, then. The guys are getting everything ready for us so just wear something comfortable."

"Sure."

When she left, I dragged myself off my bed. Changing into something better than my night clothes, I headed out to join Ryoko on the roof. Rylan and Raikidan didn't take much longer than me, and once they handed us our weapons and supplies, we split into two groups and headed out to our locations.

I rested my gun against a wall and messed with the setting on my communicator until my signal came in better. "Let me know when you guys are ready."

"Sure thing," Raikidan replied.

He had been abnormally quiet tonight. That had just been the first thing he'd said to me since I had gotten back. I had expected him to show up in my room while I was stewing, but I remained alone the entire time. Though, he wasn't my concern right now. Ryoko was also acting weird. She had teased me when I had gotten home, but now she was quiet and lost in thought. It was like something had happened in that short time.

My brow furrowed when Ryoko dropped her gun and slid to the ground against the adjacent wall. "Ryoko?" She stared at her feet instead of answering. Something definitely wasn't right. I sidled over to her. "Ryoko?"

Ryoko pulled her legs up to her chest and buried her face into her arms. I froze when she began to sob. Why was she crying? What was going on? *What am I supposed to do?*

"Eira, we're ready," Raikidan called in.

"Um, one sec. Ryoko and I are trying to figure something out now," I said.

"All right."

I touched Ryoko's shoulder. "Ryo? Ryo, what's wrong?"

Ryoko flung herself at me and continued to sob. I lightly touched her shoulders and tried to figure out what to do. "I… I can't d–do it…"

"Ryoko?"

"I… I just can't."

I sighed. I was starting to get what was going on here. "Ryoko, this is about Rylan, isn't it?"

She nodded. My lips twisted. This was a bad time, but it couldn't be helped.

I pressed a button on my communicator to start transmitting my signal. "Raikidan."

"Are you finally ready? I want to move from this spot."

I ignored his attitude. "Change of plans. Something came up and you guys will have to do this without us. Our side isn't as important anyway."

"Eira, what's going on?"

"I can't say. Just… just do your end of the job, and we'll meet up with you guys back at the house."

"Eira, wha—"

I pressed the power button to my communicator, cutting him off. He was to finish the job, and I was to tend to my comrade—no—my *friend's* needs. I rested my hand on her head and began stroking it in a soothing manner. "Talk to me, Ryo. I may not be good with words, but we both know I'm good at listening."

Ryoko pulled away and sniffled, a look of defeat clear on her face showing me how much this had been eating at her. "I'm... I..." She sighed. "I'm done. It's time I started thinking like you. I can't keep believing in fairytales."

"Ryoko, I need you to be just a little more clear, for me to understand."

She exhaled again and leaned against the wall. "He really doesn't care about me in the way I want him to. In the way you keep insisting he does. I've foolishly waited decades for nothing to happen. Even Raid seems like he likes me a little. I'm not stupid. Or blind. I see how he gets when I'm hanging out with Rylan or when I'm trying to snake out a little extra from a customer at the shop. I see that it bothers him. But Rylan... Rylan doesn't get like that. He just..."

She stopped talking and stared at her feet. I was at a loss of what to do. Rylan really did care for her and I wanted her to be with him because he could make her happy, but her waiting for what seemed like nothing, wasn't fair. *It's hurting her far too much and that's not right.*

"I'm sorry, Laz. I know you're not good with this kind of stuff, but it's nice to be able to actually get it off my chest."

I leaned against the wall next to her and stared up at the sky. "No, I'm the one who's sorry, Ryo."

"Why?"

"For getting your hopes up. I really thought I was right about this. I guess I was blind and saw nothing."

Ryoko grunted. "You, blind? What would blind you?"

"Your happiness. I just want you to be happy, Ryo. I thought... I thought he would be the best to do that. I was wrong. I don't want to see you cry anymore."

"So, you think I should see if Raid does like me?"

"Would that make you happy? Would he make you happy?"

Ryoko rubbed her leg. "Maybe. I won't know unless I find out if he really does like me, or if I'm just dumb and desperate."

I shook my head with a small chuckle. "You're neither dumb nor desperate."

"Yeah I am. It was because of your date that I lost it."

I sighed. "So it was the date. I figured as much."

Ryoko's eyes widened. "No, no, no, no, don't think of it like that! You going on a date didn't upset me. Well, it did a little, but not a lot like you think. What upset me was the fact that you went on a date with someone you don't like, and had an awful time. You were miserable, and it made me think of how I have been feeling for a while."

"But the date itself did upset you."

Ryoko nodded. "You don't want to go on dates. You don't want to find someone. But I do want that. I want someone to fill that void I feel. I guess, even though it was a bad date, I was a little jealous."

"Well don't be. You weren't missing out on anything."

"It was really that bad?"

I rolled my eyes. "Bad doesn't begin to describe it. As far as first date experiences go, I can say with certainly, that would put anyone off from ever wanting to date again. Even I know dates are supposed to be better."

"That's right… you've never been out on a date before…" She shook her head. "Well you were still asked out, 'cause the weirdo likes you."

She stuck her tongue out and I laughed. I then frowned. "For the record, Ryo, if I could be myself, like you, Zo wouldn't have ever asked me out." I stared at my hands as they hung over my knees. "He just sees me as Eira. He only knows Eira. He doesn't know Laz. He would stay as far away as possible if he knew her. Even Rylan prefers Eira. Always has. So, be glad there's someone out there who likes you for the real you."

"But we don't know if Raid really likes me."

"Well you're just going to have to find out."

Ryoko nodded and stood. "Thanks for listening to me, Laz. You've always been good at making me feel better."

"Just promise me you'll make choices that'll make you happy."

"Promise. And for the record, I like Laz more. She's real."

I sighed. "Real, but not likable."

Ryoko shook her head. "You're wrong, and one of these days you'll see that. Now let the guys know we're doing better and let's get this assignment finished so we can go home."

I nodded and clicked my power button as she headed off. I froze when my communicator powered down. *Oh shit.* I pressed the power button again and waited for the few seconds it took to power on and connect me with Raikidan. "Raikidan?"

"We haven't moved."

I gulped. "Did you—"

"Yeah, we heard. You didn't shut off your communicator."

I sighed. "Perfect."

"How's Ryoko?"

"Fine. She went ahead of me. She looks better than she has in a while. How's Rylan?"

"Pissed off and beating himself up. Stormed off before you came back to talk."

I hung my head. "Perfect. Now he's going to hate me."

"Does that matter?"

My brow furrowed. "What do you mean?"

"It's not your fault, Eira. It's his. If he had half a brain and had really cared, he wouldn't be in this situation. You were just doing what you're supposed to. You were thinking about Ryoko's happiness, which Rylan was ruining."

I sighed. "I guess you're right."

"A big question is, how are you doing?"

"What? I'm fine. Why would you wonder that?"

"Laz…"

I averted my gaze as if he were standing next to me. "Raikidan, I've told you, it's Eira."

He sighed. "All right, sorry. Meet you back at the house after this?"

"Yeah."

"It's a date, then."

My cheeks flushed a little and I was glad he wasn't around to see. "Raikidan!"

He laughed. "I'm just messing with you. Though, it's probably not the best thing for me to say after earlier."

I groaned. "Let's not bring that situation up. I'd really like to forget about it."

"Sure thing, Butterfly."

I sighed and picked up my gun. I needed to catch up with Ryoko before she ended up doing all the work.

19

CHAPTER

My ears hurt from the loud echoes in the shop. Blaze, Raid, and Zane were welding—Ryoko sanding—and Raikidan and Rylan were grinding away on sheet metal. It made it hard to concentrate as I worked with Argus. He nudged me every time my focus wandered.

The large front door of the shop creaked open, and several sets of footsteps entered the building. I wasn't sure how I was able to hear them over the noise, but I also didn't care much. They were soldiers, and I wasn't planning on paying them any mind. They were the only business the shop ever had lately. I wasn't even sure if I had ever seen a civilian step foot in here while I was around. The soldiers paid good money, so I guess it didn't matter in the end.

Zane stopped his welding and went to speak with the group. I planned on working more, but Argus took charge with some electrical configurations, so I ended up looking around again. I nearly jumped out of my skin when a bright flash hit my eyes and Argus screamed in pain.

"Argus!" My stool crashed to the floor as I rushed to his side.

Argus leaned over the workbench with his hand covering half of the left side of his face, and the other bracing himself. Blood rushed around his fingers and splattered everywhere.

Ignoring the urge that screamed to kill him, I rested one hand on his back, and the other on his face, to help put pressure on the wound. "Ryoko, get the first aid kit!"

Ryoko was in the office before I could get all the words out of my mouth. A soldier rushed over to give me a hand, but I wasn't going to have it.

"Don't touch him!" I snapped.

The man flinched. "Ma'am, I'm a medic. I can help."

"I said don't touch him!"

"Boy, do as she says," Zane urged.

"But—"

"Do as she says."

The man nodded and backed away, but another soldier who had approached wasn't as inclined to be so agreeable. "The hell he should. The man's bleeding out and Larron is qualified to stop it. She shouldn't be acting like a crazy bitch."

Zane gave the man the ugliest warning stare I've ever seen, but it was too late. The man had spoken and now he was going to get it.

"Go to hell, you low-life piece of arrogant trash!" I spat. "It's because of you and your stupid projects that he's even in this condition. If you didn't want these stupid, impossible upgrades, it wouldn't have malfunctioned while he was making it!"

"The idiot should have been wearing a face mask!" the soldier barked back.

"I gave it to her to wear," Argus muttered through clenched teeth.

"Argus, don't talk," I hushed. "You'll stretch out the wound, making it worse."

"Why the hell didn't you wear it yourself?" the soldier demanded.

I was really starting to toy with the idea of killing this soldier. "Because I was helping him with this project! Because of everything you guys want done in such short time, we haven't had the time to get more masks to go around, so some of us have to go without, to make sure all your damned deadlines are met! Now all of you just get the hell out of here!"

"Woman, stop—"

Blood splattered on him as I threw my hand out. "Out!"

The soldiers flinched.

"Damian, we're leaving," Zo said.

I hadn't realized Zo was here, but right now I didn't care, nor would I have, even if I hadn't been mad. I still wasn't okay with being around him after our unfortunate date.

Damian looked at him. "Sir?"

"You heard me, everyone out." Zo focused on Zane. "We'll come back when this unfortunate situation clears up. We'll also discuss deadlines."

Zane nodded. "That would be best."

Ryoko dropped the heavy first-aid kit on the workbench and rummaged through the content to get me the supplies I needed to fix Argus up. While she did that, I continued to keep pressure on the wound.

"Here." Ryoko handed me some cloth and a bottle of liquid.

I took the cloth from her and used it to soak up the blood.

"Eira, you don't have to do this," Argus insisted.

"Shut up and sit still, or I'll hurt you."

"You wouldn't hurt someone who's already bleeding out."

"Yes she would," Raikidan said. "And you know it."

Argus sighed and stayed quiet. When his blood saturated the cloth, I removed it from his face and took a quick look at the wound. A large gash cut into his cheek all the way up to his forehead. How his eye hadn't been damaged was beyond me, but I wasn't going to take this stroke of luck for granted. Ryoko handed me another cloth, and I soaked it in the liquid she offered me before.

"This will sting real bad, and then go numb," I said.

"Just put it on so we can get this bleeding to stop," he muttered.

I chuckled and dabbed the soaked cloth on his wound. I was quick to grab the needle and thread when the bleeding slowed and his face was numb. Argus flinched a few times, but stayed quiet and was good while I pulled buried information out of my head that Azriel had taught me long ago, and stitched up Argus' face.

I tightened the bandana around my mouth to make sure it wasn't going to fall off. It wasn't normal for me to wear something like this, and I didn't plan on getting caught, but it was better to be safe than sorry, especially with an assignment like this.

After we had gotten Argus patched up, I made a call to Shva'sika to get her opinion on how to handle the matter, and she insisted we get Argus home for her to take a look at. Unfortunately, the moment we got Argus settled, the Council had sent over an assignment for us to complete. Normally I'd be happy the Council was finally handing us more assignments like they claimed they were going to, but Argus' condition weighed heavily on my mind. It didn't help that our assignment had us searching for and swiping paper-trailed information. The information tended to be valuable, but you had to sift through the garbage to find it, and with five of us working the assignment and under such a tight time frame, it felt more and more impossible to complete as the minutes passed.

Ryoko signaled to me that she was splitting off, and Rylan and Raid followed her into a building. Raikidan and I continued until my communicator flashed, signaling I had reached my target building. I looked around before climbing down to the window below. Raikidan waited above until I had the window open, and I didn't wait for him to come inside before I started searching.

My gloves kept my fingerprints off everything I touched, so the only things I had to worry about were making too much of a mess or getting caught. I shuddered when something clattered to the ground.

I spun around and glared at Raikidan. "Be quiet."

He didn't hold eye contact with me. "Sorry…"

I grumbled and opened a filing cabinet. The files, to my surprise, were organized. Normally they were pretty chaotic, as if they were just thrown in there to be forgotten about. Unfortunately, I couldn't see anything that would help us. My lack of reading ability may have contributed to that, but usually important documents had a way of sticking out to me, regardless.

I looked at Raikidan when I realized he wasn't searching. Instead, he stared out the window. "What's wrong?"

He shook his head. "Just a bad feeling. You keep searching. I'll keep an eye out."

I went back to my task, but my pace was much quicker, matching my now-increasing pulse. It wasn't unusual for Raikidan to be on edge on assignments, but this time he was paranoid, and it was making me paranoid. My heart stopped when a siren went off. It wasn't from this building, but I had a feeling I knew which one it was from. It wasn't long before more sirens went off around the compound.

I slammed the cabinet shut. "Shit!"

I dashed to the window just as Raikidan was climbing up to the roof. He hauled me up when I was almost there, but I didn't protest. We needed to get out of there. Raikidan held a steady but fast pace as we jumped from roof to roof. As we ran, I searched desperately for one of the others' active signals.

"Laz, is that you?"

My heart leapt at hearing Ryoko's voice. "Yes, it's me. Are you guys okay?"

"Yeah, we're fine. Sorry about that. They tripped a room and I walked into it."

"Don't worry about it. We just need to lose them."

"Easier said than done."

"What do you mean?"

"The information we were given was wrong," Rylan called in. "This place was crawling with soldiers to begin with, and now there are more."

"Then we need to stay in these small groups and try to blend back in with the city."

"It's the only thing we can do at this point. Good luck."

"You as well." I cut the connection and signaled Raikidan to follow me.

I chose our direction and picked up the pace when some soldiers spotted us. I jumped down into an alley and attempted to find a place to hide, but there was none. There wasn't even a dumpster as a last resort. The soldiers were close so there'd be no way we could leave this alley on the ground, and I didn't trust my ability to climb to get me out of sight fast enough.

My brow furrowed when Raikidan handed me his bandana, and his clothes changed to his Guard uniform. My breath caught when he boxed me in against the wall.

"Change your clothes," he ordered.

"W—what are you doing?" I asked.

"Just change your clothes and hide the bandana. We don't have time to argue this."

I hesitated, but when a soldier shouted, my mind had been made up for me. I ripped the bandana from my face and had my clothes change. Once I assumed a shaman disguise, I slipped the bandanas behind my back, inside the cloak, and tied them to a small pouch I had made with the armor. My heart raced as Raikidan continued to tower over me. He didn't move or speak. He just stared at me as he boxed me in.

Just as heavy boots echoed close to the alley, Raikidan caressed my cheek. "Laz'shika—" Several people ran into the alley and shone lights on us. Raikidan growled and held up his hand to shield his eyes. "Do you mind?"

The soldiers lowered their lights, allowing us to see. I kept my head low as if acting embarrassed, but Raikidan didn't move as the soldiers stood there staring at us. "What the hell do you want?"

"We're looking for some rebels," one of the soldiers informed us. "They came this way."

"Well as you can see, we're the only ones here, so why don't you get lost? I'm a little busy here."

The soldier was not too thrilled with Raikidan's attitude, but another soldier pulled him back to speak low in his ear. "Just leave him be. He's a Guard and she's not. You know their weird rules. If they're found out, they're in a lot of trouble. You can't blame him for being defensive."

The soldier sighed and motioned for the others to move on. "I apologize for the intrusion, and don't worry, we won't rat you out."

Raikidan only watched them leave. Once sure they were gone, he pulled away from me and I let out a sigh of relief. Raikidan made a motion for me to follow and I complied.

Once I knew it was safe, I spoke. "That was smart."

"Sorry I did that to you. It was the only thing I could think of," he said. "I may be helping you with overcoming your closeness avoidance, but I didn't want to put you in that kind of situation without consent."

"How did you know they'd react that way?" I asked.

He smirked. "I hear things."

I chuckled. I couldn't help but like the fact that even though it put me in such an uncomfortable position, he had used what he had learned to trick them to see what we wanted them to. I wasn't even sure where he had learned that bit of information. I didn't know they thought that. It was dumb, but a lot of things the soldiers here thought shamans did or didn't do were pretty dumb.

"You might want to tell me where a safe house for us to go to would be," Raikidan advised. "I have no idea where I'm going."

I laughed and picked up my pace to lead. There was one close by. I didn't have a key to it, but there was supposed to be one hidden on the front porch. I prayed it'd be easy to find. I just wanted to get home.

20
CHAPTER

Raikidan and I sat close together on the couch, sharing my Library book. I let him pick the topics to see what was going on in his head, but I was also distracted, making it hard to keep the book going.

My eyes flicked every so often to spy on Ryoko and Raid as they sat next to each other on the other side of the couch, looking over a selection of car magazines. They were comparing current cars and prototypes, and even using what they saw to come up with some new, obscure vehicle that didn't even make sense. Rylan wasn't in the room, not that I was surprised. Ever since Ryoko admitted she was done waiting for him to make a move, he had lessening contact with her and had now shut himself off completely, secluding himself. But, interestingly enough, Ryoko didn't seem to notice.

She did, though, start hanging out with Raid more, and of course he wasn't protesting. He wasn't stupid. He knew he had somehow gotten the upper hand, and he didn't take it for granted, going to work charming Ryoko with everything he had. It didn't hurt that they actually had a lot more in common than I had first thought, and, strangely enough, his shifting control had gotten better almost overnight.

Maybe I had been wrong. Maybe Raid was a better match for her. Possible, but I wasn't fully convinced. Only time would tell if he would be able to make Ryoko happy.

My focus moved off of the two when Seda made her way into the room. She paid no one but Argus any mind. He sat at the bar looking over some papers, completely oblivious to everything going on around him. I knew what Seda was up to. Before Shva'sika could finish healing Argus while we had been out on our failed assignment, a small infection set into the wound. My guess, it had been from the lack of sterile environment I had to work with when trying to get him cleaned up. This stalled the healing process until the infection disappeared, which happened to be last night. Seda was now just making sure it was staying that way.

"Seda, please, it's fine," Argus insisted, pushing her hands away. "You don't have to waste your time worrying about me."

Seda reached for his face again. "Shut your mouth and let me take a look."

I chuckled. The moment her hands touched his face, he turned red. I wondered if she knew how she affected him.

"Your face is rather warm. Are you sure you're okay?" she teased. *Yeah, I think she knows.*

Argus grabbed her hands and lightly pushed them away. "Seda, I'm fine. Thank you for your concern, but you really don't need to be. The infection is gone and the wound is scabbed over."

Seda's smile faded. "All right, if you say so."

I wanted to hit him with this book. What was it with the men in this house? I doubted Argus meant any harm, but he could have just let her check. It would have been the polite thing to do.

Seda snatched something from the fridge and chose to leave, but Argus grabbed her by the wrist and held up one of the papers he was reading. She understood what he wanted and sat down next to him, which confused me. *Is she actually upset by him rejecting her help and just helping him because she feels she has to, or does it not affect her like I think it does? Does she want to help him with what he's working on?*

Raikidan nudged me, pulling my attention back to him and the book. I looked at the book as he tapped it and placed my hand on the paper surface to listen.

A voice came to me as several different ones, piecing a sentence together from different entries. *"Are you not interested in what I'm looking for?"*

It was interesting to hear, and I had no idea someone could do that, so I tried it myself. *I'm just distracted, sorry. Keep looking.*

Raikidan nodded, and the book responded to what he wanted to know. Unfortunately, my focus wandered back to Ryoko and Raid, and then Seda and Argus. I couldn't help it. Something drew me to them, but the more I watched them, the more a weird feeling pricked at me, and I didn't like it. I forced myself to focus on the book.

I shifted my weight a few times to try to get more comfortable, but it didn't help me. Something was bothering me and I didn't know what.

"I'll be right back," I whispered to Raikidan before hopping over the back of the couch and heading to my room. Once there, my feet led me to my nightstand.

I knelt and opened the bottom drawer, where I stashed all my photographs. I picked up a small collection of them. The photographs I had selected happened to be of Ryoko and me, over thirty years ago when we had still been in the military. She looked happy in these, and I had done my best at the time to be as well.

The ones after that added Rylan into the picture, and then Ryoko disappeared and it was just Rylan and me. My brow furrowed when I flipped through the photographs, and the pictures of him and me didn't seem to end. Had I always had this many photographs of us? When I started to think the rest of the photographs were just of us, they switched to Xye and me, and it was that same deal. Every so often, someone else would appear in the photographs, or they'd go back to Rylan and me real quick.

I realized, for the most part, these photographs were of just Rylan and Xye with me. But why? I don't remember having this many photos of them. And why were they making me feel weird? It was the same feeling I was getting in the living room.

My flipping stopped when I came across a photograph of Ryder and me. It was the same one Ryder carried on him. A smile crept onto my face. I thought I had lost this. Putting it on my bed, I filtered through more photographs. That was until I came to a photograph of me with a man that looked a lot like Azriel, but was also different. *Tannek…*

We stood close to each other, his hand wrapped around my shoulder. Not a single trace of negative emotions could be found on either of our faces. *I thought I put this away…* My chest ached, and I forced myself to look through the rest of the pictures. There was a reason that picture was meant to be out of sight.

My heart stopped when I came to one I never thought I'd see again. It was a photograph of my mother and a tall, tan man with a muscular build, green eyes with what appeared to be a gold ring around the pupils, a shaved head that you could tell had once been red hair, and a red beard and mustache. They looked happy and close, and the photograph was angled as if one of them had taken it. Unlike their happiness, anger boiled up inside me, and I had to resist the drive to shred this photograph. I couldn't shred it even if he was in it. I didn't have many pictures of my mother anymore.

I tossed the picture angrily into the drawer and tried to calm myself by glancing over the pictures I had already looked over. I picked up a few at a time to compare them. I had even managed to find some of just Rylan and Ryoko, but the angry feeling inside me didn't go away. It felt like it was getting worse, but in a different way.

Close bonds. Sometimes people wanted more than just friendship. Feelings others had. *Feelings I*— I began stacking the photos back into the drawer. Feelings I was not destined to give into. I threw the remaining pictures into the drawer in a hurry when someone knocked at the front door.

I hurried out of my room and down the stairs to greet whoever was still knocking. I was taken by surprise to see a group of soldiers standing on the other side of the door when I opened it.

"Good morning, Miss," the soldier who had been knocking greeted.

"Um, hi. Can I help you?"

"We're just here for a quick inspection."

"Um, all right, come on in." I led the band of soldiers up the stairs. "Guys, we have company."

By the time the soldiers had reached the living room, everyone had been ready for them, not that we had been doing anything out of the ordinary. Seda and Raid were the only ones who had to do something different, and all Seda did was activate the cloaking watch to hide her mask. Raid, on the other hand, had shifted into his dog shape and lounged across Ryoko's lap.

"Go about your business, I guess," I told the soldiers before sitting down next to Raikidan. "Just knock on closed doors."

The soldiers accepted my invitation, and most of them went about checking. These inspections were getting annoying. They were happening a lot more now, thanks to some better organizing of troop location on someone's part, and they were really putting a damper on what we did sometimes. It was even worse when the soldiers who stopped by had a psychic in their group. We were lucky enough to be have been dealing with those who were on our side, but our luck couldn't last forever.

Raikidan poked my sides playfully and I pushed him away. Taking this as a sign it was okay to be a pain, he grabbed a hold of my sides and began tickling me. The book fell onto the floor with a thump, but I was too busy to make sure it was okay. I failed miserably at getting Raikidan away, and failed even worse at keeping my laughter at bay.

"Rai, stop! Please," I begged.

"Say uncle."

"No." The tickling increased, but I refused to give in. It wasn't until he was on top of me, that I'd had enough. "Okay, okay, uncle. Uncle!"

Raikidan chuckled and let up on the assault. I laid there for a few moments to catch my breath before sitting back up. As I did, I kicked him. Unfortunately, Raikidan grabbed onto my foot and ran a finger down it as a threat. I glared at him and yanked my foot away. He picked the dropped book up off the floor and pretended to use it as some sort of peace offering. Rolling my eyes, I scooted closer to read.

"You're such an ass," I murmured.

"And you're a pain," he said.

"And the two of you together are a pain in the ass," Ryoko teased.

Before either of us could say anything back, the sound of small feet thundered down the hall. "Mommy. Mommy, mommy, mommy!"

Genesis, looking like she had before Ryder had given us the growing plans, zipped around the couch. Around her neck was a necklace with a sun pendant Argus had made. After he and Seda fixed the major kinks in the watch, he'd gone about making a necklace and had Genesis test it, since it was getting hard making excuses about why she was never around when the soldiers came by.

"Mommy!" she cried again.

Ryoko smiled at her. "What is it, Genny?"

"There's a scary man in my room." She looked over at the hallway. "And he's touchin' all my stuff!"

Everyone in the room chuckled. She was so convincing.

Ryoko rubbed her head. "It's just a soldier doing an inspection. You know that. They come around a lot."

"But he's touchin' all my stuff!" she repeated. "Mommy, make him stop."

Ryoko sighed and shook her head. After a few pushes, Raid hopped off her lap and she took Genesis by the hand to lead her back to her room. Raid scratched himself a few times before lying down with a sigh.

"Hey," Raikidan whispered. "Did Azriel ever give you that raise?"

My nose scrunched. "No."

Raikidan grunted and went to say something, but a soldier who had stayed in the living room cut him off. "I know of a place you'd be paid better."

I tilted my head. What was he up to? "And where is that?"

He strolled over confidently and leaned close to me on the back of the couch. "Well, you could go work at Midnight. We'd make sure you'd be paid well."

I froze up. *He did not just suggest that to me!* My hand flew up and smacked him across the face. The soldier stumbled back, taken by surprise by my answer. I jumped over the back of the couch and slammed the door to the roof shut behind me as I stormed up the stairs.

I plopped down on the sill of the roof and hid my face in my arms with a groan. Why were so many of the men I came in contact with deplorable? Was it just them, or were all men like that, even if they weren't so open about it? I refrained from trying to rip my hair out. I didn't want to know. I just wanted them to stop.

I lifted my head when something touched my shoulders. Raikidan knelt in front of me, a look of concern clear on his face. I forced a smile to make it seem like I was okay, but it didn't fool him.

Raikidan pulled me off of my perch and held me close. "Don't listen to him. He's lucky his friends were there to keep him safe. He wouldn't have made it out of the house alive."

"I don't remember telling you what kind of place Midnight is," I said.

A chuckle rumbled through his chest. "You didn't. Rylan did. You are to never step foot in that foul place."

Raikidan didn't act like the men I met. He didn't treat me like a toy or a game. I sighed. Raikidan also wasn't human. He didn't have the same thoughts as humans. He was different. *It's not fair, really...*

Raikidan's grip tightened as if he interpreted my sigh as if the soldier's words still bothered me. But it was okay. I felt safe.

No. I pulled away from him. That wasn't right to feel. I wasn't supposed to feel safe with him. Safe meant attachment, and that led to problems in the end. Raikidan appeared nu-human now, but he wasn't human. Nothing good could come from becoming attached to him. This small attachment needed to be stomped out, and it started with stopping him from helping me any further with my issues.

"Do you want revenge on him?" Raikidan asked.

I tilted my head. "What?"

"Do you want to get him back for what he said to you?"

"Well sure, but how are we going to do that?"

"Use his mind against him."

I gulped. That idea made me uncomfortable. "I don't know…"

"We don't have to. It was just an idea."

"And it was a good idea, don't mistake that. I'm just not sure… Oh what the hell, why not?"

Raikidan looked at me in bewilderment from my sudden decision swing. I could do this. It didn't mean anything. It was acting, and Raikidan wasn't human. It was because he wasn't human that he wouldn't take anything the wrong way and make it awkward, or any more so since this would be embarrassing to start with.

Grabbing hold of Raikidan's hand, I walked backward and held tentative eye contact as I made my way down the stairs. A smile twitched on and off my face until it finally stayed, and then a giggle faded in and out next. Raikidan continued to keep intense eye contact with me while a smirk remained planted on his face. My heart pounded a little harder in response.

I reached for the doorknob, but missed. I made several more blind attempts but it wasn't until I bumped into the door that I finally found it. I was forced to open the door quickly, as Raikidan didn't feel inclined to stop advancing. The moment the door opened, another giggle escaped my lips, catching the attention of everyone in the living room, but I ignored them. I made it look like Raikidan was the only thing I was thinking about as I led him to my room.

I had forgotten about the soldier inspecting my room, so when Raikidan grabbed him and threw him out once we had entered, it took me by surprise. What surprised me more was the fact that he had managed to do it without losing eye contact with me.

"Dude, what the hell—" The last part of the soldier's protest was cut off when Raikidan slammed the door shut.

Raikidan stared me down, and a lump formed in my throat. The look was so intense, but he didn't move. I knew he wasn't going to do anything unless I did. Swallowing the lump away, I forced myself to go through with this.

Raikidan grunted when I forced him against the door, and his inhaling breath came deep as I covered his mouth with my hand and destroyed what personal space boundaries I had left. Raikidan's hand flew up and supported my back, helping with the difficult height difference.

A feminine voice cleared her throat behind me, and I immediately pushed myself away from Raikidan and spun around. In the door frame of my closet stood a voluptuous young woman with red hair in military attire. *Stupid.* I should have remembered that she would have been in here. It was protocol that no man inspected a woman's room alone. The citizens felt that if the inspections were to be mandatory, then rules needed to be put in place to protect their privacy. Men not searching women's rooms, and vice versa, was one of those rules, though they could supervise from afar.

A devilish grin was plastered on her face and she kept her voice low. "Don't worry, I won't tell anyone. I'm actually quite interested in which of the guys you're trying to get back at, so I can go along with it."

Raikidan moved away from the door. "The one with spiked up, poorly dyed blue hair."

The woman rolled her eyes. "Tarlen. That would figure." She cracked her knuckled. "Don't worry, I'll handle this."

She crossed the room, and we moved aside so she could leave but also so we wouldn't be seen. Raikidan, to add to the situation, slammed the door shut behind her.

"I don't know what you boys did to get that woman's boyfriend all heated up, but you're all a bunch of idiots."

"B—boyfriend?" It was Tarlen who spoke. "You're joking right?"

"His clothes are all put away neatly in that nice closet of hers. But with the way he was all over her in there, I highly doubt he's her brother."

"Shit!"

"Man, you are so lucky he didn't try to kill you," a soldier teased. "And it looked like he wanted to at first."

"Wait, I think I missed something while I was dealing with my daughter," Ryoko said. "You did something to piss Ray off in regards to Eira and lived? You're a lucky man. Hot, good in the sheets, fiercely loyal, and protective to a T… she's a lucky lady. Wish I could get a man like that."

Ryoko, you would take advantage of this situation.

Raikidan decided to add to the dramatic atmosphere. He pushed me against the wall, boxing me in with his arms. I froze up as he leaned closer, but I worked out the ability to breathe finally when I realized he was only… *smelling me?* He inhaled deeply by my neck. *I hope I don't smell too bad.*

"What did you do to get him all riled up anyway?" the female soldier asked. It sounded like someone was whispering in her ear, and Raikidan and I had to stop ourselves from laughing when we heard her slap someone. "You're such a pig!"

"Man, what is up with you women and slapping?" Tarlen demanded.

The woman slapped him again and then stormed out of the house. I had to throw my hand over my mouth to stop myself from laughing and giving us away. Raikidan nudged me to get my attention. When I focused on him, he jerked his head in the direction of the bed. Grinning slyly, I grabbed him by the shirt and pulled him away from the door. I threw him onto the bed, face down, and made an attempt to keep him pinned that way. Raikidan grunted with effort as he tried to roll me off but I was going to be stubborn.

Raikidan continued to struggle, but I had the better position, making it possible to keep him pinned. He didn't utter a word, only grunts and sighs as he struggled, so I knew he didn't hate this, and I was glad. It was making me feel better for some reason, and I wanted to feel better.

It didn't take long for someone to knock on the door. I shoved Raikidan's head into the bed out of surprise, and then blinked when Ryoko walked in.

She laughed. "Blaze, you owe me some money."

"No way!"

"Yeah, Laz is only beating him up."

"Fuck me!"

I chuckled. "Were we really that convincing?"

Ryoko shook her head. "Out of us, just him. Fooled those soldiers though. Especially that Tarlen guy."

I chuckled and then gasped as Raikidan suddenly threw me off. I rolled off the bed and landed head down on the floor with part of my body still sticking up in the air.

Ryoko gasped and Raikidan swore. "Eira, I'm sorry! I didn't mean to throw you like that. Are you all right?"

I blinked a few times to wait for the shock to wear off, and then I laughed raucously. Raikidan had thought I still had a firm grip on him, even though Ryoko was distracting me, so he used too much strength to push me off.

My laugher became contagious, Ryoko soon joining in, and then Raikidan. Raikidan crawled over to the edge of the bed and reached down to pick me up. I offered my hands and he took them, pulling me up with one big heave. I moved so fast I almost worried the motion would make me sick.

I stared into his eyes when he and I came nose to nose. His hand let go of mine and rested on my lower back to support me.

"I'll leave you two alone now," Ryoko said slyly before closing the door behind her.

I barely heard her as Raikidan's gaze stayed locked with mine. Time slipped away as I gazed into those sapphire pools. I needed to look away but I couldn't, so instead I rested my forehead on his and closed my eyes. A smile crept onto my face.

"You're welcome, Eira," Raikidan murmured.

I almost chuckled. I didn't have to say my thanks for him to know. "That was a lot of fun, surprisingly."

"Surprisingly," he agreed. I yawned and he chuckled. "Looks like the little butterfly is tried."

I pulled away from him. "No, I'm not."

"Yes, you are."

"No, I'm not." I yawned again and Raikidan snickered. He lay on the bed and tugged my shirt a few times to encourage me to lie down as well. Finally giving in with a sigh, I laid back and relaxed. I yawned once more and Raikidan attempted to cover my eyes with his hand.

I pushed his hand away. "Raikidan, stop. I'm not tired."

"We have to work tonight. You should take a nap."

"We always have to work in some way."

"You know I mean the club. Besides, you need the energy. Everyone can benefit from a nap. Even dragons nap. We sleep a lot, actually."

My brow furrowed. "You don't nap."

"You're not around me all the time to see if I do."

That's fair. "I don't want to mess up my sleep pattern."

"I seriously doubt you won't be tired after working."

My nose scrunched. "Honestly, I'm half tempted to call out. Not feeling doing the waitress thing right now."

"It's better than taking up that Tarlen guy's offer."

I grimaced. "I guess so."

Raikidan covered my eyes with his hands again. "Sleep. I'll wake you when you need to get ready."

I lifted his hand slightly so I could look at him. "If I'm not already awake by then."

Raikidan covered my eyes completely again. "Sleep."

I smiled a little and then relaxed. He was right. Sleep would do me some good, so I'd listen—this time.

21
CHAPTER

Raikidan and I made our way up from the basement. He still insisted on learning how to control fire, and yet wasn't making any progress. I was patient with him, but I wasn't sure how long I could keep this up. Eventually, I was going to find myself trying to convince him to stop. By now, if he was destined to be a fire elementalist, he would have at least been able to control something, even if just a little. Raikidan opened the door for me, and my brow rose in question before I shrugged off the behavior and entered into the living room.

Ryoko poked her head out of her room. "Laz, have you seen my good walking boots?"

My brow rose. "Walking boots?"

"Yeah, my boots that don't have the steel toes," she explained. "They're more comfortable to wear on long walks."

"Why not just wear sneakers?"

"Because they don't look as cool?"

I shook my head. "I didn't even know you had a separate pair, but I'll go check the music room to see if they found a new home in there."

Ryoko murmured her thanks and went back to looking in her room. As I headed down the hall, I wondered about her boot to shoe ratio. But that thought switched over to Rylan as I neared the music room.

No one saw him anymore. He kept to himself in his self-loathing depression, to the point where Seda had to assure me he was eating when no one was around to see him leave his room.

I stopped dead in the doorway of the music room when I opened the door and stared in shock. Broken instruments—shredded papers—*It's like a tornado ripped through here.* Slowly, I made my way over to my guitar and picked it up. Something jagged and large had punctured the body, rendering it unusable. Carrying it with me, I walked over to my piano to find it in no better condition. The seat was smashed, piano keys were scattered about. One of the legs of the piano was broken, and the body punctured all over. The holes had close similarities to the ones on my guitar.

Presumably, no one had been in this room recently, except Rylan. We figured if he had this room to himself, he might start feeling better sooner. It was obvious he wanted nothing to do with this room anymore.

Two people talking out in the hall pulled my attention away. Curious, I wandered out of the room, making sure to close the door so no one else could see the mess, and ventured down the hall. I stopped when the voices became clear.

"Why don't you ask your new boyfriend?" Rylan spat.

"What?" Ryoko sounded really hurt. "What is your problem lately, Rylan? All I asked was if you wanted to go out on a wa—"

"Save it." A door slammed and Ryoko gasped. I went to move to see if she was okay, but Raid walked past me, as if he hadn't seen me at all, so I stayed where I was to see how things played out.

"Hey you rea—you okay, Ryoko?" At least he sounded concerned about her well-being.

"Yeah, I'm fine."

"You sure?"

"Yeah. Give me a second to find Laz, and we can go on our walk."

"All right, I'll wait for you outside."

I backed up a little ways so we wouldn't run into each other too soon. I didn't need her to know I had been eavesdropping.

"There you are, Laz."

I smiled in greeting. "Hey. I wasn't able to find your boots, sorry."

"Nah, it's cool. That's why I'm looking for you. I found them. One was under my bed, and the other one somehow made its way into my dresser."

I laughed. How she managed to place things in such ridiculous locations was beyond me.

"Well, Raid and I are going out on a walk. I'll catch you later."

I watched her walk away. She was acting as if nothing had happened between her and Rylan. My fists clenched. I needed to talk to him. He had no right to act that way.

Taking a deep breath, I stalked down the hall, determined to get to the bottom of Rylan's attitude. I veered around the corner and was surprise to see him out of his room. He was looking down the hall, as if he had been watching someone. *Someone like Ryoko.*

Rylan had a nasty scowl on his face, and it didn't go away when he switched his gaze to me. "What do you want?"

"We need to talk," I said.

Rylan snorted and headed down the hall. "I'm out of here."

I followed him. "Rylan, don't you walk away from me."

Rylan spun on his heels and towered over me. "What the hell do you want? Want me to apologize for being angry she's with someone else? Do you want me to go find her, and tell her I was wrong to be upset with her?"

"No. I want you to stop being an asshole. You have no right to be angry with her for wanting to be happy."

"I could have made her happy!"

"You were sitting on your ass doing nothing," I spat. "Ryoko has the lowest self-esteem I have ever seen in a person. She isn't oblivious to the way men treat her, and she goes out of her way to avoid them. Except you. You have always treated her like a person, and she held onto that and fostered feelings that were not once reciprocated. But because she didn't trust anyone else, she waited and waited and continued to wait longer than any other sane person would have! But you sat on your ass acting like the pansy you are, and she finally had enough of it and chose to focus her energy on someone who showed genuine interest in her. Stop blaming her for your mistake. Stop blaming her for looking to someone else for something you weren't ever going to have the balls to give her!"

Rylan turned away. "I'm not going to stand here and be lectured by the one person who encouraged her to make this choice when she knew how I felt."

"I told her to be happy. Rylan, don't you walk away from me." I reached out and grabbed his arm.

Rylan spun around to face me, but that wasn't all he did. His hand continued to swing, and the back of it collided with my face. Shva'sika gasped, as she rounded the corner just as this happened. If his goal had been to get me to let go, then it worked.

I held the side of my face in utter shock. I couldn't believe he did that to me.

"L–Laz, I'm sorry," Rylan tried to apologize. "I didn't mean to do that."

The voice in my head snarled. *Make him pay for his insolence!*

My shock morphed into anger, and my fist collided with his face in retaliation. Rylan stumbled back and I stormed past him.

"Rylan, I don't know what your problem is, or what the two of you were arguing about, but I know she did not deserve that!" Shva'sika said.

Raikidan tried to make sure I was all right as I passed through the living room, but I pushed him aside and headed for my room. I wanted to be alone now.

I slammed the door behind me and slid to the floor. My fingers touched my stinging cheek. That slap hurt in more ways than one. I sat alone for a several minutes, unaware of anything going on around me. I jumped when Raikidan rested a hand on my shoulder. In my distracted state, I hadn't heard him come through the window.

"Eira, are you all right?" he asked.

"I'm fine," I muttered. "I just want to be alone."

Raikidan grabbed me by the arms and hauled me into his lap. "No you don't."

I curled up into him. He was right. I couldn't deny it. "It hurt so much…"

He stroked my back. "If he weren't your friend, I would rip him part."

"He's your friend, too."

"That wouldn't matter."

I pulled away and stared at him. I could tell by the way he gazed at me, he was being serious. "I don't want you to kill him. Even if he is being an asshole."

"He just needs to see being mad isn't going to get him anywhere. The only way he's going to get Ryoko to want him, is to prove he's better than the competition."

"Yeah, fat chance that'll happen."

Raikidan grinned. "Maybe not. I have an idea."

I cocked my head, my curiosity piqued. "I'm listening."

"Rylan left after you locked yourself in here, so you can't knock any sense into him, but there's someone else who's out in the city who can."

"Ryoko?" I asked. He nodded and my eyes widened in surprise. "Are you actually suggesting we meddle in her personal life?"

Raikidan shrugged. "Why not? She's doing it to us all the time."

I grinned wickedly and jumped to my feet. "That's a great idea. At the very least, it'll help repair their friendship."

Raikidan stood so I could leave. "I'll let you handle this one. I'm pretty sure I'd just get in the way."

I nodded and opened the door but stopped, and turned around. I kissed him quickly on the cheek. "Thanks, Rai. I really appreciate this genius idea."

I spun on my heels and made a mad dash for the basement door. Once in the garage, I hopped on my motorcycle and sped off into the city in search of Ryoko and Raid.

"They're about three blocks away. I'll guide you," Seda informed me.

"Thanks, Seda."

"I think this plan you two cooked up is a little crazy, but some of your crazier plans have been the best ones."

I chuckled and took all the appropriate turns when Seda directed. A grin spread onto my face when Ryoko and Raid came into view. I pulled up next to them and my visor shot up so they could figure out who I was.

"What's up, Eira?" Raid asked.

"Have either of you guys seen Rylan?"

"No, last we knew he was still at the house," Raid said.

"Why, is everything okay?" Ryoko asked, worry clear in her voice.

"I'm not sure. He went down to the garage after you guys left, and after giving him a few minutes, I went to talk to him to figure out why he's been acting so strange. But when I got there he was gone. If you guys haven't seen him, then he hasn't come down this way then."

"Or he has and we missed him 'cause he's driving," Raid said. "It'd be hard to know if it was him if we weren't actually looking for him."

"But we should help look," Ryoko said. "If he's out in the city and still acting weird, he might get himself into trouble. I'll go back to the house and grab a car so I can go over to the shop. If he's not there, I'll spread out from there."

"All right, thanks, Ryo. I'm going to go to the club to see if he's checking in with Azriel about hours."

She nodded and took off back toward the house.

When she was out of earshot, Raid rounded on me. "What the hell is your problem, Eira?"

I blinked. "What are you talking about?"

"Don't go playing dumb on me. You're doing this on purpose, and screwing up what chance I have with her."

I grabbed his shirt and pulled him closer. "You listen here, and listen good. I want Ryoko to be happy, and I will do whatever it takes for her to find the right person for her. If you really care about her, you'll help find your brother for the sake of their friendship. If you care, you'll try to prove that you'll do anything for her. And if you don't like the competition your brother gives you, then get lost, because you're not in it for her."

I threw him away and sped off to make it look like I was heading for the club. I knew Rylan wouldn't be there. Thanks to his foul mood, his attitude was getting in the way of work, so Azriel told him not to come back until he fixed his issues.

I cruised around the city until Ryoko called in. "Hey, I found his car parked outside the shop. I'm going to go and try to talk to him."

"All right, good luck."

"Thanks, I think I'll need it."

I prayed things would go smoothly as I turned around and headed back to the house. I was glad she was the one who found him, not that I was surprised. I doubted Raid even made an attempt to look, and I hadn't been much help, for obvious reasons.

Once at the house, I parked my motorcycle out front and headed inside. I didn't want to park it in the garage until I knew I wasn't going to be needed to give Ryoko a hand. When I made it into the living room, I wasn't at all surprised to see Raid flipping through the channels on the TV, refusing to pay me any mind as I strolled to the kitchen.

"No luck?" Argus asked.

I picked up an apple. "Ryoko found him. She said she was going to talk to him."

"Well, let's hope she can figure out what's up."

I nodded and sat down at the bar to wait. It was all I could do now.

My eyes snapped opened when the front door opened and the sound of two people laughing echoed up the stairs. I left my meditative position on my bedroom floor and headed for the door. From the sound of it, Ryoko and Rylan had patched things up, but it was wise to check for myself. Raikidan's eyes followed me as I moved, but he didn't say anything.

Poking my head out, I watched as Rylan carried Ryoko up the stairs on his back. The two were laughing, and Rylan almost fell over when Ryoko yanked his ear playfully. Neither paid anyone in the living room any mind as they went through.

"Hey, Rylan," I called.

He looked back at me. "Oh hey."

"You owe me a new piano and guitar."

He smacked his forehead. "Oh, I forgot about that mess. I'll have it replaced by tomorrow."

I snorted in disbelief.

"What's wrong with the piano?" Ryoko asked him as he started walking away again.

"Well, you'll see when we get to the music room." I noticed the nervous quiver in his voice. "Let's just say I forgot about a mess I'm supposed to clean up in there."

"Ry, you promised me music!"

"And you'll get it."

"You'd better not be lying to me again."

I chuckled. The two of them were certainly entertaining.

"Well at least they're back to normal," Zane said.

A small smile tugged at the corner of my lips. "It's like old times."

I went back into my room before anyone could ask me any questions, and went straight for my closet as good memories of the past flooded through my mind.

Jasmine brushed my hair out of my face. "I may not be as strong as you and my sister, but no matter what happens, I will do my best to keep you safe. You're family and I love you."

My mother waved me over. "Eira, dear, I want you to meet our medic, Tannek."

Each memory came at random—each moment a little harder than the first to handle.

His dark eyes nullified my want to leave—to run from this. I knew I should, that this would only end in pain but—Tannek cupped my chin. "Eira…"

I pulled on my light weight motorcycle jacket and grabbed my helmet. I needed some time alone, and not in the house.

I ran outside before anyone could find out where I was going, and hopped on my motorcycle, making sure I was aware of the little space Ryoko and Rylan gave me to get out between their two cars. The motorcycle revved to life and I took off down the street, taking whatever turn I deemed necessary at the time. I didn't have a destination in mind, or a time I wanted to be home.

I squinted when I took a corner and saw a man standing on the side of the street a little ways off. The moment he saw me, he extended his arm out with a thumb facing up, and I couldn't figure out why. No one hitchhiked in a city. It wasn't until I got closer that I realized it was Raikidan. How he had gotten here so fast was beyond me.

Curious, I slowed down and pulled up beside him. "Need a lift, stranger?"

A half smile formed on his face. "Do you always offer rides to strangers?"

I couldn't help but smirk. "Only to the ones I know. Now get on before I leave you behind."

Raikidan hopped on and I sped off.

"Are you okay, Eira?" he asked.

"Yeah, why?"

"You took off after that comment you made."

"I just needed to clear my head, that's all."

"You don't like those memories."

I sighed. "It's not that. They're just… complicated."

Raikidan's grip on me tightened. "You know, you have some really crazy ways of doing things, but your plans tend to work out regardless."

"I have you to thank for it. You're the one who came up with that idea."

"Then I guess you owe me."

"I owe you nothing."

"Oh really?"

"Because I did all the leg work."

Raikidan chuckled. "Why are you so smart?"

"Because between you and me, one of us has to be." Raikidan knocked on my helmet and I laughed. "Hey now, no distracting the driver."

"Talking is a distraction."

"Hey, none of that. Only one of us can use our brains."

Raikidan chuckled and hit my helmet again. I rolled my eyes and took a ramp that led to the freeway.

"You're really good to your friends," Raikidan said.

I shrugged. "I'd be a bad friend if I wasn't."

"You do more than most would."

I was quiet for a moment. "I'd do anything for them."

"Even die?"

"Yeah."

Raikidan's grip tightened. "They're lucky to have you."

I grunted. "Not really."

"Not many would give up their one chance at life to let others continue theirs."

"Would you?" I was curious.

"At one time I had a reason to. Then things changed…"

My gaze faltered from the road for a quick second. "What made it change?" When he didn't respond, I knew that was the wrong question to ask. "Never mind. It's not important."

We remained silent after that, which was for the best. The freeway was becoming congested and I needed to concentrate.

It wasn't until we made it out of that did Raikidan speak again. "Thanks for not leaving me on that street."

I chuckled. "You didn't think I'd pick you up?"

"To be honest, yes."

"Well, if I hadn't seen you I would have."

"Well, I couldn't blame you for that."

"Oh, so now you want something to blame me for?"

"No, I'm just saying you're lucky you picked me up since you did see me."

"You know, I could just kick you off on this freeway, and you could walk home."

"You wouldn't dare."

"Try me."

Raikidan grumble to himself and I smiled triumphantly. "So, are we planning on going home soon?"

"What, homesick already?" I teased.

"No, just figured since it's getting late, you'd want to start heading back."

I took a ramp to get off the freeway. "Oh, right, I forgot you have a curfew."

Raikidan growled, and I laughed before taking the most direct route home to spend the rest of the day relaxing for once.

22
CHAPTER
(RYOKO)

I watched as he walked away dejectedly. Laz stood next to me, unaffected by Rylan's reaction to her rejection. It wasn't the first time she had done it, but the way she looked didn't seem right. Maybe it was because… well, it didn't matter. The truth was right in front of me, and I needed to accept it. Zeek had been the only one meant for me, and now that he was gone—

"It bothers you that he attempts to give me the affection you crave from him."

I shook my head. "No, of course not."

"You can't lie to me, Ryoko. I see how you react. It upsets you greatly."

I shrugged. "It doesn't matter. It is what it is. You're the lucky one."

"I'm incapable of reciprocating those feelings. You should be the one receiving his affection."

I went to reply but someone yelled out, preventing me. "Captain!"

We both turned to see a muscular young man with black hair running over to us. It was Rylan's younger brother Raid. I didn't know him well, but I doubted that would last long. He was being transferred soon to our special unit per Amara's request.

"Raid," Laz greeted with a curt nod.

He took a few breaths before speaking. "Amara wants to see you. She says she has something good to tell you."

"Do you know what about?"

Raid shook his head. "She didn't say, but if I had to speculate, you may be getting the promotion she put you in for."

"Very well. I'll go see her."

Raid nodded and then looked at me and smiled. "Hey, Ryoko."

I smiled back. "Hey."

An unusual look crossed Laz's face as she glanced between us, and then walked off without a word, leaving the two of us alone...

My eyes fluttered open. A hand shook me and I was not happy. I did not enjoy someone waking me up, especially if it wasn't an emergency, and by the light touch, this wasn't one.

"Ryoko, wake up," Danika urged.

I rolled over and squinted at her with tired eyes. "Why?"

"There's something you're going to want to see."

"What is it?"

"You'll see."

"Tell me or I'm going back to bed."

Danika chuckled. "Just crawl out of bed and you'll see. You can go back to sleeping after."

I grumbled and sat up. I rubbed my eyes to help me wake up a little more, and then tugged on my cropped shirt to make sure I wasn't falling out of it. Slowly getting to my feet, I followed Danika out of my room and down the hall. I wished she'd just tell me what was going on, but the moment I heard the piano playing, I started to get an idea.

Danika led me right to the music room. Rylan and Seda stood outside the room looking in. Rylan smiled at me when I stood next to him, and I smiled back. I was glad he was better now. It hadn't been like him at all to act the way he was. Then again, until talking with him, I wasn't aware it was because of me. He had been honest with me, and had explained how it upset him how much time I had stopped spending with him to start spending it with Raid.

I hadn't realized that I had been spending so much time with Raid, and never thought it would upset Rylan so much. I didn't know he liked spending so much time with me. It made me wonder if I was wrong to give up on him. Laz had hurt him pretty badly, but I waited so long, I really could have just been dreaming. He wasn't going to choose me, and I needed to come to terms with that. I needed to come to terms that we were only going to be friends. But after waiting this long, longer than any sane person would have, I wasn't sure if I could come to those terms.

Rylan jerked his head to get me to look into the music room, so I peered in. At the piano, playing the beautiful tune that flowed through the house, was Laz. She played flawlessly, unaware of our presence. The piano Rylan had picked out for her was nice. Instead of getting her a baby grand piano, he dished out the extra cash to buy her a grand piano. He had chosen a burgundy color, and he had plans to have someone come in and add some small details to it.

He had done this for destroying her piano and guitar, and for everyone else, as well. It was his way of showing he was sorry to everyone for the way he had been acting. He had even done something for me. When I walked into the shop, he was working on my favorite car, and it wasn't just a tune-up. He had added so many features to it, and he even took the time to do some special detailing all on his own. I absolutely loved it. He told me it was an early birthday present, but my birthday wasn't for another few months, so I knew it was an apology.

My eyes flicked to Raikidan when he came up behind me and rested his hand on the top of the doorframe as he peered into the room. I couldn't help but drag my gaze over of the length of his half naked form. It was hard not to notice every muscle and scar. How Laz managed to not see something was beyond me. Sure he was a dragon, but his body was godly, and the amount of focus he placed on something, especially her, was so intense. If someone looked at me like he did her, I'd melt into a puddle.

My attention was pulled from my ogling when Laz began to sing. I could hardly believe it. There was no fighting, no excuses, just her singing in Old Tongue all on her own. I didn't even know she knew Old Tongue. *She's full of surprises.*

My eyes widened when she pulled out another surprise. Her eyes flashed from clear to glazed over. I had seen that look only twice since she had been back, and my body tingled with anticipation. Except for when she came back knowing something new, or when she had moved elsewhere, nothing had ever happened when this change occurred. But something told me this time would be different. Like something was going to appear.

Just then, out of nowhere, translucent figures began appearing one by one. My heart almost stopped when I realized I could put names to many of the faces of these strange figures. One in particular stood out to me as she walked over to Laz. It was Amara. I watched as she sat down on the piano seat next to Laz, who seemed oblivious to Amara's presence.

"Am I going crazy?" I couldn't stop the question from falling out my mouth.

"No, they're spirits," Danika replied. "They're people who have had some sort of strong connection with Laz. You probably can put names to some of their faces, like I can. Several of them are from the village, like Valessa and my brother."

Sadness pricked my heart. I remembered Laz telling me a little about Danika's brother and that he died. I just wondered which spirit was him. I knew I had seen an image of him once, but it had been so quick I couldn't recall it. When I spotted a man with long blue-silver hair sitting on the piano, I knew right then it was him. Other than his ears being a bit different, he and Danika had similar features. He looked like a nice young man. It was a pity he was dead. *And, damn girl, can you get some nice looking men to follow you around.*

"Why do her eyes do that?" Rylan whispered. "I mean the glazing-over thing."

"It's a shaman thing," Danika explained. "Shamans, depending on their training status, will look one of two ways when spirits become involved. The eyes of a shaman in training will only glaze over, whereas the eyes of a fully-realized shaman will glow."

"Why is that?" he asked.

"It has to do with the ceremony that is performed when the shaman in training has learned what he needs to know."

"What happens at the ceremony?" I asked.

"I'm afraid I can't tell you that. We're not supposed to discuss it with anyone who isn't a full shaman."

My ears drooped. I wanted to know, but I understood, even if it made me wonder what type of secrets shamans knew. I wondered what new secrets Laz had learned. My ears pricked when a new sound joined Laz's singing. The spirits were singing with her. I watched with wonder. I couldn't make out their words, but it was such a beautiful sound.

Raikidan cranked his head over his shoulder, piquing my interest. "You okay?"

He nodded. "Just thought I heard something."

I looked back, but couldn't see or hear anything. "I think you're crazy."

"He might not be," Danika corrected.

I tilted my head. "How so?"

"When a shaman and spirits come together, it creates a type of field."

"Like a force field?"

"Kind of like that, yes. Because there is this field, if there is a lingering spirit following someone and they come into contact with the field, they can be detected sometimes."

"But only sometimes?"

"Spirits are tricky. They can allow you to see them, or they could not. It's up to them. Even a shaman can't control whether he'll see them or only hear them. So from the sounds of it there's a lingering spirit here, and I'd say it's connected to Raikidan, since he's the one who felt its presence."

I watched as Raikidan went to thinking. He was so serious when he did that. It made him interesting to study. I glanced behind me when a shadow caught my peripheral. "Blaze?" He walked down the hall, his movements stiff and uncharacteristic. "What's Blaze doing over here?" I blinked when I noticed the spirit of a young woman following him. "And who's the woman?"

"I'm not sure," Rylan replied. He sounded just as curious as me.

We watched as the woman tried to stay in front of him, but he'd walked right through her. My lips pressed into a thin line. *Is she trying to stop him?* When he grabbed the door knob of the door leading to the roof the woman became frantic. The motions sent a chill up my spine.

Just then, Argus bolted past us and grabbed onto Blaze's arm. "Blaze, wake up!"

Blaze jumped and took in his surroundings, his eyes wide. "What the hell? How did I get here?"

Argus blew out a breath. "You were sleepwalking again."

My brow rose. I didn't know Blaze was a sleepwalker.

Blaze scratched his head. "I thought I fixed that."

"So did I," Argus said. "Now get back to bed, and lock your door this time."

Blaze made his way back down the hall. "Yeah, yeah."

We all watched as he disappeared into the darkness, oblivious of the presence of the strange woman following close behind.

Argus walked over to us and looked at Blaze one last time before peering into the music room. "I'm guessing it's best not to ask about the translucent figures in this house?"

"It might give you a headache if you did," Seda teased.

Argus chuckled and then bid us good night before heading back to his room. As things calmed down, I relaxed against Rylan, listening to what was left of Laz's song. Rylan rested his hand on my shoulder, and I was okay with that. I was okay with how I still felt. I didn't want this moment to end. It was perfect. *Almost.*

I frowned when Laz's song ended and she slid the piano guard over the keys. I had hoped she would have played for longer, but the look in her eyes troubled me. She seemed… conflicted.

She pushed past us without making eye contact. We all watched her head down the hall, and instead of going to her room, she opened the door to the roof and headed up the stairs. *What's eating at you, Laz?*

I smirked when Raikidan left the room and made his way after her. Without fail, the faithful puppy followed her around. I wished the two would get their heads out of their asses and see exactly how perfect they were for each other.

Rylan grabbed my wrist when I took a step to follow. "Ryoko, don't."

I slipped out of his grasp and continued on. "I'm just being nosey."

"Yeah, and nosey is the problem," Raid said. "Leave them be."

I pretended to think about it and then continued walking. "No."

The brothers sighed, but neither made another attempt to stop me. *You guys are just as curious, but not nearly as brave.* I wasn't afraid of being caught. And meddling in Laz's affairs definitely wasn't beneath me in the least. *Honestly, they should expect it from me at this point.*

Careful of how I stepped so I wouldn't make a lot of noise, I tiptoed up the stairs and listened in on the conversation happening on the roof.

"Your voice is beautiful," Raikidan complimented.

"What?" Laz asked.

"When you sing. Your singing voice is beautiful," he clarified, though I wished he'd repeated his words in the exact manner as the first time.

Laz grunted. "It's not that great."

"Eira, you really should sing more. I'm not making that up."

"Why, so you can kidnap me?" My brow rose in confusion, and I guessed Raikidan's had, too, before Laz laughed. "Well, I always knew the story was a little farfetched."

Oh right!

"What are you talking about?" Raikidan asked.

"It's just a silly human story about dragons," she said

"Oh, well, will you tell me it?"

"It's nothing special."

Stupid, just tell him.

"Your human stories interest me."

See, tell him! I had to refrain from throwing out my arms to emphasize my mental thoughts.

"You don't tell me any dragon stories."

"We don't have many."

"But you do have some."

"Yes, but they're not relevant to what we're talking about."

"How would you know?"

Raikidan let out an aggravated sigh. "Eira, just tell me the story."

Yeah, no kidding, Laz. You're such a pain sometimes.

She snickered, showing how much of pain she was purposely being. "All right, all right. A long time ago, when dragons were more abundant, people believed that if a young maiden had a beautiful singing voice, a dragon would come and snatch her up to take her back to his lair so she could only sing for him, like a pretty song bird. It was because of this idea they forbade young women from singing while they were alone or outside, so they wouldn't be taken away."

Raikidan laughed. "They really believed that?" He continued to laugh. "That's ridiculous! The only reason a dragon would take her is if he knew her, and he'd only take her if she didn't want to be around humans anymore."

I tilted my head with curiosity as Laz spoke. "So a dragon would take someone?"

"Well, a red dragon, sure. Remember, most of them like human companionship."

"That's true. But they wouldn't just up and take them?"

"Eira, we may be thieves when it comes to precious gems or objects we like, but we wouldn't take someone against their will. That would just be dumb."

He's got a point.

Laz chuckled. "All right, all right. Not that you guys aren't above making stupid decisions."

That's true too.

I bit my lip so I wouldn't laugh when Raikidan smacked her. She also laughed, so I had to guess it was only in the arm. Though if you asked me, he should have aimed a bit lower.

"Do you have any other stories about maidens and dragons?" Raikidan asked.

"Only one type comes to mind. They're about maiden sacrifices," Laz said.

"I'm not sure if I want to know about that one."

"Not all of them are bad," she said. "Or I don't think they are. Yeah, some were killed, but most were tied somewhere in hopes a dragon would take them as an accepted offering to keep the dragon from destroying their towns or farms."

"Why a maiden? Why not just anyone?"

"I don't know. The stories just say dragons only liked maiden sacrifices."

"Humans are dumb."

She grunted. "Well if dragons are anything like you, then they must be dumb, too, since you follow a human around."

I covered my mouth so I wouldn't laugh. A good comeback on her part, in my opinion.

Raikidan smacked her again and then switched subjects, not surprisingly. "So will you sing more, Eira?"

Laz snorted. "Why would you want to hear a dumb nu-human sing?"

Oh boy, here we go.

"Eira, don't start with me. Just answer my question."

"No, I won't."

"You won't answer my question? Or you won't sing?"

My ears twitched at the sound of one of them standing up. "I won't sing."

"Eira, why not? Your voice is gr—"

"Because I'm tired of everyone making a big deal out of everything I do!" I jumped back from the ferocity in her voice. "I'm sick of people pointing out when I do something out of the ordinary, at least what they think is normal for me. I'm sick of everyone making a big deal over stupid shit! So I do what is thought to be normal of me, and everyone leaves me alone."

Laz… She didn't really mean that, right?

"Eira, I'm sorry. I was just trying to—"

"You were just trying to help." She sighed. "I know. But the only way you're going to help is if you let me do things on my terms, not yours."

"All right, I'm sorry."

"No, I'm sorry. I shouldn't have shouted."

Yeah, no kidding. A little uncalled for.

"You had a right to yell. I shouldn't have pushed. So let's forget I asked, and go back to bed. You're horrible when you don't get enough sleep."

Sounded like she pushed him. "You're no better."

I snickered and began creeping back down the stairs. Plans brewed in my head, and I didn't want to be caught. That'd just make it harder to enact them. But as I was leaving, I caught the last bit of their conversation.

"Raikidan, you won't steal me away if I do decide to do what you've asked of me, right?"

"Eira, we've been over this."

She chuckled. "All right, then I'll think about it."

I smirked. *Laz, you give me too much to work with.*

23
CHAPTER
(EIRA)

Scattered street lights illuminated the dark, quiet street—not a civilian or soldier in sight. It was the perfect place to keep under the radar. Shamans, and dragons disguised as shamans, worked around me to carry cargo from two merchant caravans into a house designated for temporary shaman living.

But the cargo wasn't supplies for selling. No, it was for the rebellion, and that's why Ryoko, Rylan, Raikidan, Shva'sika, and I were here. Genesis had volunteered us to help since we knew the shamans and dragons better than anyone else—not that I minded.

I carried a small box from a wagon and over to the building it was parked in front of. I had no idea what they had obtained for us, but now wasn't the time to find out. We needed to get the cargo unloaded and inside as quickly as possible.

Even though we had back up paperwork, thanks to some hands on the inside of the fortress, it still would be a pain to deal with the military if they did happen to show up.

I handed my box off to a North shaman waiting at the door, and went back to the wagon to grab the next. Our efficiency left me with nothing to take, so I patiently waited. Just as the female shaman was about the hand me a decent-sized box, something crashed behind me and I cringed.

I didn't want to know what had been broken, but since I was running this operation, it was my responsibility to deal with it. I exhaled through parted lips when I laid eyes on the broken crate and found it filled with actual merchant supplies and not contraband.

The dragon who had dropped the box, kept his head low and shuffled his feet. "Sorry."

"Just clean up and get it inside. And nothing better be broken. You're paying for it if there is."

He nodded and tried to pick up the items as fast as he could, while still being careful. I just shook my head. I had been keeping tabs on this one all night. Even before Raikidan told me he was young and to keep an eye on him, I could tell how twitchy he was. All night he had been looking over his shoulder and doing more standing around than actually helping. And now here he was breaking boxes.

I didn't know much about dragons, but since Raikidan had warned me about his age, I wondered if that had a significant impact on his actions. If he were young, like Rimu and his siblings, I would agree with the idea, but this dragon didn't appear to be all that young. He had the form of a twenty-six-year-old.

The woman in the caravan giggled as she placed another box on top of the one she had planned to hand me before the distraction. "You're so mean."

I watched her carefully. She had light skin and freckles, but I couldn't see her hair or eye color to be able to identify her better. *Something is familiar about her… but what?* "I wasn't mean at all. I could have chewed him out, but I didn't. I just told him to pick it up and pray he hadn't broken anything valuable."

She snickered and straightened. "For a dragon, that's a pretty big threat. We love our gold."

Her long red hair spilled out of the confines of her hood, giving her away. "Xaneth?"

She smiled and then retreated into the rear of the wagon to grab another box. My eyes scanned the area to make sure things were going smoothly before I jumped into the wagon.

"I'm going to be honest," I said. "I'm confused. Don't your unspoken laws state you can't do this?"

She smiled and pulled her hood back, allowing me to see amusement dancing in her eyes. "Our *laws*, as you put it, say it's wrong for a female to fight. They can't stop us if we insist, and helping this cause in a non-violent manner isn't going outside those preferred norms."

This intrigued me. "So why are you helping?"

Xaneth sat down on a sturdy box and her smile disappeared. "Because I don't want my children to live in a world where they have to be afraid of being seen. I want them to be able to experience the world in any form they desire. My greatest wish is for them to see a world that isn't as dark as this one currently is." She then looked at me and smiled. "And I'm doing it for you."

I tilted my head. "Why me?"

The look she gave me in response to my question made me feel a bit weird. It was like she was trying to get me to understand something secret and yet important, but at the same time wasn't sure if she wanted me to know.

I turned when someone came up to the back of the caravan. It was Raikidan. "Hey, you going to gossip all night, or are you going to work like the rest of us?"

I snorted. "I am working."

"Right."

Xaneth giggled. "I shouldn't keep you any longer. I don't need to get you into any more trouble with your keeper."

I laughed at her joke and then hopped out of the wagon. I grabbed a box and headed for the house, briefly catching Raikidan and Xaneth speaking in their native tongue, but shrugged it off.

After handing off my box to the shaman waiting in the entrance of the house, I headed back to the caravan. I passed Raikidan on the way, and noticed his intense gaze following me. *He's so weird.*

I grabbed a hold of a crate, but stopped myself when I noticed a pair of soldiers heading our way. It was obvious they intended to investigate us, and I wanted to sigh. No doubt one of the dragons being careless caught the attention of a neighbor watching from the safety of their house. It was time for me to make sure this didn't get out of hand.

"Good evening, gentlemen," I greeted.

They both tipped their head respectfully, but only the one on my left spoke. "Good evening, ma'am. We received a call from a concerned resident on this street, regarding a break-in in progress."

They thought we were stealing? I nearly laughed. Civilians never ceased to amaze me with the wild thoughts they came up with.

"I have a feeling whatever it is you and your fellow shaman are doing is the source of this claim," the soldier continued. "Care to explain what's going on here?"

I giggled. "Oh dear, we didn't mean to frighten anyone. We're just unloading merchandise to store overnight. We were supposed to trade with another caravan, to vary the selections, but one of the wagons broke down and was unable to meet with us in this marvelous city. We requested permission to allow temporary lenience on our caravan's stay, so we could get this issue resolved without us having to do the trade outside the safety of the city walls."

"May I see the papers for your approved request?" the soldier asked.

"Certainly." I turned around and focused on Xaneth who was watching the exchange. Everyone else had also stopped their work. "An'tha, would you mind retrieving the papers?"

She smiled. "Of course, Laz'shika."

Xaneth disappeared into the caravan, and a few moments later came out with a few sheets of rolled-up paper. I met her half way to take them from her, and then returned to the soldiers to hand over the paperwork. The soldier who had been speaking to me accepted them and read them over.

"Everything is here," he said before handing the paperwork back to me. "If I may ask, why are you unloading the wagons? It appears to be a waste of energy if you plan to leave tomorrow."

"Very observant of you." I smiled. "But the answer is simple. Our caravans are made out of wood, making it easy for them to be broken into in a city like this one."

"Very well. Sorry for bothering you."

I smiled. "Don't worry yourself. You're just doing your job."

"D—do you need any help?" This was the first time the other soldier had spoken, and he didn't come off as the confident type. Or maybe it was something else.

I continued to smile. "Thank you for the offer, but"—I looked behind me to the others who had resumed their jobs and then back at the soldiers—"I believe we have enough hands to get this all taken care of. We shouldn't be much longer."

The soldier frowned. "All right then."

I watched them leave and had no qualms about overhearing their conversation.

"What was that about?" the first soldier asked him.

"I was just trying to be helpful," the other one replied.

"Don't tell me you've already become smitten with her," the first said. "You could barely see her face, let alone the rest of her."

"So? She seemed nice."

The first soldier snorted and I rolled my eyes as I headed back to the caravan.

Xaneth smiled crookedly when I tried to hand her the paperwork. "What?"

She giggled. "Oh, nothing."

"No, that smile doesn't mean *nothing*," I accused. "Spill it."

Ryoko came up next to me and grabbed two boxes. "You know why she's smiling, Laz. You were uncharacteristically nice."

I grunted. "Because I have to be. Unless you would have rather them going through the boxes and see what we're actually transporting."

Xaneth giggled. "That's not what I find amusing."

"Then what is it?" I wasn't happy about her being so cryptic.

Just then, Shva'sika came around the other side of the wagon. "It's because of that young man. He was quite taken by you, and based on the conversation that continued afterward, I'm sure you could have gotten him to do whatever you wanted. And it's all thanks to that pretty voice of yours."

I shook my head. "Whatever."

"Oh don't be like that, Laz," Ryoko begged. "It's cute."

"It's stupid," I argued. "To fall for someone based solely on her voice is idiotic. You can't be happy with someone you see as ugly."

"Beauty is subjective," Xaneth said. "But that young man wouldn't be wrong to think you're beautiful."

I grunted and carried my box off to the house.

Xaneth sighed. "She's stubborn."

Ryoko chuckled. "You have no idea."

I rolled my eyes and focused on finishing the job. As I headed back to the wagon to grab another crate, I noticed that young dragon struggling. It looked like he was about to drop this box too, and I wasn't having it. I rushed over, grabbed a hold, and helped steady him.

"Thanks," he murmured.

"Let me help you get your hands right so you don't drop this one, too."

He nodded in response and allowed me to reposition his hands.

"Better?" I asked.

He smiled. "Yes, thank you." I smiled back and then headed to the wagon, but he stopped me. "Hey, wait. I did end up breaking two things when I dropped the other box. I don't know the value of them, though…"

A smirk spread across my lips. "Don't worry about it. I just wanted you to understand you couldn't be making a habit of it."

"I'll be careful, promise."

"Good. Now get back to work."

He nodded and headed for the house.

Xaneth smiled when I made it back to the wagon. "That was nice of you."

I shrugged and picked up a box. Just as I turned around, though, it was taken from me by the young dragon. I blinked as he passed me the briefest of glances before rushing off.

"O…kay…" I wasn't sure what to make of that.

Xaneth giggled. "Do you always have this effect on males?"

My eyebrow quirked up. "What are you talking about?"

She gave me a pointed look. "Don't tell me you can't see what you've just done." I stayed quiet and she laughed. "Arsors is now rather infatuated with you."

"What?" I shrieked. "Are you kidding me? Why? I didn't do anything out of the ordinary!"

A lopsided grin pressed up her face. "Maybe it's just you, then."

I rolled my eyes. "Yeah, right." Xaneth looked around and snickered, making me curious. "What?"

"The others of my kind are picking on Raikidan," she said.

I sighed. "Do I even want to know why?"

She smiled at me. "I can't be sure why, but for some reason he reacted rather negatively to Arsors' attention to you."

I pinched the bridge of my nose. "Great."

Xaneth blinked. "What? Does he do that often?"

"You could say that…" I muttered. When she smiled knowingly, I rolled my eyes. "Don't you start, too."

She shook her head and smirked. "I don't know what you're talking about. I'm just thinking."

I grabbed a box and headed for the house. "Yeah, and that'll get you into trouble." My brow furrowed when Raikidan stole my crate. "Hey, what gives?"

"I got it," he said before headed for the house.

I blinked a few times and then shook off my confusion and headed for the wagon again. I glared at Xaneth when I caught her trying to conceal her laughter.

"Don't start."

"I'm sorry, I'm not laughing at you. I'm laughing at him," she admitted. "He's such a strange male, and does things that contradict what he claims."

"Well I can agree with you on that."

She laughed and then looked around. "Appears we're out of crates in this wagon."

I peered over to the other wagon and Ryoko waved to me. *Looks like we're done.*

Several shamans went into the house, and the rest of the crew piled into the wagons. There were so many that I had to sit up with the driver, but I didn't mind in the least. He was a pleasant old man, and he was kind to the horses that pulled the caravan along.

The shaman held the reins up to me. "Would you like to drive?"

I chuckled. "Unless you want everyone in here either holding onto the frame of this wagon for dear life, or being thrown out onto the road because this vehicle is out of control, I'm going to pass."

"I'd like that not to happen, thanks," Ryoko said.

I pointed at her and the old shaman chuckled. "Very well."

But Shva'sika wasn't going to take my answer. "Don't be like that, Laz. You ride horses just fine."

"Riding and driving are two different things. At least with riding, it's easier to stop the horse if things get out of control."

The old shaman snorted. "I'd beg to differ."

Rylan leaned closer to me. "Since when could you ride well?"

I whacked him on the head. "Unlike you, I can ride just fine."

He rubbed his head. "Since when? You didn't get the chance to practice a lot back in the day."

"Since she stayed with us," Shva'sika said. "Ranchers come by the villages four times a year to see if we're interested in buying. Laz nearly did."

I chuckled. "What can I say? He was a well-bred Percheron."

"But you somehow refrained from making the purchase."

"Where was I supposed to stable it? I doubt Darren would have appreciated a large horse chilling out in the kitchen of the inn."

Laughter echoed through the caravan. Even Shva'sika couldn't help but laugh. "Yes, that's true, but we did also offer several times to build you a house of your own. We could have given you the space to have at least one horse."

"I hadn't intended on staying as long as I did," I reminded her. "Every time I made an attempt to leave, you'd drag me back—literally."

She crossed her arms and her shoulders pulled back. "Yes, I did."

Ryoko giggled next to her. "You really like to get what you want."

Shva'sika smirked. "It's just a perk of being me."

The two giggled away, and I rolled my eyes. I then sighed when the old shaman tried to hand me the reins again. "Okay, I'll drive, but if anyone dies, it's not my fault."

"If I die, I'll be sure to haunt you," Raikidan grumbled.

The wagon echoed with laughter as I drove the horses on with relative ease. I really hoped I did this right. I didn't want any issues surfacing because of me.

CHAPTER 24

I sat down on the crate and leaned against the brick wall. I had been working at the club all night, and I desperately needed a break. Rylan was working overtime at the shop, and Raikidan had disappeared earlier this morning, along with Shva'sika, so I was forced to do this alone.

My feet hurt from running around, and my ass hurt from all the slapping and grabbing it got from the drunken soldiers. Without Raikidan around, they became bolder, and it took every ounce of my will not to kill them.

I let out a long sigh. I wanted this night to just end. I wanted to go back to the house and think of real strategies to take down Zarda. I didn't want any of this stupid eavesdropping and uncomfortable provocative antics. But most of all, I wanted to go home and check on Argus. The first infection hadn't stayed away for long, and no one could figure out why. He had done a great job keeping it clean, and Shva'sika and Seda had taken turns checking him as a precaution. In the end, Azriel had come over to give us a hand and he had somehow found a small metal shard embedded in his skin.

Azriel had to sedate Argus and cut open the skin again, but as soon as he took out the small shard, he found more. It had taken over an hour for him to finally be comfortable with saying he had found them all, and allowed Shva'sika to heal Argus up as best as she could.

Unfortunately, the scar was no longer as neat as the first one, but Argus didn't mind. In fact, he liked the new look. Azriel told us the infection would go away in a few days as long as he had gotten all the fragments, and there was no eye damage for anyone to worry about, but I still felt a little responsible. Argus really hadn't been wearing protective eye wear because of me.

Low chuckling from the entrance of the alley caught my attention. I looked up to see two figures encroaching on me. I could smell the alcohol on their breath from where I was, and from the way they were dressed, I assumed they were soldiers. *Where did they come from?* How had I not noticed them approach?

"Look, Sedo, a little lost kitty."

I didn't like where this was going.

"You're right, Amon, maybe we should help her." The two of them laughed and the one named Sedo drew a knife. "Do as we say, kitty, and we won't have to hurt you."

I scrambled to my feet and searched for a way out. I had to keep up this pathetic, weak act as long as I could, even if it meant running, but there was nowhere to go. The alley was short, and the only place to sit was far from the door, which these two were now blocking.

I backed away until my back bumped into the wall. *Great.* There was no way out of this if I kept up this act, and I wasn't going let myself be manhandled by these two soldiers.

A low growl emitted from behind them. The two stopped advancing and looked back. A tall, hooded figure stood in the entrance of the ally.

"Rai…" I whispered. He had the most ridiculous timing, but I wasn't complaining this time.

"Nothing to see here buddy, so get lost," Sedo stated.

Raikidan growled again and before either man could move he closed the distance and threw them into the wall. The then wrapped him arm around my waist and pulled me close. Even with him wearing a baggy sweatshirt I could feel his tense muscles. *So much anger…*

"Stay away from my girl," he growled.

His girl? What is he talking about?

Amon chuckled as he staggered in his attempt to stand back up. "Ya hear that, Sedo? Mr. Tough Guy claims the kitty belongs to him."

"I'd like to see him prove it," Sedo responded with a chuckle.

I tensed. I knew what that meant and I didn't like it.

"I don't have to prove anything to you," Raikidan retorted.

Sedo pulled a gun and aimed it at us. "I think you do."

"You don't have to prove anything to them," I whispered. "Just give them a good beating and no one will know."

Raikidan gave me an apologetic look. Had Sedo not pulled a gun, things might have been different.

Raikidan's hot breath caressed my face and I had to force myself to breathe. It was one thing to deal with his personal space problem, or for him to be working with me on my issue with close contact, but this… this was a whole other thing I wasn't okay with.

"I'm sorry," he whispered.

His free hand came up and cupped my cheek while the grip of his other arm tightened. He pulled me closer until his lips touched mine. My heart stopped and my breath caught. His lips were soft, warm, and, unfortunately, inviting. The touch wasn't forced, like when he had been pushed into me at the house months ago.

Compelling myself to breathe and my eyes to close, I had to go with it. No matter how much I wanted to push him away and deck him, I couldn't.

My lips synchronized with his as they opened and closed, being extra careful my tongue stayed as far as possible from his lips. His facial hair tickled, but I resisted the urge to laugh.

As his lips continued to touch mine, a strong desire to pull myself closer to him and touch him in ways that were extremely inappropriate flooded over me. *Oh this is not okay.*

After moments that lasted too long, he pulled away, allowing me to breathe. My rapidly beating heart pounded in my ears.

I barely heard Raikidan growl at the men in the alley or speak to them. "You're still here?"

Sedo chuckled. "Of course. Now hand over the girl and you can go without a scratch."

Raikidan bared his teeth. "Over my dead body."

Sedo raised his pistol. "Suit yourself."

Raikidan stepped in front of me to act as a shield, and I stepped back. This wasn't going well at all. My hand reached up to touch my neck as I thought of something to change the situation. Nothing had a chance to come to mind because my fingers touched a part of my neck that was no longer soft and smooth. The spot had a slight bumpy and leathery texture. *It can't be.*

I couldn't believe what had happened. How could the effect of that kiss have been so strong it had partially broken down the one wall I tried to make sure always stayed up? Anger could, and had, twice in the past. It was a strong enough emotion my wall couldn't defend against it. But… lust? I couldn't even deny I didn't know what this recent sensation was. I tried so hard to bury that—to hide my design flaws that made me a failure in the end…

I stared at Raikidan's back as he stood in front of me protectively. *Why him?*

"What's going on here?" I peered around Raikidan to see two soldiers standing at the opening of the alley.

"Let's get out of here, Amon," Sedo whispered. "She ain't worth our hides."

"Nothing, sir," Amon lied. "Just checking to make sure these two are all right."

One of the soldiers snorted. "Don't give me your lying bullshit. I can see the pistol Sedo has in his hands. Now get your asses moving and leave these two alone or you'll have more to worry about than a few missed meals."

Amon glared at us and the two left. The soldier that had saved us gave a silent apology with his eyes and then pushed Sedo and Amon to get them to move faster. Raikidan turned to face me just as I finished wiping my mouth with my arm. I needed to make sure every trace of what had happened was gone. I prayed that in this short amount of time, the visible change on my neck had reverted. I could put as much energy as I wanted to appear normal, but once the change broke free, it was hard to make it go away without Rylan's help.

Knowing full well that I was now late from returning from my break, I headed for the door. As I passed Raikidan, I spoke, "That never happened, got it?"

He didn't respond. He just watched me enter the building.

I flopped down on my bed face first with a groan. Azriel hadn't questioned my lateness when I had arrived back to the work scene, nor was performing my job any easier than it had been earlier.

Raikidan had followed me into the club and worked at his normal bouncer position with no questions from anyone, but I wished he would have just left. His presence may have kept the harassment to a minimum, but for me, it had been overwhelming. It made it hard to forget what had happened.

Now I was home and my mind was buzzing even more. I wanted it to shut up so I could forget it all. Why was it affecting me so much? Why had it broken down that wall so easily?

I groaned again and threw my pillow over my head. Raikidan entered the room and switched to his dragon form without a word. He had been quiet all night. He barely looked at me even after our shift ended, which was just fine with me.

I shut my eyes and tried to force myself to sleep, hoping I'd forget everything. Eventually sleep came, but the memory stayed.

25
CHAPTER

The TV channels flipped by at a rapid pace as I looked for something to watch. Ryoko begged me to stop at a few of them, but I ignored her and kept going. It wasn't that I didn't want to watch them, well it was a little bit of that, but I mostly just liked to see her complain when I didn't listen.

Rylan sat between us and watched us with delighted amusement. Raid, surprisingly, was nowhere to be found. He had still been persistently competing for Ryoko's affection, regardless of the fact that Ryoko was starting to show interest in Rylan again, so the fact that he wasn't here to keep an eye on his older brother was a little surprising to me. I blinked when something hit my ear. It was small and soft, and I wasn't sure if I had actually felt anything at all until it happened again. My gaze flicked down at my lap to see two pieces of popcorn lying there. I narrowed my eyes at Ryoko accusingly, since she had a bowl of the stuff, and then I was hit in the face by a handful of the buttery treat.

Ryoko laughed. "Just pick a channel already."

"I'll pick a channel when I feel like it."

Ryoko tossed another handful of popcorn at me, and I retaliated by scooping up what she had thrown and threw it back at her. It only took seconds after that for a full-out popcorn war to break out, and Rylan became the victim stuck in the middle of it all. When he had finally had enough of the stuff bouncing off his face, he grabbed both of our arms. Even though we each still had a free one to continue, we both stopped and glared at him.

"I think it's time for you two to actually eat this stuff, instead of hitting me with it," he said.

Ryoko and I looked at each other, and then she tossed a small handful at him.

He exhaled. "Ryoko, don't push me."

A wicked grin spread up Ryoko's face and then she dumped the bowl right onto Rylan's head. Rylan let out a tight, slow exhale and let me go, but not Ryoko. He removed the bowl from his head slowly, and then picked up a handful of thrown popcorn and tossed it at her. Ryoko blink furiously and I laughed.

"Well then," she said when her shock wore off. She picked up a handful of popcorn and shoved it in his face. He choked on the treat and the room echoed with laughter.

When he managed to push her away, he gathered up the scattered popped kernels, and retaliated on her. Seda, from where she and Shva'sika hung out in the kitchen, pushed forward a new bowl filled to the brim with popcorn, and I rushed over to it, before Ryoko or Rylan could think to use that, too, for ammunition.

"Give it to me!" Ryoko begged.

"All right." I dumped the bowl over her head, and Rylan howled as she growled out an irritated complaint.

Ryoko glowered at me, but did something no one would have expected. She gathered up a handful of popcorn and then tackled Rylan, landing on the couch, and shoving popcorn into his face.

"Eat it!" she ordered.

"Ryoko, no," Rylan complained. "Get off me!"

"Eat the popcorn."

Rylan managed to knock the popcorn out of her hand, but that didn't stop her from torturing him. She grinned and then grabbed his sides. He laughed and bucked as she tickled him.

"Ryoko, stop," he begged. "You know I'm extra sensitive there!"

She snickered and increased her assault. Shva'sika shook her head. "How did it get to this?"

I shrugged. "The gods only know. This is Ryoko."

Tears streamed down Rylan's face, and his bucking grew worse with Ryoko's relentless attack. I laughed when one thrash was strong enough to not only send her flying to the floor, but him as well. The room grew quiet as the two stared at each other. Shva'sika held a hand over her mouth to stop her from laughing, and I bit my lip. This was all too perfect.

"S–sorry," Rylan finally said, pulling away from her quickly.

Ryoko laughed. "I deserved it."

To my disappointment, Rylan jump to his feet, and collected up the scattered popcorn. When he gathered a bowlful, he noticed Ryoko had only sat up.

"Need held getting up?" he asked.

"Maybe."

He bent over and offered a hand to help her, but instead of her taking it, she tossed a handful of popcorn at him. He exhaled tersely and then dumped the bowl he collected on her. She ducked her head instinctively, but that caused several of the popped kernels to go under her chin and lodge in between her breasts, and Ryoko instinctively began fishing them out right in front of him. I lost it when Rylan's face turned several shades yet didn't look away. I stumbled for the roof door. I needed to get away from all this. It was too much.

I sat down on the edge of the roof and stared up at the sky to get myself under control. I wasn't alone for long. Raikidan showed up and sat down next to me, watching me.

I took a deep breath. "All right, ask away."

"What just happened, did that fall under your human rules of flirting?"

I chuckled. "You catch on quick."

Raikidan shook his head. "You humans are so confusing. You make these choices for mates. How do you know they're the right one?"

I scratched my head. "We don't. It comes down to trial and error and hope that you don't get hurt too bad in the process. That's why many are hesitant to try since most feel the pain isn't worth it."

Raikidan stared at his feet. I could tell he was thinking. The concept didn't make sense to him, and I wasn't good at explaining it, so that didn't help him in the least.

"Eira, if you could, would you try like them?" he asked.

I shook my head. "Monsters like me don't get that choice. That's just how it is."

Raikidan grabbed my wrist. "Don't say that."

I tried to pull away. "I only say the truth."

Raikidan tightened his grip and cupped my chin so I'd look at him. "You're not a monster, Eira. I can't believe that… no… I won't believe it."

I stared at him. Why did he resist the truth so much? I sighed and averted my gaze. Raikidan let me go, allowing me to have the space I wanted.

"Raikidan, what's it like for dragons?" I asked. "I mean really like? You said you guys just know, but that doesn't make any sense. You can't just know they're right just by looking at them, especially if you stay together for life after that choice."

Raikidan stared at the ground and didn't speak. After a few moments I got it. It was how it always was. The information was always one-sided.

I stood and began to walk away. "Forget I asked."

Raikidan grabbed my wrist. "Eira, don't. Don't mistake my silence for unwillingness to speak. I'm just trying to figure out how to tell you without you thinking I'm lying."

I sat back down and waited. Raikidan worked his jaw so much, it had to be an interesting response. "We hear her voice."

My brow rose. "What?"

"It's all on the male's side. We hear our destined mate's voice and we seek her out until we find her." I sputtered out a laugh. Raikidan sighed. "Eira, please don't laugh."

"I'm sorry, but did you just hear yourself? You've basically just said you're all crazy."

Raikidan looked away. "This is why I didn't want to say anything."

I sighed. "Raikidan, you hear a voice in your head. How is that not supposed to sound made up?"

He gave me a pointed look. I swallowed. My laughter upset him, I got that. But it was hard to believe what he said.

"All right, tell me more about this… voice."

Raikidan's eyes narrowed. "Why should I?"

"So I can understand more and don't think you're crazy."

He worked his jaw before speaking. "There's nothing really else to tell. We don't choose our mates. The gods do. They make us wait until the right dragon comes along, and when she does, a voice starts talking in our heads until we find her and she accepts us. Not that convincing her is an easy task, either."

I pursed my lips. "So basically, you guys are just handed happiness."

"That's… one way to see it."

My head cocked. "Sounds like not all of you see it that way."

Raikidan shook his head. "Because we don't make the choice, some don't want it. Some also don't want that kind of responsibility."

"What happens to those who don't want it?"

"They try to ignore it as long as they can, but eventually they're forced to look for her. Unfortunately, it typically goes south from there." Raikidan focused hard on the ground, his next words hesitant. "Instead of trying to get her to accept him, he kills her."

My breath caught. "W–what? Why would—how could he do that? I thought it was the worst thing for you guys if you ever did that."

Raikidan nodded. "It is, that's why most have someone else do it for them. They think they can turn a blind eye if it's done that way. But there's supposedly a repercussion for it, no matter how they go about it."

I leaned closer. "Go on."

"It's said that if our mate dies by unnatural causes, particularly if it's our fault, we go insane."

My brow furrowed. "How so?"

"It's claimed that when she dies, her voice doesn't go away like we would hope. It gets worse. She becomes hateful, and never lets up until it drives us to insanity."

"But it's only said to do that."

"It could be that the male drives himself insane over guilt or the voice does get worse. No one knows for sure, and the only ones who do are too insane to tell."

"Does her voice go away once the two have become a mated pair?"

Raikidan shrugged. "I don't know. No one talks about those things. That part of a dragon's life is private. Not even my parents told me everything. They told me how things were, and that was that."

"Like, you mate for reproductive purposes only?"

Raikidan chuckled. "Yes. I don't know if that's true or not. I figure, by how my parents acted, and by how Corliss acts with his mate, it's possible to not actually be the case."

"Corliss has a mate?" Even though I already knew the answer to this question, this was the best time to get the information from him so I wouldn't screw up later.

Raikidan nodded. "Yeah. He was one of the few dragons who received a mate early in life."

"How early?"

"He was only a century old, which is young for a dragon. Most aren't given a mate until they're around two to three centuries but it's been more common lately for them to have to wait even longer given how few in numbers we are."

"So Corliss is older than you?" I asked, confused based on the dream I was given back when I was visiting the South Tribe.

He scratched his head. "Well not exactly. Technically we hatched around the same time, so that would make us around the same age. But had I hatched when I was supposed to, I would have been older, so we say I'm older."

I held up my hands. "Wait, back up. What do you mean, 'hatched when you were supposed to'? Were you not supposed to stay in your shell for two centuries?"

Raikidan laughed, and my face twisted. Why was he laughing? "I'm sorry. I'm just surprised you remembered I said that. No, we don't normally stay in our eggs that long. We're only in our shells for about half a century, so we can handle the shapeshifting process later in our lives. I was just a very rare case."

"How rare?"

"Rare enough to be the only one in over eight hundred years." He grunted. "My mother said it was because I was special. Not sure why she hadn't given up when most would have. I'm not special in the least."

I smiled. "Because you were special to her."

"How would you know?"

I turned my gaze up to the sky. "Because I'm a mother, too, and I'll tell you a little secret. We know things about our kids that wouldn't make sense to know."

"Eira, what's it like for human females? You don't seem the type to lay eggs like dragons do."

I laughed. "No, we don't. Human women carry their babies inside them for about nine months."

He cocked his head. "What?"

"We have live births."

Pure horror blanketed Raikidan's face. "How do you birth something like that?"

I laughed. I knew exactly what he was thinking. He hadn't seen a baby before; only small children. "Relax, Rai. Human infants are small. They generally weight in at only six or seven pounds, and rarely come out longer than fifteen to twenty inches. Of course, that's not to say birthing them is a walk in the park, even at that size."

He pursed his lips. "That's… tiny. How do they survive?"

"Their parents take care of them. Human babies are helpless, so their parents are there for them until they're able to take care of themselves. That's around seventeen or so, but some stay with their parents longer if they don't feel ready."

"I've noticed you humans choose not to live in large groups. Why is that?"

I shrugged. "I couldn't tell you. While it's not uncommon for a few friends to live together, or families to start out large until the children are grown and choosing to move out, it's nothing remotely close to what I'm learning dragons do. Our grouped living here is more out of necessity than anything.

Raikidan nodded, understanding but not quite happy I couldn't satisfy his curiosity.

A thought came to me. "Going back to the destined mates thing, Zaith's… offer to me, it was political, wasn't it?"

Raikidan chuckled. "Well yes and no. With everything I told you, it's hard not to see how it was a bit political. But somehow, between you not caring about what he had to say, showing how powerful you were, and the gods know what else, he became infatuated with you. Of course, you wanted nothing to do with him, and that didn't make him too happy."

"And I had you to thank for letting me know what he was up to."

His lips pressed into a thin line. "It wasn't right for him to try to trick you like that."

"You sure he didn't just think I knew because of you?"

Hi nose scrunched. "Positive."

"So it's safe to assume he doesn't have a destined mate yet."

Raikidan shrugged. "It'd be a wise guess. I can't see why he'd try to trick you if he was destined for someone else already."

I chuckled. "I pity the dragon who has to put up with him."

Raikidan laughed but didn't say anymore so all conversation ended. But I wasn't done talking for once. One question ran through my head. However, I wasn't sure if I should ask it. It could possibly answer my big question of why he was really here, but it might be too personal.

"You want to ask me something."

I worked my jaw. There was no thinking about it any longer. "I was just wondering… do you have a voice?"

He chuckled. "No, thankfully."

"Don't want one?"

"I like living on my own, and only having myself to worry about."

I pursed my lips. I wasn't convinced. "All right. I was just curious. It just sounded like it would be annoying to have one."

Raikidan grunted. "You have no idea."

I grinned as Raikidan groaned and rested his head on in his hands. "So you lied to me."

He sighed. "Yes."

"Is she the real reason why you're here?"

He nodded. "You gave me an incentive to actually go looking for her. I don't think she's here, but I promised to help you, so she can wait."

"How long have you been hearing it?"

"A few decades."

My brow lifted. "That's a bit of time to ignore it. You really don't want a mate."

"I told you, I like having to only worry about myself."

I regarded him for a moment. "You're also under the average age when dragons are assigned a mate. Why is that?"

He shrugged. "I don't know. Mostly likely reason is because I hatched so late. My development was a bit different than the average dragon because of it.

I nodded. "How will you find her if you did choose to look?"

"Besides me being able to pick her voice out of a crowd because of how often I've heard it, there are a few hints she gives that help, but they're not open for discussion."

"I understand." I thought for a moment and then frowned. "Will you kill her?"

He didn't respond. He just stared at the ground so I waited. "I told myself I'd never look for her. I didn't want to hurt her. She deserves… better than me."

I shook my head. I knew he was a half-color and all, but that didn't mean he had to think so low of himself like other dragons did. "Raikidan, do me a favor." His gaze flicked to me. "When you find her, don't kill her. She doesn't deserve that, and you… deserve to be happy."

I hopped down onto the fire escape. "And if you want, when you're really ready to look for her, I'll help when this is all over. It's the least I can do for you bringing a sense of peace to my life."

Raikidan didn't respond, a thoughtful expression coming over him. I left him to think about it. If Seda was right, and my fate could be different, then maybe I'd be able to help him. *Maybe.*

The cool water lapped over my feet and the coarse sand slipped between my toes as I wiggled them. I squinted my eyes, looking for the island in the middle of the lake that I loved gazing at from afar. I wanted to find some way to get over there, to discover the hidden secrets it may hold, but the fog around me was too thick. I shivered from the slight chill that hung in the air. I didn't know why I didn't leave to go elsewhere. Thanks to the fog, I had no reason to stay.

I spun around when footsteps crunched behind me. A dark shadow appeared in the thick fog and I took a step back, but only one. My body wouldn't budge as the shape drew closer, even though I wanted it to. I tilted my head when the shape became clear enough to identify as a male humanoid.

Most of the fog dispersed around the figure, revealing a tan-skinned man, wearing only black denim pants, his face remained obscured. An aura of familiarity surrounded him, but I couldn't place who he was. The man didn't speak; he only offered his hand to me and waited.

"Go to him." I blinked at the sound of the voice that came from all directions. "Remember who he is, and go to him."

"Stay away from him." There was another voice that sounded similar to the first, but colder. "Stay away—and stay safe."

"Remember."

"Forget and leave."

The man, oblivious to the voices, continued to offer his hand. A part of me wanted to remember. A part of me felt that it was important, and that if I remembered I'd be safe. But another part told me it wasn't safe. That side told me I was only safe when I was alone.

"Trust him."

"Forget him."

"Stay."

"Leave!"

Before I could make the choice for myself, the fog around me darkened and began to distort. It wrapped around me and pulled me away.

"No!" I shrieked. "I want to make my own choice!"

I struggled but the fog tightened its grip on me.

"Eira!"

I looked up to see the man moving closer to me. The fog tried to push him away, but he fought against it and continued his advance.

"Remember."

I wanted to remember. He was trying to get to me. He was trying his best to help me. My eyes hooded when his hands grabbed my waist and pulled me close. An aura of safety fell over me, like a blanket had been tightly wrapped around me. And for a moment, I thought I could place his face in my mind.

"He'll only hurt you!"

I gasped as I was ripped out of the security of the man's embrace. He reached out for me again but the dark fog engulfed me and plunged me into darkness.

"Remember the pain of the past and stay away."

26
CHAPTER

I pulled out several bottles of liquor from the cabinet and placed them on the counter with the rest I had pulled out. Shva'sika took out glassware next to me, and Ryoko grabbed several of the bottles on the counter and brought them into the living room. Seda and Genesis sat on the couch watching us, the latter wringing her hands and bouncing her knee.

Since Genesis had finally been able to age her body, Ryoko thought it best she had her own *coming of age* party. This meant forcing her to consume copious amounts of alcohol since she was long overdue. Genesis had been a bit unsure, but when the boys offered to let it be a "girl's night" affair, she became a bit more comfortable with the idea. I suspected that since she didn't know how she'd act under the influence of alcohol, she didn't want to run the risk of making a fool of herself in front of the men. Why we women were different, I would never know.

Raikidan left my room and poked his head into the kitchen. "You sure you don't need help?"

I went to speak, but the bottles on the counter began levitating and then shot into the living room where Seda set them down on the coffee table. "Nope, we're all set."

He stared at all of us for a few moments longer, as if hoping we'd change our mind, and then secluded himself in my room again.

"Is it me, or did he look disappointed?" Shva'sika asked.

"Oh, he was," Seda said. "Poor thing is bored."

"He needs a hobby," I said.

Ryoko eyed me slyly as she left the kitchen with some snacks. "He does, she's just here with us."

I glared at her. "Don't you start."

"What, I'm just stating a fact. He could be down in the garage with Rylan and Raid working on their lost-cause project car, but instead he's silently hoping he can hang out with us girls."

Raikidan poked his head out the room. "Am not."

He then closed the door and the room filled with laughter. We all sat around the table and I mixed several drinks for Genesis to try—some she liked, and others she didn't. Those she didn't like, typically the less sweet drinks, Ryoko downed like a champ, regardless of whether she'd like it or not.

"My head feels fuzzy," Genesis said after consuming four full drinks, four shots, and at least seven sips of drinks she didn't like.

Ryoko giggled. "Lightweight."

"To be fair, these sweet drinks she likes have higher alcohol contents," I said.

Genesis held up her shot glass with an amber liquid with cream layered on top. "I really like this quite a bit. I didn't like the other shots you gave me, but this one is nice. What's it called?"

I grinned. "A slippery nipple."

Genesis choked on her drink and everyone laughed. "That's not what it's actually called."

"Yes, it is," I said.

She shook her head. "What an absurd name."

Ryoko giggled. "There's some pretty interesting ones out there."

I mixed up a red sweet drink and passed it to Genesis. "Like this one."

"What's it called?" Genesis asked.

"Drink it first."

She puffed air through her lips and sipped it. She smiled at the taste and drank more.

"Bend over Shirley."

Genesis choked on the drink and I laughed. "That's not funny!"

Ryoko gasped. "I know what she should drink!"

She looked at me and popped her lips. I laughed, understanding what she was thinking, and mixed a layered yellow and orange drink. Genesis took the glass, but hesitated to down it.

"It'll taste good," I said. "Weird name, but don't let that stop you."

Genesis sipped the drink and her eyes lit up. She drank more and Shva'sika grew curious. "What's it called?"

I waited for Genesis to stop drinking so she shouldn't choke this time. "Pop my cherry."

Ryoko slammed her hand on the coffee table as she laughed and Shva'sika's hand flew up to her mouth. "I never thought I'd ever hear something like that come from your mouth."

"Isn't it great?" Ryoko said. "She's growing up!"

I pushed her. "Shut up. I've been working at the club long enough to get used to these names."

"Right, it's not like she'll use any of these words seriously around another person as if she's interested in them," Seda teased.

I tossed my thumb in her direction, agreeing with her.

"Yeah, we'll see about that," Ryoko said.

I shook my head and made her another drink to keep her quiet for a minute or two. I also made up a drink for Shva'sika, who admitted she wasn't as experienced with our "city drinks", and also made one for myself.

"Seda, you need to have at least one," Ryoko said when Seda refused to try something.

"Sorry to disappoint you, Ryoko, but psychics can't drink," Seda said. "Alcohol reacts negatively to our power, and can cause people around us a lot of pain, or worse."

Ryoko pouted. "That's no fun."

Seda laughed. "It's okay. I can still have fun watching you four get wasted."

"Well, I think we need to do something more than just drink," Ryoko said. "Let's play a drinking game!"

My brow rose. "What do you have in mind?"

She grinned wickedly. "Truth or dare."

I rolled my eyes. "That's not a drinking game."

"It can be," she protested. "You pick truth, and refuse to answer, you take a shot. You answer and it's a lie, you take two shots, and every time you are caught lying, or you refuse to answer, that number goes up. Same with choosing dare and refusing the dare or failing it."

"I like it," Shva'sika said. "Sounds like it can get rather interesting as we drink, and Seda can catch a lie."

Seda smiled. "I can also make it easy for us to see a dare if it has to be done in another room."

"How?" I asked.

Seda stood and left. After a few minutes, she returned with a large, clear sphere in one hand and a golden circular stand with hexagram designs all over it.

"Is that a crystal ball?" Ryoko asked.

"Of course," Seda said. "There are reasons stereotypes exists. We use crystal balls to concentrate our abilities. This will make it easy for me to show you all what happens in another room.

Ryoko's eyes lit up. "You're so smart! This will make this game so much more fun."

Everyone but me was on board for this game. I knew better than to get excited, because I knew Ryoko. She had a master plan, and I knew it involved Raikidan, and me being intoxicated enough to be convinced to do a few things. She was too predictable for me not to know this. But being the odd one out, I'd have to agree or I wouldn't hear the end of it.

"So, how do we want to figure out the turns and such?" Genesis asked.

Ryoko thought for a moment and then snapped her fingers when she came up with an idea. She left the room, and after about ten minutes came back with two pieces of cardboard no bigger than her hands. "I may not be all artsy-fartsy like Laz, but I can make something neat in a pinch." She placed the cardboard pieces on the table, revealing a drawn circle on each, with our names written in colored sections and a plastic needle fastened to the center. "We can take turns at random. This spinner, with the reds and oranges will be the person who asks the truth or dare, and the one with the blues and purples, will be the person on the receiving end."

I nodded. "Creative. Could be a bit one sided, but I'm going to guess you hope it is."

Ryoko placed a hand on her chest, her expression of fake insult. "Whatever could you mean?"

Shva'sika giggled. "You're not fooling anyone, Ryoko. We all know what you're up to."

"I just wanted to play a fun game with you ladies," she tried to claim.

"Yeah, sure." I poured several shot glasses full with a clear, pure alcohol that didn't have much of a smell. "We'll drink this premium agave liquor if we fail our truth or dare. We'll all take one shot before we start. Might as well make this an interesting game from the get go."

Ryoko clapped her hands. "I like the way you think!"

Everyone but Seda picked up a shot and took them like champs. Even Genesis downed hers in one swallow.

"Okay, let's see who goes first!" Ryoko spun the needle on each name chart and when the needles stopped, I groaned. "Danika gets to challenge Laz something!"

"Truth or dare," Shva'sika said, wasting no time.

"Dare." I needed to get one dare in, or Ryoko wouldn't let me hear the end of it for playing too "safe." And since this was Shva'sika coming up with something this round, I thought I'd be safe. I was wrong.

Shva'sika grinned. "I dare you to seduce your dragon Guard."

The girls burst out with laughter and I stared at Shva'sika in shock and mortification.

"Wow, right out of the gate!" Ryoko cheered. "And you were trying to pin the attempt on me."

I shook my head. "What is wrong with you? No way in hell am I doing that."

Shva'sika shrugged and then pointed to the drink waiting on the table. "Take the shot then."

I picked up the glass and downed the liquor.

Shva'sika spun the two needles. The spinner for the red and orange names landed on Ryoko and the spinner for the blue and purple names fell on Genesis' name. Ryoko beamed and Genesis looked worried.

"Okay, truth or dare?" Ryoko asked.

"Um… let's go with truth," Genesis said.

Ryoko grinned. "Now that you've had time to adjust to this new you, including the new hormones, you found a guy or girl that catches your fancy?"

Genesis made funny faces as she thought. "Well, I don't know, honestly. I've found guys to be very attractive, and that's been weird for me, but I've been so caught up with adjusting and dealing with the rest of the Council, that stuff hasn't really crossed my mind. Doesn't help I don't come in contact with other guys much beyond our housemates and members of the Council, and I haven't found myself wanting to cozy up to any of them."

We waited for Seda's assessment, though most of us were pretty convinced Genesis was telling the truth.

"Truth," Seda announced. She then smiled. "Though, future dictates that she has met someone with potential to change that."

Ryoko squealed. "Who, who?"

Seda turned her head toward me instead of replying. Everyone set their eyes on me and I remained puzzled. Then it dawned on me. "No."

Seda shrugged. "Nothing may come of it, but it's a potential."

"No!"

Ryoko's brow rose. "'Kay, now I want to know why she's mad."

Shva'sika giggled. "She's not mad, just being overprotective."

Ryoko gasped when she got it and Genesis' eyes widened. "No…"

I reached over and spun the needles. "Let's focus on something else."

The two needles spun, and one landed on Genesis, to ask the question, and the other landed on me, to be the victim. "Truth or dare?"

I sipped my drink. "Truth."

"Have you ever been in love?"

Of course she'd ask that. "No."

Seda chuckled. "That's a lie."

My livid eyes snapped to her and she smiled. Genesis and Shva'sika glanced at each other wide-eyed in surprise and then looked at me. Ryoko smiled, but otherwise said nothing. I couldn't believe Seda said that.

"I have never been in love," I said.

"That's not what your past says," Seda said. "Just because you want to ignore the past, doesn't mean it didn't really happen."

I ground my teeth together and then begrudgingly took the double shot for "lying." Now that this had gone down, I was going to have to deal with either a dare from Ryoko that I knew she was dying to use, or more truths about that part of my past I refused to revisit.

Ryoko flicked the needles and the spun until one landed on Shva'sika to ask, and me to answer. *Of course I wouldn't get a break.* "Truth or dare?"

"Truth," I said, knowing it was risky.

"What was the name of the guy you loved?"

I took three shots and leaned back on the couch. The girls stared at me with surprise at my quick refusal, but they didn't understand. This wasn't something they should poke at.

Seda spun the boards, and the needle landed on Ryoko to challenge and the other on me to be challenged. *Seriously? Another one for me?*

"Truth or dare?" Ryoko asked.

"Truth."

Ryoko grinned. "Do you love Raikidan?"

"No."

Ryoko looked at Seda, obviously hoping for a particular answer. Seda remained quiet for a moment. "Truth."

Ryoko's brow rose. "Why the long pause?"

Seda chuckled. "Because love is complex and I needed to analyze the extent of her feelings before coming to a conclusion."

"It didn't take you that long with Genesis."

"Genesis hasn't had the same life experiences."

Ryoko pouted, but I was glad. Seda's mention to the complexity of feelings made me uneasy, since it sounded as if she were hinting my feelings were close to love, as absurd as it was, but luckily Ryoko didn't catch it. *Or I hope she didn't.*

I spun the needles and they landed on Genesis asking and me being challenged. *Okay, this is getting old.*

"Truth or dare," Genesis said.

"Dare." Somehow, I knew Genesis wouldn't be able to come up with something that would be humiliating or awkward, and I didn't need her asking another question about my past.

"Rylan and Raid are working on that project car. Steal a tool they absolutely need, without getting caught."

I grinned. "Too easy."

"Well, then," Shva'sika said. "Let's up the stakes."

Ryoko's eyes widened and she made impressed and excited sounds. "I like how this is going."

"I add to Genesis' dare by having you take the tool, and store it on one of them, without either of them knowing," Shva'sika said. "Fail, and you have to take seven shots, and your future truth and dare failures start from that point forward."

"Challenge accepted." I stood. "I also have a counter challenge. If I complete your dare, and am also capable of taking another item of important use, and bring it back with me, both of you have to take on the drinking addition."

"Fine," Shva'sika said.

Genesis frowned. "I don't think I'm going to feel very good by the end of the night."

I chuckled and headed downstairs as soundlessly as I could. I doubted either of the boys could hear me with the noise they were making, but I needed to be as careful as possible. Keeping low, I snuck into the garage and slipped between some cars near Rylan and Raid. I observed their work habits and noticed one particular wrench they always went for. My time in the shop had me aware of its use, and for such an old car, I knew this was the tool to move on them.

Nearly crawling on my stomach, I slithered closer, and waited for both of them to be preoccupied. When the opportunity presented itself, I snatched the tool and hid in the shadows. I watched when Rylan went to use the wrench again, only to find it missing. He asked Raid about it, but Raid pointed out Rylan had it last. The two searched, and I was careful to stay out of site. As their search continued to turn up nothing, their irritation grew until they began arguing. I bit my lip so I wouldn't laugh and give myself away. Rylan stormed off, and Raid went back to working. I took this opportunity to sneak closer.

Raid bent over the front of the car and worked on something in the engine bay. I grinned and snuck closer, waiting several moments before reaching out and tucking the wrench through his belt loops. Raid, concentrating too hard on his work, never noticed. I slipped back into the shadows and waited for Rylan to come back.

Minutes passed before Rylan returned. He looked just as irritated as when he left. I grinned and watched the show that was about to start.

Rylan spotted the wrench in Raid's belt loops and lost it. "Are you kidding me? You did have it, jackass!"

Raid stopped working and gazed at his brother, confused. "What are you talking about?"

"You tucked it in your damned pants!"

Raid reached behind him and found the tool. "Dude, I swear I didn't put it there."

"Yeah, sure you didn't. It's just the two of us down here, stupid, how else would it have gotten tucked where it is?"

"I'm telling you, I didn't put it there!"

The two argued relentlessly and I continued to bite my lip so I wouldn't laugh. I spotted an impact gun sitting on one of their tool boxes and took it, slipping back into the house. The two of them would definitely miss having this around, even if it wasn't as important as the wrench. The girls were roaring with laughter when I made it upstairs. Rylan and Raid could be seen fighting in the crystal ball. I bowed for my performance.

"That was too perfect!" Ryoko said.

"Agreed," Shva'sika said. "Even though it means I've lost out on this bet, I am thrilled to have been able to witness that. Well played, Laz."

"What are you going to do with that tool you took?" Genesis asked.

"Well, since I got Raid in trouble, I thought it only fair to do the same for Rylan," I said.

Seda chuckled. "He did go to his room in his fit of frustration, so it works out perfectly."

"Yeah, he was so ticked off, he didn't even notice us looking at you with the crystal ball," Ryoko said.

I grinned. "All the more perfect."

I left the room and headed for Rylan's. After placing the impact gun down on his bed in plain sight, I returned to the living room and took my place on the couch. Seda had already set up the seven shots for Shva'sika and Genesis, and the two took deep breaths before downing them all. Genesis struggled to finish them, but Shva'sika had no problems. *It's as if she has done this before.*

Raid came upstairs at this point, clearly irritated. He didn't say anything, just stalked down the hall. When he reached Rylan's room, he entered and I bit my lip when he swore. He stormed out and back down the stairs, impact gun in hand.

Ryoko pointed to the crystal ball. "Show us!"

Seda chuckled and held up her hands to the crystal ball. It pulsed with light and then revealed a moving picture of Raid entering the garage and shouting at Rylan. Seda also used her psychic abilities to allow us to hear what was going on. We all laughed as the two argued.

When they were no longer amusing to watch, Ryoko spun the fate makers. She smiled when it landed on her and me as her victim. *By the gods, seriously?* "Seda!"

"*You just have bad luck.*"

"*Fantastic.*"

"Truth or dare?" Ryoko said.

Since she was asking, I knew I should go with truth, but my buzz had me taking a risk. "Dare."

She smirked. "As seductively as you can muster, go kiss Raikidan smack on the lips."

I contemplated this. I could drink more, or, since I knew she would bring it up again once I had more booze in me, I could get it over with. *Now, when I'm more sober, would result in a better experience. And it's not like I haven't had to kiss him before. At least this time it'd be on better terms.* "All right."

Ryoko's eyes widened, as did the others. "Really?"

I stood. "Won't be all that seductive, but I can do the latter."

"Just sway your hips," Shva'sika said. "No way he'd be able to keep his eyes off you with your hips, dear."

I grunted and I strolled to my room. Raikidan jumped when I flung the door open and tore his gaze away from the library book from his place at the foot of my bed.

"Something wrong?" Raikidan asked. He took a closer look at me. "You okay? You look a little off."

"Been drinking."

"Right. I overheard you were playing a game that would force you to consume more alcohol. "

I walked closer to him, exaggerating my hip movement more like Shva'sika said. "Still playing it."

Raikidan's brow rose, his eyes wandering over my form a bit from what my intoxicated brain processed. *No, he's not doing that.* Before he had the chance to say anything, I rested my hand on his chest and grasped his chin with my index finger and thumb. We inhaled deep in unison when I leaned in and captured his lips with mine.

Raikidan's body tensed, his hand reaching up and touching my elbow. His strong scent enveloped me, my mind drifting back to the alley next to the club. I managed to push through the alcohol fog and keep that memory at bay, focusing on the dare.

The girls made a mix of loud noises, displaying their enjoyment and surprise that I had gone through with this. I pulled away slowly, smiled, and then strolled out, continuing my accentuated hip movements.

Ryoko smiled widely at me, impressed with my ability to go through with the dare, but her smile faded when she realized that was all it was. *Sorry, Ryo. No matter how much you wish, it's not like that.* I sat down on the couch and reached out for my drink. I leaned back and sipped the drink. Ryoko went to open her mouth to speak, but I held up my hand. She waited and soon after, Raikidan came out of the room. I casually glanced back at him.

"What was that about?" he asked.

"Just me playing our game," I said. "Got a problem with it?"

He opened his mouth to reply, but then shut it as he struggled to have a proper response. The girls giggled. "I'm just really confused."

"It's truth or dare," Ryoko said. "And Laz chose dare and performed it well beyond our expectations."

Raikidan struggled with a response. His tongue dragged over his lower lip, and for some reason my eyes followed, my mind buzzing for a moment. In the end, he gave up trying to understand and headed back into the bedroom. The living room echoed with laughter.

Shva'sika flicked the spinners, and the arrows chose their victims. I was chosen to ask, and Ryoko became my prey. "Truth or dare?"

She thought for a moment and then smiled. "Why not. Dare."

I snickered. "Go downstairs and give Rylan *and* Raid a kiss right on the lips."

Her face turned scarlet. "I–I can't do that."

"I triple-dog dare you."

She gasped. Ryoko may have come up with this game as a way to get at me, but I knew her too well. She couldn't deny a triple-dog dare, and I was going to get her good. *Payback is a bitch.*

Ryoko swallowed hard and stood, her fist clenching. Seda activated her crystal ball when Ryoko headed for the basement and the four of us watched as Ryoko made her way to where Rylan and Raid were working on their vehicle. She twirled a lock of hair as she approached the two, who were oblivious of her presence. She shuffled her feet. "Hey, um, guys."

Rylan looked up and smiled at her. "What's up, Ryo?"

Raid went to react in the same manner but frowned when he noticed her posture. "What's wrong?"

"Um, I need your help with something," Ryoko said. The two abandoned their work and walked over to her. Ryoko chewed on her lip. "I can't believe she's making me do this…"

Rylan's brow rose. "What?"

Ryoko slowly met their gaze and gave a weak smile. "Sorry about this."

She reached out for Raid first and placed her hands on both sides of his face. She pulled him closer and his eyes widened when their lips met. I watched Rylan's negative reaction to this, as the women around me laughed. Rylan's expression switched to match his brother's when Ryoko detached from Raid and did the same to him.

Ryoko pulled away and laughed nervously. "Thanks for being good sports."

She then spun on her heels and ran, leaving the two men standing there, dumbfounded. I kept myself under control until Ryoko opened the door and I got a look at her crimson face.

"Yeah, yeah, keep laughing," Ryoko muttered.

I held up a bottle of liquor and calmed myself. "Want a drink?"

She sat down on the couch and hid her face. "I think I want to hide in my room for the rest of my life."

I snickered and tossed the bottle to her, which she guzzled down.

Genesis flicked the needles and they chose her to ask, and me to answer. "Truth or dare."

"Dare," I replied.

She poured a tall glass with the expensive agave liquor. "Dare you to chug this."

Ryoko and Seda laughed and I shrugged. "All right. If I'm going to have a hangover tomorrow, might as well go all out."

I took the glass from her and drank the liquor as quickly as I could without choking. Genesis stared with wide eyes, and Shva'sika, Seda, and Ryoko egged me on with cheering and laughter. Raikidan popped out of the room to investigate all the excitement.

I placed the glass down on the table when I finished the last drop and stretched as if there had been nothing to it. *That'll hit me in about five minutes, and then I might have a problem with this game.*

Genesis stared at me. "H–how?"

"I got many more years of drinking on you. You'll get there." I stood abruptly and then rocked as the liquor spread through me. "I'll be right back."

"You okay?" Shva'sika asked.

"I gotta piss."

Ryoko's nose scrunched. "Wow, TMI much?"

I grunted and headed for the bathroom. While in there, I overheard Raikidan asking more about the game, and then Ryoko whispering to him. *What is she up to?*

When I left the bathroom, nothing appeared out of the ordinary. The girls were still clustered around the coffee table, and Raikidan had taken a position leaning on the kitchen bar on the living room side. I assumed he wanted to figure out more what this game was about.

"All right, whose turn is it now?" I asked as I went to sit down.

A yelp came out of my mouth and warmth rushed over my body when a strong, masculine hand smacked my ass out of nowhere. I turned around, holding my rear with my hands to protect it, to find Raikidan right behind me.

I stared at him, mouth agape, and Ryoko burst with laughter. "Raikidan's!"

I fixed my eyes on her. "That's what you two were whispering about?"

Ryoko nodded. "Yep!"

Raikidan chuckled and headed back toward my bedroom. "Consider it payback for going along with her dare."

My cheeks flushed. I took a deep breath and an idea came to me. "Fine. Two can play that game."

Ryoko's laughter stopped. "What's that supposed to mean?"

Raikidan halted in his tracks to find out the answer as well. I opened the basement door without explaining, and headed for the garage.

"It's killing Ryoko, but I'm not letting her know what you're up to," Seda messaged. *"I don't want to ruin your fun."*

"I appreciate it."

Raid and Rylan were working away on their project car, but stopped when they noticed me walking over.

"Oh boy," Raid said. "Do you need something from us too?"

I laughed. "Yes, but not like Ryoko did."

Rylan let out a breath. "Well that's a relief. What are you guys doing up there anyway?"

"Truth or dare." I slipped between the two and hung my arms over their shoulders. "How's the project car coming?"

"We might actually get her up and running one of these days," Raid said.

"Cool. Now, I'm wondering if you two are willing to do something for me as payback to Ryoko."

"If it gets on Ryoko's bad side, then no," Rylan said.

"I'm intrigued," Raid admitted. "What's on your mind?"

"Ryoko needs to understand if she's going to use a game to her advantage, it can also be used against her. I want one of you, or, preferably, both of you, to go up there and grab her boobs."

Rylan pulled away. "No. I know better than to do that."

"Well I'm interested," Raid said.

Rylan stared at his brother. "Are you kidding me?"

Raid crossed his arms. "Got a problem with it?"

I backed up so the two could duke it out.

"Of course I do. Besides the fact you don't just go around grabbing a woman's breasts, Ryoko's self-esteem is pitifully low. Touching her like that is not going to do her any good." He gave me a pointed look. "You should know this best of all."

I grinned and backed away. "Or it could boost her self-esteem. I'll let you two work this out, and I'll tell Ryoko you both decided not to go along with my plan, just so if you do, it'll be quite the surprise."

Rylan sucked in a hard breath. "Neither of us are going to do this."

"Speak for yourself," Raid said, hitting Rylan in the chest. "I'm not afraid to show her I'm interested. And I'll make sure my hands are nice and greasy so they leave a reminder."

Rylan stared at his brother with livid eyes. I grinned and walked away. If Rylan knew what was best for him, and his chances with Ryoko, he'd go through with it. As odd as it was, Raid was right. Grabbing her would show some indication of interest in her.

"Oh, by the way," I called back, "she is still on the fence between you two. This choice will push her closer to one of you."

They continued to squabble and I made my way up the stairs, though the alcohol I'd been consuming was finally starting to kick in, making it a bit difficult. When I reached the living room, the others looked at me expectantly, but I shook my head. "Ryoko has all the luck. They refused to play."

Ryoko let out a relieved exhale. "Good. Now we can go back to our game."

I took my place on the couch and began drinking again. No reason not to at this point. As I did, I noticed Raikidan still hadn't left the room and I caught him watching me.

"Since he's never seen you drink so much, he's concerned about your wellbeing," Seda messaged.

"That's sweet of him."

She chuckled. *"I like it when you drink. That was cute of you to say."*

"Don't get used to it. I'll be back to my normal self tomorrow."

Genesis' turn was next, and Shva'sika managed to get a dare out of her and made her down five shots. I noticed how tipsy she was getting and did my best not to laugh. She was holding out better than I expected, but she was still a lightweight compared to Ryoko and me.

The basement door opened and Raid entered the living room, cleaning his hands on a dirty rag. Though, I could tell he was only pretending. *This should be good.*

"You guys sound like you're having fun up here," Raid said.

Ryoko tipped her back and smiled. "Sure are. What about you? Done working on that piece of junk?"

"She won't be a piece of junk when Rylan and I are done with her."

She turned away. "Yeah, yeah."

"I should grab the bathroom sink before Rylan gets up here. But first…" He walked up behind Ryoko. "Laz, I'm accepting your dare."

Ryoko's eyes widened, her face reddened, and she squealed when he reached around her and grabbed her breasts with his greasy hands, leaving large handprints behind when he pulled away. I couldn't stop myself from laughing as he walked away with the biggest shit-eating grin on his face. Ryoko had the biggest shocked look I've ever seen on her, and it intensified my sick enjoyment. I could tell she wasn't sure if she should be mortified, embarrassed, or accepting of what had just happened.

"I can't… believe… you had him do that!" Ryoko finally said.

I continued to laugh. "That was so much better than I expected!"

Shva'sika giggled. "Were the greasy handprints your idea too?"

"The what?" Ryoko shrieked as she looked down at herself.

I shook my head. "Nope. That's all him."

Ryoko's face turned several shades darker. "You're lying."

I grinned. "Nope. He accepted the bet downstairs and told me he was going to make sure his hands were nice and greasy so they'd leave a *reminder*."

She looked down at her lap to hide her face, but her ears twitched, giving her away. He had just won more of her favor. "And Rylan?"

"He refused. Said it wasn't right to do, no matter what you had done to me."

"Sounds like him."

I caught the disappointment in her voice. She disguised it well, but not enough. *Rylan only has himself to blame for messing this one up.*

The basement door opened just then and Rylan entered the room, his hands tucked in a rag, though it was obvious he wasn't sure if he should clean them or not. "My brother go through with your little dare?"

I giggled. "Oh yeah."

Rylan shifted his gaze to Ryoko and noticed her twitching ears. His eyes widened a little, surprised to see she actually liked what happened on some level. Raid came out of the bathroom and looked our way. Ryoko lifted her head to peek at him. He grinned and her face flushed, her ears twitching a few more times. She looked down at her lap and he chuckled before heading down the hall. Rylan glowered at the thought of his brother getting a leg up on him. But instead of changing his mind, he headed for the bathroom to wash up. *Of course, not even that can get him to change his mind. His loss.*

I sipped on my drink, preparing for another round of truth or dare, but we didn't go back. Seda, Shva'sika, and Raikidan were busy watching Ryoko, and Genesis struggled to stay awake, overcome by all the alcohol in her system.

Rylan exited the bathroom. Ryoko didn't look at him. She wasn't expecting him to do anything, but I noticed water still dripped from his hands. *What's he up to?* It wasn't like him at all to not dry his hands. Instead of heading down the hall, he came back into the living room— his eyes fixed on Ryoko.

"The mongrel I call a brother has no tact," he murmured. "None at all..."

He came up behind Ryoko and she lifted her head. With his right arm, he reached around and clasped his hand around her neck and chin, and with his left arm, he reached under her left breast—lifting it up—and squeezed her right. The water on his hands dripped down her skin and soaked her bikini.

"The stray has no idea how to handle you."

Ryoko froze, and her face flushed several shades, though she wasn't the only one to freeze. Everyone in the room stared at the pair, taken completely by surprise, even myself. I really thought he wasn't going to go through with the dare. Rylan grinned when Ryoko's ears began twitching, even more so than when Raid pulled his stunt, and withdrew from her. When the shock wore off, I couldn't stop the laughter. Shva'sika and Seda also found it impossible not to giggle. The others remained quiet, unable to comprehend what had just happened. Ryoko's cheeks flushed even more, and she ducked her head as her ears continued to twitch.

My laughter became so strong, I fell off the couch. The others gasped, and Raikidan even yelled out my name, but I continued to laugh. I couldn't stop it. That had been too perfect.

"I–I can't believe you told him to d–do that," Ryoko managed to say.

I shook my head. "I didn't! He told me he wasn't going to accept the dare."

The crimson in her face spread down her neck to her shoulders, and Genesis and Raikidan joined in on the laughing. I couldn't believe Rylan actually did that. I knew daring him would have been a long shot, unlike Raid, but how he pulled it off… I had no idea he had that in him.

The front door opened, and Zane and the boys came inside.

"Why is my niece laughing on the floor?" Zane asked.

"She laughed so hard she fell," Shva'sika said through her giggling.

"How does someone as coordinated as her manage that?" Blaze asked.

Argus pointed at our setup. "By the looks of all the empty bottles on the table, she's more than just a little tipsy. Though I'm curious what got her to laugh that hard."

"I managed to successfully dare Raid *and* Rylan to grab Ryoko's boobs," I said. I looked up when none of them responded, and I laughed at their shocked faces.

"Why is it I always miss out on the fun?" Blaze asked.

Argus punched him in the arm. "Because you make it go from fun to creepy."

Blaze rubbed the tender spot. "I do not."

Shva'sika snickered and looked at Seda. "Seda, I have a dare for you, if you're up for it."

The two stared at each other, silence falling over the room. I guessed they were speaking telepathically, and it intrigued me. Why the secrecy? When Seda's cheeks flushed I started to get it.

"All right then, I'll give it a shot," she said out loud.

Everyone in the room watched as she slipped around the furniture and headed straight for Argus. I pulled myself up so I could rest my arms on the seat of the couch and watch. *What is she up to?*

"Seda, what are y—" She cupped his face with both her hands and pulled him in for a deep, and passionate, kiss. Zane and Raikidan took a step back, and Blaze stood there with a surprised, but very interested gaze.

When she pulled away, Argus was left with flushed cheeks and a confused look in his eyes. Seda sashayed her way back to her seat while I continued to look at Argus. Something told me Seda had done more than just kiss him. She wouldn't have been so unsure if it were that. Sure, kissing someone could make things awkward, but I could tell her unsureness wasn't because of that potential. I fell back on the floor, laughing, when I realized what she had managed to do.

"Did the alcohol finally mess up her brain?" Blaze asked.

"I can't take it. Seda, tell them," I begged. "That was too perfect!"

Everyone looked at her, and she smiled before taking something small out of her mouth. She opened her hand, revealing a curved labret stud.

Shva'sika, Ryoko, and Zane cracked up and Genesis gasped. "You didn't…"

Argus grabbed his lower lip to be sure it wasn't a trick, and Blaze ran his hand through his hair. "That's some impressive tongue control."

Seda levitated the piercing, and then sent it over to Argus, who took it, though still a bit dazed. "I didn't even notice…"

Zane chuckled as he patted Argus on the shoulder and walked off. I sat up and drank some more. As Zane passed the couch, Shva'sika stood and dashed toward him before he could disappear down the hall.

"Whoa!" he yelped when she slapped him on the ass.

"Counter dare complete!" she announced.

I choked on my liquor and then started laughing. Ryoko and Genesis also laughed, along with Blaze and Argus, and Zane looked at Shva'sika, and then Seda, who merely smiled.

"You ladies are something else when you drink," he said.

We continued to laugh more, and he left. Argus was soon to follow, still wrapping his head around what Seda did.

Once I finally got myself under control, I peered around at the others. Genesis looked ready to fall asleep, and I guessed if Shva'sika drank three more glasses she'd be down for the count. Seda, of course, looked ready for anything. I felt like I could drink, but not play any games anymore. Ryoko, on the other hand, she looked ready for both.

"So, what now?" I asked.

Shva'sika glanced at Genesis. "I think the birthday girl is going to bail on us soon."

Genesis yawned. "Sorry. I guess this stuff makes me sleepy."

Seda chuckled. "You're not the only one that happens to."

"I think I might call it soon too," Shva'sika admitted. "I've never drank this much myself."

Ryoko pouted. "But I want to keep playing."

Blaze walked over to the couch. "I'll play with you, Ryoko."

She stuck her tongue out at him. "Not a chance."

"It just went to creepy again," Raikidan said.

Blaze sighed and hung his head. I snickered and held up my glass. "Why not end the game now when we're all in good spirits and just drink until we drop."

"If you do, I want in," Blaze said.

Ryoko shrugged. "Well, if people are going to bail, why not."

I grinned and looked back at Raikidan. "You want in?"

He held up a hand. "I'm going to continue to watch all of you make fools of yourself. It's been entertaining."

Ryoko giggled. "You just don't want Laz kissing anyone else in her drunken state."

He glared at her and I thought I could see his cheeks reddening a bit. *My tipsy mind is playing tricks on me.* "Don't you start with that, Ryoko."

"Wait, Eira kissed someone?" Blaze asked as he sat down on the couch.

I grinned. "Yeah, I kissed Ryoko."

His eyes widened and Ryoko winked. "It was so good, it almost turned into a fantastic make-out session."

Color drained from his face at the thought of his hormonally-driven brain missing something like that, and then shook his head. "You two are just trying to mess with me."

I grinned. "Maybe we are, maybe we aren't. You'll never know."

He stared at the two of us, and then turned his gaze to the other ladies. When they didn't reveal the truth, he looked at Raikidan, who only chuckled. Blaze frowned. "Let's just start drinking."

Seda and I poured, and the group of us hammered out the drinks. Unsurprisingly, Genesis was the first to fall after one drink. Shva'sika was next, but lasted longer than I expected, with four. We forced Blaze to drink faster than us, since he was behind, and only managed to down nine before he was on the floor. We'd be sure to make fun of him tomorrow.

This left Ryoko and me, and I knew I wouldn't last as long as her. She was one hell of a heavy-weight. I didn't know anyone who could drink her under the table.

I downed my eighth glass, while Ryoko outpaced me with her twelfth. When I finished my drink, I decided to haul my intoxicated self onto the couch, only to fall over and face plant into the cushion. The room spun a little, and my hearing muffled. "I think… I've reached my limit."

Ryoko started clapping. "Oh yeah! Still undefeated!" She stood, but immediately fell back down. "Oh, I shouldn't have done that."

Those of us who were still conscious laughed at her.

"I think this means it's time to get everyone to bed," Seda said.

"I'll clean up," Ryoko slurred.

Seda held up her hand. "I'll do it. You two can't even stand properly. You'll only break something, hurt yourselves, or both."

"I'll help them get to bed," Raikidan offered.

"I can get to my room on my own," I said.

He chuckled and walked over to Ryoko. "No you can't, and you know it. I'll help you first, Ryoko."

Ryoko smiled. "Aw, you're so sweet."

He lifted her off the couch and cradled her in his arms. While he carried her to her room, Seda used her telekinesis to help Shva'sika stand, and lifted Genesis' sleeping form. The three of them left the room. I looked over at Blaze as he stirred. "What happened?"

"You're a lightweight, that's what," I slurred.

He grinned at me. "Maybe. But I make up for it in other areas. Why don't you crawl over here and I can show you?"

Creepy again. I grimaced. "You'll never get me drunk enough to do something that dumb."

He pouted. "Why are you so mean?"

Raikidan's voice came from behind me. "Because you deserve it." He lifted me up in his arms and carried me to my room, but didn't refrain from looking back and shooting a nasty scowl off at Blaze.

"Great," Blaze muttered. "No way I can compete with him."

"Raikidan, I may be drunk, but I can walk," I said. "You don't have to carry me."

His chest rumbled, soothing me a bit. "You're funny. You can't even stand up on your own."

"Can too…"

He chuckled and carried me into my room, placing me down on the bed. "Lie down and sleep."

"I need to change into new clothes."

Raikidan rummaged around in my drawers and pulled out a tank top and thin shorts. He held them out to me and grinned. "You think you can dress yourself, or do you need help?"

My cheeks burned. "Get out."

He snickered and left, but didn't refrain from looking back briefly. *Why is he acting so weird?* I went about getting dressed instead of worrying about it. Or tried to. My intoxicated state was far worse than I predicted and I found myself struggling to get my new shirt on. I abandoned the effort and attempted my shorts, but only wound up falling off the bed. "Ow…"

My bedroom door flew open and Raikidan ran in. "Are you—"

He stopped and stared at me as I lay awkwardly on the floor, half naked. My cheeks flushed. "I need help…"

"You sure you want me to help? I don't need you freaking out at me."

I pouted, and he chuckled. He shut the door and made his way over to me. "You're so different when you're drunk."

"Yeah… whatever…"

He helped me to my knees, and I covered my bare chest with my arms. Raikidan grabbed my shirt and knelt behind, helping me get the garment on.

"We'll ixnay the shorts and get you into bed," Raikidan said. "It's warm enough out that you don't need pants anyway."

"I'd rather wear more than just panties…"

"You're fine."

I sighed and did my best to get up, with his help of course. The room spun and it made my stomach queasy. *I'm going to have a horrible hangover tomorrow.* When standing proved to be too big a task for me, Raikidan picked me up and set me down on my bed. He sat next to me and I remained sitting up until the room stopped spinning.

"How do you feel?" Raikidan asked.

"Like I'm drunk."

He chuckled. "I don't know what that feels like."

"Well, if you drank with us, you would."

Raikidan shook his head and then pressed on my shoulder. "You should lie down."

I fought his urging. "Not just yet. My head is still spinning."

He smiled. "All right then. I'll let you do that on your own terms."

My eyes widened when Raikidan cupped my chin. He leaned in and captured my lips with his. My heart stopped and my drunken brain couldn't process anything. A warm, tingling sensation flooded through my body that encouraged me to lean in and close my eyes, and in my intoxicated state, I struggled to fight that urge.

Raikidan pulled away, taking my breath with him, and my eyes fluttered. "Good night."

"Wait," I managed to say through my confusion fog. "Why did you do that? Did Ryoko do one last dare?"

Raikidan chuckled and then shifted to his dragon shape. *Jerk…* Why wouldn't he tell me? *"Seda, what just happened?"*

"Sorry, Laz, but I can't tell you."

I lay down and stared up at the ceiling. That confirmed it. Ryoko had to have dared Raikidan and convinced both him and Seda not to tell. Why else would he have done that? *It's not like he would have done it on his own.* That kiss also had enough passion for it to be a dare from Ryoko. I closed my eyes. I wanted to be convinced of this, but my intoxicated brain couldn't be coerced into agreeing.

27
CHAPTER
(RYOKO)

I chewed on my lower lip as I scanned the two photographs on my bed. One pictured Rylan and me, and the other Raid and me. I groaned and fell on my back. *I'm so pathetic.* Even after everything that had happened over the past few days, I couldn't make up my mind. I thought I could give Rylan up and try to see if something could become of Raid and me. But when Rylan got upset I stopped spending so much time with him, I thought maybe I was wrong to give up so soon.

And after what happened last night with Laz's dare… My heart thumped in my chest at the memory. *Who am I fooling?* I was just seeing what I wanted to see. I knew Laz insisted he did care, but it was hard to see it beyond hopeful wishing.

I looked at the photograph of Raid and me. Raid paid a lot of attention to me, and he had for a long time. Like Rylan, he also had a lot of things in common with me, but when I hung out with just him, it wasn't like when Rylan and I spent time together. It was almost like he didn't understand me on the same level Rylan did.

I buried my face in my hands. *What is wrong with me? Just pick one!* I knew I struggled with this because I couldn't trust myself with this choice. I'd waited like an idiot for decades for one of these guys to see how I felt about him. It wasn't like that kind of wait was uncommon for us nu-humans. Our perception of time was different than the shorter-lived races.

But Rylan showed no obvious sign of seeing me the same way. It didn't help that I wasn't treated well by a large percentage of the men I'd met. He and… Zeek… were the first to treat me like a real person. Raid came into the picture later, but by that point, I had latched onto Rylan.

I reached for a framed picture on my nightstand. In it, was me with a bronze-skinned, muscular man with amber eyes and dark brown hair. I slid my thumb over his face, desperately trying to remember what it felt like to be near him. *Zeek, I'd give anything to have you back… What did I do wrong to be cursed with this pain? Why can't I have what I want?*

I placed the picture back down on my nightstand and sat up. I needed to talk to Laz. I knew she wasn't the best choice to talk about love, but even if she couldn't give me any advice, maybe just talking out loud would help me. *It made me feel better last time.*

Slipping off the bed, I searched for her in her room, only to find Raikidan to be the only one there.

"If you're looking for Eira, she's up on the roof," he said. "After she recovered from that miserable condition you call a hangover, she wanted some fresh air."

I smiled. "Thanks for the heads up."

I left and headed up the stairs for the roof. Why she liked it up here, I'd never understand. My pace slowed as I neared the door when I heard two people talking. My nosey side kept me quiet, and my ears picked up Rylan and Laz's voices.

"Don't go jumping to the same wild conclusions Ryoko has," she said.

Rylan chuckled. "Don't worry about that. Your and his relationship may be different, but I'm not about to instantly think the way Ryoko does."

Well maybe you should. I hated feeling like I was the only one in this house who could see the truth behind everything going on.

"Speaking of Ryoko…" she said. "When are you going to tell her how you feel?"

I perked up and listened intently.

"W–what?"

"Oh don't be like this, Ry," she complained. "Just be honest with me."

He sighed. "It's… complicated…"

"No it's not. You're just afraid. You know how she feels about you, Rylan. You overheard that conversation because I didn't shut down the communicator properly. And yet you still dance around her."

My eyes widened. She was lying, right? He didn't actually hear what I had said. My fingers curled. *But now that I think about it, it made sense.* His emotional state after that matched perfectly.

"It's not… it's not just fear. She deserves better than me." My ears dropped at the tone of his voice. There was so much pain in it. "I should have seen it. But I didn't because I was hung up on you and then afraid I'd do the same exact thing with her. And let's be honest, I've struggled to come to terms with what happened to—" He sighed, cutting off the thought. *What was he going to say there?* There were some parts of Rylan's life, pieces from before I'd been released from my tank, that not even I knew about. "I'm such an idiot, I don't deserve her."

I leaned on the wall of the staircase, my hand against my chest. It felt as though my heart had just been ripped out. *She was right. She was right this whole time…*

"And you think your brother does deserve her?"

"I don't know if he's right for her, but he sure as hell deserves her more than me. He's been chasing after her since he first met her. He'd go to the ends of Lumaraeon for her if it meant she'd notice."

"And you wouldn't?"

"I'd give her Lumaraeon if that's what she asked for. But I don't have any right to be in that position."

"So, why did you go through with the dare last night if you feel this way?"

"Because when my brother has the chance to get a leg up on me and tries to rub it in my face, I feel like I can't back down. And I know it was wrong to do what I did, especially considering it was at Ryoko's expense. It's why I've decided I need to pull back and let him get in my way. Since I don't deserve her, I can't get mad when he tries to be there to make her happy and look his way instead of mine."

"Are you sure about this?" I detected a frown from her voice, matching my own.

"Yes."

I ground my teeth together. I came up here to figure things out. I got my answer just now, and there was no way was I going to let him wallow in self-pity or for me to lose out on the guy I've been waiting for all this time. I threw open the door and the two of them jumped, but remained sitting on the curb of the roof.

"Ryoko?" Laz said with a raised brow of confusion. "What's up?"

I locked my gaze on Rylan and stalked over to him. He swallowed. "Ryoko, you look really angry. If you're mad at me, whatever I did, I'm sorry."

Laz scooted away, keeping a close eye on the two of us. I grabbed Rylan roughly by his shirt and crashed my lips into his. He locked up in shock, not that I wasn't expecting that. Although my advance was aggressive, the feeling of his lips on mine sent a flood of warmth through me.

I pulled away, but kept my hands grasping his shirt. "You're going to take me out on a date tonight, and it's going to be dinner and some sort of movie, I don't care what. Got it?"

His mouth moved wordlessly as his brain took a moment to catch up. "What?"

Laz sucked in a tight breath and clapped her hands together. "All right then. I'm just going leave and let you two *talk*."

She left, but I was too intent on Rylan to care much. "I heard everything you just said to her about me." His eyes widened, his pupils dilating. He swallowed hard. I continued before he could say anything, "And you're right, you are being an idiot. But not because you didn't tell me how much you want me, or that you couldn't see that I want you just as much. You're an idiot for thinking my stubbornness is your fault, and for giving up because of self pity."

"Ryoko, I—"

I sat down on his lap, facing him. "I want you."

"Are you sure?"

I kissed him again, softer this time, making my heart skip a beat. "You'll be my idiot."

Rylan grinned and cupped my chin. He kissed me passionately, and I thought my heart might jump right out of my chest. "Are you sure you want dinner and a movie? We could stay home and spend time together talking about this."

"I want a real date."

"Very well. We'll have dinner at seven, and a movie after."

"And before all that, we'll talk about us," I said. "And how we're both idiots."

Rylan laughed and rested his forehead on mine. "It's a date, then."

CHAPTER 28

(EIRA)

I handed Rylan the sheets of paper to look over. The song came to me suddenly, so I thought it was a good idea to write it down, even if the boys didn't like it. I didn't care if they approved or not. It was out of my head now.

Rylan smiled and made a few changes to the vocal notes, and then added the instrumentals. The fact he liked it without questioning the meaning surprised me, though, I shouldn't have been. Ever since he and Ryoko had gotten together the other day, he'd been okay with just about anything.

Raid, on the other hand, had been crushed. He'd convinced himself that he was going to have a good shot at it this time. Then again, a part of me wasn't convinced he was ready to give up just yet.

He was still overly friendly with her, and tried to compete for her attention whenever possible, but it wasn't working so well, now that her attention was completely glued to Rylan. I had to admit, he was stubborn. It had to be in the genes, because even now, as Ryoko watched eagerly from her seat by the piano, he was still trying to gain her affection.

Rylan showed me his corrections and I just nodded. I didn't care what he did to it. When I approved, he showed the boys, who wrote down copies for themselves. I sat on the piano and observed them work out the instrumentals. It wasn't a beautiful thing to listen to, but it wasn't the worst they'd done. Ryoko couldn't help but laugh. She knew it was just practice, but no one could deny it sounded awful.

Rylan struggled with his part, so I hopped off the piano and peered over his shoulder. I rolled my eyes. He had decided to put in some power chords he always had trouble with. I didn't understand why he insisted on using them when he hadn't perfected his talent, but I guess it didn't matter. It was what he did, and there was no changing it. Luckily, I knew this power chord well, and I picked up my new guitar to give him a hand.

He watched me as I showed him the way I did it for him to try. He continued to struggle, but after a few more times of watching me, he got the idea and was able to do it on his own.

I smiled and stepped back, to allow him to play without me getting in the way. All three of them were so good at this it seemed almost wrong. I only hoped they didn't butcher the lyrics. If anything was worse than instrumental practice, it was vocal mess-ups.

I closed my eyes and let the tune engulf me—sooth me—compel me to do something. My lids cracked open and I strummed my own tune that harmonized with the one already being played. I wasn't sure where the tune came from, or where it would go, but I didn't stop it. It wasn't often I came up with anything more than lyrics. What surprised me more was when I began to sing along. No one said anything, but I sensed a few extra pairs of eyes on me.

"Zo, what are you doing here?" Zane whispered.

I stopped immediately and looked up. Sure enough, there was Zo, and few of his lackeys, standing just outside the doorframe. Awkwardness flowed over me. I could put up with my friends hearing me, but not someone I wasn't fond of.

"I'm sorry I interrupted. I just had to let you all know we're here for an inspection," he explained.

I slipped off the piano and put my guitar back in its stand. I excused myself quietly and pushed my way out of the room.

"Nice going, Zo," Raikidan muttered.

"What did I do?" Zo asked.

"It may not seem it, Zo, but Eira is pretty shy," Zane told him. "Particularly when it comes to singing."

"But she sang in front of hundreds of people," Zo defended.

"She did it because she owed her friends a favor," Rylan said. "She wouldn't have done it otherwise."

"We didn't mean any harm," a soldier told them.

Zane exhaled. "That may be, but she won't see it that way."

Footsteps headed my way, but I didn't stop walking. I needed to be alone.

"Eira, hold up," Zo called to me. I took a deep breath and came to a stop. Zo touched my arm lightly, but I wouldn't look at him. "Hey, we didn't mean to upset you."

"I know."

"You really have nothing to be shy about, Eira." I still didn't look at him. "How about I make it up to you?"

Now I turned my gaze to him. What could he do to possibly make me feel better about this situation?

He smirked. "It's a little last minute to do today, but how about I treat you to lunch tomorrow?"

Great, another date I'm going to have to sit through. My gaze fell to the floor as a worked my jaw. "Well that's… thoughtful of you, Zo. But…"

"But?" He sounded upset over my hesitation.

"But she's busy."

I looked up when Zane spoke. I hadn't heard him walk over. "I am?"

He held up a communicator. "I just got clearance to bring some custom vehicles to a dealer on the sea coast, and you're coming with us."

Joy and excitement welled up in my chest. "Seriously?"

"I figured you could use a change in scenery."

I threw my arms around his neck and gave him a tight hug. "Oh, thank you, Zane! I've never seen the ocean. Thank you, thank you, thank you!"

He patted my back. "You're welcome. Ray said you've never had the chance to see it, so I figured now was the time."

I pulled away and scrunched my nose. "He's not coming, is he? He's already had the chance to see the ocean without me."

Zane chuckled some more. "Someone has to keep an eye on you while the rest of us work."

My shoulders slumped. "But I don't need to be watched like a child."

He rubbed my head. "That's true, you're not a child, and your memory is doing well, so that's why I'm letting you come with us, but it's still not safe for you to go out on your own, even in a small seacoast city. It's still a city."

I huffed. "Fine."

Zane smile. "Then go get your things packed. We're leaving early in the morning, and it's a long drive there and back."

"How early?"

"Try one A.M."

I groaned, hanging my head back. "I don't want to be up that early."

"You can sleep in the truck. Now get ready. And, Zo, I'd appreciate it if you and your boys would get this pointless inspection over with quickly, so we can get to work with getting ourselves ready."

Two women poked their heads out of my and Ryoko's room and cleared their throats.

Zane held up his hands. "My apologies, ladies. Meant no disrespect, but you both are smarter than the men and know this is just as pointless as it seems."

The two giggled at his flattery and went back to their *pointless* searching. *Zane, you're such a ladies man.* I slipped away and packed a bag for the trip, making sure not to get into the female soldier's way. It had been true. In all my years, I had never seen the ocean. I was excited to finally see it with my own two eyes.

The feeling surrounded me. Warm and fuzzy—something I hadn't experience in a long time. I knew I should push it away, but I didn't want to.

Her aqua hair blew in the wind and her smile radiated like the sun. Everything felt all right when she smiled—like it dispelled the nightmare that threatened to consume me.

Strong arms wrapped themselves around me from behind. They were protective, caring arms and I was okay with them. Her smile brightened and I knew this was okay. It was more than okay. It was right...

I jolted awake and looked around. The truck's engine rumbled as it idled. It was too dark to see much outside, not that I would see much anyway, thanks to the bright light that was shining through the truck on the opposite side of me.

Zane pulled his hand away from my shoulder. "Easy, Eira. I just need you to be awake for a few minutes for some procedures, and then you can go back to sleep. Can you hand me our identification cards?"

I rubbed my groggy eyes. "Oh, okay."

Reaching into the glovebox, I pulled out a few thin, rectangular objects with small buttons and glass domes in the center. I handed them to Zane, who proceeded to hand them to someone outside the truck, beyond the light. As I waited, I glanced around the large cab of the truck. Ryoko was curled up against Rylan and looked as awake as me. Rylan, on the other hand, appeared wide awake, and stared out the window. Blaze sat next to them in the roomy back, leaning on his knees while Argus relaxed in his part of the seat next to him.

Raid had opted to stay back at the house so no one would feel cramped, but I had a feeling it was because he wasn't going to be able to stomach watching Ryoko and Rylan interact with each other. It wasn't like he'd have any opportunities to try to impress her.

Raikidan lounged behind me, exhaustion rolling off him in waves. I pitied him. Unlike the others and myself, he wouldn't be able to sleep.

"You going to be okay?" I whispered.

"I'll be fine," he muttered.

"All right, I just wanted to make sure…" I curled up to my pillow and stared out the window. "You didn't have to bite me…"

I closed my eyes and waited for us to be cleared to leave. My eyes bolted open when my pillow was yanked away from behind. I stopped my head from hitting the window and spun around in my seat. I glared at Raikidan as he tucked my pillow behind his head and relaxed. "Give it back."

"I'm using it now."

I grabbed it and yanked it away from him. "If you wanted one, you should have brought one."

Raikidan grabbed a hold of the pillow and pulled. "I don't have one."

"Not my fault." He had a tight grip, making it difficult to take it away from him. I narrowed my eyes. "You're going to rip it."

When he didn't show any signs of caring, I reluctantly let go. I slipped back down in my seat and sulked. Now I wasn't going to be able to sleep either. I jumped when someone knocked on my window. Ryoko snickered but I ignored her. I pressed the window button and the glass rolled down so the soldier on the other side could speak with me.

He held up a thick metal bracelet that wasn't at all appealing. I hated these things. "Ma'am, you'll need to wear this tracking device. This is your first time out of this city since you've become a citizen, so I'm going to show you how it's put on, just in case you choose to leave some other time."

I held out my arm for him. He held my arm and secured the tracking bracket around my wrist. I flinched when he tightened it too much, and he immediately loosened it with a key. I frowned at the device and the soldier hopped off the truck. I glanced back at the others as they secured their tracking bracelets to their wrists as well. Even Raikidan had insisted on putting his on without help, and when he was done, he remained leaning on his knees with his hand wrapped around the bracelet.

When the soldiers looking in determined everyone had a tracer, they hopped off the truck. Soldiers ran up to Zane's side of the truck and informed their commanding officer of their findings, or lack thereof. Once they deemed the towed cars clear, the commanding officer handed back the identification cards and gave us the clearance to leave.

Zane handed me the identification cards and we headed through the gate. I played with the cards while I waited for us to get to the outer wall. I pressed the biggest button I could find and it started up a hologram on the dome in the center of the card. The card I had, happened to be Zane's. It showed his face and as I pressed buttons, the display changed.

I put the cards away when we reached the outer wall gate and stared out the window. We wouldn't need them, and this drive was going to be long.

29
CHAPTER
(RYOKO)

The soldiers barely paid us any mind when we reach the gates of outer wall, not that I was surprised. Once you passed the first wall they assumed you were good to go through the second. It almost made the second wall pointless.

The moment we cleared the gate, Raikidan threw his tracer on the floor. My eyes widened, my mouth falling open, and Laz laughed. He had used his body posture to conceal the fact he wasn't wearing the stupid thing.

"Why didn't I think of that?" Blaze exclaimed.

Laz snickered. "'Cause you're not smart enough."

He took his hat and threw it at her. She caught it and tossed it back at him.

"All right you two, settle down," Zane reprimanded. "You should all be trying to get some sort of sleep. It's a long drive, and you'll need the energy when we get to the harbor."

I curled up against Rylan. "Which harbor town are we going to again?"

"Larkren."

I yawned. "Okay."

Laz relaxed in her seat and stared out the window as everyone else relaxed, but Raikidan's open eyes caught Zane's attention.

"Raikidan, that means you too," he told him.

"Not a good idea." Laz corrected. "Unless of course, you want everyone in this truck to be crushed."

I perked up. "You mean you can't sleep like that, Raikidan?"

Raikidan shook his head. "Not possible."

My brow furrowed. That didn't make sense. He had slept on the couch with Laz that one day. Unless… unless he didn't know. It was possible, but that idea didn't make any sense either. I wanted to rub my temples. I was hurting my brain.

"Well if I had known that, I wouldn't have made you stay up the whole night helping up load up the truck," Zane said.

Raikidan shrugged. "I'll manage. It's just one day without sleep. Nothing to it."

Sadness pricked deep inside me as I watched Laz look out the window, completely unaffected by this information. Raikidan was a dragon through and through, and she knew this. She accepted this.

Raikidan was different from others. He understood her in ways others couldn't, but even still, she pushed him away like others before him, and I was starting to see why. There would be no strong arms to hold her at night. There would be no warm body to wake up next to. Even if something was possible between them, she would feel lonely in certain ways, and it would be far too difficult for them to be together.

Rylan wrapped his arm around my shoulders and I snuggled into him with a sigh. I peered up at him as he watched Laz. I knew that look. He was sensing out her feelings. He was thinking the same as me. I resisted the urge to sigh unhappily.

She was lucky. She was able to share a sensation with him that I wanted to share with him. She was handed something that she didn't want and I did. That's how it always was. She was given things she never wanted and I was right there wanting, hands out. Only when she rejected them did I get that opportunity. I was the second choice; second best. Rylan's grip tightened and he rested his head on mine as if he knew I was being negative.

"Shit! What the hell?" Blaze shouted.

I sat up and my eyes widened. Raikidan had nodded off and his body was slowly shifting. I had only seen his true shape a few times, and I wasn't keen on getting crushed to see it again. I snapped my gaze to Laz but she, too, was out. "Laz!"

She jerked awake. "Shit, what?"

"Do something!" I shrieked.

She turned to look at me in question but once she saw Raikidan, her seat belt slammed against the side of the truck and she was reaching into the back. My eyes widened when she slapped him to wake him up, and was even more surprised when he didn't react.

"Raikidan, wake up." She smacked him again and then pushed him by the shoulder but he still didn't wake up. He just continued shifting. "Raikidan, you stupid, overgrown lizard, wake the hell up!"

Her treatment of him astonished me. I didn't realize she was so violent with Raikidan. She grabbed him by the shirt that was almost gone and slapped him, much harder than before, and he reacted this time. His body shifted back and his eyes snapped open.

His brow creased, and his eyes flashed in anger. "What the hell, Eira?"

"You fell asleep, that's what, you dick!"

He tilted his head a little. "What?"

She shoved him backward and climbed back into her seat without repeating herself.

Raikidan's head bounced off the window and he rubbed it unhappily. "Sorry, I didn't mean to…"

"Yeah, well sorry doesn't make up for you almost crushing us all," Blaze muttered.

"Shut up, Blaze," I snapped.

"Why don't you? You weren't nearly crushed by him," he shouted back.

"It's not like he meant it to happen. I don't see you having to fight sleep after working all night. Not that you did as much work as him anyway, giving you any right to sleep."

"Are you serious? I did just as—"

"That's enough!" Zane barked. "Both of you shut up now, or I'll throw you both out of this moving truck myself."

Blaze crossed his arms and muttered to himself. I, on the other hand, didn't sulk. I looked at Raikidan sympathetically instead, except he wouldn't have known. Raikidan was more focused on staring at the back of Laz's seat as if he were trying to figure out what she was doing.

He looked almost sad, as if he was regretting yelling at her, or was he thinking about something else? I couldn't tell with him. He wasn't easy to read, but he did act differently with her, like he was afraid to displease her in any way.

"Hey, Raikidan," I said. He shifted his gaze to me. "What if you shifted first and then slept? I know you can make it so you can fit into Laz's room, so would you be able to make yourself small enough to fit in here?"

"I'm not sure." He took in the size of the truck. "I've never tried to be that small."

I picked my feet up off the floor and pulled them up onto the seat. "We'll just give you the floor if you wanna try. I don't see the truck having any issues holding the extra weight, do you Zane?"

"I think she'll do just fine," he replied.

"I love how the rest of us don't have a say in this," Blaze said.

Argus slid to the corner of the connecting seats near Raikidan and relaxed. "I'm okay with it. If Raikidan's comfortable on the floor, that means more room on the seats for us, and I don't have to worry about waking up with you in my face."

Blaze grunted. "I don't swing that way."

"I don't know. You were pretty comfortable cuddling up to him on our last trip," Rylan teased.

I giggled at the memory. Argus, on the other hand, wasn't too thrilled to think about it, and I couldn't blame him. Blaze hadn't been keen on letting go that time, no matter how much Argus struggled. He couldn't even wake Blaze up.

"Go screw your girlfriend," Blaze muttered.

"I'd like to not see that, thanks," Argus said.

"I'd put you to shame anyway, Blaze," Rylan taunted. "I don't think you'd want to witness that."

I giggled and cuddled up to him. I always found it funny when he said things like that. Rylan acted different around the guys now that we were together. He seemed… more confident. I was okay with that, though. It made me feel good about my choice. I hadn't realized he had been as worried about what I'd say to him as I was about what he'd say to me if I told him how I felt. We were so stupid.

"Hey, Eira, since you're the only smart one to have thought to bring a pillow, and you're not using it at the moment, mind if I do?" Argus asked her. When he didn't receive an answer, he became confused. "Eira?"

"She's asleep," Zane said.

"Again?" Blaze shook his head. "What is with her?"

"Besides the fact that it's only three in the morning?" I replied sarcastically.

"She doesn't normally fall asleep this fast, or that many times," he clarified. "That's what I was getting at."

"I think she's just relaxed," Zane said. "You know how tense she is in the city. Elarinya told me she's much different outside the wall."

I nodded. "You'd be right. She relaxes so much when she's out here. It's like she feels she has nothing to worry about."

Argus propped his feet up on the seat when Raikidan slipped off of it. "Well, I'll leave it there then if she wakes up and wants it."

I barely heard him. I was more interested in what Raikidan's process. He'd closed his eyes and now took slow, concentrated breaths. Then, he began to shift. Everyone kept their feet up as he took over the floor. When he was done, he was much bigger than I expected him to take, but I wasn't going to complain. I was more interested in the fact that he rested his large head over the console facing in Laz's direction.

My curiosity got the better of me as he lulled to sleep quickly. I walked over the boys to get to the other side of the truck. I peered over Laz's seat and smiled. She had rolled over onto his snout and curled up against him, sleeping more soundly than I'd seen from her in a long time. There was no twitching, no mumbles, no sign of nightmares at all. It was like they were being taken away.

My eyes widened when Raikidan began to shift, but he didn't shift into a larger dragon shape like I expected. Instead, his form shifted back into a nu-human, and that meant Laz had no support anymore. I grabbed onto her so she wouldn't fall and wake up. I didn't need that happening right now. Not until I figured out what was going on.

Argus came over to help me with Laz by placing her pillow under her so I could let her go. Once she was situated, we looked at Raikidan, who was leaning over the console. He had moved a bit when he was shifting. Now his arm hung over the console on Laz's side of the cab. He didn't seem the least bit uncomfortable, although I was noticing small movements from him where he appeared to be moving closer to her.

Taking a few subtle hints from Argus, we pulled away and I took my place by Rylan's side again. He sprawled out for me to use him as my pillow, but I only laid there. I wasn't tired now, and I wanted to watch Raikidan to see what was going on.

Unfortunately, Rylan had other ideas. He rubbed my back and it was far too soothing for my liking. I fought the urge to sleep by pure willpower alone, and was successful for the next few hours that passed.

Raikidan didn't do much more than sleep, but Laz had moved around enough so that the two were quite close. I resisted the urge to smile. My plans weren't foiled yet, not after this recent event. Raikidan had no idea what he was capable of doing, and I was sure it had a lot to do with Laz.

I yawned as the sun began to rise over the horizon. And as if the sun were a trigger or reminder of what he truly was, Raikidan shifted back to his dragon shape and took up the floor once more. I yawned again and didn't resist the urge to sleep anymore. I needed my rest for what lie ahead, and since Raikidan was no longer shifted into his nu-human form, neither would know what happened. This would give me time to plan, and neither needed to know. Not yet, anyway.

30 CHAPTER

(EIRA)

I gazed around eagerly as we drove through the main gate of Larkren. The entrance only had one gate, and wasn't guarded by a multitude of soldiers—just a few, and they didn't seem to care who came in or out, as if it were more for show than anything.

My excitement ebbed when the old and sometimes run-down and abandoned buildings around us were the only sight to see. But as we drove further, the building status improved. Angled shingled roofs, wood, sometimes stone, siding, and large windows; each structure carried similarities along with their own uniqueness, unlike most of the homes of Dalatrend. Only those with money, like the wealthy Fourth Quadrant citizens, could afford to stand out.

The people here seemed happier than the ones in Dalatrend, and it didn't appear as though any of them were forced into staying here.

Zane pulled the truck up to a large car dealership, and I peered at the cars on the lot. They weren't the standard cars you'd find at a dealership. No, they were all custom built and unique-looking, just like the cars we transported. Ryoko began squealing and we all laughed.

The first out of the truck, she ran off to look at the selection of cars. She was out of sight before the two owners of the business were even able to leave the building to greet Zane. Unlike the others, I wasn't interested in the custom vehicles. I wanted to explore this town and find the ocean. The salt in the air teased me, and the more the wind brought it in from the bay, the more I wanted to see it.

I waited by the front of the truck as Zane and the boys spoke with the owners. The owners spoke with Zane with eager enthusiasm. I could only guess this delivery would be a highlight of their day.

Raikidan stood next to me. He appeared distracted, and I had a feeling it wasn't the new surroundings. Something was up, but I wasn't going to ask. If it was important he'd tell me.

Zane held up his hand to the two owners and looked over at me. "Eira, you can head out now. We'll call you when we're going to head back."

I smiled. "Thanks."

I slipped back into the truck and grabbed my side bag. Securing my communicator to it, I grabbed Raikidan by the hand and headed in a random direction. He didn't protest, showing genuine interest in our excursion.

I finally let go of him when I figured I wouldn't lose him. We walked around and socialized with some of the locals and entered a few shops and markets, having a bit more fun than I thought I would have had. I was interested in a few of the trinket shops and what they had to sell—they had large selections of shells I had never seen before, and I even bought a few out of pure temptation.

Even Raikidan was having fun. He pulled small pranks on me every now and then, and when a shop had clothing, he had me trying on the most ridiculous ones, and of course I made him do the same. He had me laughing so much, and I couldn't remember the last time I had this much fun.

The markets were nice, each one more interesting than the last. There were so many different types of fish for sale; I half expected to see a whale or shark at some point.

The locals we came in contact with were friendly and helpful, and none of the shop owners were overbearing or pushy like I was accustomed to. The people of this city were laid back, and enjoyed the free lives their ruler gave them. But if Zarda had his way, this city would be under his control, and the people would be subjected to massive change.

Once I grew bored of what the city had to offer, I was determined to find the ocean. I was surprised I hadn't seen even a glimpse of it. This city was bigger than I thought.

As we walked, a soldier approached us. "You two look lost. Can I help you?"

I was reluctant to speak with him. I wasn't sure if the soldiers here would be like the ones back home. But Raikidan wasn't so apprehensive. "We're looking for the ocean. My friend hasn't seen it before."

The soldier smiled. "I had a feeling, from the tracking device, that you weren't from here."

I hid my bracelet and glared at him. "You have a problem with that?"

The soldier held up his hands. "Easy, I didn't mean to offend you. Dalatrend is the only city I know that makes it hard for its citizens to leave, so I'm not surprised you haven't had the chance to come here. But if the ocean is what you're looking for"—he pulled out a hologram map—"then you'll want to follow this route."

I pulled out my map and copied the path. "Is it worth it?"

The soldier smiled. "You'll have to see for yourself."

I eyed him, but decided it was the only option I really had. I thanked the man, and we followed the course he set us on. The route led us down small streets lined with homes and stores, and it was easy going. I was still skeptical about this route until we rounded a corner and caught a glimpse of the harbor. Excitement bubbled in my stomach, and my feet picked up the pace.

Raikidan followed close behind, and soon the path we traveled on veered off the main road and onto a dirt one. My eagerness rose as the buildings disappeared, and all that remained was grassy land. Until it dropped off. I knew that on the other side of the drop off was the ocean—I could smell it. I could hear it.

The land curved up to a cliff where a large lighthouse stood, overlooking the ocean, watching out for boats. That's where I'd go. I wanted the best view. I continued on, but halted when Raikidan stopped following. I turned and watched as two men approached us. They were tan, muscular, well-groomed men with red hair and green eyes. Something didn't feel human about these two men, and with the way Raikidan was now positioning himself in front of me, I knew something wasn't quite right about them.

Raikidan began growling at them, but the other two didn't react in the same fashion. They glanced at each other and then Raikidan as if they were confused by his aggressive reaction to them. Then the talking began. It wasn't my tongue, that was for sure, but it didn't take much more than knowing a dragon to realize what tongue they spoke.

I became uncomfortable when glances fell on me more often. Even Raikidan looked back at me. I didn't like the fact that they were talking about me—who would really—but the fact I couldn't understand the language… that didn't improve the situation. Displeased and unwilling to deal with the treatment any longer, I walked away.

"Eira?" Raikidan said.

I continued on without acknowledging him. The breeze was light, and small birds hovered above in search of their next meal in the tall grass.

"Call to them," a kind but unfamiliar voice whispered. Normally I'd be concerned by this, since everything was different from the voice I normally heard, but my relatively good mood kept me in an uncaring state.

Smiling, I pulled out a small loaf of bread from my side bag and broke off a small piece. Once the large piece was back inside my bag, I cradled the piece of bread I had left and whistled to the birds above.

They weren't wary like I expected them to be. Instead, a few of them flew down and eagerly pecked at the treat. I could only assume the locals and tourists fed the birds regularly. Once they had devoured all the bread, they peered up at me for more, but when I didn't procure any after a few minutes, they flew off in search of more food. I continued on my way as well. I only had a few more yards to go.

A smile spread across my face when I reached the top of the cliff. The ocean was so big and uncontained. I listened as the waves crashed against the rocks, and felt the salt air sticking to my skin. The soldier had sent us to the highest point of the harbor. I could see for miles. Sitting down, I took it all in. It was nothing like I had ever imagined, and I had the best view.

Raikidan sat down next to me and gazed out at what lay before us. "Is it what you thought it would be?"

"It's so much better," I said, my voice a bit breathy.

"Then you'd love the shores in the south. It's just crystal blue water for miles."

"That does sound nice."

He looked down at my side bag. "Can I have some of that bread?"

I smiled and pulled out the loaf, cut in half. I gave him his portion and kept the other for myself. "You want some cheese with that?"

He nodded. "Sure. It was a good idea to buy these."

"I figured we'd get hungry. I'll buy some more when we head into town. That way we have something to snack on later on our way back to Dalatrend."

"Sounds like a good idea."

"Sharing this food isn't going to confuse your instincts again, right?" I was hoping the answer was a safe one.

"Don't worry. Not this time."

"How is this time any different?"

"It just is."

I grunted and shook my head before digging into my snack. We ate silently for a little while—it was nice.

"You haven't asked what we were talking about." Raikidan finally said.

My brow rose. "What?"

"You knew the others were my kind, and we were talking. You're not dumb."

I shrugged. "It doesn't matter."

"You seemed upset."

"You were talking about me."

"Then why do you say it doesn't matter?"

"Because I don't—"

"Don't. Don't say it, Eira."

I sighed. "Because in the end it doesn't matter."

"But you want to know."

I leveled my eyes with him. "How would you feel if someone was blatantly talking about you to someone else, a stranger, in another tongue you didn't know, as you stood right there?" I ripped a bite out of my bread and went back to staring out at the ocean.

"So you are mad." He sighed. "If it's any consolation, nothing bad was said about you."

I still didn't look at him. It didn't matter whether it was good or bad, he had still done it.

"They thought you had stolen my heart."

I looked at him funny. "What?"

"They wanted to know why I was with you, and if you had stolen my heart," he repeated.

"Stolen your heart?" That was a new phrase for me.

Raikidan nodded. "It's a story. It's said if a dragon is to spend too much time with a human of the opposite sex, there is a chance the bond they make causes the dragon to give his heart to the human."

"They obviously don't know me if they think I'm capable of something like that."

"I told them they were wrong, but because they think their brother has fallen to that fate, they don't believe me—not that I care whether they do or not."

I cocked my head. "Why would they care if you associate with me?"

"It's not common for a half-color of my colors to associate with humans. I may be half red dragon, but my darker scales have an effect on me too. It's that way for most of us. One scale color will have a greater effect, and it's usually the color we have most of. In my case, black color traits typically dominate."

"I see. So they've been watching us for a while then, haven't they?"

He nodded. "They sensed me the moment we reached the front gate. They'd been keeping an eye on me, just in case the same was happening to me as it was their brother."

"Let's just hope they're wrong about their brother." I rose to my feet to head back down to the city. "Because he's cursed himself if he has."

Raikidan followed. "You really believe that?"

"There is a fine line between human and dragon. It's there for a reason, and to cross that… well, you can't help but see it as anything but a curse at that point. It's doomed to fail."

"You think all relationships are doomed to fail."

"Not all, just most."

"Why?"

"Because I have seen so few work out."

"You fear for your friends, then."

I nodded. "I worry about them, yes."

"It'll work out for them."

"I hope you're right." My communicator flashed, signaling someone was calling me. I answered it. "Hello?"

"Laz, where are you?" Ryoko called in.

"Leaving the lighthouse, why?"

"Oh, wow, you really went out there to see the ocean. How'd you like it?"

"It was nice."

"Good. Do you guys have plans to do anything else? We've finished with the sale, so we're just chillin' and doing our own things until everyone is ready to leave."

"Well, we're just heading down to the markets to pick up a few things before heading back to the truck."

"Okay, take your time. I'm going to test drive a really nice car."

"Ryoko, you can't have it."

"I know, but that doesn't mean I can't drive it for a little bit. Oh, and just a heads up. Blaze said he called shotgun on the way back so you're stuck with us in the back."

I shrugged. "All right, no biggie."

"Well, you two continue having fun now," she teased.

"Don't you start. Ryoko?" She had hung up so she wouldn't have to listen to me scolding her. I glared at my communicator. "Stupid mutt."

Raikidan snickered. "You're so nice to her."

"Someone has to be."

Raikidan shook his head and followed me back into town, but well before we arrived, I stopped when we passed a dilapidated building. The structure, while made of stone like many of the buildings around it, resonated a different aura. It used to be big, and by the looks of it, it used to have large pillars on the inside. Curious, I ventured closer.

"Eira, what are you doing?" Raikidan hissed. "That building looks dangerous."

I waved him off and ventured inside. My breath caught at the sight. The roof of the building had crumbled away in the center, but there was enough left for me to see part of the intricate painting that was once up there. The roof painting didn't keep my attention for long—instead, I found the writing and paintings on the wall more interesting.

Jogging over to one of the walls, I ran my hand over the writing carved into it. My heart leapt. I couldn't believe what I had just found.

"Eira," Raikidan hissed. "We shouldn't be here. I just found a sign that says 'keep out.'"

"I'll only be a moment," I said. "I can't pass up this find."

"Eira…"

"Hey, what are you doing?" a man yelled.

I pinched my nose, letting out a tight breath. *Nice going, Raikidan.* Here he was telling me we needed to get out of here before we got caught, and he's the one who got us caught.

"I'm sorry, sir," Raikidan tried to apologize. "My friend ran in and I didn't see the sign until just now."

I was surprised by how pleasant he was being. He was usually more standoffish.

A soldier poked his head into the building and narrowed his gaze at me. "Miss, you can't be in here. It's dangerous."

"I'm sorry, but I can't pass these up," I told him as I pulled out a piece of paper and pencil out of my bag. "I need to catalog these Old Tongue writings."

"Y—you understand these?" he asked, his surprise clear.

I shook my head. "I know how to interpret the pictures but not the writing. Though I do know someone who understands both and he'd be ecstatic to see this place."

"What's your colleague's name?" he inquired.

"My colleague?" I laughed as I held the piece of paper to the wall and rubbed the graphite of the pencil over it to collect the etching from the wall. "We don't work together, but his name is Me'kunar. He's always complaining he's missing information on our ancient past. Looking at these pictures, I believe I might have found him something."

"Me'kunar, huh? Sounds like a shaman name."

I nodded and pulled out my communicator so I could take a few pictures. "He is, as well as his colleagues. They run the largest library of our ancient history. They're going to want to know about this place."

The soldier nodded. "Then I'll send word to show him this place if they visit."

I smiled. "Thank you. And thank you for not throwing me out of here. I've gotten what I need to send him to pique his interest."

He nodded and ushered us out. Once we were back on the road and pointed in right direction, we headed off.

The town was bustling with life now that it was later in the day, making it harder to get to the shops without losing each other. We finally found a food shop, and sought refuge. I took my time looking around. I'd need to make sure I had enough for the trip back, and there wouldn't be much doubt that the others would want some as well and wouldn't be smart enough to think of buying anything themselves.

Every time I chose an item to purchase, Raikidan would take it away and carry it for me himself, without telling me why. *Come to think of it, he hasn't spoken since we left that old building.* He didn't look like he was deep in thought, or taking them away for any special reason, so I decided to keep an eye on him.

Once I figured we had enough for the trip, I took our purchase to the counter. The clerk tallied up the total, but before I could pay for it, Raikidan placed money down on the counter. I looked at him questioningly, but he waited for the clerk to give him his change without looking at me. He then grabbed the bag of food to show me he was ready to leave.

I waited until we were outside to speak to him. "I had the money for it."

He began to walk away. "So did I."

I didn't follow. "You're acting weird on me again, Raikidan."

He fixed his gaze on me. "How I'm acting, it doesn't please you?"

"No." I walked past him. "And stop asking if things please me. It doesn't feel right."

I weaved around the congestion of people but stopped when a young man and woman caught my eye. They weren't doing anything out of the ordinary, but they still stuck out to me.

"That's them," Raikidan whispered.

The woman had long, raven hair and bright blue eyes, and the man, like his brothers, had short red hair and green eyes. Unlike his siblings, though, this one had facial hair. The two of them appeared happy, but I knew the look in the dragon's eye.

My lips pressed into a thin line. "His brothers are right to worry."

"How do you know?"

"I've seen that look before. He's made his choice clear, and has cursed them both if she has chosen him as well."

"She doesn't know what he is," Raikidan said. "The other two were surprised you not only knew my identity, but were completely comfortable with the knowledge, too."

"He fears she'll push him away if he told her." I shook my head. "And that is why it's doomed to fail."

Raikidan tilted his head. "I don't understand."

"It comes down to the fine line between humans and dragons. Not only do we have different biology, but we have different social structures. We both know our differences have caused us major issues, so think about what it would do to someone who would struggle to accept the existence of dragons, let alone find out the person they've been interested in is one. So he doesn't trust that she will be okay with the truth and won't push him away. Without that trust, there is nothing for a relationship to build on."

"I see what you're getting at."

I faced him. "Do you see this line, Raikidan, or do you struggle with it?"

Raikidan grunted, his brow knitting briefly. "Are you listening to yourself? Of course I see this line. It's clear as day. Now let's get back to the others."

I followed him. At least I wasn't the only one who saw the line. Dragons and humans were too different. I sighed, my eyes falling to the ground. But if that was true, why did we get along so well? Why did I get along better with him than I did with anyone else?

CHAPTER 31

The shadow of the irregularly-shaped roof concealed me as I waited, the sound of Dalatrend's normal nightly sounds roaring in the distance. I was about to do what I did best, assassinating single targets. Though a small war raged inside me. It wasn't just soldiers I was assassinating. Civilians who had their hands deep within Zarda's pants were on my list, and some of them had families.

Back in the day, it wouldn't have mattered to me. A target was a target. But now I thought differently. Could I really break apart a family for the sake of our cause, even though the target deserved it?

"You can do this, Laz," Seda encouraged. *"Have courage. Everything will be all right in the end."*

"I hope so."

I leaned against the half-wall and continued to wait. I wasn't stalling, no, I didn't want to stall. I was waiting for my signal to get this over with. The others had wanted to see what I was about to do. I didn't understand why they'd want to witness me kill someone. Sure, killing others in battles and an assassination were different types of deaths, but they were deaths nonetheless, and my former military friends were no strangers to death. Regardless, Ryoko had insisted on seeing me in action once. Even in the military, no one had been around to witness what I could do. I had always gone ahead and done my job alone.

"Babe, you're all set," Aurora called in. "I have the computer set up to your signal, so we can see what you see."

I exhaled. "All right. Just to make sure you guys understand this, this isn't going to be pretty."

"We're former soldiers," Rylan said. "We've seen death more than anyone should. We just want to actually see how you work."

"Very well."

I snuck out of the shadows and over to the edge of the building. I looked around as street lights reflected off my armor. I would have preferred to not wear my assassin uniform, but this armor had been designed for this activity, and it would have been stupid of me not to use it.

Checking to make sure my daggers were in place, I mentally willed my gloves to disappear around the pads of my finger tips, and the soles of my boots to melt away to utilize the hidden spines under my skin. Clinging to the edge of the roof, I made my way down. This target always left his study window open, so it would be easy getting into his place. He wasn't home right now, but according to the intel I had, he'd return soon.

I surveyed the large study decorated with priceless objects as my boots and gloves went back to normal. The man had money, but that was to be expected when you sucked up to Zarda. I rummaged through the shelves and tossed things on the ground, not caring if they broke or not. There wasn't anything of real value to me in this room, so I went to the next. Unfortunately, it was a small child's room. I left immediately once I'd realized this. I wasn't going to touch that.

A jewelry box smashed on the floor as I rummaged through the contents on top of a large dresser in the master bedroom. Curious about the contents, I rifled through them. *Bingo.* I snatched the most expensive-looking pieces and stuffed them into a bag. I continued to search around the room and tore it apart, grabbing whatever I found pretty or worth something, and threw it in my bag.

My rummaging stopped when footsteps by the front door caught my attention. The bedroom was no place for a murder, so I made my way back to the study, stopping at the stairs to the foyer. I glanced down, staring at the front door until the locked clicked and the door knob began to turn. Silently, I snuck back into the study and hid in a dark corner to wait.

I could hear a man and a woman talking down in the living room. I didn't catch a child's voice, and for that I was thankful. I didn't want a child to witness the horrid act I was about to commit. The moment the adults saw the mess upstairs, things would end for one of them. As far as I was aware, the woman who lived here was also innocent, and I prayed she wouldn't get in my way.

I listened as the two came up the stairs and headed for the bedroom. I didn't react when the woman screamed, or when the man began cursing. I only waited.

The man ran down the hall toward the study, and I prepped myself. The cracked open door flew open and crashed against the wall. The man bolted in, looking around at his disheveled room. The gawking didn't last long, though. He collected himself and went directly to a safe I had been unable to open earlier.

His back turned to me, I drew a dagger and advanced. The man opened the safe and pulled out a pile of papers, letting out a relieved breath. I made a mental note to take those with me once I dealt with him. I stopped advancing, and hid my dagger as the man turned around.

The man jumped and stumbled backward, knocking over a plant. "By the gods, I hate it when you soldiers do that, especially you assassins. You're far too quiet for my liking. But I'm glad you're here. I want you to find out who did this to my home." I didn't react. "Are you deaf, woman?"

"Slit his throat for his impudence," the voice in my head said.

I revealed my dagger and his eyes grew wide. "Zarda has no more use for you."

"No, no it can't be." He stumbled backward. "You're lying. I've done nothing wrong. I've done all that he's asked!"

The man ran for the door. He was fast, but I was faster. I knocked him to the ground and dragged my dagger across his neck, slicing deep into the skin. I then stabbed him in the back twice as an extra measure, although I knew the man was already dead. A slice to the neck was my favored move, even over breaking the neck. It was faster, even if it was messier.

I turned away from his lifeless body and froze. The woman of the house stood in the doorway. Contrary to what I expected to see on her face, there were no traces of fear or even sadness. No, she looked... happy.

"Thank you," she whispered. "I know you are not one of them, and now I don't have to worry about my son becoming like his father."

"Don't trust her."

I gave a curt nod. I wasn't about to believe her and give away my voice. Only the dead ever heard it.

The woman tossed me a small bag. "Take the rest of it. I have no use for the jewels he gave me. I don't want memories of what he became."

"Don't trust it. Kill her too. No loose ends."

I eyed her and then picked up the papers the man had pulled out of the safe before dashing to the window. Putting extra strength into my step, I pushed off the windowsill and set my sights on the building across the small street. I landed on the roof of the targeted building and disappeared into the shadows of the night.

I had several more targets to get to, and I was losing moonlight, not that it could be helped. It took patience to be an assassin, and if I could only get to two or three targets out of five or six, then that was good. Not a concept Zarda could ever grasp, but his opinion never mattered to me.

I slipped into the shadows of my greenhouse and peered into the structure. My messenger hawk slept peacefully, and nothing moved within. *Good to see he's back.* Someone had been using him without my permission, and I didn't like it. Shva'sika had tried to claim to be the culprit, but in truth, I knew she was too polite to use him without asking first.

I made my way inside the house. I had only been able to take out three of my targets before I had to abandon the assignment. I had almost taken out a fourth, but I hadn't factored in the security, and almost got caught just sneaking around. The best course of action was to stop while I was ahead.

I opened the door to the living room and was greeted by the others lounging about as if nothing was amiss. I unstrapped one side of my mask. "Shouldn't you guys be sleeping?"

"We just wanted to make sure you'd get home safe," Ryoko admitted. "You know us."

I smiled. "All right then. Off to bed with you now."

"Yes, mom."

I chuckled and shook my head as I headed for my room. I closed my bedroom door behind me and smiled. *Just the guy I wanted to see.* Without fail, Raikidan sat on the window sill. At this point, it felt dumb to even have a separate room for him.

"Here." I tossed him a bag filled with some of the stolen goods as I walked past him.

"Don't do that, he doesn't deserve your treasure."

"What's this for?" he asked.

I shrugged as I rummaged through my long dresser for a special box to hide away the remainder of my newly-obtained treasure. "I figured you could add it to your hoard or something."

I watched from the corner of my eye as he rummaged through the bag. His eyes glowed with delight, but it faded as he switched his gaze to me. "Thank you, but you don't have to give this to me. I told you before that I didn't want payment for helping you."

Finding my desired box, I unlocked it and stored away my new treasures. "Rai, it's not payment. I just figured you'd like to have some of what I managed to steal."

"I'll give you something in return. Not sure what, but when I find the right thing, you'll know."

I shook my head and slipped into my closet after storing my box away. There were no words that would get through that thick head of his. I spoke the truth, but if he didn't want to believe me, then that was his problem.

CHAPTER 32

A quiet sigh escaped my lips as we walked. There had been nothing to do, so Ryoko insisted on dragging me around town on foot. Rylan and Raikidan opted to join us, thinking it would curb their boredom, but we still hadn't done anything yet, making the boredom worse. Ryoko would take interest in a store, but the moment she scanned the items in the display window, she lost interest and went to the next store.

Ryoko gasped and rushed over to a store with a small display. I rolled my eyes and followed. I stood next her as she continued to look over the display of jewelry excitedly, even though there was no reason to. These items weren't just a few gold coins. The lowest-priced pieces sat in the double-gold-coin digits. Most of them were several platinum coins. No way could we afford them.

Ryoko looked at me. "Let's go inside."

"Wow, you finally found a place to check into," Rylan teased.

"Too bad it's a place where we can't afford anything," I muttered.

Ryoko grabbed my arm. "Don't be a buzz-kill. We don't have to buy anything; sometimes it's just nice to look. Besides, we need to find you a new necklace."

I tried to pull my arm away. "Did you not hear me just say we can't afford this stuff?"

Ryoko rolled her eyes, and again dragged me into the store. It was a small place, but clean. The floors were made of wood with a dark finish, the jewelry displays were glass with silver accents, and all the jewelry in the displays were complimented by satin drapes or pillows.

Ryoko didn't hesitate to rush over to a random display and look at the riches it held. She had let go of my arm in the process, allowing me to peer at another display that was closer. I had to admit, the stuff in here was nice, but the prices made me uncomfortable.

"So, find anything you like?" Ryoko asked.

I shrugged. "Not really."

Ryoko peeked at the jewelry I had been looking at and frowned. "They're diamonds. How can you not find something to like in this display?"

My eyebrow rose. "Do I look like a girl who would wear diamonds?"

"Well, if you got all dressed up, then yeah."

"Well… I need something that doesn't require me to dress up."

"Why? Maybe you should just dress up more often."

I shook my head and went to look at another display. I ended up passing by several before one caught my eye. My eyes shone with slight delight. They were so beautiful.

Ryoko giggled. "Sapphires. Of course you'd like those." I glared at her and she giggled again. "You have good taste, though. I can't argue that."

I half smiled and went back to my marveling. There were mainly blue sapphire jewelry displayed, but some of them were red, and some were a bit of a mix.

"Can I help you ladies?" We glanced up to see a neatly trimmed gentleman towering over us. "Or are you just window shopping?"

"We're trying to find something for my friend here," Ryoko replied.

The man looked me up and down real quick. "I don't think you'll find anything fitting for her."

My eyes narrowed. "Excuse me?"

Raikidan growled. "You dare to criticize how she looks?"

"On the contrary. I'm just stating that these fine body ornaments wouldn't be fitting for her."

Raikidan pushed away from his position on the wall and made his way over to us, barely glancing at any of the displays. He placed a hand on both of our shoulders. "Let's go."

"But we're not done looking," Ryoko objected.

Raikidan's intense gaze snapped to the retailer. "We're going to Black Starlight."

I noticed the store man gulp, piquing my interest.

Ryoko tilted her head. "What's Black Starlight?"

"It's a better quality jewelry store, with better pricing."

Ryoko smiled. "Sounds nice."

The man composed himself. "Your friend is lying to you. That store's prices are much higher."

Raikidan grinned. "Depends on who you know."

"I think we should go." I didn't take my gaze off the man as he sweated like crazy. "I'd like to see this place, and see what it has to offer."

Raikidan's grin grew. "Excellent. We'll be leaving now, ladies."

Ryoko waved goodbye to the retailer, and we followed Raikidan out of the stupid building and down the street. I was curious about where he was going to take us. Raikidan didn't leave the house much, unless someone else was with him, and I seriously doubted he would go into a jewelry store if he was with one of the guys. So what was this place he was showing us, and how did he know of it?

The building was tiny, much smaller than the other jewelry store, but far more unique in appearance. The entrance of the building had a neat little tunnel instead of a straight-up door. It also had an old rustic appeal that gave it a village-craftsman-shop feel.

"Is this the place?" Ryoko asked.

"No, of course not." I said. "It's not like it says Black Starlight on a large sign above us or anything."

Ryoko glared at me. "How would you know? You can't read."

It was my turn to not like her words. I place my hands on my hips. "At least I don't act like a blonde."

The boys chuckled at the two of us as we stared each other down. Raikidan touched my shoulder, bringing me out of my mood, and led us down the tunnel, to the real door of the small shop. I gazed around the room as we walked over to the main counter. The interior was just as rustic as the outside with wood panel walls and timbered beams striping the ceiling, but it also had a sort of elegance that lived up to other Sector Eleven businesses. Ryoko ran over to a display before we could reach the counter. I swore she'd burst from excitement any moment.

"These are so amazing!" Her eyes sparkled. "Eira, you need to see these."

I didn't move, too preoccupied with scanning the room. *We're being watched…*

"You act like something is about to jump us," Raikidan whispered. "You need to relax."

I grunted and eyed a display to ease my nerves. I knew Ryoko was feeling the same as me. She would have used my nickname had it not been the case.

"Eira, c'mon, you really need to look at these," Ryoko insisted.

Rylan chuckled. "I don't think she's going to be interested."

"Diamonds?" I guessed.

He nodded. "Diamonds."

"Pass."

I went back to looking at several displays, containing jewelry with topaz, emeralds, and amethyst, but there was a display of sapphires that kept catching my eye. It wasn't unusual for me to like this gemstone, but I tended to gravitate to emeralds first.

"You have good taste."

I glanced up to see a handsome man who had sapphire eyes with silver rings around the pupils walking out of a doorway that had been covered by strings of wooden beads. He finished smoothing out his thin, black mustache, and quickly ran his hand through his slicked back black and red hair. He wore a black long-sleeved shirt with the sleeves partially rolled up, and denim pants that fit his tanned, athletic build well. The man had a bit of an accent to his voice that sounded similar to the one those from the North had, but his wasn't as strong as what I was used to hearing in my travels. *Why does it feel like I know him?*

The man turned his attention onto Raikidan. "It's about time you showed up. I thought you might have gotten lost."

Raikidan crossed his arms. "Hardly. I just didn't feel like dropping by until now."

Ryoko raised her hand. "Okay, confused. You know him?"

"He's Raikidan's brother," I said.

His brother focused on me at me with a curious eye, and then shifted to Raikidan, who only shook his head. He hadn't told me. He never talked about his past, let alone his family. I had figured it out on my own.

The accent his brother had almost threw me off, since Raikidan didn't have much of one, although occasionally I had picked it up. It was the eyes and facial shape, particularly the jaw, that gave me the right clues. But it was this guy's hair that made me feel like he was more significant in Raikidan's life. The red, although slicked back with the rest of his black hair, was in a noticeable stripe-like pattern. *Why is he so familiar? This is going to eat at me…*

"How the hell did you figure that out?" Ryoko asked.

I shrugged and went back to looking. "Similar facial features."

"Yeah, sure."

"Yeah, I don't see it," Rylan said.

"That's because you suck at facial recognition," I stated.

Ryoko nodded. "She's got a point. You scored really low on those tests."

Rylan narrowed his eyes at her. "So did you."

She stuck her tongue out at him. "Still better than you, though."

I rolled my eyes and ignored them. Raikidan's brother, on the other hand, found amusement in their bickering. "I should introduce myself. My name is Ebon. Welcome to my shop. And yes, I am Raikidan's older brother."

Ryoko grunted, indicating he had answered the question she was about to ask. I picked up a necklace on display outside the glass cases, and held it up briefly before putting it back down.

Ryoko gasped. "Raikidan, I thought you said these prices were better! They're twice as expensive as the other store."

Ebon chuckled. "Any friend of Raikidan's is a friend of mine. The prices you see won't be anywhere close to what I would charge you."

"Well that's a nice perk." She placed her hands on her hips. "Raikidan, you've been holding out on us."

I narrowed my eyes as I viewed some earrings. Something didn't add up. Raikidan had claimed he'd had no desire to learn about humans in any way until I showed up, but here he was, in his brother's shop, in the middle of a nu-human city.

Raikidan shrugged. "Not really. I didn't know his shop was here until recently."

My gaze snapped onto him. "You're the one who's been stealing my messenger hawk!"

Raikidan held up his hands. "I borrowed him."

I narrowed my eyes. "You didn't ask to use my bird."

"It's a bird!"

Ryoko wagged her finger at him. "Raikidan, you should know by now to never take her stuff."

"I borrowed the bird," he insisted. "And he came back fine every time."

"Sorry, brother, I didn't mean to get you into trouble," Ebon said.

"I'm always in trouble with her," Raikidan muttered.

Ebon chuckled. I turned away angrily and knelt to look at the display in front of me. *I knew Shva'sika was lying to me!* But since it was Raikidan who had used my messenger hawk and my hunch was right, Ebon did play a significant role in Raikidan's life. Why else would he seek him out?

"Dammit, what is that weird rumbling noise?" Ryoko asked.

"The two of them are just talking. Ignore it," I mumbled.

Her brow furrowed. "What? You're crazy. Talking requires actual words."

I shook my head as I chuckled, and continued to look for something to catch my interest. There wasn't a large selection, making it hard, and I didn't want to explain anything to Ryoko.

Ebon opened his side of the display and pulled out a necklace I had been eying. "This is the one you were looking at right?"

I pursed my lips. "Uh, yeah."

Ryoko wandered over to us. "How'd you know she was looking at that one?"

"I've been doing this a long time."

"Laz, let's see what it looks like on you," Ryoko said.

I took a step back. "I don't think that would be a good idea."

"Have some fun, will you?"

I blew air out of parted lips and Ryoko took the necklace from Ebon to hold it up in front of my neck. She shook her head and gave it back to him. Ebon pulled out another necklace and Ryoko tried that one instead.

"So, Ebon, do you make these yourself?" Ryoko asked.

"Yes."

"I didn't think dragons held jobs."

Ebon shrugged. "We may not be human, but that doesn't exclude us from the same activities as humans. I enjoy the craft and making a profit, so it's a win-win for me."

Ryoko nodded and held up another necklace up to me. This time she approved, and I did as well, but it still wasn't a necklace I would wear casually.

Ryoko frowned. "You don't like it do you?"

I shrugged and handed the necklace to Ebon. "It's not casual enough."

"It'd be nice for a party."

"She wouldn't have a dress to go with it," Rylan said.

He did not just bring that up. I turned and gave him a nasty glare, but it was too late.

Ryoko squealed. "Can we do that next?"

"No," I said.

"Do what now?" Raikidan asked.

"Dress shopping," Ryoko said.

"No!" I repeated.

She narrowed her eyes at me. "Your opinion doesn't count. You'd say no to going down to a burger joint."

"Because the food at those places is nasty. And we're not shopping for dresses."

"Don't be so lame!"

"Ryoko, don't make her do it," Rylan said. "She won't have fun."

Ryoko glared at him, and he lowered his gaze. I didn't feel bad for him at all. He was the one who gave her the stupid idea.

"Do you wish to look at anything else?" Ebon asked, saving us from the storm that was starting to brew.

Ryoko crossed her arms to think. "I dunno. Do you have anything else that isn't on display?"

"I'm afraid not. I prefer to make custom jewelry. I just put up a few displays to give patrons an idea of what I can do."

"Fair enough." I headed for the door. "Nice meeting you, Ebon."

"The pleasure's mine."

"Wait, Laz, where are you going?" Ryoko questioned.

"Home." I wanted to get back there soon so I could talk to Raikidan about his brother. *It's too important to ignore.*

I sat quietly on my bed as I thought. It wasn't like me to want to go out of my way to know something about someone, so this was going to be hard for me to do.

"Eira." I glanced over at the windowsill where Raikidan sat. "What's eating you?"

I gazed back down at my lap. "Nothing, just thinking." *Really, Eira? You can't even ask this simple question? Everyone else and their grandmother can.*

Raikidan walked over and sat down next to me. "You want to talk about something."

I avoided eye contact. Was it really that obvious?

He scooted closer. "Talk to me, Eira. You know you can, or at least, I hope you know."

I scratched the back of my neck. "I wanted… to know more about you… I guess."

"You want to know more about me?"

I looked as far away from him as I could. When he didn't say anything, I knew I shouldn't have asked. It had been a bad idea. No, it had been stupid. "Look, forget I said anything, okay? It was—"

"No, Eira, you misunderstand my silence. I was thinking of what to tell you."

I peered at him through my lashes. "Really?"

Raikidan smirked. "Yeah, really." I smiled. That was a better response than I had been expecting. "I just don't know what you want to know."

I shrugged. "I dunno, maybe, what it was like growing up?"

Raikidan lay back on the bed. "That's a good one. I'll need a second to think about that."

I waited a few moments before lying next to him. "I guess I should narrow it down better. You told me you grew up alone, and it was hard since you were a, uh, half-color. You could tell me about that."

"You really don't like that term, do you?"

I shook my head. "I don't like it any more than I like the term halfling."

Raikidan rolled on his side and messed with my bangs. "It's not a happy story."

I made a pathetic complaining noise as I swatted him away and attempted to fix my bangs. "Can't be any worse than mine."

Raikidan sighed. "Growing up was a little tough for me, since I hatched long after my siblings grew up and left. I had to teach myself how to do things where my parents couldn't, even if it meant I'd get hurt."

"What was something you had to get hurt to learn?"

"When whelps cross territory boundaries and are caught, they're usually given lenience, but when they're a half-color, they're attacked as if they were a full grown adult." He touched his right shoulder. "That's how I got this."

I touched the scar, but then immediately retracted fingers. It wasn't right to do that.

"I wasn't completely alone though. I had Ebon for a while." I focused hard on him. This was the information I had wanted earlier. "He was from my clutch, and the only one who had stayed when the others left. He taught me a lot, and promised he wouldn't leave until it was time to find his mate."

I was starting to realize why Ebon had such a strong familiarity to him. "But that's not what happened, was it?"

Raikidan worked his jaw. "No. Our father wasn't the easiest to live with, and Ebon, well, he was an oddity for half-colors and didn't embrace his black scales at all, making him more like our mother. He enjoyed learning about everything, and obtained skills humans and elves knew. That's how he mastered his craftsman skills he uses at the shop. My father didn't like that, and after tensions grew too thick between them, they fought, and Ebon left. It upset my mother, but out of the others, she was the most okay with him being on his own. She always said his stripes represented how well he could blend in with anything."

I cocked my head. "Stripes?"

Raikidan nodded. "He had an interesting pattern to his scales. Like me, his predominant scale color is black, but his red scales streak across his body in differently sized and shaped lines."

My heart slowed. *I knew it.* "So, like a tiger, just reversed."

"Yeah, it was exactly like that, except he didn't have any red scales on his face."

I was right. Ebon had been in that dream I had about Raikidan. He had been the dragon leaving the cave and flying away. That also meant Corliss had been in his life before he had been full-grown.

"I get the feeling you weren't completely alone after that."

Raikidan blinked and then chuckled. "Well, I guess you're right. Ebon would come back for visits every now and then, which was nice. And I had Corliss."

This was my chance to get this information from him directly. It'd reduce the risk of slip up later. I chose to play ignorant. "I don't get it."

He chuckled again. "Corliss isn't just my neighbor. He's also my cousin. His father and my father are from the same clutch. So every once in a while, Corliss would be brought over for visits."

"So is Corliss a black dragon?"

Raikidan shook his head. "My father's sire thinks he's cursed. Not only did my father take a red dragon as a mate, but Corliss' father took a green dragon as his mate."

"And there's Rimu's father as well."

"Yes. Anahak would be the son of one of my uncle's daughters on my father's side. My uncle and his daughter both took black dragon mates, while some of his other offspring, along with their offspring, took dragons of other colors as mates."

"Well your grandfather can go cut off his wings and jump off a cliff."

Raikidan chuckled and I was glad he found humor in my dislike of his family member who didn't approve of him.

"So, what does Corliss look like, scale color-wise?"

"Interesting. His scales are mostly green, but he has black ones that are scattered all over, making him look like the night sky."

"If he was like the night sky, then he'd be mostly black."

He poked my nose. "You know what I mean."

I laughed and then quieted down when a new thought came to me. "Raikidan, how long have you been in contact with your brother?"

Raikidan scratched his head. "Well, only recently, to be honest. Shva'sika mentioned she had seen him while out doing some shaman thing, and said we looked a lot alike, so she thought we might be related. I didn't think it was him right off, so I brushed the idea off. But then after a while I started thinking about it, and then sent your bird to deliver a message to him. Sorry for not asking, by the way. I just really needed to know."

My gaze was soft as I looked at him. "It's all right. Family is important. It good to keep those good relations when you can. Besides, when they're around, you're less likely to accept living alone as the best thing for you."

Raikidan stared at me. I had to look away. *I shouldn't have said that.*

"I guess you're right." I focused on him again. "I thought I had been alone growing up, but I wasn't as alone as I could have been. I guess that's why I wanted to find him when I had the means to."

"Rai, how many siblings do you have?"

Raikidan let out a sorrowful sigh. "It's just me, Ebon, and our older sister from a previous clutch, I think."

My brow rose. "You think?"

"No one has heard from her in about a century, so no one knows if she's still alive."

"How many clutches did your parents have?"

"Four."

"And how many were in those clutches?"

"The average. Between two and four."

I frowned. That meant he could have had up to fifteen older siblings, and only two of them have possibly survived.

"What's the likelihood of dragons surviving to their first century?"

Raikidan huffed. "Depends. If they lived in a clan and chose to stay that way, the chance is pretty high, but the clutch rates and egg numbers tend to be lower. If they come from a pair of dragons who live alone, the likelihood of them surviving their first half-century is fifty percent, and once they leave to be on their own, it drops to twenty-five percent. For half-colors, it's unlikely for them to survive on their own."

"They're actively pursued and killed, then."

Raikidan nodded and my gaze lowered. His life was hard for a born creature. To be killed in cold blood for being different, it was no better than being a tank-born.

I stared up at the ceiling. There was one more question lingering in my head. "What's it like to have memories of growing up?"

"Huh?"

I looked at him. "What is it like to remember growing up?"

"Well, that's hard to say. The memories are in pieces. Some here and some there. Some are important and some aren't. It's not something I can remember entirely, but sometimes I remember pieces I could never remember before. They feel like normal memories. Why do you ask?"

I gazed back up at the ceiling, and then raised my hand to look at it. "I'm a tank-born. I don't… have any of those kinds of memories. The tank feeds us images of things to learn, like animals, trees, the ocean, and, if we're really lucky, a person we're supposed to know. But that's all we get. We don't get fake memories of being children, or memories of someone taking care of us, or even memories of sharing something with a sibling." I sighed. "The first thing I remember was waking up too early and everything going wrong in vivid detail."

My eyes shut, but the memories surfaced, so I opened them again. "I remember the confusion, and the struggle to survive because I knocked my breathing mask off when it stopped giving me oxygen. And I remember the tank malfunctioning and not releasing me like it was supposed to, so Jasmine had to break the glass in order to make sure I didn't drown. I remember a large chunk of what I did that first day, but that first day was when I was seventeen. I wasn't a child. I didn't have memories to look back on. I didn't get a life like most did." I clenched my hand into a fist and held it close to my chest. "I just… wanted to know what it was like to have that."

"Eira…"

I chuckled. "Sorry. I went off into a weird place on you again. Well, now you know something about me, and why I don't talk about myself much. There isn't much to know after that."

Raikidan suddenly rolled over on me and tucked his arms under my body. I tensed and my cheeks burned. I tried to speak, but nothing came out. His grip tightened as he nuzzled my neck, and my body warmed up all the way down to my toes.

I finally found my voice, but it wasn't strong like I needed it to be. "R–Raikidan, w–what are you doing?"

"Just shut up and let me give you a hug."

I gulped. "This isn't a hug."

"It is to me," he whispered in my ear, sending a tingling sensation down my spine. *Not a comforting sign…*

"Raikidan, please. This is… making me very… uncomfortable…"

Raikidan let go and raised himself until he hovered over me. "There's nothing to be uncomfortable about, Eira. That's why I've been working with you on all this."

I pushed on his chest, but he didn't budge. "Please…" He huffed and moved so I could sit up. "Thank you."

He took several moments to respond. "Eira, I don't want you to be afraid of me."

"I'm not."

"Then why are you fighting this so much?"

My eyes found more interest in the patterns of my comforter than him. "I'm not fighting it."

"If you weren't, you'd be making a lot more progress. One day you're good, the next we're back to square one."

I sighed. "Rai, it's not that easy to just up and get over…"

He pulled me into his lap. "Then what else haven't you told me?"

A lot… "You know what you need to."

"That's not an answer I want to hear. Don't you trust me?"

"It's not that I don't trust you. It's just…" The words died on my lips. There wasn't a way for me to come up with a believable excuse, because Raikidan was right, I was fighting this. As much as I wanted to be free of Zarda, I didn't want to face other parts of my past I had tried so hard to bury. I didn't want to risk repeating those same mistakes…

Raikidan rested his chin on my shoulder, refusing to give up on this space issue, but willing to change topics to ease the tension. "You know, the jewelry Ebon made that you tried on, it looked nice on you."

I turned away so he wouldn't see the blush emerging on my cheeks. "I looked all right."

Raikidan chuckled in my ear. "You can't deny a compliment. You had a deal with Shva'sika."

The flush went away and I rolled my eyes. "That was weeks ago. It doesn't stand anymore."

"I think it does, because you won the challenge. It didn't take more than a day before Shva'sika realized the truth you were trying to get her to see, but that also means you have to keep up your end of the deal from now on."

I snorted and climbed off his lap, much to his dislike, evident with his protest grabs. "You have this all wrong. She only had to go a week and so did Ryoko and I. That was it. It was her choice to go longer. Missed your chance."

Raikidan shook his head. "Do you enjoy being difficult?"

I winked. "I might."

He rolled his eyes. "Well, you should go back to his shop and buy something when you have the extra money."

"None of it is casual enough."

"You could pull it off."

I grunted. "Right. But since we're on the topic of his shop, I do have a question. How does him being a shop keeper work with your hoarding instinct?"

Raikidan grinned. "You and your curiosity on that instinct. You can't just let it be, can you?"

I frowned. "Humans don't have those instincts. We like and collect things, sure, but it's not something that compels us. Your instinct is so strong it's interesting to learn about. That's all."

Raikidan held up his hand in defense. "Easy. That wasn't meant to be an attack on you. Hoarding is normal to me, so it's just a bit strange to have someone ask about it."

"So are you going to answer my question or not?" I muttered.

He smiled. "Our hoarding instinct is strong, that's true, but we also understand value. My brother can sell his crafts because he's getting more than he had before."

"So basically he can swap for one item for another as long as it has equal or higher value."

Raikidan nodded. "Exactly. It's common for dragons to barter with each other, especially those in colonies. And before you ask, yes, dragons have separate hoards in colonies. We don't like to share unless it's with a mate."

"Bartering hoarded items," I mused. "Sounds like you guys get bored a lot."

He chuckled. "We can live a long time under good conditions. Sometimes we need to pass the time. Not like humans can't get bored, either, in their short lives."

I crossed my arms. "Our lives aren't that short."

"Elves and dragons outlive you by far."

"Wogrons, dwarves, and other races don't."

He grunted and pushed me down as he stood, as if he had used me as some sort of leverage. "Whatever. You should get some sleep. I have a feeling you're going to need it."

"I get that feeling every day."

He chuckled. "Well now I'm getting it, so it must be something big."

"Perfect." I curled up and snuggled into my pillows. "Good night, Raikidan."

"Good night, Eira."

A smile crept onto my face before I emptied my mind and willed sleep to take me.

33
CHAPTER

Everyone was quiet while we waited for Genesis to come back into the room. She had summoned us for a meeting on our next group mission, but then received a call from the rest of the Council.

I leaned on my knees patiently, but Blaze was another story. His leg bounced, and he was fidgeting with a pen.

"Blaze, that's annoying, stop," I ordered. He sighed and stopped, but didn't stay that way for long. "Blaze!"

He threw his hands up in the air. "What do you want me to do? Sit still while Genesis takes her sweet lovin' time chit-chatting with the Council?"

Ryoko held out a hand. "Uh, duh."

"She's taking forever," Blaze muttered.

"Keep your panties on. It's only been five minutes," I said.

"Seven actually," Argus corrected.

"Whatever."

Just then, Genesis ran into the room. "Sorry. The Council was divided on something and felt the need to involve me, but not listen to what I had to say."

I chuckled. "That would figure."

She sat down on the couch between to Ryoko and Raid and let out a breath. "Okay, now for the assignment you all will be needed on."

My eyebrow rose. "All?"

"Well, almost all," she corrected. "Zane won't be participating for obvious reasons, and I'd still prefer Shva'sika to keep a low profile due to her active shaman status."

Shva'sika nodded. "I understand."

Zane smiled. "I'll give my support from afar. How does that sound?"

Genesis giggled. "That's perfectly fine. Now for what this assignment entails. It's rather complex so I need you all to listen carefully. Thanks to information Argus and Eira uncovered at the hidden research facility, we tracked down a high-grade weapons and surveillance manufacturing plant hidden deep in the largest military outpost in Quadrant Three."

"The Helvan street one we found Arnia hiding in, correct?" I asked.

Genesis nodded. "Yes. With the information collected we're pretty sure there are some weapons and surveillance equipment we could use that could give us a great advantage."

"Only pretty sure?" Blaze asked. "We're not dealing with a definite?"

Genesis frowned. "Sadly, no. Security is tight for this building to the point where we couldn't even get moles close enough to give us any confirmation. This tight security is why all of you will be needed. Normally a high security situation would require us to use assassins to infiltrate the facility undetected, but we're sure not even an assassin could go undetected in this place without help."

Blaze pounded his fists together. "Please tell me we get to cause a commotion."

The room echoed with laughter. Even Genesis found his enthusiasm amusing. "Yes, as a matter of fact, you do."

He threw a fist into the air. "All right!"

"Ryoko, Raid, and Raikidan will also be helping," Genesis continued. "In order for us to get a small squad in to grab plans and other information we believe having Brutes and foot soldiers with either strength enhancements or high destructive abilities causing a commotion on a destructive level to two parts of the compound will draw most of the security away from the manufacturing building. Eira will join other assassins to sneak into the building and grab what they can as fast as possible. Rylan, you'll be assigned to watching the building to let them know if they need to get out quick."

Rylan nodded. "I understand."

Shva'sika cleared her throat. "If I may make a suggestion. I believe the dragons could be a great deal of use. They're a hardy race and as Raikidan has proven, even in a human form, they're quite resilient. I believe some shamans could also be of use. Guards especially are strong and many have elemental abilities. Other elemental shamans would be excellent at causing destruction. We may try to keep ourselves in check but we will never deny how dangerous the elements are."

Genesis nodded, her eyes thoughtful. "The dragons I can agree to if they wish to help with this. The shamans I'm not so sure. I know most of you hide your identities rather well, and I'm not doubting you could handle yourselves out there, but this is a battle and there's a huge risk of casualties, even with the type of bullet proof armor we have at our disposal. We're taking a big risk creating this confrontation in the first place."

Shva'sika smiled. "We're a proud people. Death doesn't scare most of us and we're willing to die for what we believe in, just like any of you."

Genesis tapped a finger to her lips. "Very well. I assume you'll want to inform them?"

"I think that would be wise. I'll be able to tell the dragons at the same time since most are sharing living quarters with shamans," Shva'sika said.

Genesis nodded again. "I'll leave that up to you then."

"When will this go down?" Raid asked. "I doubt by how calm you are this is happening later tonight."

"You'd be correct," Genesis said. "We're going to execute this tomorrow night. That way we know everyone is accounted for and there are fewer potential surprises waiting for us."

"So, Argus," Ryoko began, "is there anything else you and Laz uncovered that could give us a hand in this battle that wasn't related to the discovery of this manufacturing plant?"

Argus grinned. "I'm glad you asked. I've been working hard on some of the plans I found and one of them I'm pretty sure you're going to like, Ryoko." He reached under the coffee table and grabbed a bag he had brought in with him earlier. The first thing he pulled out was a pair of enormous metal gauntlets. "You can thank Eira for these. They were one of the better finds."

Ryoko took one and examined the glove. "They look cool. What do they do?"

"Put it on and flex your hand," he instructed.

Ryoko slipped the gauntlet on and flexed her hand as instructed. We all watched in amazement as sparks of electricity crackled around the palm of the gauntlet every time she closed her hand.

Blaze got all excited. "Yeah, that's what I'm talking about!"

"This is really cool," Ryoko said. "How does it work?"

"Attached to the glove is a canister stored with electrical energy. It's released when a plate in the palm of the glove is touched. The plate is sensitive, so the smallest movement can activate it. I can't take all the credit for this though. Shva'sika deserves a lot of recognition. She helped me work out a way to charge the storage canister since the original plans had no stable way of creating it on its own."

Ryoko turned her head toward Shva'sika. "Really?"

Shva'sika smiled. "Thanks to the way my ability manifests, I can sense electric potentials in objects. I also store my energy in my body so I've got firsthand knowledge on how it works."

Ryoko grinned. "Cool." She then turned to Argus. "You said these gloves can't make the electricity on their own, so that means they have a set amount of charges, right?"

Argus nodded. "We're still working on a way for the gauntlets to produce their own electricity, but for now you'll have to use them sparingly."

"So can I use one?" Ryoko's eyes pleaded.

Argus smiled. "I'd be happy if you did." He then tossed one to Blaze. "And you too. I made two different sizes on purpose since I only had time to make two."

"Did you make anything else?" I asked.

He nodded. "I was able to make one other thing in the short amount of time I had. Well, improve upon something existing, really." We watched as he pulled out two communicators from the bag. "The military was working on some advanced features for the communicators. Many of them were useless, but two in particular turned out to be quite interesting." He held the communicator out toward me. "Eira, would you mind helping me demonstrate?"

"Uh, sure," I said, taking it. "What do you want me to do?"

"When I call you, I want you to press that oval-shaped blue button next to the tone dial," he instructed.

I nodded. He stood and walked to another area of the room. When he called, I answered it and a projection of Argus appeared in front of me. It wasn't the best hologram I'd ever seen, but it was easy to figure out it was him.

"Whoa," Ryoko breathed.

"Cool, right?" Argus said. "Eira, if you could, please click the blue button again and then face the communicator away from you and press the red button."

I nodded and did as he asked. When Ryoko gasped, I spun my head to look back at Argus. His communicator projected an image of the room on the wall. But it wasn't just an image. Genesis and Ryoko projected from the device, and they were moving. *A video feed?* I turned the communicator and the feed followed in real time. Video feeds were slightly different than moving holograms. Unlike holograms, which could only show one object at a time, video feeds were able to capture large areas. It was technology few had access to, mostly just news stations and the military, and they usually required larger equipment to function properly.

"Now that's even cooler," Ryoko said.

"How come Eira's side isn't projecting anything?" Raid questioned.

Argus grinned. "Glad you asked, because I'll be able to explain how these work as well. Using wavelength technology, science theories, and the proper mathematical equations, I was able to engineer a sensor that acts as a beacon and converter for sound waves. The sensor is capable of detecting two types of distinct signals that come from each projection mode, and by triangulating the exact—"

"Uh, Argus," I interrupted.

He blinked. "Yeah?"

"That doesn't make any sense to us," I said.

Ryoko waved her hand. "Yeah, speak dumb-person, please!"

Argus laughed as he rubbed the back of his head. "Sorry about that, I guess I got a little carried away there."

"We'll I'm not sure what they're talking about," Seda joked. "It was perfectly clear to me."

Ryoko snorted. "Then why don't you go have your smart-people party elsewhere?"

Shva'sika giggled. "Argus, how about if you try to explain in it a much simpler way, instead."

Argus nodded. "I'll try. Basically, I've installed a sensor that can send and receive images and live feeds. The sensors are currently only one-way, so only one person can work the projection at a time, requiring some coordination. Whoever activates the feed sensor first in the conversation will get the active projection. I'm hoping to figure out a way to change this soon."

"That's pretty impressive," Shva'sika complimented. "I think this advancement is an excellent find."

Genesis nodded. "I agree. How many have you made, Argus?"

"Just these two, I'm afraid," he admitted. "Naturally, they were more complicated to work on than the gauntlets. But they do interface just fine with the ordinary communicators."

Genesis nodded again. "That's fine. I want you to help Eira on her end of the assignment, so I believe two will suffice for now."

Argus nodded and then looked at me. "I'll give you my portable computer and teach you how to use it, so you can hack into any computer systems and grab valuable information."

"Okay," I said. What else could I say? I doubted I'd be able to use the device properly, but it didn't hurt to try.

"Now, does anyone have any questions?" Genesis asked. When no one replied, she nodded. "Good. I'll let you all prepare in any way you need. And if any questions should come up, I'll be in my room."

We watched her leave before going about our own business. Argus tapped me on the shoulder and I followed him back to his room so he could try, and likely fail, to get me to understand how his computer worked.

Rylan and I waited in silence on top of a building. No one else had shown up for our end of the assignment yet, but I wasn't going to worry, since the others executing the distraction hadn't reported in. Instead, I played with the night vision mode of my communicator that Argus had implemented last minute, and Rylan watched with amusement.

"We're in position on the south side of the compound," Ryoko called in.

"We're still getting ready on the northeast," someone replied. "But we'll be ready shortly."

"Rylan and I are the only ones here for the infiltration," I said. "Let's hope the others make it here soon, because I'm limited with what I'm able to carry."

"We are here," a woman replied back. "You're the one who isn't here."

Rylan and I glanced at each other before I spoke again. "Uh, I'm pretty sure I'm waiting on the east side of the compound."

"East side? The building is on the west side," she argued.

"No, it's on the east," Rylan said.

"Wow, really guys?" Ryoko chimed in. "This assignment is off to an amazing start already."

"Shut your mouth, Brute," the woman spat.

My lip curled. "And you watch your tongue. Or I'll be cutting it out."

"If you do, Eira, I wouldn't mind having it," Raikidan said. "Human tongues make for a nice stew ingredient."

Laughter from the two distraction groups came through the communicator, and I couldn't help be amused myself.

Of course the woman was far from happy. "Can we get back to the matter at hand?"

"We could if you'd admit you were on the wrong side of the camp." Rylan and I ducked when a large light shone up near us, and I kept my voice low when it went away. "Then we could actually start this assignment. This place is crawling with soldiers."

"The correct location is on the west side. If I have to I'll even call the Council for confirmation," the woman said smugly.

I was undeterred. "Go for it."

Everyone was quiet for some time before a guy spoke. "Alra is too shocked by the answer to tell you herself. We'll be arriving at your location on the east side soon."

Rylan and I chuckled and continued to wait until the group showed up. Unsurprisingly, they were all assassins, and I could only assume they were from Team One. Most greeted with a nod, except for one alluring woman, whom I could only assume was Alra.

Choosing to skip formalities, I spoke quickly. "Rylan will be keeping watch while we go inside. I have a modified communicator and portable computer that will help us break any security codes we run into."

They nodded, but it was the sandy blonde-haired man closest to me who spoke. "Several of us will also be staying out here as lookouts as well. Those heading inside all have separate assigned rendezvous points to drop off any finds."

I nodded. "Very good. Let's get this started. Ryoko, Blaze, you hear that? Do your stuff."

The response I received was a large explosion on the far end of the compound, and the group of us chuckled as soldiers panicked below us.

"They really know how to make an entrance," someone said.

Just then, the other side of compound lit up with activity and I laughed. "Looks like they didn't want to be outdone."

Rylan and the others laughed. All except one person. He was looking around.

"What's up with you?" I asked.

"I'm trying to find Chameleon," he said.

My eyebrow rose. "Chameleon?"

"Yeah, the Council assigned him to this assignment last minute, and he was with us until we had to meet up at this location."

"He's probably already inside," Alra said. "He'd be reckless enough to try to sneak in before it was time."

I grunted. "I'll drink to that accusation."

All conversation ended when Rylan held up his hand. He was peering through the scope of his sniper rifle. He flicked his gaze to us and nodded when he noted the area was clear enough for us to start getting to work.

I jumped to my feet immediately and slunk around the top of the building until I found an area that would be safe to jump down to. The rest of the assassins who were going inside followed. I kept the pace slow, as there were still several soldiers roaming around, but we were sure to knock out and hide the ones who weren't avoidable.

When we reached the door to the factory, I went to inspecting the special lock and found out rather quickly that I was going to need Argus' help. I dialed my signal to his communicator and waited for him to pick up.

"I'm here," he called in.

"I need guidance to open this door," I said. "It's a digital entry."

"Press the blue button so I can see it," he instructed. I did as he said, and bent closer so I could give him a better look. "Okay, that one is pretty easy. You see that small port on the side of the lock? Insert the smallest cord hanging off the portable computer. I'm at Aurora's computer station, so I'll be able to hack it from here."

I obeyed his instruction and watched as the computer came to life on its own and went to work. The others fidgeted behind me. When approaching footsteps echoed around the corner the muscles in my neck tightened, and I shifted my weight multiple times. *Hurry it up, Argus.*

The lock on the door clicked suddenly, and we entered the building and closed ourselves in before being seen. It was quiet, as if no one was inside, but well-lit unlike what I had anticipated. This made me rather paranoid as I activated the map of this place on Argus' computer and we crept down the hall.

I spun around and several assassins drew weapons when Alra gasped. Sticking out of the wall next to her was the disembodied head of a man with multi-colored hair and kaleidoscopic eyes.

I relaxed and tried to keep my voice quiet and stern, but not too harsh so I wouldn't spark any conflict. "You really shouldn't do that, Chameleon."

He rolled his eyes, his head movement causing his skin to shift colors rapidly. "Whatever. I just popped in to tell you I've temporarily disabled all building security systems. Ezhno says we have fifteen minutes before they're active again."

I nodded. "Then we move quickly. Everyone spread out and search every room you find. If you happen upon anyone working here, disable, but don't kill."

The others nodded and dispersed through the building. Only Chameleon and I remained, and he was just staring at me.

I gave him a funny look. "What?"

"Nothing," he said before disappearing into the wall.

I shrugged it off and set a quick pace down the hall until I came to a room that should have a computer to hack, based on the information my computer read to me. This room was dark, requiring me to activate the night vision on my communicator. There were already two other assassins in this room checking out the paperwork and weapons on the table, so I went straight to the computer to work. I did well with remembering what Argus taught me, but in the end, I had to call him for help. He, of course, found it amusing how close I had gotten before giving up.

Unable to do the hack remotely due to the sensitive nature of the computers, he walked me through the process. Once I was in, he relayed any algorithms needed to get past random security checks while stealing any information that I came across.

When things started to go a bit smoother, he let me take over and went about checking on the others in case they needed a hand.

When I was sure I wasn't going to run into any issues, I dialed my communicator's signal to Raikidan's to check in. "How are things going over there?"

"Yahoo!" Blaze hollered in the background. I couldn't help but laugh.

"That answer your question?" Raikidan asked. "I'm not sure who's having more fun, him or Ryoko. I think they have some sort of competition going on. They keep yelling out numbers to each other."

"That doesn't surprise me. If those two called the shots, they'd try to have more confrontations like this. It's what they're built to do, and they like it that way."

"And now he's down on the ground because he was shot in the leg."

He was so calm about the statement I couldn't help but snicker. "You know, that's not usually something you should be calm about."

"Well, I'm not overly fond of him."

I laughed. "You're such a jerk."

"And besides, he's getting back up like it was nothing."

"That's because of his early Brute design."

"Come again?"

"While our previous leader, Lord Taric, didn't modify experiments to the extreme, he did look into ways to improve us. During his time, he tried to give Brutes the ability of self-regeneration, and Blaze is one of those attempts. The project was failures overall, but most of the experiments did get an advantage out of it. Blaze has a slow healing ability that numbs him to pain, and regenerates certain wounds. That bullet hole will need proper healing in the end, but not nearly as much as someone else who would have gotten shot."

"And what about Ryoko's design?"

"Hers is a more perfect Brute design. Zarda traded the healing and regeneration idea for straight defense to add to their unnecessarily strong offense. Most Brutes now can harden their skin and can withstand a great deal of heavy fire."

"Interesting."

My communicator started to flash, indicating an incoming call. "Gotta go, new call." I cut the connection and picked up the other. "Yeah?"

"How are things going?" Argus asked on the shared mission line.

"Good so far. Transfer is slow, but these files are pretty big."

"That's a good sign. Usually their bigger files are the better ones."

"Let's hope."

Everyone in the room froze when a blaring alarm went off in the building and red emergency warning lights started flashing. *Oh shit.*

"I tripped a hidden security wire!" an assassin shouted through the communicator. "Everyone, get out now."

The assassins behind me grabbed whatever they could and ran for the door, but stopped when they realized I wasn't following.

"Commander, let's go!" one called.

"I can't," I said. "I need to get out of this computer properly or I'll lose everything."

"Don't worry about it," the other said. "Our lives are more important than the information."

"I'll be fine. Just get out of here. I'll be right behind you."

The two glanced at each other with uncertainty in their eyes, but left as I asked. I continued working quickly to finish my task.

"Eira, just unplug it and go," Argus urged.

"You told me if I just pulled this out while extracting information, I'd kill your computer," I reminded him. "I'm not doing that."

"Don't worry about it. I can replace it. I have all current files backed up."

"We need these files. I'm getting them."

He sighed. "I hope you know what you're doing."

My heart started to race when rushed heavy footsteps echoed down the hall. *C'mon, c'mon, c'mon. Move faster, computer!*

I almost snapped the transfer cord when I yanked it out the moment the transfer was complete. Tucking the computer away into a pocket for safe keeping, I ran for the door, but backed up immediately when I realized it was too late for me to leave that way. I searched for a place to hide but there was none. I was sure I'd have to fight for my life, until I noticed the corner of the room to my left was empty.

Taking a chance, I powered down my communicator and had my

armor cloth do away with my boots and gloves before I scaled up to the ceiling, where I suspended myself by using the two connecting walls and the hidden barbs in my skin. I gritted my teeth as I attempted to ignore the pain and tried to remain as still as possible. Not many understood these barbs weren't as great as most thought. Sometimes I found myself sticking to objects when I didn't want to, and they weren't strong enough to keep me suspended for long without causing pain. It was why I tried to only use them when scaling walls.

I slowed my breathing when three soldiers entered the room and swept the room with guns and flashlights at the ready. At the same time, I could feel myself slipping, and tried to be quiet as I tried to fix my positioning. The soldiers took their time searching the room, but I sent a prayer of thanks to the gods for their lack of intelligence to look above them or even turn on the lights.

The soldiers spun around and aimed their guns when a small creature scurried into the room. I tilted my head when they startled the cat, and watched as it reared up its hindquarters and fluffed out its tail. The soldiers relaxed and one made a call.

"We found a cat. I'm pretty sure it's what tripped the alarm."

I bit my lip as I watched the cat relax and become friendly with the soldiers, rubbing against their legs while the one soldier argued with someone else over the possibility of the cat being used as some sort of distraction. As cute at the cat was, I found the argument far more amusing.

We knew of the shapeshifting abilities the dragons had, but for some reason we never utilized it. I made a note to bring this up with the Council. This feline, and these idiot soldiers, made me realize just how useful the ability would be.

When the arguing ceased, the soldier went to pick up the cat but it scurried out of the room and down the hall, away from the door leading out of the compound. The soldiers pursued the cat, allowing me to climb down. *That's a bit convenient.* I couldn't help but feel bit skeptical about the situation now. Sure, it could be luck the cat went the way it did, but I wasn't so sure.

"Laz," Seda messaged.

"Yeah, I'm leaving," I said.

"No, you can't yet," she said. *"Chameleon is stuck inside with you. He was*

too reckless, and wasted too much energy to escape when the alarm went off. He's stuck in the room just down the hall to your left."

Left. Perfect. I knew it was too good to be true. *"Okay, I'll get him. Not sure how we'll get out together, but I have to try."*

"Check your right back pouch."

My brow furrowed with confusion and I checked. When my fingers touched an object that felt like a watch, I grinned. *"Did you put this in here?"*

"I saw two possible outcomes for this assignment. I thought I'd prepare you just in case."

"Seda, you're the best."

She chuckled, but didn't say anything more so I could concentrate on the task at hand. Peering around the corner, I noticed the cat was still scurrying around with the soldiers hot on its heels. *Slippery little beast, aren't you?*

I slunk down the hall and slipped into the next room. I looked around the room, but didn't see Chameleon. *If he moved, he's—*

Just then, Chameleon popped out of the wall near me and gasped for breath. I jumped.

"You shouldn't do that," I hissed. "You're going to get hurt if you push yourself."

"I thought you were a soldier," he muttered. "Why do you care anyway?"

I snorted. "I'm far quieter than those lumbering warthogs. And I care because we're in this together, regardless of any personal issues we may have. Seems in our time away from service, you've forgotten that's how I work. But that's not my problem. We need to focus on getting out of here."

"No shit."

"No need to be rude."

"Well unless you have a plan, then I'm going to be."

I held up the watch. "I do, but its success relies on you."

"Is that one of those prototype cloaking watches everyone is talking about?"

"Yeah, Argus is the one who developed them. Now, I need to know, if we get out of here, will you have enough energy to use your ability to get out of the compound? And if you can, can you use it on both of us?"

He nodded. "To both of your questions, I can, if you have water."

I chuckled and reached into one of my left back pouches and pulled out a water skin. "You're lucky I come prepared. Why do you need it?"

"If you must know, my design allows me to rearrange my molecular structure so I can merge with any substance, but in order to do so, I need to expend water. This makes my daily water need far greater than the average person. When I get too dehydrated, I can't merge my body with anything."

"No need to be rude about it," I muttered as I handed him the water.

"Not like you would have given me the water if I hadn't," he shot back before taking a swing.

"Actually I would have, but thanks for assuming I'm a heartless bitch like everyone else seems to believe. Now drink your water so we can get out of here. We don't have much time. That cat won't keep them distracted for long."

He watched me for a moment before taking another swig. "Tell me about your plan while I do."

"It's simple. I'll change my looks a little bit and pretend to capture you. Then I'll get us outside without issue and you get us out of here. We head our separate ways after that."

Chameleon nodded. "Simple enough. Soldiers are too afraid of us assassins to try to argue a possible order."

I also nodded. That reason was exactly why I didn't feel the need to be so sneaky about getting out of here. Other soldiers feared all assassins, I just happened to be feared more.

"Okay, I'm done," he announced.

"There's still water in the bag."

"I'm going to spill it on the floor, to make your convincing job easier."

"You don't need it?"

He shook his head. "There isn't enough to make a difference. I'll only be able to get us two blocks away, three at most, if we start just outside this building."

I nodded and activated the watch, turning my hair to a dark brown, and my eyes a pale blue. "Let's make a commotion then."

"Before you do, my real name is Asix." He shrugged. "Just in case you need to use it."

I nodded. What else could I do? I thought Chameleon was his true name. It wasn't uncommon for experiments to have unusual names like that.

Taking my silence at a cue to just continue, he dumped the water on the floor and then slammed the bag hard on the ground. I let him noisily knock things off a nearby table before I ran at him and tackled him to the ground. Using the armor cloth to my advantage, I crafted fake handcuffs and slapped them around his wrists just as a squad of soldier came running into the room.

They watched as I wrestled with Chameleon for a few moments until I came out victorious. I let out a hard breath, as if I had expended a lot of energy to grab him. "Finally caught you, you shady fox."

I climbed to my feet and forced him to follow.

"Well, it looks like the assassin gets the credit," a soldier grumbled.

I chuckled. "Credit for what? My hunt that has finally ended? Your little *cat-burglar* is your own issue. This is mine. Asix here has been giving me the slip for months. Though, your little kitty cat is the whole reason I caught him, so I'll think about giving you all some credit. Now if you'll excuse me, I have a captive to deal with."

"I can't let you do that, ma'am," one of the higher-ranking officers said. "Because he was caught during this infiltration issue, I can't allow you to take him."

I stared him down. "You will not take the credit for my capture. Now move out of my way."

He attempted to stand his ground but the longer my eyes bore into him, the more his nerves got the better of him. In the end, he relented. Chameleon struggled like he was supposed to as I hauled him down the hall, but his false struggle made it a bit difficult for me to get him out the door—not that I was going to complain. We just needed to keep up this act for a few more minutes.

I finally shoved the door open and pushed him outside. Chameleon calmed down and glanced about. The compound swarmed with soldiers, but as long as he wasn't going to ditch me, it wouldn't be a problem. Of course, if he managed to escape, I had this disguise and I could run after him.

The door didn't close behind me, as the other soldiers from before followed. I glanced back at them as the cat from before shot out into the open. I stopped walking and watched it skid to a halt. The little creature's head swiveled back and forth before approaching me and rubbing up against my leg, convincing me this cat definitely wasn't a real one. Not a chance. *It has to be Raikidan.*

So I bent over and scratched his head before picking him up with one hand. He purred and rubbed his head against mine, or tried to, as I made it hard for him by holding him down and away from my face.

"Assassins are so weird," someone murmured.

Someone hushed him. "Don't question their soft spot for animals."

I nearly chuckled. That accusation was pretty spot on. Almost all assassins did have a soft spot for animals. Most of us would refuse an assignment order if there were any threat of animals being harmed.

"I thought she was in a rush," someone whispered suspiciously.

"Her captive isn't struggling anymore, either," someone else observed.

I glanced over at Chameleon slyly, and he grinned at me. Immediately, I released him from his fake bindings and he grabbed me around the waist.

"Hold your breath and close your eyes," he ordered. "You too, cat."

I did as he said, and a strange sensation rushed over me. My body's molecular structure changed and moved through several types of materials. The sensation wasn't a pleasant one. *And I thought shifting was uncomfortable.* I was pretty sure I would have preferred shapeshifting.

I wasn't sure where we were, or how long we had been moving, but I held my breath as best as I could. I even held it once I suspected we had stopped.

Chameleon pulled away from me. "You're good."

I opened my eyes and took in a deep, quiet breath while taking in our surroundings. We stood on a rooftop several blocks away from the compound, its blaring alarms easily heard from here. Then I noticed Chameleon breathing rather heavily. "You okay?"

"I'm fine," he replied tersely. "It's just difficult doing that to someone else as well."

I nodded. "Thank you."

"Whatever. Who is your cat friend anyway? You never mentioned he'd be coming with us."

I flicked my eyes to Raikidan. "Yeah, about that…" Just then, he squirmed around and jumped out of my hands. When he shifted, I was taken aback to see a tall man with a muscular build like Raikidan, and appeared the same age as him, but this wasn't Raikidan. He had bronze skin, and hair that was so many colors I was certain he'd globbed it with paint. "Uh, you're not Raikidan."

The man's kaleidoscopic eyes danced with amusement at my revelation. "No, I'm not Raikidan. He was a bit tied up, so I came to help instead."

I eyed him. "Who are you?"

"It doesn't matter," he said. "We need to focus on getting to safety."

I didn't like that answer. He couldn't have been a dragon, and a druid or shaman would have known better than to avoid that question. He may have assisted with getting us out safely, but I didn't trust him.

I turned to tell Chameleon to head out on his own, but he was already gone. "Well, at least I don't have to worry about him anymore."

The mystery man chuckled. "Not much of a friend, is he?"

I walked to the edge of the building and looked around. "We're definitely not friends. I half expected him to leave me behind in that mess. Glad he didn't, but still surprised."

"Eira, who are you talking to?"

I whipped around to find Raikidan standing a little ways off. The mystery man was nowhere in sight.

"Raikidan? When did you get here?"

"Like three seconds ago, and I didn't see anyone with you while I had you in my sights, so why were you talking to yourself?"

"I wasn't talking to myself. I was talking to someone who evidently ditched me while I was speaking," I said. "What are you doing here?"

He had a look of disbelief but chose not to argue with me. "I'm here to help. Seda told me you could use some assistance, so I came to find you."

I nodded. "I appreciate it. I just need help blending into the city. I was planning on jumping down into this alley and pretend to be a jogger who likes to do her workout late at night."

He grinned. "Would you like a four-legged companion to complete that look?"

"I wouldn't protest."

He nodded, and the two of us climbed down into the alley below. Once I had my clothes changed into appropriate running attire, I changed a few of my features with the cloaking watch, and then used the armor to create a collar and leash for Raikidan, who had chosen to take the shape of an Alsatian.

As we jogged down the street, I couldn't get that mystery man out of my mind. Who was he, and where did he disappear to?

CHAPTER 34

The needle pricked my finger and I flinched. That was the third time in the past five minutes. Raikidan observed from his spot next to me on the bed. According to him, he had never seen anyone sew before, and since my explanation skills hadn't worked, he chose to watch me instead, although I was not the best person to watch. I sucked at sewing, but I needed to get this skirt made.

Shva'sika had told me I needed to get my shaman clothes ready for something, but she wouldn't tell me why. She had been running around like a headless chicken, so I wasn't surprised she had forgotten to explain, but a part of me felt she had intentionally not told me—it was just like her to do that.

I sighed and continued sewing. I wasn't going to be using my armor, so I needed to make new bottoms, and I decided to make them look like the ones I had come up with when we left the city for our vacation. Luckily, Seda knew a lot about making clothes, so she had made the cloth to the correct size it needed to be, and all I had to do was put it all together.

A knock sounded on my door, and Ryoko poked her head in. "Danika is back. Looks like she's going to explode with excitement. You may want to get out here."

I chuckled and put my work down. "All right, I'll be right there."

Ryoko poked her head out into the living room and nodded before looking back into my bedroom. "She says Raikidan too."

Raikidan slipped off the bed, and the two of us followed Ryoko into the living room. Shva'sika sat on the end of the couch closest to the window while everyone else in the house filed in. She didn't look to me like she was about to explode, but she could have calmed herself down by now, too.

"So are you going to share with the class this super-secret mission you've been on?" I teased.

She gave me a mild warning look and shook her head. I chuckled and remained standing when she gestured for people to take a seat.

Ryoko was nearly bouncing out of her seat, looking more excited to hear what Shva'sika had to say than Shva'sika herself did about telling us. "Well, spill the beans already!"

Shva'sika chuckled. "All right, all right. Genesis asked me to come up with an assignment for as many of you as possible, so I did some digging, and found out from several other shamans in the city that there's a meeting between the shamans and military tomorrow night."

"So a party?" Ryoko asked for clarification.

"In a sense, yes, but there's more to it. It's meant to strengthen the bond between the alliances, in hopes of keeping both sides happy. Apparently, according to my sources, the alliance Laz made with the South Tribe has something to do with it. Care to shed more light on this?"

I nodded. "Rick, a power hungry general, was leading a misguided attack on the South Tribe when Raikidan and I were in that location. That's what sprung my alliance with them. They agreed to come to the city and told me they'd find a way to convince Zarda that Rick had been wrong. This may be the end result."

Shva'sika nodded. "That sounds about right. Does the name Tla'lli ring a bell?"

I nodded. "That would be the shaman who contacted me first in the city. She's the South Tribe chieftain's daughter. Nice young woman. Will she be there?"

"Yes, she's a major figure in this meeting, as is her assigned body-guard... Talon, I think it was?"

"He's a soldier," I said, "and it doesn't surprise me he'd be assigned that duty. I gave Talon the order to convince Zarda the attack was misguided, and Rick had been executed on the spot for treason, since attacking a shaman tribe violates the pact made between the tribes and Zarda. It would only make sense Zarda assigned Talon to watch Tla'lli once convinced. Talon got along with her well making it rather fitting."

"Well that clears up a lot," Shva'sika said. "Now the question is, are you willing to go?"

I nodded. "Of course. I'd like to see them, and see what's going to happen during this meeting."

Ryoko's hand shot up. "I wanna go too!"

Shva'sika looked at Raikidan and Rylan. "Will you two, as well?"

The two of them nodded. There wasn't a reason for them not to. As my Guard, Raikidan didn't have much of a choice since I was going, and the two of them were just a bit over-protective anyway.

Zane answered, "We will be, just not in disguise. We were invited to this meeting already, so we're unable to say no at this point. I'll just have Blaze, Argus, and Raid join me. We'll come up with an excuse for everyone else's absence."

Shva'sika nodded. "I'm glad you're all on board with this. I just have one big favor to ask of Ryoko and Laz."

Ryoko and I glanced at each other, and then I eyed Shva'sika. "We're listening."

"The other shamans don't have an issue with us being there, but they requested something of us. To keep bonds strong, each side does something for the other. The military throws the party, and the shamans bring the entertainment. Unfortunately, the three shamans who were supposed to perform aren't going to be able to fulfill their end of the agreement, and we've been asked to fill their place if possible."

"Perform what?" Ryoko asked.

I suspected I knew what Shva'sika was getting at. There was one thing shamans prided themselves on when it came entertainment, so it didn't surprise me in the least that this was what they offered. "The entertainment we've been asked to provide is dancing, isn't it?"

Shva'sika smiled. "I figured you'd catch on."

"Is it a requirement to do this?"

Shva'sika shook her head. "No, it was just a friendly request, as it would help them out tremendously. We'll make sure no one knows it's you, if you're worried about that."

I nodded. "I'll do it."

Her brow rose in surprise. "Really?"

I shrugged. "Yeah, what's the harm?"

Ryoko's eyes flicked between us several times before shaking her head. "Wait, what? What are we doing? What did I just miss?"

The two of us chuckled and then Shva'sika spoke. "We're going to teach you something, if you're up for it."

"Um, okay."

"Do you think she'll be able to learn it in time?" I asked. "A day and a half isn't exactly long enough time to learn something so complicated."

"We need a third person. That's what will be expected for this dance. We'll just have her learn the basics and incorporate it. You know how diversified these dances can be."

"True."

"Can someone tell me what it is I'm going to be learning?" Ryoko demanded.

Shva'sika chuckled and pulled her off the couch. "Bellydancing."

"Whoa, Eira knows something like that?" Blaze relaxed on the couch. "That's hot."

I rolled my eyes and headed down the hall. "We'll take the music room. It's the biggest and most private. Oh, and, Ryoko, make sure you wear something loose and comfortable."

"But you're not." My clothes changed into a loose cropped shirt and comfortable cotton pants in response. "Okay, never mind. I'll go change."

"I'll finish your sewing project for you." Seda said telepathically.

"Thanks, Seda. I owe you."

"Don't worry about it. It makes me feel useful."

"I'll see if I can get you into the party, how does that sound?"

"I... I don't think that would be a good idea..."

"Worried you won't get a nice date to bring you?"

"Laz, stop it! You know there will be psychics there and that's the reason. It would definitely be too dangerous for me to go."

I chuckled and continued down the hall. She was lying, but if she didn't want to go, then I wasn't going to make her—or convince a certain brainiac to take her.

I looked around, as the small group I pretended to converse with gave me a little cover. The atmosphere was much different at this party than it had been when it was just military and military supporters. *It's far tenser.*

So far I hadn't found Tla'lli, but then again, I hadn't met any shamans I knew. Most of the shamans I had come in contact so far were from the East and North Tribes, including the ones I was supposedly speaking with now. Shva'sika, on the other hand, knew everyone she ran into, but that didn't surprise me.

"Your friend is here now," Raikidan whispered.

I scanned the room until I found her. As she was forced to converse with every soldier who tried to speak with her, the poor elven woman struggled to keep a pleasant expression on her face, and her shoulders every now and then rolled forward, as if fighting the need to protect herself. Talon, who stood next to her, put on a calm façade, but I could see how on edge and unhappy he really was with all the attention Tla'lli had to endure.

"Looks like it's time to say hello." I looked back into the small group. "Please excuse us."

"Of course, Ambassador," they murmured.

I rolled my eyes as I left. *Ambassador.* Another one of Shva'sika's *brilliant* ideas. No, I couldn't blame her. She was just the messenger. Apparently, because of the alliances I was offering, the tribes had decided to bestow me with the greatest honor title they could offer. I was to be their *ambassador,* even though I was leading them down a path of war and bloodshed, not peace. Not to mention—I wouldn't be acting politically with Zarda in a direct way. I wasn't going to have contact with him at all, which is what an ambassador would do. It was a stupid title, and a stupid idea.

I put on a smile as I approached Tla'lli. "Tla'lli!"

Tla'lli turned her gaze on me and a smile spread across her face. "Laz'shika!" She embraced me with a strong hug and I returned the gesture. "It's good to see you again."

"The feeling is mutual, my friend. It's been far too long," I said.

"A few weeks isn't that long," she argued.

"It depends on how you look at it."

Tla'lli shifted her gaze to Raikidan. "I see Raikidan still follows you around as faithfully as ever."

Raikidan crossed his arms. "Do I have to remind you again that I'm no dog?"

She smirked. "Every time."

He grunted and she and I both laughed. I was glad he was able to go along with things so well. It would make life far too difficult had he not been able to.

Tla'lli controlled herself and gestured to Talon. "You both remember Talon, yes?"

"Of course," I said.

Talon nodded respectfully. "It's a pleasure to meet you again, Ambassador Laz'shika."

I couldn't help but roll my eyes. "As with you, Talon, although you seem a little more uptight than the last time we met."

Talon's eyes shifted elsewhere, showing how unhappy he was about me pointing that out. He didn't like being uptight.

"How's your father doing, Tla'lli?" I asked.

"He's about the same. I worry about him, especially since I haven't been able to go home to see him myself, but he won't lie to me, so I know his letters are truthful, and that keeps my mind at ease."

"Good. I believe he still has a lot of fight in him. He won't be gone from this world any time soon."

"I hope you're right." Tla'lli pulled a crystal orb out of a pouch and looked at Talon. "Would you mind getting me something to drink?"

Talon nodded. "Of course."

"Raikidan, why don't you go with him?" I didn't take my eyes off the orb.

Raikidan followed Talon wordlessly, and Tla'lli placed both hands on the orb. It began to glow with a white light, and then the world around us grayed and slowed down. We were the only ones who weren't affected.

"This must be important," I said. "No one just uses a *time relic* on a whim."

"I don't know when I'll get the chance to stop by your place and talk with you," she admitted. "They expect me to do so much right now."

"It's because Zarda doesn't trust you. But don't take that personally. He doesn't trust anyone because he himself isn't trustworthy."

She nodded. "It was hard convincing him that general was lying. I had to come in and give Talon a hand."

"He's never been a good liar."

Tla'lli nodded again. "That was what made it hard. He had a silver tongue once he was able to tell the truth."

"How did you get stuck with him anyway?"

"Well, it's not all that complicated. Once we explained the situation to Zarda and I spoke with him in hopes of strengthening our alliance, he assigned Talon to protect me. It didn't matter if I was here or back in the village."

I thought that over. That didn't seem right. "It sounds like Zarda thinks Talon will act as a spy and report to him if anything is amiss."

"Well, good thing we don't do anything wrong."

I poked her arm. "Now you guys are."

"Well then it's a good thing Talon is on our side."

I laughed. "I can tell you're getting along with him well."

She nodded. "He's really nice. A little on edge when he's talking with me or the other women of the village, but that's the only thing that bothers me about him so far."

"You'll get used to that. He does his best to not offend women as much as possible, so it makes him a bit paranoid."

"But not everyone can be pleased."

I shrugged. "Try telling that to him. I gave up."

"Then I won't tell him about how unhappy he makes the older women, in particular the elven women."

My brow rose. "How does he do that?"

"Well, since I'm of age to marry now, they think I should be looking for a nice suitor, and not just friends. They don't think he makes good suitor material, so they feel he needs to keep his distance."

I chuckled. "Let old people be old. You don't seem to care either way."

She let out a deep sigh. "I don't want that lifestyle right now. I'm young and I don't need someone by my side when I take over the tribe. It's not a requirement."

I nodded. "Well at least you're doing what you want. I've seen many in your position sacrifice their own happiness to make others happy."

I watched her as she glimpsed back at Talon, who moved slowly at a table. "Although, I'm getting the feeling your thoughts and choices may be changing."

She glared at me. "Don't you start. Others have that crazy idea in their heads too."

I held up my hands. "Easy. I'm just making an observation. That doesn't make me right. No need to get your panties in a knot." She snorted and I refrained from smiling. "So is there anything else you needed to speak to me about?" I peered past her, spotting the two men making their way back to us. "We're running out of time."

"I can't think of anything else. The convincing went well with the other tribes. I know you've had help with various shamans in these past few weeks, but now that the other tribes have officially decided to help, they're going to be sending more shamans they feel are qualified for this task in small groups, so they don't draw any unwanted attention. I'll be notifying you or Shva'sika when everyone is ready to help out more."

"Shva'sika would be a better choice. She's more involved with sha- man affairs than me, since I have a public image to maintain."

"Then maybe we should make her the Ambassador instead of you."

I blew out a heavy breath through my lips, my shoulders sagging. "Please do."

Tla'lli laughed. "It's not that bad. I'm not sure if Shva'sika told you, but the position of Ambassador is real. It's rarely given out since there are so few worthy of the task. The Ambassador's job is just to keep peace between the tribes, which may sound easy to most, but it can be quite difficult since we all think a bit differently. You won't have to worry about the military at all. That's the job of the tribe leaders."

I grunted. "Fine by me."

"It would be a bad idea to put you in that kind of position anyway."

I nodded in agreement before looking past her to see that the men were now much closer. Tla'lli noticed as well. We needed to end this before they reached us. Tla'lli sent a pulse of energy through the time relic, and the world sped itself back up to normal. She hid the orb before Talon and Raikidan reached us. I took a deep breath to make sure I was collected. Times orbs were one of the last remaining *magic relics* left in Lumaraeon from before the time of the War of End. Using one sometimes messed with the body, so it was best to make sure I'd be capable of functioning normally after participating in its use.

Raikidan handed me a small glass filled with an amber liquid. "This is all I could find that I figured you'd like. I think it's alcoholic."

I nodded my thanks, but before I could take a sip of the liquid, Shva'sika and Ryoko came over to us. They didn't say anything, so I knew it was time. We weren't to speak about the performance around the soldiers. That was the rule she had placed down. They weren't supposed to know who was performing.

I gave my drink back to Raikidan. "Please excuse me."

I followed the two out of the crowded room through a pair of double doors concealed behind a wood room divider screen, and into a small side room that had been converted into a dressing room.

Ryoko pulled down her hood when the doors were shut. "Hey, Danika. Can I ask you something a little weird?"

Shva'sika chuckled. "You never ask anything weird."

"I beg to differ," I muttered.

Ryoko shoved me, and I fell down on a bed of pillows and laughed. "Anyway, my weird question is, why don't the four different shaman tribes have actual names, instead of just compass point names? From what I've gathered, they're not in those exact point positions, so it doesn't make much sense."

Shva'sika sat down in the bed of pillows near me and patted a spot next to her to encourage Ryoko to sit. "That's not a weird question at all. To be forthright, the tribes don't actually have names. Ages ago, when there were more villages, they were places where shamans congregated during pilgrimages and jobs. Things changed after the War of End pushed most life to the east side of Lumaraeon."

A melancholy expression briefly crossed her face. "Only four villages endured the devastation. This is when they became true places of living for shaman; going as far as developing distinctive cultures for each. Those outside the culture insisted on giving a name to each place, even though we didn't want to. So that's how we ended up with directional names, given that was their placement on the new maps of the time"

"Why didn't you want to name your homes?" Ryoko asked.

"Because it would defeat the purpose of being shamans. It's about the shamans, not the villages, and that's why it's the shamans who receives the special names, and why it doesn't matter what you call the villages." A smile crossed Shva'sika's lips. "Of course, for cartography and travel purposes, it does make sense to come up with names, so I do agree those in charge at the time should have come up with something. Would have been better than what we work with now."

Ryoko tilted her head. "The shamans get the good names? I thought they were just earth shaman, fire shaman, water shaman and whatever else you guys can be."

"Well, you're partially correct. The way you just described them is one common way, but there are others."

"Okay, so—to make it less confusing to me, give me examples while you explain this to me."

Shva'sika smiled. "I'll use Laz as an example then. To everyone who knows she is a shaman or sees her in her shaman clothes and uses fire, she is called a fire shaman, or on rarer occasions, a Shaman of the Flame. But her true title is a Shaman of the Rising Sun."

Ryoko's eyes widened. "That is a really cool name! What are all the others?"

Shva'sika chuckled at her enthusiasm. "Well, there are the water shaman, who are also called Shaman of Water, and their true title is a Shaman of the Rising Tides. Then we have the earth shaman, who are also called Shaman of the Earth, and have a true title of Shaman of the Fractured Crystal. Next we have wind shaman, or Shaman of the Sky, and their true title is a Shaman of the Whispering Winds."

Ryoko looked like she was about to explode, and I couldn't help but finish off the titling. "Then there's the ice shaman, who are also known as Shaman of the Snow, and their true title is a Shaman of the Frozen Waste. Next we have lightning shaman, who are also called Shaman of Lightning, and their true title is a Shaman of the Dancing Lights. And lastly we have healing shaman, who are also known as Shaman of Healing, with a true title of Shaman of the Cleansing Spirit."

"Those are severely cool names!" Ryoko then began to count her fingers. "So there are a total of seven elements then?"

"Well ice is considered a sub-element, but there are also metal shamans, since metal is considered a sub-element as well." I turned my head toward Shva'sika. "Then again, metal shamans don't have titles. Why is that?"

Shva'sika shrugged. "I'm not fully sure, but it might have to do with two factors. One, they're rarer than Shamans of the Whispering Winds, and two, they can only bend impure metal, so they feel like they're still Shaman of the Fractured Crystal."

"That makes sense," I mused.

"What do you mean by impure metal?" Ryoko questioned.

"I mean it still has a high concentration of earth in it. Copper and steel are good examples. This is why it's a sub-element. It relies on the main earth element to bend this new form."

"So in the case of ice, it needs water in order to freeze, making it a sub-element?"

"That's exactly right. Some believe lightning is a sub-element of fire, but in fact, they're completely different."

Ryoko giggled. "I feel smart."

The two of us laughed at her. She was too cute for her own good sometimes.

"Now I have another question. Why is it that we're wearing cloaks and the shamans from the South Tribe aren't?" Ryoko asked.

"That has to do with the pact we signed. In order for us to remain neutral, we're not supposed to hold jobs in the city, aside from the traveling caravans," Shva'sika explained. "The South Tribe shamans have no desire to own shops or work in the city, so they freely show their faces. The rest of us like holding jobs outside our tribes, so we hide our face so our true identity is never found out, giving us that freedom. The South Tribe shamans think of us as cowards, but we prefer it this way."

Ryoko blinked. "How does being neutral prevent you from having jobs?"

"We would take away from others having jobs, meaning wouldn't be neutral in the eyes of Zarda."

"So why are caravans allowed?"

"They aren't permanent. They come with wares and trade-goods from all over Lumaraeon that the local shops won't have, and they only stay for short periods of time, so shops don't lose all their business and money."

Ryoko's nose scrunched. "That's so dumb."

"When does anything we're forced to agree to have a smart backing to it?" I questioned.

Ryoko grunted. "Good point."

"I just worry about the South shamans," I voiced. "They aren't going to change their ways and if they're going to aid us, their lack of privacy is going to get them into trouble."

Shva'sika nodded. "I agree, and they're also going to have a harder time blending in since they have such a unique appearance."

Ryoko nodded. "They are hard to miss."

Our conversation ended there when three figures walked into the room. They were shamans, but it was best not to talk about shaman affairs with them in front of Ryoko. Shamans were friendly and hospitable, but not all were okay with the idea of non-shamans meddling in the affairs of shamans.

The three shamans pulled down their hoods and smiled at us. All three were women; one appeared to be from the South Tribe and the other two from the North Tribe. I guessed the South Tribe shaman to be one of fire, while the North Tribe to be ice and… earth, since her hair color was quite *normal.* In their arms they carried folded bundles of clothes and body jewelry.

"Those must be our costumes," Shva'sika observed.

The fire shaman was the first to answer. "There are costumes for the Shaman of the Rising Sun, Shaman of the Dancing Lights, and the Shaman of the Fractured Crystal."

Ryoko's head snapped in multiple directions. "Where's the earth shaman you're talking about?"

"It's you silly," the ice shaman scolded playfully.

That would make sense why these women don't appear upset with Ryoko being here. They think she's one of us. They weren't too far off, that was for sure. Ryoko had quite a few earth shaman qualities.

Ryoko's brow furrowed. "What? I think you're a little confused. I'm the last person you'd want playing with the elements. It'd be a disaster zone."

Shva'sika giggled. "Ryoko, you have a lot of qualities of an earth shaman, or at least, an earth elementalist."

"Yeah? Then prove it."

"Strong," I listed.

"Stubborn," Shva'sika remarked with a smile.

"Sexy as hell," I added.

Ryoko's face scrunched. "What does that have to do with anything?"

The earth shaman holding Ryoko's clothes handed them over to Ryoko. "Earth elementalists and Shaman of the Fractured Crystal have a high tendency to be easy on the eyes, so to speak."

"Well, nu-humans are supposed to have a higher than average rate of being lookers, so it's not that hard for someone like me," Ryoko mumbled. "But I'm still not convinced about any of this."

"Ryoko, how hard can you hit?" Shva'sika inquired.

"Um, pretty hard I guess."

"Hard enough to crack earth?"

"Well yeah. That's easy."

Shva'sika smiled. "You say it's easy when not many would find it that way."

"Yeah, but I'm altered to do that. That doesn't mean I'm an earth shaman or elementalist. Just means I'm freakishly strong like I was designed to be."

"Laz was altered and can use fire, but does that disqualify her from being a shaman and elementalist?"

Ryoko thought this over. "No, I guess not."

"Then you being strong because of alterations doesn't disqualify you either. With training, it is possible for you to control the earth, like other elementalists."

"Still don't think it's a good idea," Ryoko muttered.

We laughed at her. She wasn't going to give in, and that only reinforced how right we were.

I stood when the fire shaman handed me my clothes. I laid them out on a table and my brow furrowed. "Shva'sika, I think there's a mistake."

Shva'sika glanced up from looking at her clothes. "What do you mean? They look right to me. You knew the tops would be small."

"There isn't anything in this bundle that'll hide our faces." I held my hands out at Ryoko when she answered for me.

Shva'sika giggled. "Of course not. Your face needs to be seen for the dance. It adds to the atmosphere. Laz, you know that as well as I do."

The corner of my eyes tightened. "We can't do that! Soldiers in there know us, and if they see our faces, we're screwed."

Shva'sika smiled. "We're not if they can't remember it's us."

My brow furrowed. "What?"

"We spiked the drinks," the fire shaman said. "The drug we put in them makes it so the memory of anyone who drinks it gets all screwy. When they look at you, they won't be able to piece together who you are, and by tomorrow morning they won't remember much of what happened tonight, so they'll think they just drank too much."

I narrowed my eyes. "Which drinks?"

She blinked, her eyes innocent. "All of them."

Ryoko gasped. "But Rylan and I drank some of that stuff!"

Shva'sika chuckled. "Calm down, Ryoko. Do you remember the blue pill I gave you?" She nodded and I also recalled the pill she made me take. "That pill negates the effect of the drug. So unless you drink too much, or your memory is bad to begin with, you should remember everything that happens tonight."

I laughed. "That is absolutely diabolical! Do you guys do this at every party you're forced to attend?"

"Yeah, basically," the three shamans replied together.

I laughed some more. That was the worst thing I had ever heard of a shaman doing. I could barely believe they were actually doing it. "So Zane and the boys, did they get a pill too?"

"Well I gave one to Zane, Argus, and Raid, but I might have *accidentally* forgotten to give one to Blaze," Shva'sika said.

Ryoko and I laughed. If what they were telling us was true, there was so much potential to rub what he forgot in his face tomorrow.

I shook my head. "Man, now I wish I could find some twins and convince them to give him a quick kiss."

Shva'sika's brow rose. "Why?"

Ryoko giggled. "Because Blaze has a thing for twins. If we had some twins give him a kiss, he won't be able to remember it happening, and we could rub it in his face."

"I think we can help you on that one," the ice shaman said.

My brow rose. "Really?"

The fire and ice shamans exchanged a glance and then the ice shaman smiled at me. "We know two ladies who wouldn't mind doing you that favor. It's the least we could do, since you are filling in for this dance on such short notice."

I waved my hand lazily. "The soldiers must be entertained. But if you could get that done for me, I'd appreciate it. It would make having to do this that much better."

The shaman laughed and excused herself so she could talk to the two women she had spoken of. I just hoped if they did agree to it, I'd be able to witness it. That would make the taunts that much more rewarding.

Looking down at the clothes I was supposed to wear, I sighed and dressed. The top and pants were simple enough, but when it came to the body ornaments and makeup, I was at a loss.

The fire shaman cocked her head. "You looked confused."

"I've just never worn so many ornaments when dancing before." I chewed my lips. "And my makeup skills aren't the best. I can manage the basics, but this is a whole other level. I don't know where to start."

The shaman chuckled. "I see. Well, then you've never worn a traditional tribal dance costume, have you?"

It was my turn to be amused. "No, I guess I haven't."

The woman assisted me with the makeup first, and then the ornaments. "Many of these belong to Tla'lli. She insisted you use them tonight, so don't ruin them."

"I wouldn't dream of it."

The woman smiled. "Good, now let's get this veil on you and we'll get you on your way."

She secured the veil, and I turned and faced my companions when I was ready. Ryoko and Shva'sika wore outfits different from mine, veil aside, but ones I was more accustomed to wearing.

Ryoko spun in circles. "Does this make me look fat?"

I snorted and Shva'sika laughed. "Of course not."

"It doesn't make me look too large in the chest, right?"

"Ryo, you look fine, stop fussing," I chided.

Her ears twitched. "How come we don't get clothes like yours?"

Shva'sika giggled. "Because Laz has to take the place of the tribal dancer from the South Tribe while we are filling in for the West and North."

Ryoko cocked her head. "No East?"

Shva'sika shook her head. "They're not ones for these types of dances. They're usually too focused on inventing to bother with learning traditional dances and customs."

"Fair enough. So what's with the veil we have to wear?"

Shva'sika shrugged. "It just completes the outfit."

"So I could not wear it? It's a little annoying."

"Yes, but what reason would you have to not wear it? It can help with concealing your identity up front, even if it's only a little bit."

"I'll deal with it, then."

My eyes squinted as a smirk twitched onto my lips. "Besides, I think Rylan might find it quite enjoyable."

Ryoko face reddened. "Laz, stop teasing me about that!"

"Aww she's so cute when she's embarrassed," Shva'sika joined in.

Her fists curled by her side. "Guys!"

Shva'sika grabbed Ryoko's shoulders and leaned close. "You'd worry if we didn't."

Ryoko huffed. We peered over at the door when a knock rapped on it. The ice shaman from before reentered. "Everything is set up for all of you. I am going to warn you, the soldiers are a bit rowdy right now. I think they're having a little extra to drink tonight."

I rolled my eyes. "Oh wonderful."

"Zarda is probably going to send them off to take over some town or city tomorrow," Ryoko said.

I nodded. "I wouldn't doubt it. Even during peace talks, he's plotting war tactics and scheming over the best areas to conquer."

Shva'sika rolled her eyes. "You two need to stop thinking about work and start thinking about this dance."

Ryoko pouted. "But I'm not going to be any good."

"You'll do fine." Shva'sika pushed Ryoko toward a door I hadn't noticed before. "For someone who had never done it before in her life, you did well during practice."

"But Laz does better!"

"I've been doing this longer," I reminded her.

"Since when do you know how to dance anyway?" Ryoko asked.

I shrugged. "After being at the West Tribe for a while, I felt obligated to participate in the customs. Plus, I needed something to help keep my female figure, with Daren trying to fatten me up."

Ryoko laughed and then stopped when something crossed her mind. "Wait a minute. You mean to say you've known how to dance all this time? You were always telling me you didn't know how to dance and had no desire to learn."

"Ryoko, I know real dances, not that repulsive form you do at the club."

She winked. "You wouldn't find it so repulsive if you picked a particular hunky dance partner."

I did my best to repress the flush that threatened to spread across my face. "Ryoko, don't start."

"Oh, will you just admit it already? There's no shame in it."

"Ryoko, I mean it."

"Laz and Raikidan sitting in a—"

"Ryoko!"

Shva'sika and the other shamans laughed. "Can't you two get along, even for a little while?"

Ryoko and I both tilted our heads a bit. "We are getting along."

Shva'sika laughed again. "If you two say so. Just stop bickering and collect yourselves."

"Where does this hall lead us to anyway?" I asked.

"To a small, secret room under the main party hall," the ice shaman explained as she led us. "It's been modified to have a lift that will bring you up to the small platform where you'll dance."

"You guys obviously do this a lot," Ryoko said.

"Well, we used to," the shaman said. "But over the years, our ties with this city have worsened, and the parties stopped happening. Now that we've pretended to put some effort into improving them, they'll be happening a lot more."

"What are your standings like with the other cities Zarda doesn't control?" Ryoko asked.

"We have more freedoms, if that's what you're wondering." We stopped walking when we came to a room filled with blankets and pillows. "But we don't have time for that. Enter the room, and once you're in position I'll have it lift you up. I'm not sure what your dance consists of, but when you face me, your backs will be to the audience."

The three of us filed in and sat down in a line facing the door. Shva'sika nodded and the shaman pressed a button. Creaking and clicking noises were heard and then the floor of the room we were in began to move. The ceiling over us slid away, allowing us to see the dimmed ceiling of the main party hall and hear the music we were to dance to as it began to start up softly.

I folded myself over so I laid partially on the floor in front of my body. As we drew closer to the room, my heart began to pound. Even though half of the audience wouldn't remember this, there were quite a few who would, many of them I knew and would have to put up with long after the party.

"Take it easy, everything is going to go well," came a feminine voice.

I narrowed my eyes. *"Who are you? I don't enjoy psychics in my head."*

"A friend." I refrained from snorting. *"Just relax. You won't do well unless you do."*

"I thought you said it's going to go well."

"It will once you relax."

I sighed and did my best. The floor stopped moving when we came level with the platform, and I listened. There were very few who were talking, and it was making my heart beat even faster, making it hard to hear the music for my start cue. I wasn't doing well when it came to relaxing.

"Eira, they're too drunk and drugged to know it's you."

"They're not the ones who are getting me worked up." The music cued the note I was looking for, and I began to move my shoulders like we had rehearsed.

"Your friends won't say anything after. They'll enjoy this performance but they're supportive, and won't say anything that would upset you. I promise."

I took a deep breath and slowed my heart to match my movements. I forgot about the crowd watching. I forgot about wondering what they were thinking. It was just the music and my slow arm and hip movements. Or it was, until the routine made us face the crowd. My heart raced again, but I did what I could to make it look like nothing was bothering me. I needed to keep this dance looking as sensual as possible.

Nothing worked. I needed something to keep my focus. My eye scanned the room as I turned my head with the music and locked onto one person. Raikidan sat at a small table next to Rylan, surrounded by friends and enemies alike, relaxing in his chair with an arm over the back of it and another grasping a small glass of liquor on the table.

"If you get too nervous, find something or someone to focus on." I remembered Shva'sika explaining to Ryoko during practice. *"It's easier if it's a person, though. You can pretend you're dancing just for them."*

Could I pretend I was dancing for him? I locked on to Raikidan where I thought I'd be having eye contact if his hood hadn't been blocking his face. Raikidan pulled the glass up to his lips and he relaxed more in his chair and a grin spread across his face. My heart slowed to a normal pace. *I can pretend. He's the only one I can pretend with.*

Soldiers made comments and whistled as we performed moves that I already knew they'd react to, but none of that mattered to me. My focus was Raikidan and as long as he reacted in ways that made this easier for me to do this, then that was all that mattered.

The lights began to dim and my movements slowed. This was the part of the dance I had been dreading. Shva'sika had decided that we'd do small solos, and I was going to be the last one so I could end it. For now, I was to remain still as Ryoko did her part in a light spotlight, but that only made my heart race again. I wouldn't be able to use Raikidan as a focus.

Shva'sika was next, as the spotlight dimmed from Ryoko and sparks flashed from Shva'sika's fingers as she clicked them together. They were her light, and they made her movements look slower than normal. The audience approved of the spectacle. But all too soon, her lights began to fade and my turn arrived.

Taking a slow breath to calm myself, I moved one hand over my mouth to snatch a small flame and the other to untie the thin scarf on my hips. When Shva'sika's part ended, I grasped the scarf with the hand with the flame and lit it. It was only show fire, but that didn't matter to the audience. My movements were fluid, and the scarf acted as a beacon and lit up my movements.

The scarf floated over me as my *snake arms*, as Ryoko called them, moved in slow motions over me and my legs moved below me. I briefly switched my show fire to real fire to destroy the scarf, and then organically moved the fire around my body's sensual movements.

I sensed Ryoko and Shva'sika moving behind me as they got in position, signaling the dance was finally ending. My feet moved me backward as I lined up with the others. My movements became bigger and the fire larger, lighting up the stage.

Shva'sika and Ryoko matched my arm movements and when the music queued, we clapped our hands together. The fire exploded into a bright light and the floor below us dropped. I blinked frantically to try to get my eyes to adjust to the new darkness, but the blinking didn't helped. The only thing I knew was that the audience liked what they had seen.

"Laz, you okay?" Shva'sika whispered.

"Yeah, just trying to get my eyes adjusted."

"Keep them closed for a few moments. That should help better than blinking."

I nodded and did just that. When the platform reached its lowest point I opened them again. My sight wasn't perfect, but it was better and improving by the second.

"That was quite impressive," the ice shaman complimented. "Of course, I didn't get a chance to see all of it, but from what I saw, it was nice, and from the sound of it, the end was better. We might just have you fill in more often."

"I'll pass," Ryoko muttered as she walked into the hallway.

I cocked my head. "Ryoko, you okay?"

"Yeah, I just need to sit."

I followed her into the dressing room and sat down next her as she relaxed with a sigh into the bed of pillows. "Are you sure you're okay?"

"Yeah, just trying to calm down." She took a deep breath. "That was stressful."

"You did well."

Her ear drooped. "I nearly screwed it all up."

"Didn't look like it."

Ryoko snorted. "Yeah, right."

"Ryoko, you did great!" Shva'sika encouraged. "You really did."

Ryoko sighed. "I don't feel like I did."

A sly grin slipped up half my face. "Just ask Rylan when we get back out there. I bet he'll let you know what he thought."

She pushed me over and I laughed. A shaman I had never met before came around the room divider screen with a bundle of clothes in her hands and handed them to us. We thanked her and dressed ourselves in our normal attire. Once dressed and the dance costumes were folded and piled neatly, we made our way into the main party hall. I could feel eyes on us everywhere as we came around the divider screen, but I ignored them, which helped Ryoko keep calm.

When we joined our little group of friends they didn't act out of the ordinary, much to my surprise. Blaze didn't seem to know who we were, but that was to be expected by now. Rylan grabbed Ryoko and pulled her closer to him so he could whisper something in her ear. She laughed in response and pushed him away playfully, her nervousness now gone. Whatever he had said must have helped.

Raikidan slid his glass of liquor to the edge of the table and motioned me to come closer. Complying, I took the glass and nodded my thanks but before I could take a sip he grabbed hold of me and pulled me into his lap. But that wasn't all he did. He slipped his hand inside my cloak and rested his hand on the opposite hip, preventing me from getting back up.

"Raikidan, what are you doing?" I asked.

"Nothing."

"Let go of me."

Raikidan grinned. "I don't think so."

I attempted to get away. "Let go."

Raikidan pulled me closer. "Nope."

"I said let go." He was starting to make me feel weird.

Raikidan continued to grin and rested his chin on my shoulder. "No."

I couldn't believe him. What was with him? Yes, I could smell the alcohol on his breath, but he couldn't be drunk yet.

A soldier chuckled behind us. "Watch it, boy. You might go and get yourself into trouble."

I turned to see Zo. *Why can't I escape this guy?*

Shva'sika laughed. "Too late. He's always in trouble with Laz'shika."

"That's not what I meant," Zo said.

"Don't tell me you believe that rumor."

"Of course I do."

"What rumor?" Ryoko asked.

Shva'sika smiled. "That's right, this is your first time here, Ren'ka. The soldiers here believe it's forbidden for Guards to have personal relationships with their charges."

Ryoko turned her head toward Rylan. "I guess I have to stop seeing you then."

Rylan chuckled and took a sip of his drink.

"Wait, she's a Guard?" Zo sounded shocked.

Shva'sika smiled. "Oh, that's right. They also think only men are Guards."

Ryoko laughed. "Okay, I'm sorry, but you guys are dumb."

"Ren'ka," Shva'sika scolded.

Ryoko lowered her head. "Sorry."

"Go easy on the girl, Shva'sika." I looked up to see two identical South Tribe shamans strolling up to us. "She's always been one to speak her mind, and it happens to be the thoughts most of us are thinking."

"It doesn't make it any less rude, Ne'la," Shva'sika said firmly.

The one called Ne'la fixed her gaze on me. "Thank you, Ambassador, for filling in for our older sister. She would have loved to see it."

"How is she doing?" I asked, playing along as if I knew her.

"Stubborn like always, so healers won't be giving her a hand for some time."

I chuckled. "You and your sister would be the same in her situation."

"That is true."

Ne'la's sister tugged on Ne'la's elbow and it was apparent her sister was either one of few words or mute. Either way, Ne'la understood what her sister wanted.

"Please excuse us. El'na has reminded me of someone we must find."

The two women excused themselves, but as they passed Blaze they took great interest in him. With small grins, the two moved closer to Blaze and planted a kiss on his cheeks at the same time. I grinned. Tomorrow morning was going to be fun.

Blaze blinked with bewilderment as the two pulled away and walked off. "Hold on. Tell me what I did right so I can do it again."

Neither woman acknowledged him as they walked away and the group laughed at him. Blaze pouted but my attention left him when Raikidan began acting weird again.

"I told you to stop it," I said.

"Raikidan, Laz'shika, why don't the two of you cool it outside for a bit. We don't need it getting too hot in here," Shva'sika teased.

I went to reply, except Raikidan stood suddenly. I lost my balance but he caught me, and before I could really get my footing back, he escorted me toward the balcony. I hoped the balcony was empty. Then I'd be able to get Raikidan to spill what was up with him. I was wondering if someone was putting him up to this. It wouldn't surprise me in the least.

I leaned against the balcony railing once we were outside. No one was around, making it possible to talk to him, which was good since he wasn't acting any different now that it was just the two of us. Actually, it was getting worse.

I faced him and tried to push him away. "Raikidan, you can cut the act now. It's just us out here."

Raikidan grinned and boxed me in. "Who said I was acting?"

My eyes widened. "W—what?"

Raikidan leaned closer. "You did it on purpose, didn't you?"

I gulped. "Raikidan, w—what are you talking about?"

"Eira…" I gulped again and my heart began to pound in my ears. His hood now touched mine. "If you're going to make me feel like a human"—he chuckled quietly and brushed my cheek with the back of his fingers—"then I'm going to make you squirm like one in return. It's only fair."

My mind buzzed as I tried to figure out what he meant. It wasn't until he rested his hand on my lower back and pulled me closer, did I realize what he meant.

"R—Raikidan…" I couldn't figure out what else to say. My mind wasn't working the way I needed it to.

His face was now near my neck, and a strong, warm sensation tingled throughout my body. There was no way that dance could have really made him feel this way. He had to be acting. It was just one big bet of how long he could make me uncomfortable. But who would he bet that with? We were all undercover.

"Lazmira…" he murmured.

I placed my hand on his chest and pushed him away from me. I stared at him in slight shock for a minute. "Who did you just call me?"

Raikidan hesitated, as if he too was surprised by his words. Before I got the chance to demand him again to explain himself, someone cleared his throat behind us. Raikidan grumbled as we turned to see who was getting our attention. I was surprise to see Zo standing a little ways off.

"I'm sorry to interrupt, uh, whatever you're doing, but your friends have requested your presence," he informed us.

I forced a smile. "Thank you, General. We'll be right in."

Zo nodded and went back inside. I stared Raikidan down for a moment before pushing past him. I wasn't going to get any answers from him about the situation now, thanks to Zo's interruption. But I wasn't honestly sure I wanted to know at this point. *How did he know—*

Ryoko waved at me. "Laz'shika, hurry up! I have something to tell you."

I shook my head and picked up my pace. It didn't matter. I was curious about what Ryoko had to say though. What had I missed while I was outside? Unfortunately, fate didn't want me to know. Just as I reached her side, a loud *boom* was heard. The room grew quiet as everyone became interested in the strange sound and stared at the large double doors of the main hall. We waited to hear something else.

It wasn't long before people shouted in the hall outside the party room and then something heavy was hitting the door. Soldiers drew closer to the doors as something began pounding on them. They threw themselves to the ground when the doors burst into pieces. A group of people flooded into the room, and from the artillery they carried, it was apparent they weren't friendly.

"Rebels," a soldier muttered.

I wanted to argue with him, but I kept my mouth shut. These weren't rebels. We wouldn't do anything like this. These guys wore bandanas over their mouths to cover part of their faces and their clothes looked as though they stole them from rebellious teenagers or thrift stores.

I watched as none of the soldiers attacked these supposed rebels. I couldn't figure out why. Why wouldn't they try to stop them? Then it dawned on me. None of the soldiers had weapons. Of all the times they wouldn't carry weapons, naturally it had to be during a peace party. I narrowed my eyes. That made this attack far too convenient. How would they know it'd be a good idea to attack this party? Something wasn't right here.

A man pushed his way through the group of rebels and scanned the room. "This will be easy. Kill them all."

Before the rebels and party guests could react to the order, I retaliated. Moving swiftly, I used a table as leverage and shot fire blasts at them as fast as I could. These supposed rebels weren't skilled in fighting by the way they clumsily dodged my attacks.

My attacks ceased and I stared down the leader of these rebels. "Leave now, or you will pay the consequences."

"For a peace lover, you're not too peaceful," the man taunted.

"For an imposter, you're not too convincing."

The man narrowed his eyes. "You don't know what you say, woman."

"I don't? I am an ambassador of the Tribes. I seek to maintain peace between them. I research and learn to obtain that knowledge to do so. Now we wish to integrate within the society of the cities. We wish be a part of something more. I watch and learn how the city and its citizens interact. I watch how things fall into place. You do not fit into that. You do not fit in. You do not work like the true rebels of this city. You have too much chaos controlling you."

"Everything is chaotic."

"Not everything. Even a wild animal driven mad with hunger still has a goal. The rebels have goals and priorities. You follow neither."

"You sound like a supporter."

"I am neutral. I watch but I do not participate. I listen but I do not speak. Now leave or reap the consequence of your choice."

The leader scowled. "Kill them all."

As the rebel imposters made their assault, the shamans retaliated, forcing the soldiers to stay back if they weren't going to be of any use. Rylan and Raikidan came to aid me, while Ryoko stayed back with Shva'sika to protect her as she charged herself up. Psychics aided us, and even Talon joined in by the use of his unique ability. He also appeared to be trying to make it so Tla'lli would stay back, but she wasn't having it. With a strong whistle, she carried the wind on her breath and pushed a handful of the rebel imposters back. With the force we had, it didn't take us long to take care of the problem. These people were untrained, ordinary civilians. They weren't a match for trained combatants.

I turned away from the group of lifeless bodies. So many lives wasted. Why would they do this? Why would they throw their lives away?

"Grenade!" someone yelled.

I turned and froze when a pin-pulled grenade came rolling at me.

"Ambassador, move!" someone yelled.

But it was too late now. I wasn't able to get away in time. This was it. I grunted when Raikidan tackled me to the ground and a table flew over us and onto the grenade. It wouldn't help and was probably going to make things worse, but I understood how someone would think it would help in such a situation.

Raikidan held up my hood as he shielded me with his body. I clung to him and waited for the worst. I flinched when the grenade went off and things sounded like they were blowing up. Raikidan flinched and grunted in what sounded like pain. My grip tightened, but that was the worst of it.

My eyes darted around. Everything appeared untouched, as if it was only in our heads. It wasn't until I noticed the psychics did I understand that the blast had been contained in a force field.

I tried to get Raikidan to move so I could get up, but he wasn't responding. "Raikidan?"

When he didn't respond again, I tried to move him by force and he moaned in pain. I tried again, and again he moaned but this time, something else made me aware that there was something wrong. I smelled blood.

35
CHAPTER

I finally managed to wriggle out of Raikidan's tight grip and pull myself from under him a little, only to be horrified by his condition. Large wooden shards protruded from his back and lower body, with blood pouring out of the wounds. The psychics hadn't been fast enough, and Raikidan had been hit by pieces of the wooden table that had been thrown over the grenade.

No, not again… "I need a healer over here!" I shouted, my voice cracking. I fought the wave of panic rushing up within me. If he couldn't fully heal or be healed at all and he died, I'd never forgive myself.

Two healers rushed over to us, and they weren't alone. Two young, blonde psychic women followed them. One of the psychics used her ability to gently move Raikidan without hurting him, so one of the healers could help me move out of the way and check on my condition. My leg bled from a small gash, but that wasn't a concern to me. I watch as the two psychics worked together to remove all the shards from Raikidan's back.

One of the psychics turned her face toward me, a soft smile on her lips. *"You don't need to worry. He's going to be just fine."*

Her voice… At least now I could put a face to the mysterious psychic that had spoken to me earlier. I had to admit, she sounded a lot older than she appeared.

"Trust me, I've already seen it."

"Shaman healing doesn't work right for him," I said. *"He's going to need more than just two healers."*

"Don't worry. He'll be good as new in a moment. You need to focus on shaman matters, though. Questions won't be answered unless they're sought out."

I couldn't argue that. We needed to know who these people were, but now that they were all dead, only shamans could speak with them. The healing shaman protested as I limped away, but I ignored him. My leg could wait.

I walked over to a high-ranked soldier who was taking the liberty of kicking what was left of the bodies as he checked out the mess.

"You shouldn't be so disrespectful to the dead," I scolded.

"Rebel scum don't deserve respect."

"And how do you know they truly are what you think they are?"

"I just know. What else do I need to have?"

"Proof. Facts showing who they are."

"They attacked us. What more is there to know?"

"You are blind to what is the truth, because of what you want to see."

"If you think you can give me proof, then please, *Ambassador*, be my guest."

I didn't like the sarcasm in his voice, and it made me hope I could prove him wrong. Sure, these people weren't from our rebel group, but that didn't mean another with different motives and ideals wasn't springing up.

Kneeling down on the ground, I closed my eyes and sought out the spiritual plane and any lingering spirit who would have a connection to what happened. My breath slowed when I made the plane connection, and when I opened my eyes, I found a gray, lifeless world before me. I looked around until a spirit manifested in front of me. I wasn't surprised at all to see that it was the leader of this rebel group.

Terror oozed out of him, his eyes wide. "Where am I? What is this place?"

"You're on the spiritual plane."

He gulped. "I'm… dead?" I nodded. He shook his head and backed away. "No, this can't be happening. Sara is waiting for me to come home. The kids… I promised them I'd be home from work on time this time."

Something wasn't right with this man, as if he had no idea what had happened to him. He turned away and his head scanning in a frantic panic for a way out. That didn't settle well with me. I needed answers, even if I had to piece them together.

"Wait!" He looked at me. "Who are you, and why did you attack us?"

"Me attack you? Why would I do that?"

I shook my head. "I don't know. That's what I'm trying to figure out."

"I don't know what you're talking about. I'd never attack anyone." He turned to leave again.

"Please don't go! My friend almost died because you guys attacked us." The man stopped again. "Please try to remember. I don't hate you, I just want to know what happened and why. Try to remember."

"I don't—" His brow furrowed—"wait, maybe I do. I was walking home from work, my car had broken down, and our funds were too low to afford a cab. I didn't want to be late getting home, so I thought I was taking a shortcut. It was dark and the street was deserted, or, so I thought. I wasn't actually alone. Someone was following me, and they weren't trying to hide it…"

His gaze absently drifted as if he was forgetting again.

"What happened with the person who was following you?"

"What? Oh, right… I picked up my pace, but he kept following me, so I panicked and ran. I was confused I took a wrong turn and was jumped by a group of people. They tied me up and blindfolded me, so I couldn't see who they were. Then someone hit me on the head, and everything went silent…"

He gazed down at the ground, disappointed in himself for some reason. He then began to fade. "I… I really am dead…"

"Hey wait! Tell me your name."

He stopped fading, focusing on me. "What?"

"What's your name?"

"My name? My name is Delmon."

"Delmon." I smiled. "It's a nice name."

He smiled back. "Thank you."

"Delmon, do you remember anything after you were jumped by those mysterious people? Anything at all?"

He shook his head. "No, I—wait, maybe…"

"Take your time. There's no rush." I prayed that was true and that my body wouldn't pull me back before I could get some answers.

Delmon's brow creased with concentration. He sighed with defeat after a few moments. "I'm sorry… I can't…"

I held out my hand. "It's okay. Maybe you can show me instead?"

He looked at my hand skeptically. "What's in it for me?"

"I will tell your family what happened and you can move on."

He scanned the lifeless world. "Does the afterlife always look like this?"

I shook my head. "No. It's much nicer once you move on. This is only the Plane Between."

"Purgatory."

I nodded. *Ordinary people and their names for the planes.* I felt bad for lying to him, but if it got him to pass over then it didn't matter. In truth, no one knew what was on the other side, not even shamans. Spirits never told, as it was forbidden to. It was why I never asked Arcadia when I met her.

Delmon extended his hand. "Please, tell my family I'm sorry I wasn't able to keep my promise."

I smiled. "I'll tell them whatever you want me to say."

He rested his hand on mine and I was instantly transported elsewhere, but not all of me. It was as if only my eyes were. All I could see was bits of Delmon's memory. The memory was in shades of grey, and a little fuzzy in areas that weren't the focus. There wasn't any sound, but it was obvious things were moving and should have made some sort of noise.

Delmon, no longer blindfolded, was tied to a chair in a windowless room. Men in strange uniforms that resembled soldiers' uniforms surrounded him. Delmon looked only half-conscious and unresponsive to the men around him, which pleased them.

A man behind Delmon grabbed him by his hair and pulled his head back. Another came up to him and held up a syringe gun. Delmon became more conscious when he saw the gun. His eyes widened and he began to struggle. The men around him began to laugh, and the man with the gun held him down by the shoulder and injected something into his neck. Delmon's eyes widened and he screamed in pain until he passed out.

The man holding Delmon's head let him go, but they didn't leave—as if waiting for something… or someone. Finally Delmon stirred and lifted his head. But something was different. His eyes seemed… colder.

The man who had injected him with the solution in the gun began speaking with Delmon, and he responded by looking at and listening intently to this man. Delmon nodded and smiled wickedly as if he were agreeing with what the man was telling him. When the man finished speaking, another cut the ropes that bound Delmon to the chair. Delmon stood, rubbing his wrist.

The man who had been speaking with Delmon motioned him to follow, and he did so without a fuss. He didn't attempt to run. He didn't attempt to fight these men. He stood among them as if he were on their side. It was like he was a completely different person.

The memory changed, and was now more chaotic than before. It showed Delmon being trained, and then him working with others that reminded me of the other fighters he had been with when he had attacked us. It then showed him and that same group sneaking around and planting bombs somewhere. It showed them watching from afar, as buildings blew up, both civilian and military, and then of them planning some more.

In the midst of these memories, some other, more vibrant ones showed. They were pleasant memories of his family. While he had been doing all of this he could still remember them. I wanted the memories to stop. I knew what was going on now, but they weren't finished.

The men from before were now back, and they handed instructions to this group. The group moved out with their weapons and moved through the city like shadows. The memory then showed them slipping into a building and attacking some soldiers that looked like ones from this city. They moved down a familiar looking hall, and then were confronted by more soldiers. The rebels took the weaponless soldiers out with ease, and broke down the large double doors to the main party hall we had all been in.

The memory slipped away and I stumbled backward.

Pain gripped Delmon's face. "I really didn't do all of that, did I?"

I shook my head. "No, Delmon, you didn't. Someone controlled your body and made you do those things. They took your life away from you."

Delmon gazed at his hands. "I'm sorry. I'm sorry for what I did. Tell my family I'm sorry I never kept my promise."

"I'll tell them," I promised. "I'll tell them you tried. I'll tell them you loved them and you never meant for this to happen. I'll tell them you thought of them even while you were forced to leave them behind."

"Thank you." He smiled at me before he began to fade away, and I was okay with it this time. I had the information I needed, and it was now time for him to move on.

"Be wary, young freedom fighter." His disembodied voice came. "They come from the outside. They turned us into a distraction so they could get in. They don't want their presence known until it's too late. Stop them, before they destroy everything."

Color returned to the world around me, and air rushed back into my lungs. I took slow, controlled breath, so as to not show any signs of weakness in front of these soldiers. We didn't need them knowing what happened to untrained shamans and then twisting that knowledge to think it applied to all of us.

The young man who had tried to heal me before was waiting beside me. I nodded and he fixed up my leg.

"Well?" The soldier I had argued with before questioned impatiently.

I didn't speak or stand up until the healer completed his task. "They were not rebels."

The soldier snorted. "Do you have proof? And I mean real proof, not just words."

"I saw it. I saw what they did to him. To all of them."

"Who did what to them?"

"I don't know who, but they controlled these innocent people to commit vile acts against their will."

The soldier snorted again. "I'm sorry, but I can't take only your word on this matter."

"Then take mine as well." We looked at a young psychic woman as she advanced toward us. It was the woman who had spoken to me earlier. "I can see what she experienced. I can show you the same, if needed."

"Very well," the officer said. "We will clean up this mess in the mean time."

"This will not take long," she informed us both.

The soldier grunted and walked off to shout orders.

The psychic focused on me. *"This won't hurt."*

"This won't be the first time a psychic has read my mind, but I will apologize

in advance for anything disturbing you see. In this form of reading, it is hard to hide... certain events."

The psychic held out her hand. *"I'm well aware of the torture you went through, Eira. I'm also close with a friend of yours and sometimes what she knows gets transferred to me by accident."*

I took the woman's hand and instantly felt her enter my mind. It didn't hurt, but it was uncomfortable, though less so than seeing all the memories she probed. Most of the memories were of the conversation I had with Delmon, but every once in a while a random personal memory came up. Sometimes it was a bloodstained memory and other times it was something that happened more recently, like the event Raikidan and I shared in the alley next to the club. These types of events were more common for some reason. I wasn't sure if it was because they were so fresh or I had done a much better job at suppressing the bad memories.

I could tell this woman was still training. She wasn't anywhere near Seda's talent. Most of the time, you didn't feel her presence, and you didn't see the memories she observed.

The young woman retracted her touch when she had seen what she needed to, and tore her focus away. "Captain Drengo, the Ambassador is telling the truth."

The soldier from before strolled over to us, his head tilted at an angle toward her. "Excuse me?"

"These are ordinary civilians who were taken and controlled by an outside source."

"What was controlling them?"

"A serum. I cannot say what kind, but it was injected into the bloodstream. It is fast-acting, only taking a few minutes at most."

"Who is doing it? Rebels, I can only imagine."

The woman shook her head. "No, not rebels. They have no need for such methods. These people had more funding, and they wore uniforms. We're looking for an outside invader."

Drengo eyed me and I wasn't having it. "You're accusing us of doing this?"

People began to murmur, their words filled with hate and worry.

"It's convenient you want to enforce peace when this all happens."

Tla'lli advanced. "You attacked my village during a celebration, under false pretenses. Of course we want to enforce peace. We've done nothing wrong, and here you are pointing fingers again."

"All the more—"

"That's enough!" Zo stormed over to us. "Drengo, leave. I won't tolerate this behavior, or your accusations."

"But, sir."

"Leave! I'll deal with you later."

Drengo scowled. "Yes, sir."

It wasn't until Drengo was out of our line of sight did Zo speak to me. "I apologize for his rudeness. He was out of line."

Tla'lli opened her mouth to speak, but I didn't let her say anything. "It's all right. I can see where he is coming from."

Zo gazed at me with slight confusion. "You can?"

"I am a neutral figure. It's my job to see both sides and find an outcome both sides can be happy with."

Zo nodded. "I see. Then in the interest of our side and possibly yours, can you help us anymore than you have?"

"What this woman now knows is all I can tell you, except for one piece of information I don't think this young psychic knows, and I'm not quite sure if it's of any use."

"Any information you can offer is useful."

"The man I spoke with, the one who led this attack, his name is Delmon."

A soldier approached us. "I'm sorry to interrupt, but did I hear you correctly? You said his name was Delmon?"

I nodded. "Yes, that is correct."

"Corporal, you know the man?" Zo inquired.

"Not personally, no, but coincidentally, I wrote up his missing persons report."

"How long ago was that?"

"A few months ago. I'd have to look at the report to know the exact time."

"From the memories Delmon showed me, it would be around spring time," I said.

"Early spring, to be exact." The young psychic corrected. "I have calculated his disappearance to be one month prior to the mid spring attacks that first began this whole problem. That month would be enough time to make them look like real rebels, even if their goals were not the same."

"Corporal, I want you to dig up that report, along with all the other missing persons reports from around that time to now. We may be able to identify some of these other civilians."

"I will help with that," the psychic offered. "I will be able to identify them with the information I have by looking at their pictures."

"Someone will have to inform any living relatives if they are identified," the corporal informed.

Zo nodded grimly. "Not a favorite task, but a necessary one. I'll do them, along with anyone else who volunteers."

I almost smiled at Zo's selfless offer. He may be a creep around women, but he seemed to genuinely want to help civilians. Maybe he wasn't as bad as I made him out to be.

"Someone is going to have to tell Delmon's wife the grim news," the corporal stated.

"I'll be doing that," I said. "I promised Delmon I would."

"Wouldn't that go beyond your neutral terms?" Zo questioned.

"If he weren't dead, you would be right," Tla'lli said. "But since she spoke with him on the spiritual plane, it becomes a shaman matter, giving us the jurisdiction to do something."

Shva'sika approached us. "We would be able to help identify the ones who have died tonight, if you would like that."

"Wouldn't that go against the standing you're trying to enforce tonight?" Zo asked.

She shook her head. "It is our job to keep peace between the spiritual plane and the living one. The men and women who have died will more than likely be restless and could pose a problem, though few of you would recognize those signs as anything more than ordinary accidents and such. If we can speak with them, we can put them to rest and identify them for you to ease your search."

Zo nodded. "It would benefit us both. Very well, I will agree to this."

The corporal looked at me. "If you're going to speak with Delmon's wife, you should know her name is Sara. I remember that much. I'll have to dig up the files to give you the home address." I nodded, remembering that Delmon had mentioned the name Sara while we were speaking on the spiritual plane.

"I'll come with you," Tla'lli decided. "You may need some help. This woman will be distraught after hearing the news."

"I agree, but for another reason. There will be children at the house."

Tla'lli let out a sorrowful breath. "All the more reason for me to go then. They will need a distraction while you break the news."

"Talon." Zo motioned for him to come over and he did as asked. "You'll be going with them, correct?"

Talon nodded. "That would be correct, sir."

"All right, then if Delmon's wife stabilizes enough for you to talk to her after the news is broken to her, see if she can think of anything that was happening out of the ordinary. Anything that would give us a clue as to why Delmon was chosen to be controlled."

"I will see what I can do. If she isn't stable enough, I'll provide her with the means to contact us when she's ready. It might be a good idea to assign someone to watch her place once we let her know, just in case her knowing puts her and her family in danger."

Zo nodded. "I agree. I'll get on that right now, so when you three leave her place there will be someone around to monitor them."

"Make that the four of us." Tla'lli turned her gaze to me. "You're going to want to make sure Raikidan is okay before we leave tonight. He's going to want to go no matter his condition, and he won't be happy you left without him or had someone to take his place."

I chuckled. "He'll be especially unhappy if someone took his place."

"That's right, he doesn't think anyone can do the job as well as he can," she teased.

"After tonight, I doubt he's wrong."

Tla'lli smiled and then jerked her head in his general direction. "Go check on him, then."

I nodded and excused myself. Tla'lli and Shva'sika went about shaman business, and the soldiers, except Zo, went about their business as well. As I headed over to check on Raikidan, I overheard the psychic speaking to Zo.

"General, I feel as though you need to know this. The men I saw in the shaman's memories, the ones controlling these people, they were wearing uniforms."

"What kind of uniforms?"

"Military, but not from this city. I fear we may be under attack."

"Thank you for telling me, Saléna. I'll put that information to good use."

"I am sorry I did not say something sooner. I just thought that knowledge should be for just us and not the shamans."

"It's all right. You did the right thing. We don't need panic to spread."

Raikidan tilted his head up when I reached him. He didn't try to stand, so I knew he was still recovering. Instead I knelt.

"How you feeling?" I whispered.

"Fine." He seemed a little reluctant to talk.

"Are you sure? I know how little shaman healing works on you."

"I said I'm fine."

I nodded. "That was brave of you to do, taking the blow like that."

"It's my job."

I leaned closer to him so our hoods touched, hiding our faces from the rest of the room. "Except it's not your job, Raikidan, and you still chose my life over yours."

He held eye contact with me, though his were rather wide, as if he was overcome by my words.

"And for the record, only one other person has ever chosen my life over their own." My lips made contact with his and Raikidan locked up, surprised. I knew it was weird of me to do, but how else could I thank him for something like this? *I can't lie, I don't hate the feeling of his lips on mine…*

I pulled away. "Thanks, Tiger." A grin spread across his face as I rose to my feet, but he said nothing. "I need to leave, to speak with someone about this situation. It's up to you whether you come with me or not."

I headed for a door that had been cleared of debris without waiting for an answer. He'd catch up fast if he decided to join me. Tla'lli ran over to me once she noticed I was leaving, and Talon, of course, wasn't too far behind.

"Eira, would you mind doing me a favor?" the young Psychic, Saléna, messaged.

"Depends."

"It's simple. Just let Seda know that Saléna and Nyra say hello and that we're doing well."

"Sure, I can do that."

"Thank you."

I sighed with slight relief as the wind picked up while I sat on the railing of the small balcony attached to the living room. Today was hot, and the *lightly used-but new to us* air conditioner had broken only after an hour of using it. Now it laid in pieces on the coffee table, enduring the brain power of Ryoko, Rylan, and Argus to figure out what was wrong with it. But the heat was the last thing on my mind right now. The events of last night still plagued my mind.

Raikidan had chosen to come with us to see Sara, and naturally, it wasn't a pleasant visit. It had been late by the time we reached the house, thanks to Talon's communicator not receiving the coordinates in a timely manner, but Sara and the children had been still up, much to our surprise. Sara was the most surprised to see us on her doorstep, although she was still quite pleasant and accommodating by inviting us in.

She was obviously stressed, due to the months-long disappearance of her husband. Even as she made room for us, it was clear that our appearance made her even more nervous. Understandably so, especially after Tla'lli brought the children into another room without explanation.

I could tell something wasn't right, beyond the stress of her missing husband and our sudden appearance. Once we disclosed who we were, she became visibly agitated, though she kept herself controlled as she sat patiently on the couch. I ended up pulling my hood down to make it easier for her to connect with me. Unfortunately, my action only made her start to fall apart. She knew at that moment that her husband wasn't coming back, but I still told her, and of course, it had only gotten worse. She had been so distraught over the news that I had to restrain her and hold her close to me so she wouldn't get violent.

In the middle of her crying, she would lash out and pass the blame and try to get away, but I wasn't going to budge, and I wasn't going to blame her for what she said. These situations were always difficult. It was the other reason, on top of my spirit walking problem, that my training hadn't gone as planned. I wasn't able to deal with these kinds of situations as well as I should have back then.

Once Sara had calmed down enough, Tla'lli had allowed the children back into the room, and I let Sara go so she could be with them. Talon had written something down on a piece of paper and had given her instructions on how she could speak with the military when she was ready, but she surprised us by telling us she was ready now—and the information she gave was disturbing.

She told us how before Delmon disappeared, she would see strange people standing across the street, and they would just stare at the house. Delmon had been at work every time, so when she told him about the men, he would just shrug it off. She told us how over time, she would notice them more and more until it felt as if they were there every day, but Delmon continued to shrug it off—until one day, he called out of work per her request and saw them for himself. Delmon chose to confront the men, but when he stepped outside, they had disappeared as if they had never existed. She told us it was about a week and a half after this that Delmon ended up disappearing, along with some other people they knew.

When Talon had asked her if there was anything she was worried about, she admitted she felt like they were still watching them. She had been so afraid that she had pulled the kids out of school and taught them from home. It was only when she gave us this bit of information that I realized Raikidan had been acting weird. He wasn't paying attention to anything going on inside the house. Instead, he stared out the window of the front door.

I had gotten up to see if he was okay, but he had me sit back down and made sure no one made any moves out of the ordinary. Sara and the kids became scared, and I demanded Raikidan to tell us what was going on. He reluctantly told us we were being watched. Unfortunately, that frightened the family more, and I chose to steal a peek. I had pulled my hood back over my head and sneakily peered out of the kitchen window.

Across the street, three people stood in the shadows on the street, just outside the reach of the lamppost. They had a creepy aura about them, and I wasn't going to just stand here and let them just scare this family. I left the window and pushed past Raikidan to confront them. The men weren't expecting such a move, slowing their reaction time, allowing me to easily chase one of them down after they all split up. The man I tackled was strong, and able to struggle his way out of my grip, but Raikidan was stronger and apprehended him. Talon had come over and tied the man up while Tla'lli stayed in the doorway of the house and kept the family inside where it was safe.

The man wasn't at all cooperative. He ignored Talon's orders to explain himself, and rambled nonsense about how it was going to be too late, and that we weren't going to be able to stop the inevitable. Before we could get anything out of him, a gunshot echoed through the street and the man fell over—blood pooling around him. He was dead and this situation was getting worse by the second for this family.

Talon called in for more men to watch the area to make sure the family stayed safe. One or two guys weren't going to be able to protect them at this rate, and once school started back up for these kids, they were going to need to be able to go. Sara wasn't going to be able to provide for them without a job, and she couldn't home school them if she was working.

My thoughts were pulled away from that night when Blaze shuffled into the living room. He looked as though he hadn't slept at all—or was recovering from a hangover.

"You okay, Blaze?" Argus asked him.

Blaze shook his head. "My head is pounding."

Ryoko giggled. "Don't tell me you drank too much."

Raid snorted. "He had two drinks. What a lightweight."

"I don't remember drinking anything. Why was I drinking again?"

Ryoko giggled again. "Oh boy, tell me you remember the party."

Blaze's brow lifted. "Party? What party?"

Zane's eyes flicked up from his newspaper on the bar. "Don't go saying that now, Blaze. It was the party of a lifetime. You would be missing out if you couldn't remember Eira's dance."

Blaze's brow furrowed. "She danced?"

"Yeah, it was real sexy, too," Ryoko teased.

I poked my head inside the room. "Aw, that means you missed the outfit that matched my dance, as well. Ryoko was even doing it with me."

"Fuck the goddess!" Blaze looked distraught over missing this.

I gasped and I climbed back in from the balcony. "Tell me you remember the twins."

He blinked. "Twins? What twins?".

Ryoko giggled. "Oh man, he doesn't remember the twins."

"What are you two talking about?" he demanded.

I did my best to contain my enjoyment while the room echoed with quiet snickers as they all realized what the two of us were doing. "I can't believe you don't remember the twins. They were so into you. But you must have been really drunk or something, because you didn't give them the right signals, and each of them only gave you a kiss on the cheek and left right after."

"Both of them?" he asked.

I smirked. "At the same time."

Blaze ran his fingers through his hair. "Fuck me! I'm going back to bed. This is just one hell of a bad dream."

Once he was down the hall and around the corner, the room erupted with laughter. His reaction was better than anticipated.

"Someone please tell me what the hell happened there," Rylan managed.

"Yeah, seriously," Raid agreed. "He really didn't drink that much."

"Even when he does drink a lot, he doesn't usually forget," Argus said.

Shva'sika got her laughter under control and pulled a blue pill out of a box she had brought out earlier. "Do you remember me making all of you take these?"

Raid nodded. "You gave one to all of us except Blaze, saying he was the only one who wasn't going to need one."

Shva'sika smirked. "Well he didn't need it—unless he needed to remember what happened last night."

The guys all had clueless expressions, but Zane's laughter boomed through the room. "You spiked the drinks!"

Shva'sika giggled. "It's possible."

The boys stared at her, astonished. Even Genesis looked surprised. Zane continued to laugh. "That, my dear, is the most diabolical thing I can imagine a shaman doing."

"And letting it all happen to Blaze was her idea," I added.

"But it was you and Ryoko who chose to make it go as far as it did," Shva'sika corrected.

"Who cares?" Raid said. "Here I thought you were a sweet lady who had no bad bone or thought in her body. I never want to piss you off!"

"You never want to piss off any woman," Zane corrected. "Unless you want to be dead."

"Or wish you were dead," I added.

All the ladies in the room laughed. I stopped when I remembered something. "Speaking of the party, Seda, a woman named Saléna wanted me to tell you she and Nyra say hello and they're doing well."

Seda smiled. "Thank you. I was beginning to wonder about that."

"Who are they, may I ask?"

Seda didn't respond. She actually appeared reluctant to tell, as if it were a major secret.

"Seda, it's okay. You can tell them," Genesis allowed.

Seda nodded. "Saléna and Nyra are my younger sisters."

"So why the reluctance to tell?" Argus asked.

"They're also psychics," I said.

Rylan looked at Seda curiously. "Is that true?"

She nodded. "Yes, but… they were planned."

Raid grimaced. "That doesn't sound good."

Seda sighed. "They've figured out there's an actual psychic gene— and it's hereditary."

"Does Zarda know?" I asked. It was the most important thing to at this point.

Seda shook her head. "Not at this point. It was a geneticist's theory, so they went with it. They don't know the gene yet, but even if they find it, they aren't planning on telling Zarda. They believe if they can track down the gene, they can prevent it in future experiments, and their goal is for it to only occur in natural humans and other such beings."

"So what made them choose your DNA?" Ryoko asked.

Seda shrugged. "A chance happening. From what I know, they took three different sets of DNA and tried to recreate them, but only my sisters made it through the tank process. When they came out, they had the active gene, so they knew it was a hereditary process."

"I'm assuming you'll be working close to this development, by the friendliness Saléna gave me," I said.

Seda nodded again. "I'm going to make sure they stay safe, and to find out more of what the geneticists can discover. It might help the rest of us with any issues we may currently have."

I nodded. "Just be careful. Is there anything else significant about these siblings?"

Seda shifted in her seat as if struggling with this question. "Well—I have noticed every once in a while that I feel a connection with one of them that is similar to the one I feel with Nioush, but it's also different."

"It's the reason you've been leaving from time to time," I guessed.

She nodded. "Yes. We're trying to understand if a larger psychic connection is starting to form. If it is, we're trying to figure out if it's going to get as strong as the one Nioush and I have with each other, or if it will be less intense. There's just so much going on with this. It's gotten to the point where Nioush has begun cooperating just so he can get this put to rest."

"Well, again, be careful," I said. "We don't need you getting hurt."

Seda smiled. "You know I will. Oh, Genesis, I think your communicator is going off."

Genesis blinked and then dashed off to her room. She came back moments later.

"Anything good?" Ryoko asked.

She shook her head. "Just a recon for later tonight, but I passed it along."

Ryoko shrugged in acceptance and went back to working on the air conditioning unit. I, on the other hand, found that a little strange. Genesis had been doing that a lot lately. I couldn't understand why, since in order to end this rebellion, we needed to do our assignments. But maybe there was some genius plan going on in that head of hers that I didn't know about. In the end, it didn't matter. She had already passed the assignment to another team, so we were stuck here.

36
CHAPTER
(RYOKO)

My heavy boots thundered on the asphalt as Laz led us down the abandoned street. She set a quick pace, but just slow enough for the rest of us to keep up with her. I understood her rush, but I wished she knew how to set a pace we could all keep up with just a little more easily.

The sounds of battle closed in, pumping adrenaline through my body, making me numb to my desire to slow down. This was why we were running. We were reinforcements for an unfortunate battle that transpired as a result of the recon assignment Genesis had passed on earlier. We were going to try to win a losing battle—but that was nothing new.

"Everyone spread out, and help whoever you can," Laz ordered. "Once we get the odds evened out, we can regroup and push forward. Understood?"

"Yes," we all replied.

"Good, now move."

We acted quickly. It was hard not to when Laz was leading. Calm and confident, she thought with a level head and thought of us over the mission even if it meant losing.

Argus and Blaze veered right, into an alley, and Laz kept running straight, with Raid and Raikidan, not surprisingly, following her.

Raikidan still interested me. I couldn't tell if he was just taking this battle partner thing very seriously, or if he willingly followed Laz blindly into any situation like a lovestruck puppy.

Rylan tugged my arm to follow him down a side street, heading to the left side of the battle. I complied and followed. If Raikidan was a lovestruck puppy, I could totally relate. It was hard not to try to please someone when you cared enough.

Rylan and I ran through side street after side street, avoiding direct contact with the military and helping those we could. It just didn't feel like we were doing much. It felt like for every one person we helped, five more needed it.

"We're losing the right flank!" someone called in through the communicators.

"Left flank isn't looking that great either," someone on our end called in. "How is the center holding up?"

"Peachy," Laz muttered.

I refrained from laughing. This was too serious to turn into a joke. Rylan pulled me into an alley, and when we came out on the other side, I froze. *No, can't be…* Laz and Raikidan fought the military in front of us. We had been pushed into the center.

"They're corralling us!" Rylan yelled into the communicator. "We need to push forward if we have any chance of winning."

"It's too late," someone rang in. "We're out-manned and out-gunned. There's no way we can push forward unless we want heavy losses."

"We can't afford any heavy losses," Laz said. "Our numbers are too few as it is."

"We need to fall back." The sound of Xantar's voice surprised me, though I knew it shouldn't have. There were so many of us fighting, it was only natural for more from our team to have been pulled to handle this.

"I agree." Laz didn't sound happy, but who would? "Fall back."

No one argued with her. There was no point when the truth was right there in front of us. We'd lost, again.

We began retreating, but I stopped running when I realized not everyone was moving. Laz and Rylan weren't with us. I turned to see them facing the military as if Laz had never called for the retreat to begin with.

"Laz, Rylan, what do you think you're doing?" I yelled.

This caught the attention of others, and they stopped to figure out what was going on, even though the military hadn't ceased their fire.

"Everyone keep going," she ordered. "Rylan and I will hold them off as long as we can."

"But you can't!" Raid argued.

"They'll kill you!" I screamed.

"They'll follow us if we leave with you now, and that will put more people in danger." Laz wasn't going to budge on this, and I couldn't believe they were going to do this. How could they do this to us?

"We won't die," Rylan promised. "We're just going to distract them long enough for you guys to get out of the radar and disappear into the shadows."

"Promise?"

I thought I heard him grin. "Promise."

I wanted to argue some more, but Raikidan tugged my arm. *How could he go along with this?* But when I looked him in the eye, I could see this wasn't something he was doing too willingly.

"We have to trust them," he whispered. "If they believe this to be the only way, then we have to believe it too."

I nodded and ran as fast as I could away from the approaching military. I glanced back to see Rylan shifting to his wolf-dog form, and that scared me. He wasn't putting up a fuss like he usually did, and he looked much more serious than I was used to seeing.

"Please don't die…"

I bit my lip and resisted the urge to cry. Seda told us they were still alive, but it had been two hours since we had gotten back to the house. I was on the verge of a panic attack.

Some of our teammates and others from other teams had come with us to wait, and even Azriel had come over, just in case. Danika held a cooling cup of tea but she had yet to touch it. I had a feeling she was using it to keep her from freaking out and I wished I had something like that myself. It didn't help that Raikidan's and Raid's rising anxiety levels slammed into me every passing minute. Raid, I could understand, being Rylan's bother. Since close family was hard to get when you are a created soldier, it's hard to accept you might have lost one.

But Raikidan I couldn't fully justify. He was naturally protective of all the women in the house but Laz held a greater weight with him, and I couldn't figure out why. Neither would admit there was something between the two, but here he was, about ready to have a heart attack from worry.

My ears twitched. *Did I hear something in the basement?* For a second, I thought I was hearing things, but then I heard it again and this time, Raid and Raikidan noticed as well. The sound came again and it sounded weird. It sounded like a sloshing, smearing sound, or even… my brow furrowed. Or even a dragging sound. The dragging and smearing became louder and thumping was added into it, catching everyone else's attention.

I jumped when something collided with the door. Everyone was on edge. Some even readied a gun to ease themselves. The door of the basement jiggled and flew open. I gasped as two bodies crashed to the floor.

"By the gods!" Danika shrieked. "Azriel, help me with them."

The two of them weren't the only ones to rush over to Laz and Rylan as they lay in a crumpled, bleeding heap. I helped Azriel roll Rylan off of Laz, and I begin to shake as I got a good look at their injuries. *How had they made it back in this condition?*

Raikidan cradled Laz in his arms, horror blanketing his face. Tears welled up in my eyes and I tried to hold them back. They promised they wouldn't die. My eyes widened when Laz coughed and then stirred.

"Laz, dear?" Danika held our injured friend's hand. "Laz?"

"El–Elarinya… fix… fix Rylan first. P–please."

Danika's brow furrowed. "W–what?"

"P–please…" Laz's eyes shut and her body relaxed.

I gulped and fought back tears. "L–Laz?"

"C'mon." Azriel hauled Rylan onto his back. "We need to get them downstairs now, or we're going to lose them both."

Danika nodded, rising to her feet. Raikidan cradled Laz better and stood. I went to accompany them as they headed for the hidden infirmary, but Danika stopped me. "You need to stay up here."

I shook my head. "No, I'm going with you."

"You are to stay."

She was firm, but I was stubborn. I wasn't just going to sit up here and wait for some sort of bad news. I was going to help. "I'm going down with you to help."

"Someone make sure she doesn't leave this room," Danika ordered.

Argus grabbed onto my arm and attempted to coax me to sit back, but I ripped free of his grip and tried to follow Danika. Argus wrapped his arms around my waist and attempted to pull me back, but he wasn't as strong as me. Blaze and Zane tried to give him a hand, slowing me down quite a bit, but it still wasn't enough.

"No, I'm going to help!"

"You're just going to be in their way," Blaze said. "You need to stay up here so they can get Eira and Rylan fixed up without any issues."

"No!" Their grips began to fail as I fought them. "I'm not going to sit and do nothing while my friends are dying."

"I told you to hold her back!" Danika yelled.

"You try holding back a train," Blaze muttered.

"Seda?"

"You need to get downstairs," Seda said through gritted teeth. "I can't hold back the bleeding forever and between the two of them, that is taking all of my concentration."

"Oh for the love of Le'carro!" Danika stormed over to me and pressed two fingers against my forehead. "Everything is going to be fine, Ryoko. Now rest."

I tried to struggle, but the moment Danika's eyes began to glow, a wave of peace rushed through me. It felt like nothing was wrong in the world—like I could sleep forever. Then, darkness overtook me.

CHAPTER 37

(EIRA)

Gunfire was heavy in my ears. The ground exploded all around me, but there was no fear in my body—only the lust for blood. The ground exploded in front of me, and blood flew everywhere.

It smeared all over the walls and dripped in pools as I dragged myself along the wall. My vision was weak, but I kept moving. Something that resembled a door blocked my way until I found the part that moved it. My body gave out and I hit the ground. Blood filled my view, and then darkness took over that...

My eyes fluttered open, only to be blinded by a bright light and overwhelmed by the heavy smell of medicine. I didn't like, it so I closed my eyes in hopes it would disappear.

My eyes didn't open again until a familiar, light chuckle hit my ears. "About time you came back to us. You've been out for a few days."

I smiled. "Good to see you too, Az."

"I was afraid you were actually lost to us. It took us a while to get you stable, and even then, that was a tentative status." I grunted, which sent searing pain through my body. "Hey, take it easy. You're better, but not back to normal."

"How's Rylan? Is he okay?"

Azriel nodded. "Thanks to you, yes. If you hadn't carried him back here and told your friend to tend to him first in your weakened state, I don't think he would have made it. I had no idea you knew real healers."

"You're a real healer."

"Medic, not healer."

"Same thing."

He shook his head. "I use modern medicine, not natural healing abilities and herbal remedies. That makes it different."

I rolled my eyes. "Whatever."

Azriel knelt next to me. "How are you feeling? You looked like you were on your way to another plane by the time I was able to get you in here and tend to you while your friend helped Rylan."

"To be honest, I'm feeling really numb. I only feel pain when I make sharp movements."

Azriel nodded. "I figured as much. Between my medicine and your friend's healing, it was assumed that would happen."

"How bad is it, Az?"

Azriel's gaze faltered. "I don't think you want to know."

"I need to know."

He sighed. "I thought Ryoko was distraught after seeing you when you stumbled through that door, but when she came in here to check on you after we had you stable, she broke down. Raikidan took one look at you and left. He was barely able to stay calm enough to bring you down here. You still have all your limbs, so that's a plus."

"I'd like to see for myself."

Azriel chewed his lip before standing. "Very well."

He walked over to a table and came back with a small mirror in hand. He held it up so I could take a look at the damage. My heart stopped at the sight of the face looking back at me. *Is that really me?* There were so many bruises and scars, and even cuts still trying to heal naturally. An alibi was going to be near impossible to come up with. I looked like I had come from war.

I took a slow breath. "And the rest of me?"

"About the same. Some areas are worse, but not many. With our biggest concern being Rylan, we had only been able to get you stable before tending to him again. It put your healing process at a standstill and caused scars to form when we finally got around to progressing your healing."

"All right. I'll think of something that'll throw off any suspicion."

"How do you do it, Laz? How do you face such burdens without any hesitation or regret?"

"If I don't, who will?"

"It doesn't always have to be you who does something. Why can't you let someone else take that burden?"

"Tell me, Azriel, who else would take that burden? Who else would protect those who deserve it with no worry about their own life?"

Azriel frown, hesitating on an answer.

"Exactly," I said, knowing his reluctance was due to a lack of names for the list. "Someone has to take the burden, so I might as well elect myself instead of waiting for it to be thrust upon me. I don't have as much to lose as others, anyway."

He knelt beside me again, his hand cupping my cheek. "I wish you wouldn't say things like that."

"The truth hurts sometimes." I leaned my head into his touch, a constricting sensation tightening around my chest. "It hurts…"

Azriel wrapped himself around me in a tight hug, but I didn't fight it. Instead, I pulled a bandaged hand over his back and returned the gesture. Azriel didn't come into my life too long after Ryoko and the others did. He came in at a time I was the most suspicious of other's intentions, but somehow he wormed his way in, and the two of us had been capable of forming a certain type of bond that made him feel more like a brother than just a friend.

Azriel pulled away. "I'll leave you to rest. Will you be up for visitors?"

"Sure."

"All right. I'll let the others know you're up for a few. Rest, and I'll come and check on you in a little bit." He opened the door of my temporary room and then gazed at me. "And, Laz, please don't do something so reckless again. I don't want another heart attack."

I chuckled. "I'll do my best, but can't promise anything."

Azriel nodded and left, leaving me alone to think, which was rarely ever good. I lifted a bandaged hand and unwrapped it, even though I knew it wasn't the best idea. My hand looked as bad as I thought. Large scars crossed everywhere, and scabs covered areas the scars had yet to touch.

As I examined my hand, the memories of what happened bubbled to the surface. The bloodlust—my built-up walls crumbling with ease—the pain of the change—my hunger to kill as I tore soldiers apart one by one. It had been so easy for me to revert back to that…

monster. I hadn't really wanted to do it that way, but it had been the best distraction—and also the most destructive.

I clenched my hand as I spoke aloud in my room, alone. "I'm sorry, Rylan. I should have thought of a plan that only involved me getting hurt."

"You should have thought of a way where you hadn't gotten hurt at all."

Surprised by the voice, I tried to sit up, only to regret it a little when pain shot through me. "R–Raikidan. How long have you been there?"

"Not long." He came into the room more. "How are you feeling?"

"All right, I guess. I'm awake and have some energy. Definitely in better shape than I could have been."

Raikidan knelt beside me. "Well you look better."

I grunted and flinched a little. *Numbness is wearing off now… great.* Raikidan reached over and caressed my cheek. I flinched from pain.

Raikidan retracted his touch. "I'm sorry. I didn't mean to hurt you."

I shook my head. "Don't worry about it. The treatments Shva'sika and Azriel used on me caused my body to go numb. It's starting to wear off now. I don't think I'll be doing much for some time."

"Is it a surface pain or is there internal pain too?"

"Surface mostly. I doubt I'd be doing as well as I am if I was still having internal problems. Besides, Shva'sika would've seen to any lingering internal issues."

Raikidan stood. "Get up."

"Excuse me?"

"You heard me. Get up."

"I just told you I'm in pain and don't have a lot of energy, and you're trying to tell me to stand up?"

"Yes. You need to stand up—and don't bring the blanket with you."

"Like hell! I have no clothes on, from what I can tell, and you expect me to just stand in front of you? I don't think so."

Raikidan closed his eyes and his hands clenched into fists. "Eira, don't argue with me. Just do it, or I'll pull you out of that bed myself."

I propped myself up better. "You even try and I'll have my hands around your throat!"

Raikidan's eyes flew open. "Just do it, Eira!"

I flinched. The harsh tone and the intensity of his stare made me extremely uncomfortable.

Raikidan sighed and his gazed softened. "I'm sorry, Eira. Please just do this for me. You don't have to face me. I just really need you to do this. Please trust me."

I held eye contact with him for several moments, wary of listening since he wasn't telling me what he planned to do. But determination won out. Slowly, I pushed myself up, which was a taxing effort, without a doubt. I made sure as I moved that the blanket came me, careful not to allow it show too much of me, as I discovered I really didn't have anything on but the blanket and a few scattered bandage wraps.

I lost my balance as I rose to my feet, but Raikidan caught me. His hands slipped into place on my upper and lower back, fitting perfectly. Heat rushed to my face at the mental image of him lightly caressing my skin flashed through my head. I forced myself away from him and fought for control over my wobbly legs. I breathed out once I finally had that handled, and glanced at Raikidan warily. Raikidan returned my gaze with a calm, patient one. I managed to turn around, but letting go of the blanket was a little harder. After more internal struggle, the blanket fell to the bed, exposing the rest of me.

"It's been hard dealing with the scars you have," Raikidan murmured. "It's been hard seeing you get more over time. But this? This I can't handle. These scars are unacceptable."

My eyes widened when I realized what he was going to do. Flames crackled behind me and warmth spread all over my body. I watched tendrils of fire snaked their way around my arms and down my torso. My scabs healed, and my scars faded to nothing. The heat of the flames burned away the bandages, but it didn't matter to me. I stared at my scarless body long after the flames stopped burning and healing.

Raikidan left without a word, but my focus remained on what he had done. I sat down on my bed and traced my arms. I hadn't seen my skin so flawless is decades. *This is just a dream. No way I look this good again…* My tracing stopped when I felt scars that hadn't gone away, or even faded for that matter. My gaze lowered as I realized I was only nearly scarless. One scar was the one Raikidan had given me when he saved my life. My hands wrapped around my body and touched my sides. *And the others are from that day…*

"Laz, dear," Shva'sika called. "We just saw Raikidan leave, are you still up for—Laz?"

She rushed over to me and knelt. I looked at her, the sensation of awe and shock preventing me from greeting her.

Shva'sika touched my face and then my shoulders. "Laz, did he do this?"

I nodded slowly.

"Um, Laz, you're naked," Ryoko stated. "You definitely didn't let him do anything to you."

"Ryoko, hush," Shva'sika said.

"But—"

"Her complexion was bad. Azriel and I had a discussion about it earlier. He also told us a moment ago Raikidan was waiting to be let in when he left this room. We saw Raikidan leave here in a hurry, and he has told us he can heal with fire. Who's to say he can't heal up scars as well?"

"But she doesn't have clothes on. Laz would never let him see her like this."

"Who's to say he saw her?"

"All her bandages are gone and there are ashes on the floor. If he used the fire to heal her, the bed sheets and blankets would be gone as well."

As the two bickered the wheels in my head turned. "Clothes."

Shva'sika tilted her head. "What, Laz?"

My head frantically swiveled in several directions. "I need clothes, now."

"Um, here." Ryoko grabbed a scrap of cloth from a table and tossed it to me. "Armor will work right?"

Instead of answering, I had it change into something to wear and bolted out of the room. Flawless skin wasn't the only thing Raikidan had given me. I had a lot more energy now, too.

"Laz, he's on the roof. I figured I'd save you the trouble of looking for him."

"Thank you, Seda."

I bolted up the stairs. I didn't acknowledge anyone in the living room as I went to the door leading to the roof.

"Uh, Azriel, I thought you said she was barely awake," Blaze commented.

"And battered all to hell," Raid remarked.

"She was," Azriel replied. "What's going on here?"

The door flew open and I burst through the threshold out onto the roof—my breath coming in short, exhausted heaves. Raikidan stood by the edge of the roof and that was what mattered right now.

Raikidan turned around when he heard me. "Eira?"

I took a few deep breaths before taking a couple steps forward. Raikidan watched me with interest. I took a few more small steps before running the rest of the distance and embraced him with a tight hug. His body tensed.

"Thank you," I whispered. "Thank you."

Raikidan wrapped his arms around me. "You're welcome, Eira."

We stayed like this for several moments and a small prick of sadness hit me when he was the first to pull away. He turned to face the edge again, confusing me. "Raikidan?"

"I'll be back."

Before I could respond, he flew away in the shape of a large raven. *Where is he going? Why did he leave?*

CHAPTER 38

My muscles ached and pain pulsed in my head. That assignment had been the worst yet. Well, almost the worst yet. That battle the other day definitely held the top spot, but this assignment was pretty close, and the outcome had almost been the same. I didn't want to shower. I didn't want to eat. I just wanted to sleep.

I barely had the energy to close my door, let alone walk to my bed. The moon and streetlights guided me to my bedside, but I didn't collapse onto it like I had wanted to. Instead, I stared at the two objects that lay on my covers. There was a flower cluster and something that resembled a necklace.

Forgetting my fatigue, I picked up the flower cluster. It was a cluster of pink and yellow honeysuckle flowers and violet hyacinths. Holding them close to my face, I inhaled deeply to take in their sweet scent. I would have to get a vase so they'd last longer. Placing them back down on the bed, I picked up the necklace. *It's beautiful.*

The pendant had two elaborate, white gold wire-wrapped amethyst gems. The smaller of the two gems was a marquise-cut, and was held into the piece in a woven teardrop shape, while the larger amethyst was shield-cut and wrapped into the weave with intricately-shaped wire that resembled plant vines or thorns, and one piece on the top that resembled v-shaped animal horns, giving the entire piece a modern-but-tribal look. The pendant looked like it could function as both an aesthetic piece and possible weapon, with all the sharp edges. The chain for the pendant was made of white gold and was long enough to wrap twice around the neck. I ran my thumb over the pendant and smiled.

"You wouldn't believe how hard it was to find the right gems for that."

I jumped, my gaze snapping up. Sitting on my windowsill was none other than Raikidan. I should have known. The flowers were the calling card. I wondered how long he'd been there. Knowing my luck, he was there when I had walked in.

"So, this is what you've been doing this whole time?" I hadn't seen him since he had healed me days ago.

He shrugged. "Mostly."

I raised my eyebrow. "Mostly?"

"Most of my time was trying to find the right gems, then a jeweler from the North to make it."

He found a craftsman from the North to make this? I was a little confused. "Why'd you do this?"

Raikidan just shrugged. I walked to my floor length mirror and put the necklace on. It was even more beautiful when worn.

"It's perfect," He said in a low husky voice behind me.

I shook that thought out of my head immediately. It had to be my imagination playing stupid tricks. It wouldn't be the first time. But he was right. *It is perfect.* My smile turned into a frown. *Too perfect…*

His dark eyes snared me. I couldn't find the will to pull away as he caressed my cheek. "Eira…"

I stared at my reflection, as the memory pushed its way to the surface. This was wrong—all wrong.

"Don't do this to yourself. You know what—"

"You aren't his to have. Not when you don't want to be."

It was all too perfect, just like… that lie. I took the necklace off.

Raikidan's expression changed from pleasure to confusion. "What's wrong? Don't you like it?"

I knew he was upset, and I felt bad. He went through all of that just to see me take it off.

"No, I don't." I paused. "I… I love it. It's just…" I sighed. "You wouldn't understand. I'm sorry."

Walking over to my bed, I clasped the chain together and hung it on my light. Because of the chain's length, the pendant touched the nightstand top at an angle. I grabbed the flowers off my bed and placed them next to the pendant. Unclasping my hair clip, I set it on the nightstand on the other side of the necklace and fell, face first, onto my bed. Glancing at the walls, I watched as the light from the window danced across their faceted surfaces. I had to look away. So I did, right into my pillow.

"Rai, just go away," I muttered.

He couldn't expect me to not hear him breathing near me, or to feel the heat from his body. When he didn't go away, I groaned and pulled my pillow over my head, sinking my fingers into until I could hear them rip the fabric. The whole time, I squeezed my eyes shut as tightly as I could. I wanted the world to fade away. I wanted to be left alone. I drifted to sleep, and as I did, I prayed I'd never wake up. That way, I wouldn't have to feel this way.

The next few days, I avoided Raikidan as much as possible. It got to the point where I barely ever left my room, and rarely let anyone in. This forced Raikidan to sleep elsewhere, since no matter what, I made sure he couldn't get back in. I couldn't look at him. How could I when I was so confused?

I leaned against the mountain of pillows on my bed and stared at the necklace Raikidan had given me, along with a few photographs. I knew I shouldn't look at any of them, not until I figured everything out, but I couldn't help it.

Just then, my bedroom door burst open, crashing into the adjacent wall. Shva'sika stormed in and slammed the door shut. *Perfect.* She wasn't in a good mood, based on her entrance, and neither was I, so I knew this wouldn't go well. Luckily I had the photographs in my hand. While I was using them to reflect, they also doubled as a good way to hide the necklace. I didn't want anyone knowing about it until I got my head straight.

"Can I help you?" I asked.

Shva'sika crossed her arm. "Yeah, let's start by you telling me what's wrong with you."

I sat up. "Hmm, last I checked, I had every right to keep to myself while I think some things over. And last I checked, that was a larger right than having someone rudely barge into my room while barking out commands."

Her eyes narrowed. "Well—sorry for being concerned for your wellbeing."

I snorted. "Seriously? You're going be rude to me and try to claim you're doing it out of concern? Get out of my room."

"No," she said. "Not until you talk to me about what's wrong with you."

"If I don't want to talk, I don't have to."

She noticed the pictures in my hand. "What are you holding?"

"Just some photos. Looking them over has been helping me think."

"Let me see them," she ordered as she walked over to me with her hand outstretched.

I folded them closer to my body. "No. They're mine."

"You've been acting out of the ordinary for days. And if you're not going to tell me what's wrong, I demand to know what you're looking at."

"Ordinary? What the hell would you know is ordinary for me?" I spat. "What you deem is ordinary? Because last I checked, I'm allowed to act any way I please. And, so that everyone would keep their noses out of my damn business, I've only ever acted in ways anyone would ever expect of me, so I don't have to hear any of you fuss over me like some dimwitted child!"

Shva'sika reeled from the insult, but recovered quickly. "Well, maybe if you'd actually talk to us, we wouldn't make assumptions."

"Get out of my room."

She ground her teeth and then lunged for the photographs in my hand. I did my best to fight her off, but in my attempt, the necklace fell onto the bed, and then the worst possible thing happened to the pictures. Shva'sika reached for the photographs, misjudging because of the struggle, and grabbed a few of them roughly, crinkling them. My heart stopped. *No…*

Shva'sika immediately let go and backed away. "Laz, I'm—"

"Get out."

"But—"

"Get the hell out!" I shouted. "Had you minded your own business, this wouldn't have happened. They are the only copies I have, and you've ruined them."

She opened her mouth to speak, but closed it and lowered her gaze as she backed away. I plopped down on my bed in despair when the door closed behind her. I did what I could to unwrinkle the photographs one-by-one, but the damage was already done.

I sighed and ran my finger over the photograph on top. Pictured was me with a man with olive skin, rich brown eyes, dark hair, and a dual set of ears, like Azriel. One of his arms hung over my shoulder while the other rose above us and out of the image as if he had been the one taking the photograph. The two of us smiled wider than I thought I could anymore, and my eyes were alive with a light that had long since died. *Tannek…*

I gazed at the necklace Raikidan had gifted me as I held it in my hand by the pendant. I remembered how I felt when I saw it around my neck. *Did I almost feel that light again? Is that why I feel this way? Is it why so many weird things are happening to me when he's around?*

"Don't give into it," the voice in my head whispered. *"You'd be a fool to go through that again."*

I rubbed my temples. *"How can I give into something when I'm so confused about how I feel?"*

"Don't be weak," it said, surprising me that I received a response back. *"You know how to feel. Indifferent. You're incapable of reciprocating those feelings."*

"But that's not really true if you're warning me, now is it?"

This time I didn't receive a response. My room and mind remained quiet, and making a decision on how to feel became no easier.

"Laz, do you want to talk to someone who is a bit more calm and rational?" Seda messaged telepathically.

"There's nothing to talk about," I muttered.

The air was quiet for a moment before she contacted me again. *"Yes, there is. You overreacted to Raikidan's gift."*

"Did I over react? Or did I not react the way he would have preferred?"

She chuckled. *"You know you can't play that game with me. So why not talk this out, just the two of us? You don't have to leave your room, and I can stay here in mine, and no one will know."*

I sighed and fell back on my bed. *"I don't know where to start."*

"We'll start with your reaction. Instead of accepting the gift with a 'thank you,' like most would, you pushed him away as if the gift meant more than you wanted it to."

"He went out of his way to have this thing made."

"It's not that uncommon for friends to give gifts that are specifically created for each other."

"It is when the gift is easily several hundred gold pieces."

"So the value of the gift is the issue?"

I worked my jaw. *"No, not entirely."*

"Then be honest and open with me, Laz. You know you can trust me. I won't tell anyone anything that is said between us."

I swallowed hard and my hands clenched. *"I'm afraid…"*

"Of?"

My lip quivered. *"Of the possible bigger meaning behind it…"*

"Tell me what you think it could mean."

She knew the conclusion I had come to, but she was going to force me to talk this out. I almost chuckled. Force wasn't the right word. Seda wasn't holding a gun to my head, but the way she spoke to me, she challenged me. I had to work this out.

"The idea is illogical," I said. *"There's no reason why it should have even—"*

"What thought?" she asked. *"You have to assume I'm not a mind reader."*

I laughed. *"You would use that joke."*

"Good, I got a laugh. That's a start. Now tell me, what thought came to your head that has you acting so out of sorts?"

"That… he may care more than just as a friend."

"And you think that's illogical, why?"

"Because he's promised to someone else."

She chuckled. *"You sure? I happened to be quite aware of that conversation the two of you had, and he was rather reluctant to talk to you about it. He may have made it look like it was because he's reluctant to have a mate, but with the way you acted over a small gift gesture, he may have been afraid of you finding out the real truth until he knew you could handle it."*

I threw my hands up into the air. *"So, what, now I'm dealing with a liar? That makes me feel a whole lot better, with my past."*

"Don't you start twisting my words," Seda scolded. *"If you reacted this way to a gift, you would have acted even worse if he had been talking about a heavy topic such as eternal bonding."*

I took a deep breath and sat up. *"His promised mate is a dragon, Seda. I'm human—a failed human experiment at that. I'm not worth much…"*

"That's not true, and you know it. That's why you're struggling with this. You're worth something, and he sees it. Whether it be as a friend or more, and you know he does."

"Doesn't change the fact that his mate is a dragon who is out there somewhere."

"No one said his mate had to be a dragon. It's just assumed. Mixed partnerships can—"

"Not this kind," I interrupted. *"I learned that from my mother. My father wasn't human. He wasn't anything remotely close to that. And he fed her with lies, and then left, with no real intention of returning. He abandoned us…"*

I thought I could feel her nodding, as if the telepathic connection was stronger than other times we had connected this way. *"Now we're getting somewhere. Your fear stems from that."*

I chewed on my lip. *"Yes… and no. Something else, too…"*

"We'll talk about that other thing, but first, we'll address this current problem with your parents. You're assuming you'll end up like your mother, based on one experience. I know that was a painful ordeal, but it's rather unfair to assume all males, regardless of species, would do what your father did."

I held my chest when it began to ache with pain. *"I'm not willing to risk feeling that kind of pain. I've felt enough in my life…"*

"We've moved on to the other half of your relationship fear," she observed. *"Easily, too. Why? Is this half a larger part of your fear?"*

I closed my eyes. *"I'm supposed to learn from the past, but every time I try to make choices from what I learned, it never turns out right."*

"Learning is only part of it, Laz. Overcoming it is the other. And your first task is to admit what happened instead of running from it. You don't make any progress running, you know this."

"I can't let go of that pain… Seeing what happened to mom… losing Tannek… I just can't…"

"You can face this. You just have to let yourself and follow your heart."

"Seda, you're the one who gave me a prophetic warning. I can't trust my heart. It'll betray me…"

She sighed. *"I didn't want to have to tell you that. I shouldn't have, but it was the only way I knew to get you to trust me so quickly. There's more to a prophecy than the surface. You have to think about it on a much deeper level. It's why we're not supposed to give them out to just anyone, like we had long ago."*

"Then tell me what it really means," I begged.

"I can't. That's something you need to figure out on your own." The necklace lifted off my bed, displaying Seda's excellent control over her psychic abilities, and hovered in the air. The clasp unhooked and then wrapped around my neck twice. *"Now, go to the mirror."*

I hesitated, but then did as she'd asked.

"Now tell me how you feel."

"Well…" I looked myself over and my heart rate picked up. I was sure Seda would know, but I needed to stay rational, so I gave her a low-key answer. *"I do like it—a lot."*

"Good. Now go tell Raikidan this," she encouraged. *"How you may or may not feel about him beyond friends, and how he may or may not feel about you beyond friends, is irrelevant. As a friend, he gave you something nice, and because you've been so caught up with worrying about the past, you forgot how to react to a gift from a friend in the present. Tell him you're grateful for the gift, and worry about everything else later."*

I smiled. *"Thank you, Seda. I needed this talk."*

"Don't be afraid to talk to others when you need to. We're here for you." She chuckled. *"And your admittance to fear, that's going to stay between you and me, unless you say otherwise."*

"I appreciate it."

"Now go on. He's moping on the roof."

I giggled and looked myself over one last time, my heart skipping a beat in the process. I did like how the necklace fit me. I felt pretty, and I was okay with that for once. *Maybe Seda is right. Maybe I do need to face this differently.* I walked away from the mirror and opened my window. I could think on that later. I had something else to deal with.

Climbing out onto the fire escape, I sauntered up the creaky metal stairs and poked my head above the curb of the flat roof before reaching the top. My search for Raikidan didn't last long, since he stuck out where he lay on the flat portion of the roof, staring up at the blue sky.

I stood there like an idiot, chewing on my lips thinking about how to approach this. A normal person would just come out and apologize, but then again, a normal person wouldn't have overreacted like I had. The fire escape creaked as I shifted my weight, and Raikidan's attention snapped over to me. Why the creaking had caught his attention when me walking up the steps hadn't was beyond me.

I waved my fingers at him tentatively in greeting while trying my best to smile and he immediately jumped to his feet and sprinted over to me. This took me by surprise. I hadn't expected this kind of reaction to seeing me.

"Are you okay?" he asked. "You and Shva'sika were yelling, and then you were quiet for a while."

"I'll be fine," I said. "I actually came up here to thank you for the necklace. I should have when you gave it to me, but I wasn't in the best mood when you gave it to me, so my excitement was short-lived. I'm sorry for that."

His brow rose. "So you weren't upset because of me?"

"No," I lied.

"Laz, don't lie to him," Seda messaged. *"It won't help you or him."*

I ignored her and smiled at Raikidan. "Trust me."

He smiled back and nodded, but I noticed how his smile didn't reach as far as it normally did when he was happy, and his eyes didn't reflect how he tried to appear. *He knows I'm lying.* But I couldn't figure out why he wasn't calling me out on it.

I walked up the rest of the stairs of the fire escape and motioned for him to come closer. He complied and I wrapped my arms around his neck and hugged him tight. "Thank you. I do like the gift. It's pretty."

Raikidan hugged me back and then lifted me up from the top of the fire escape onto the roof. A startled squeak escaped my lips, and he chuckled. "I'm glad you like it. I thought I had done something wrong by doing so."

"No, you did good. Even though I still don't understand why you went through the trouble."

"Because you deserve something nice. And you were being so damned picky about a replacement for your lost necklace, someone had to make a decision for you."

I chuckled and tried to pull away, but Raikidan tightened his grip. "Uh, Rai?"

"Not yet."

My heart skipped a beat. "Any particular reason?"

"Just because."

My brow rose in question, but I remained quiet and still. When a minute or two passed and he still hadn't let go, I started to understand. "I'm sorry. For upsetting you so badly."

"Stop saying sorry," he mumbled.

"No."

He pulled away and tapped my forehead with his palm. "Yes."

I chuckled and stepped back. When he realized how I tricked him into letting go, he pointed at me and I laughed. I ran my fingers through my bangs and my laughter immediately stopped when I noticed how odd of a stare Raikidan gave me. The way he looked at me, it sent an uncomfortable tingling sensation down my spine, making me feel a bit self-conscious. "What?"

He shrugged. "Just thinking."

I sat down on the curb of the roof. "About what?"

He seated himself next to me. "What were you and Shva'sika yelling about?"

My gaze lowered. "She tried to force me to talk to her, and in the process ruined some pictures that I don't have backup copies for."

He frowned. "That was rather unkind of her. There's no way to fix them at all?"

I shook my head. "They're pretty bent up. I did try to fix them the best I could, but there's only so much I can do. Granted, they're not completely destroyed, so it's not all bad, but it still sucks."

Raikidan stood. "I just had an idea. I might be able to fix them."

My brow furrowed with confusion. "How?"

"It's a surprise."

Before I could protest, he had opened the door to the house and disappeared. I couldn't figure out what could possibly help at this point, but I'd give him the benefit of the doubt and let him try. I touched my necklace and smiled. Such a thoughtful creature he was. I needed to try to be like that to him. I had told myself not to get too close, but at this point, that rule had been long broken and I couldn't lie to myself anymore. I just needed to be careful how close I got.

Pain pulsed in my chest. I clutched my shirt and bent forward in reaction. The pain subsided quickly, allowing me to sit up soon after. "Ow… What was that about?"

Movement next to me caught my eye and I turned, only to find myself alone. *What the—*

I touched my necklace again and my chest started to hurt again.

"Don't be stupid," the malevolent female voice in my head warned. *"Don't be stupid."*

"What are you?" Today had been the first time I had ever talked back to it. I usually ignored it or listened to it. Didn't seem right to speak to it, but with everything going on in my life, I might as well now.

"You know what happened last time," she warned.

"It won't go like that. I'm not that stupid."

"You thought his gift meant that."

"And it was stupid to think so. I'm just a friend. That's all this means."

"We'll see. But don't say I didn't warn you."

I frowned. He couldn't be happy being with someone like me. I knew this. I wouldn't fall into that trap of falsely thinking it could work. I was smarter than that. *Right?*

39
CHAPTER
(RYOKO)

Bacon sizzled and popped as it cooked in the pan. The smell of the meat and fat made my mouth water but I forced myself to keep cooking them. I wasn't going to give in and eat these raw. I didn't feel human enough unless I ate it fully cooked.

I gazed around as I waited to flip the meat. It was strange not having anyone around. Zane told me he didn't need me at the shop today, and Laz, Danika, and Raikidan went off to do shaman things. Even Seda and Genesis were gone somewhere. Rylan was the only one who was still here, and he was in his room doing… well I wasn't sure what he was up to. I wouldn't doubt he was sleeping. He had worked late last night.

Thinking of Rylan had my mind wandering to Laz, and then of her and Raikidan. I smiled as I thought of how much he'd changed her. The day they had arrived here, she hadn't looked any different. Sure, she'd lost some weight, but the way she saw the world was the same. Getting her to laugh was easier than a smile, but even then that was still a chore. Now neither was hard for her. She laughed and smiled all the time and even more so when he was around her.

My smile grew when I remembered seeing the necklace he gave her. It had been a bit of a task to get her to talk about it, but I won out like usual. He had good taste. Not something I'd wear, but it was so

Laz. And I could see she liked it by the amount of times she'd fiddle with it. They both said it had been a late birthday gift, a "just because" gift, but they couldn't fool me. *No way am I buying that.* Not with how she acted around the time he gave it to her.

I prayed he was the right one for her and that she'd let him in. I desperately wanted it to be that way. She deserved to be happy again, and I wanted her to have a sense of peace in her life. But, the thing I wanted most was for her to not have to be afraid of one man trying to be close to her. Sure, he wasn't human, but she wasn't exactly full human herself.

I sniffed the air, and panicked when I smelled the bacon burning. I grumbled when I finally managed to flip it over. I wasn't a good cook, that was for sure, but food was food at this point, and I wasn't getting any unless I made it myself.

Strong arms snaked their way around me. "Something smells good."

I scrunched my nose. "It's a little burnt."

"I like my bacon crispy." He chuckled and kissed the back of my head. "But the bacon wasn't what I was talking about."

I rolled my eyes and flipped the bacon. Noticing it was done, I scooped it up and put it on a plate I had already set aside for it. I reached for two more strips, but Rylan stopped me.

I sighed. "Rylan, please, I'm hungry."

"Then let me make you something," he said.

"No, I want to make it."

He took my spatula away. "It'll be better than just bacon."

I turned off the burner, knowing full well this was going to take a while, and turned around to face him. I reached for the spatula but he kept it out of my reach.

"Please, Ry, I want to make it myself."

"Let me do something for you."

"Ry, I don't want to play games right now."

"I'm not playing games. I want to do it for you."

I reached for the spatula again, but he still wouldn't give it to me, so I pouted. To my surprise, it didn't work. He grinned instead and didn't give an inch. I had to think of something different.

A devious grin spread across my face when something came to mind and Rylan's expression changed to confusion. Pressing against him, I wrapped my arms around his neck and cocked my head to the side, tossed my hair with it. He visibly swallowed, and I continued to grin playfully.

I leaned into him until my nose was touching his. "Fine, if you won't let me have my first choice, I'll just have to choose something different."

I captured his lips with mine and he didn't fight me. My heart leapt when his lips became more demanding. The spatula clattered on the counter, but I didn't care about that anymore. My body went into autopilot mode the moment Rylan pushed me back against the counter. My mind wasn't allowed to think, and my body wanted one thing.

I dragged my hands down his chest and his muscles responded like they always did when I did this. The moment my hands reached the hemming of his shirt, they grabbed on and tried to pull it off him, but as usual, it wasn't going to happen.

Rylan pulled away and grabbed onto my hands to stop me. "Ryoko, no."

I exhaled and pulled my hands out of his grip, doing my best to hide my disappointment. "All right."

Pushing past him, I went to the fridge to look for something to add to the meal I had started. This wasn't the first time I had tried and he'd pushed back. I knew it was best to just go back to making my meal than to keep trying. "Ryoko, please don't be mad."

"I'm not mad," I said as I selected some eggs. "I'm just removing myself from a position of want but can't have."

Rylan stopped me when I tried to make my way back to the stove. "I'm sorry if this upsets you, but—"

"Ry, you don't have to apologize," I said, moving around him and turning the burner back on. I cracked an egg into the skillet. "You already told me how anything further would make this a permanent thing because of your instincts as a human hybrid. It's the same with me being half wogron. It's why loosing Zeek had been so—"

Rylan touched my elbow and rested his forehead on the back of my head. "Please don't think about that... I know that was hard for you."

I cracked another egg. "I'm getting ahead of myself because of how long I waited. I need to step back and stay clear of positions like this so I don't cause any problems. If you're not ready to make this permanent, then that's fine. It's not like we've been together that long." *I've waited this long, I can continue to wait longer. Rushing isn't something I want anyway...*

Silence fell over us as I continued cooking. While I didn't mind him watching me, a part of me wished he'd just go do something else after everything I said.

I slid my cooked eggs onto my plate. "Do you want anything to eat?"

"Yes," he said in a deeper-than-normal tone.

"What do you want?"

His hand snaked around my waist and pulled me into him as his other hand reached up and pulled my hair to the side. "You."

My heart thumped in my chest when he planted a strong kiss on the nape of my neck. "R–Rylan, we just got done t–talking about this."

"No, you finished talking about the conclusion you'd come to," he murmured. "The wrong conclusion, at that." He kissed my neck again. "I want this to be permanent. I don't want anyone else to have you. But I wanted to give you time to make sure you wanted that, too."

I clicked the burner off. "With all the time I spent waiting, only Raid had me questioning how I felt at the end. But even he couldn't get me to give up on a life with you."

"Why didn't you choose my brother? From the start, he did a better job at showing you the affection you deserve."

I turned around to face him. "You're right, he did, but he doesn't understand me the same way you do. And... as much as I had hoped it would work out and become something more, I felt like he wasn't meant for me. So I continued to hold onto you when I knew I should let you go."

Rylan cupped my chin. "I'll make it up to you, for waiting so long. I'll make that wait worthwhile."

He claimed my lips with his. I pressed myself against him, feeling the strength of his muscles in his chest, and his kiss became more demanding. My heart thumped and I leaned into him more. I wanted to memorize his taste; his touch; him. I wanted everything he could offer, and give him the same back.

My hands found the hemming of his shirt again. This time Rylan didn't stop me from removing it. A smile crept onto my face as I tossed it, not caring where it landed. We were most definitely going to get into trouble from that, and any other clothes that came off out here. Such activities were supposed to stay in bedrooms with so many people living here, but I didn't care.

Rylan's free hand found one of the strings of my bikini top and pulled, only for the bow to be the only part to come undone. His confusion broke our kiss and I couldn't help but giggle. "I knot my tie job. If I didn't, I'd have far too many wardrobe malfunctions."

He bent closer and spoke in my ear. "Well, here's the thing, I want a wardrobe malfunction."

I wrapped a hand around the back of his head and pulled him closer. "Your wish is my command."

My free hand found the button of his pants, and within seconds, they hit the floor. I then slipped past him, playfully running my finger along his jaw line and neck, and giving his neck chain a light tug. I made it mere feet out of the kitchen before I was pinned against the wall. Warmth spread throughout my body as Rylan trailed a kiss along my neck and collar bone.

"So, you are that kind of guy," I teased, remembering the last time he pinned me again the wall in an attempt to get me to stop messing with Laz and Raikidan.

Rylan grinned. "You're about to find out what kind of guy I am."

My pulse quickened and my face flushed. He let go of my arms and snaked his around me, lifting me up and carrying me away. Rylan laid me down on his bed carefully, and hovered over me before kissing me deeply and fumbling with the button on my shorts. I shimmied out of them when their tight nature proved too difficult for him to handle on his own, and found my bathing suit bottoms didn't want to stay on and prolong this undressing.

Both became stuck on my large boots, but Rylan managed to release their hold and prevent me from sitting up to remove my boots. "They stay on."

"But—"

He kissed my neck, his teeth grazing my skin and sending a shiver down my spine. "They stay."

Rylan's hands slipped behind my neck and fussed with my bikini strings, while continuing to kiss me. Each one sent bursts of tingling sensations through my body, enticing a quiet moan from my throat. The sound excited him, hastening his attempt to remove my top. When he succeeded in undoing the knot, he splayed the strings out around me instead of immediately pulling down my top, and revealing my turned-on form. Rylan's hands trailed down my sides and then behind me. I arched my back, and he made quick work of the strings.

He pulled away and slowly removed my bathing suit top. Although he gazed down at my naked form with appreciation, I struggled to fight the impulse to cover myself. I knew better than to give into the urge. Zeek had gotten on my case numerous times when I pulled that move.

Rylan leaned over me and claimed my lips with his, our tongues wrestling with each other hungrily for several minutes before his lips left mine and trailed down my neck and collar bone. His teeth nipped and his hot breath tickled my sensitive skin. My back arched, and he ran his fingers down my spine, intensifying the heat rising in my body.

My heart raced as his lips slowly kissed lower, and his hands migrated from behind my back to my sides. Rylan glanced up at me, his eyes dark with lust. The gaze sent a hunger to my core, and my taut nipples throbbed. Rylan grinned, aware of my aching desire, and his hands reached up and cupped my supple breasts. His thumbs circled my rosy buds, while he kissed between my breasts. A moan of pleasure escaped my lips.

Rylan's kisses shifted to the side of my breast until they captured my erect nipple. I threaded my hands in his hair as he sucked and flicked his tongue, moaning with pleasure. His hand let go of my breast and slid down my stomach to my hips. Desire throbbed between my thighs. I lifted my hips hoping—begging—for more. I gasped when intense pleasure shot through me as Rylan fulfilled my heated desire.

Incoherent words mixed with my moans. My hips bucked as pleasure coursed through me, and Rylan continued his rhythmic motion. My grip on his hair tightened, my back arched, and I cried out as ecstasy flooded over me.

Rylan remained still while my breath came in short, heavy bursts. I gasped when he kissed my sensitive skin and he chuckled. He then reached up and brushed away a damp tassel of hair before pulling away and gazing down at me. I stretched and let my arms lazily lay above my head. Rylan's eyes lit up at the sight of the view I gave him.

I frowned and sat up when he suddenly left the bed. "Where are you going?"

"To get you some water. Don't worry, I'll be right back."

I licked my dry lips. I could use some water, but I didn't want him to leave. Hydration could wait. But he left before I could voice an argument. I huffed and twirled my hair. When he took longer than I liked, I began chewing on my lower lip.

"You're cute when do that," Rylan said when he came back and caught me. In his hands he carried two glasses filled with water.

My cheeks flushed. "What, no food, too?"

He walked over to the side of the bed and placed the glasses on the nightstand. "I can go grab your plate."

I swung my legs over the bed and grabbed him by the hem of his boxers. I pulled him closer and kissed him just below the navel.

He sucked in a tight breath. "Ryoko…"

"You're not going anywhere," I murmured before pulling his boxers down. I leaned back and Rylan placed his hands on his hips as I allowed my eyes to take in every inch of him.

"You appear pleased."

I smirked and then kissed him just below the navel again. "Hope you didn't have plans for later."

He threaded his fingers into my long hair. "Only with you."

I kissed a little lower. "That's what I like to hear."

My kisses continued to migrate down, taking a detour toward his hip and back. My teeth occasionally nipped at his skin and he'd inhale sharply. His grip on my hair tightened the more I teased. He sighed with pleasure when I grabbed his erect member and slowly eased my lips over the tip. Rylan groaned and tightened his grip, but then loosened as I sucked and slid his shaft in and out of my mouth rhythmically.

"Ryoko…" he moaned.

I gazed up at him as I continued to pleasure him. His eyes dark with lust, hooded as pleasure continued to flood over him. His grip continued to loosen until they slid to the side of my head and his fingers rubbed my ears. My cheeks flushed as a mix of pleasant sensations hit me in one large wave. A new hunger—need—surged inside me, my rhythm picking up speed.

Rylan moaned my name and rocked his hips, his ear-stroking never letting up, knowing full well what this did to me. His hard member swelled more as this continued. Then suddenly, he pulled away and forced me to lie on my back.

I stared up at him in confusion. "Why?"

"Not yet," he said, before leaning over me and kissing my collar bone.

"But—" I gasped when he dragged his tongue down my chest, deliberately choosing a path over my taut nipples. His teasing continued after circling my sensitive tips several times, and trailed down the center of my body, occasionally switching to kissing or nibbling.

"You're n–not being f–fair," I struggled to say through the pulses of pleasure.

His hunger-filled eyes flicked up at me when his lips touched my inner thigh. "Not being fair would have been allowing you to continue and end our fun far too early. I'm being more than fair, Love." My heart skipped a beat at the sound of the new name. "Now be good, and enjoy."

He spread my legs father apart and kissed my inner thigh until his lips met the moistness between. I gasped and clutched the blankets when warm pleasure rocked through me. Moans of pleasure came from my mouth as he continued, and one of my hands released its hold on the blankets and grabbed a fistful of his hair.

He held me down as my hips started to buck as I was stimulated closer to my release, but before I reached that point, Rylan stopped. I growled with frustration and he chuckled as he lifted himself onto the bed and hovered over me.

"You're getting too much enjoyment out of my frustration," I grumbled.

Rylan kissed me on the lips so passionately, my breath left me. "You know you love it." I snapped my teeth at him and he chuckled into my ear before nipping my neck. "Careful, I can continue to tease you instead of giving you what you want."

"Then you'd be denying what you want."

He grinned and kissed my collarbone. "True, but I'm in no rush to end this."

"No one said it had to end."

Rylan slid his hands down my sides and rested them on my hips. "You sure?"

I lifted my legs and pressed them against his hips, urging him to come closer. Rylan kissed my collarbone again and lifted my hips toward him. I gasped and my back arched as he filled me. Rylan took several breaths as he accepted the sensation that flooded through him, and then began thrusting into me. I moaned and grabbed fistfuls of sheets, embracing the pleasure that pulsed through me.

Rylan's momentum increased and he placed his hands on either side of my head as he held himself over me. I met his thrusts and matched them, increasing the pleasure for us both. Everything felt right about this—about us. Our breaths came rhythmically with each thrust.

"Ryoko… Ryoko, I love you."

"I… love you too."

Rylan slipped his hand between my legs and increased the pleasure coursing through me, until we both cried out in merged climactic release. We remained still, breathing heavily and embracing the remnants of the pleasure coursing through us.

Rylan kissed my forehead. "I love you."

He kissed my forehead again, then my cheek several times and then my neck. Each time murmuring the same phrase. I grabbed his face and forced him to look at me. I pecked him on the lips. "I love you too."

I pulled him closer and had him lay on me. Rylan wiggled his arms under me and snuggled into me. I hummed happily and closed my eyes, getting some rest before we went back at it.

My eyes fluttered open as I stirred. An arm hung over my shoulder and hot breath hit my neck. I wiggled my free toes, forgetting exactly when the boots had come off, but remembering Rylan had put up a bit of stink about it. I made a note to find out if I was going to need to invest in some *special* clothes, just for him.

"I was wondering when you were going to wake up," Rylan murmured in my ear.

"Hmm?" I said. "I didn't hear you."

He moved his arm and grabbed my breast. "How about feel?"

"I don't know… Might need a little more to tell."

He chuckled and kissed my head. "I love you."

I turned to face him and kissed him on the nose. "I love you too." He stroked my cheek and I looked around. "What time is it?"

"You were asleep for about two hours."

I thought about how long we'd spent making love and added the two hours of sleep. I sat up immediately. "I need to take my meds."

Rylan wrapped his arm around my hips. "Easy. They're on the night-stand. While you were sleeping, I went to grab my discarded clothes. I thought you might panic and try to get your meds, so I retrieved them."

"Thank you," I said with a smile.

I reached for the bottle, but Rylan stopped me. "Ryoko, wait. I don't want you taking these anymore."

I frowned. "Rylan, I need to."

"No, you—"

"Yes I do! Yes I do…" I stared into my hands. "You don't under-stand. You don't want to see what I am."

Rylan touched my chin and forced me to look at him. "I love you, Ryoko. I want to know everything about you. We all have things about us we don't like about ourselves. Do you think I like feeling more beast than man?"

I smiled. "I think you're cute when you're a dog."

He grinned. "And it's because of you I've become more okay with that side of me again. I don't care what these pills hide. I don't want you to hide."

I smiled and kissed him. "Then I won't take them anymore. You'll see why I take them, and then you'll have to make your final decision."

He pulled me into his arms. "I already have."

"So, are the others home?"

"Yeah. They came home before I could gather my clothes."

I bit my lip. "Did we get into trouble?"

"No, Laz just made a snarky comment."

My brow rose. "Laz, really? What did she say?"

"She handed me the clothes and told me she was glad we had the decency to make it to a room. She even correctly guessed the order my clothes came off, as well as yours."

I rolled out of his arms as I laughed. "That sounds like the new her."

"New her? Is that what you're calling it?"

I nodded. "Yeah. The old her would have definitely not been bold enough to make that kind of guess. I'm glad she's changing, even if it's too slow for my taste. But… I have Raikidan to thank for all this."

Rylan snuggled into me. "Just don't forget what I said. Don't meddle too much. We don't need her shutting down and going back to that dark version of her that neither of us ever want to see again."

My fingers lazily traced the back of his hand. "Be honest with me. Do you think something will happen between the two of them?"

Rylan thought for a moment. "I don't want to get too far ahead, since I know Laz has quite a ways to go before she'll be ready to let someone in, but… do you remember how I reacted when Tannek got in my way when I wanted her?"

"Yeah, you were not a happy camper. I thought at one point you were going to seriously kill him."

Rylan chuckled. "Yeah, if Amara hadn't put her foot down, I'm sure I would have tried."

I shook my head, doing my best not to let my insecurities rile up unfair and pointless jealousy. "So what does this have to with Raikidan?"

"Well, I noticed how Laz and Tannek acted around each other long before they started to become a thing, and I predicted if I couldn't get a leg up on him, I'd lose her to him. Fast forward to now, if I still felt the same way about Laz, I would have preferred Tannek as an obstacle over Raikidan. This path they're on is very similar, but stronger, and I'm sure there's no man alive who could compete with him."

I smiled. "That makes me happy."

Rylan rolled on top of me and kissed me passionately. "And you make me happy."

I grinned. "Haven't had enough yet?"

"Never."

He kissed me again and we melted into a pool of love and pleasure.

40
CHAPTER
(EIRA)

The cool breeze of the wind blowing in felt good as I sat on the couch reading. Nothing the book gave me to read held my interest long, but I had nothing better to do. Shva'sika and I had managed to patch things up. Raikidan and she had worked together to temporarily obtain a *time relic* and help me fix the pictures she'd damaged. Once fixed, I stored them away where they couldn't be damaged again. Shva'sika had planned to return it on her own, but Raikidan and I wanted to get out of the house, so we joined her—wrong choice.

She had borrowed it from a scholar who was staying with a group of shamans. The shamans, happy I had shown up, insisted on speaking to me about something that had nothing to do with the rebellion, which annoyed me a bit. A great deal of these shamans were taking this ambassador thing a little too seriously.

I glanced up from my book when Raikidan came down from the roof. He appeared deep in thought about something as he headed down the hall. Shva'sika looked up from her book and also watched him curiously. My eyes widened when he reached Rylan's bedroom door and put his hand on the doorknob, intending to go in.

The book fell to the floor. "Raikidan, don't go in there!"

He didn't hear me and still opened the door. "Hey, Rylan—"

An immediate silence enveloped the house.

"Babe, who is it?" Ryoko asked.

Rylan chuckled. "Need something, Raikidan?"

I bit my lip when Raikidan slammed the door shut and set a quick pace back down the hall, with his head low and his hand covering most of his face. Shva'sika and I erupted in laughter the moment he slammed the door to my room closed, although I felt bad for doing so. He wouldn't have known. He had gone to be on his own the moment we had gotten back, so he didn't make the discovery we had.

Shva'sika jerked her head in the direction of my room and finally spoke once she got her laughter under control. "You should go see if he's okay. That's not exactly the most comfortable situation to walk in on. I can't even imagine what's going through his head, being a dragon and all."

I nodded. I had my laughter under control, but I couldn't rid myself of the smile stuck on my face as I got off the couch. Grabbing hold of the doorknob, I opened the door and peeked around it. Raikidan sat on the windowsill like he usually did, but instead of staring out into the alley, he was covering his face. An unfortunate giggle escaped my lips when I realized his cheeks were still red with embarrassment. Raikidan looked at me in pure instinctual reaction to my now-announced presence, but then focused his gaze out the window, his face reddening even more.

I closed the door behind me. "Raikidan, it's all right. It happens. It's the risk we run with so many of us living together. It's why I've tried to caution you about knocking on doors."

"It's not that. I didn't think…" He sighed and covered his face. I watched as he tried to shake the memory out of his head.

"It's okay, Rai. You don't have to talk about it."

Raikidan shook his head more. "I just… I just didn't think you humans did it like that."

I chuckled. It amused me how there was an obvious a part of him that didn't want to talk about it, but he still was. It was like that other part of him wanted me to help him understand.

"I did tell you humans did it for fun. If they think it's going to be enjoyable or fun in any way, they're going to do it."

Raikidan's eyes squeezed shut. "It's another reason I live alone. Living in a clan… you run into this a lot. It's not something I…" He sighed and stopped talking finally.

I smiled. "Raikidan, look at me."

Raikidan's eyes opened and he began to look up at me, but his eyes darted to look out the window, his cheeks growing redder again.

I shook my head and grabbed his hand, getting his attention. "Rai…"

Slowly, he shifted his gaze to me, revealing eyes filled with turmoil. His cheeks remained red, giving away how badly this affected him.

"Come with me." I tugged on his hand but he didn't budge. "C'mon, I wanna show you something."

Another tug got him onto his feet, and I walked backward to the door until I knew he was going to follow on his own. I led him to the basement, looking back at times to make sure he was doing okay, since his pulse was jumping erratically. *This situation really has him all worked up.* Fresh air would do him good, which was perfect, because where I was taking him he'd get plenty of it.

Leading him through the secret passage in the basement, we reached the sewers. His pulse was slowing now, and I was glad. It meant I could trust him to follow without the threat of him running off in his weird state. I didn't let go of his hand, though, just in case I was wrong.

He crashed into me when I stopped suddenly the moment we reached a corner. A great deal of light came around this corner, and I knew we were close, but I also knew it could be dangerous.

I let go of Raikidan's hand and kept my voice low. "Stay here. I'll be right back."

Raikidan opened his mouth to protest but I shushed him by placing my fingers over his mouth. He grunted and I slipped around the corner. Taking slow, careful steps, I snuck down the tunnel that led to a bright opening to the outside. I peered around the opening real quick to check for soldiers, and then snuck back to where I had left Raikidan. To my surprise, he hadn't moved.

I grabbed his hand again. "C'mon, the coast is clear."

"Eira, where are you taking me?"

"You'll see, now let's go."

A single tug was all it took to get him to follow. I peered around the opening of the tunnel to make sure it was still clear, and then made a mad dash for the trees on the other side. Unfortunately, Raikidan was so bewildered about where we were that he was slowing me down.

"Raikidan, c'mon," I hissed. "You're going get us caught!"

Raikidan snapped out of the weird mindset he was in and picked up the pace. I didn't slow much, even when we were safely hidden by the trees. I was determined to get to our destination.

"Eira, where are you taking me?" He sounded like he was trying not to laugh. "And where are we?"

I didn't answer. I just kept pushing through the brush. I finally stopped and let go of Raikidan's hand when we came to a small clearing that didn't appear to be anything special on the surface. There were just a few flowers and other small wild plants growing about, and a large tree stump in the center that was rotting away with age.

I headed over to the stump just as Raikidan spoke to me. "This is where you wanted to bring me?"

I sat down on the tree stump and closed my eyes. My arms rested on my legs as I relaxed. "Yep."

"Why? What's so special about this place?"

"Listen, what do you hear?"

He was quiet for a moment. "Rustling leaves. Some crickets." I smiled and waited. He looked around. "I hear nothing but sounds of a forest, and no city. Eira, where are we?"

I continued to smile. "The one place I always told you to never go, not that you've listened."

His eyes widened. "We're outside the city."

I nodded and allowed my gaze to wander. It had been a little while since I had escaped here.

Raikidan sat down on the ground next to me. "Why'd you bring me here?"

"It's peaceful. My mom showed me this place. She let me come here whenever I needed to get away and think. I figured it could help you."

He smiled. "Thank you. The sorry excuse of a forest the city has doesn't come close to how peaceful this place is. It's so calming to only be able to hear natural things. Crazy to know we're only a few yards away from that wall of the city."

I chuckled little. "Mom always tried to tell me this place was touched by magic. It was the reason you couldn't hear the city. Not sure if she's right, but it'd be interesting if it was." I leaned back. "You know… you can come here whenever you want."

"Really?"

I nodded. "I've been the only one who knows about this place for such a long time. It's nice to be able to share it with someone again. Besides, you seem to like not listening to me about leaving the city. I don't know the method you've chosen to use to leave, but at least now I know if you leave, you'll use a safer way. They do patrol around the outer wall so you have to be careful, but it's easy to stay hidden until they're gone."

I squeaked when Raikidan pulled me into his lap and hugged me. "Thank you."

I smiled. "Welcome."

He rested his head against mine, and I blinked with confusion when a strange noise escaped his lips. But I knew this noise. It was that strange growling purr he had done before. I didn't ask him about it, for fear he'd stop. I just listened. It was so soothing, it tempted me to relax in his arms, but I resisted. *It wouldn't be right for me to do that...*

The sound stopped, and Raikidan spoke. "Thank you for bringing me here, Eira. It really has helped."

I chuckled. "You already thanked me."

"I know, but I want you to know how grateful I am."

"I do know."

"Tell me how to make it up to you."

I shook my head. "Raikidan, you don't need to make it up to me."

"Yes, I do. You're always going out of your way to do something for me."

I shrugged. "It's nothing, really."

His grip tightened. "Give me something."

I tried to get out. "Raikidan, let go."

"No."

A small chuckled escaped my lips. "C'mon, Raikidan."

He began to tickle me. "No, now give me something to go on."

I laughed and squirmed. "No, no, no, no, no! Please, Raikidan, stop. That tickles too much!"

He refused to relent. "Tell me how I can make it up to you and I will."

I shook my head. "No, just stop the tickling!"

He didn't listen. It got to the point where I was squirming so much we fell over—both of us laughing. Raikidan supported himself over me but I wasn't about to complain since the tickling had stopped.

Raikidan's chuckling quieted. "*Aio eny suvy.*"

My laughter ended instantly and I stared at him with confusion. "What?"

Raikidan blinked and then shook his head. "Nothing."

I pushed myself back up, forcing him to sit up as well. "No, what did you say to me?"

He chuckled. "It's nothing, really. Don't worry about it."

"Raikidan, you've said that to me before. What did you say?"

"Eira, don't worry about it. It's honestly nothing."

"All right…" My gaze drifted away, only to snap back to him when a thought came to me. "Would you teach me?"

His brow rose. "Teach you?"

I nodded. "Would you teach me your tongue?"

"Why would you want to learn?"

"Well, you're forced to speak our tongue…" I shrugged. "I guess it'd be nice to see you not have to all the time."

"It's not easy to learn, if not impossible for a non-dragon. I can't say you'll be able to do it."

"I won't be surprised if I can't. Remember, common was hard enough for me." I grinned. "But I like challenges. And I managed to learn Elvish, so maybe I'll get lucky."

Raikidan grinned back. "All right, but you have to teach me that symbolic writing of yours."

I nodded. "Deal."

He pulled me into his lap. "We start tomorrow."

I smiled and nodded. The sooner I began to learn, the sooner I'd figure out what he said to me. I'd also find out what he wrote in the book in the Library that one day.

I just hope I'm competent enough to learn.

41

CHAPTER

A slow, deep, frustrated sigh escaped my lips. Raikidan's language was really hard. Well that wasn't completely true. It was difficult, but not as bad as I thought it would be. Although unnatural to a human, the way the words were put together were primal and natural. What I had the most difficulty with was accepting how weird I sounded.

"*Zudy*," Raikidan encouraged again.

"*Zu…*" I licked my lips. "*Zud…*" I sighed. "I suck at this."

"You almost had it. Try again. *Zudy*."

I gnashed my teeth. The word was easy, it was the way it was pronounced and how the dragons spoke that made it hard. Not to mention that my language-learning skills were barely worth calling even subpar. "*Z–zudy. Zudy*."

Raikidan smiled, but it faded away when I didn't show any excitement. "What's wrong? You did it."

I shook my head. "It didn't sound right."

He chuckled. "It sounded fine."

I snorted and then spotted the pad of paper and two pens I had set aside on the bed. Grabbing them, I held out a pen for him. "Let's do something different."

Raikidan nodded. "All right, have it your way. What are you going to teach me?"

I wrote down a few symbols on the paper. "The same words you've taught me." I pointed to the words as I spoke. "Death, birth, and life. Now let's see how well you can write them."

Raikidan studied the three words for a few moments before he wrote them down. His quickness surprised me. His handwriting was also incredibly nice—even nicer than mine. I eyed him and then wrote down a list of words. I told him what all the words meant and he went to work. When he thought he was done, he held out his paper for me to compare.

I laid the papers together. "This word, wind, is almost right, but not quite. It needs more of a curve here."

Raikidan nodded and retried writing the word. I shook my head, and he tried again, but he still didn't get it quite right.

"Like this." I leaned over and wrote the word. "See how it flows?"

"It's like the actual meaning behind the word."

I smiled. "Right. Now try again." He did and this time he did it right. "Good. You're doing exceptionally well."

He shrugged. "It's not that hard."

I snorted. "Well then, if you feel that way, use the words I've given you and make them into sentences."

"But you haven't taught me the structure."

"It's the same as common. Just write, and I'll check to see if you do it right."

Raikidan grunted, and picked his words carefully as he wrote them down. I watched and was surprised at how well he was doing. When he finished, he looked up at me, and I turned the paper so I could see it better. All the words were written correctly and all the sentences made sense, but that didn't mean he wasn't just lucky.

"Do you know what you wrote?"

He snorted. "Of course."

"Then tell me what they say."

"Listen to the teacher. Fight to live." He chuckled. "And just for you, I will never breathe fire on peasants."

A raucous laugh tore through my throat. It was funnier when spoken. "You've done well. I didn't think you'd pick it up as quickly as you did. Not many are able to get it in such a short period of time."

Raikidan's eyes flicked down to the pad of paper. "To be completely honest, the way you've made these words, they're really close to my tongue."

"Say what?"

Raikidan took the pad and wrote something down on it. I peered at it closely when he finished. *Why does this look familiar?*

"Our lives are connected. That's what it reads. Now write your version under it."

I nodded and took the pad to write the symbols. When I was done, I laid it back down on the bed for us to examine. My brow furrowed when I noticed how similar they really were. Two symbols even looked exactly alike.

Raikidan took his pen and connected the symbols. "These two words, lives and connected, are exactly the same. These other two are similar; you'd just have to flip them to be the same. The way you speak is a little different from us, so not all word positions are the same—but it's pretty close, just like this phrase."

I scrutinized the two sentences, and then looked up at him. "Show me more."

"All right."

He took his pen and wrote several sentence until the pen stopped cooperating. When ink wouldn't flow any more Raikidan began to shake it. He shook it a little too hard and the pen went flying. I laughed as he stared at his empty hand with confusion.

After realizing the pen wasn't magically coming back, his gaze snapped to the pen that was in my hand. "Give me your pen."

I clutched my pen. "No, it's mine. Go get yours."

"Eira, just hand over the pen."

"I said no."

He lunged at me. "Just hand it over. It's just a pen."

I laughed as I fell back. "No, go get yours!"

Raikidan chuckled as he fought with me. It was hard to keep him from getting the pen since he was over me, but I did my best. We froze when the doorknob jiggled and then turned completely.

"Hey, Laz, can you help—" Ryoko stopped dead when she saw us.

I kicked Raikidan off of me. "It's not what you think."

A grin spread across her face. "Sure. I'll just leave you two alone."

"Ryoko!" She giggled and shut the door. I sighed and tossed the pen at him. "Here, take the stupid pen."

"You're embarrassed, aren't you?" Raikidan said.

"It's nothing."

"It's something if you're upset."

I grabbed the pad of paper to focus on. "Can you teach me these words?"

A frown graced Raikidan's lips for a moment before he leaned closer. "Which ones?"

I pointed to the sentence. "The one you compared to my writing."

"*Ion zutyl eny xivvexmyk.*"

I chuckled. "Yeah, those ones."

He smiled. "Prepare to be frustrated."

I laughed, and then took a deep breath to prepare myself for the torture I had asked to put myself through.

My eyes darted around as Argus and Blaze drove us to our destination in the limousine. Raikidan's and my language session had been interrupted by the Council's need, and although I honestly wasn't thrilled to be doing this assignment, my feelings didn't matter. The guys had been doing this assignment for some time now, so there was no negotiating this. I watched as Rylan and Raikidan fussed with suit cuffs, and Raid, in his dog form, swiveled his ears and panted.

Although Rylan did this a lot with Argus, Blaze, and a few others, and I couldn't blame the nerves. Gangs were not people you messed with, and that's exactly what we were doing. Intel told us some of them knew things that would be helpful to us, but this particular gang our team was dealing with was supposedly loyal to Zarda, and was only putting on a front to infiltrate other gangs and have them removed.

Ryoko fidgeted next to Rylan. Seda seemed to be the only one who was calm in this car. This was the first time the women of the team were going to be included in this type of mission, and yet here she was, calm as could be. It was like she knew how this was going to end.

I tugged on the hem of my short dress and wiggled my toes in my uncomfortable heeled shoes. I couldn't believe I was being forced to wear this. At least I didn't have to talk. I was told all I had to do was look pretty. *Look pretty.* I snorted mentally. *Right.* Luckily, acting stand-offish wasn't out of the question, so I had that going for me.

I gazed around when the limousine came to a halt. Argus and Blaze looked at each other and then climbed out of the vehicle. The two doors on the right side of the limousine opened, and Rylan and Raikidan stepped out. Raid followed, and Ryoko and I were next. I accepted Raikidan's hand as he offered to help me out of the limousine. When I was out of the way, Argus extended his hand and helped Seda out. While he was helping her, I took in our surroundings. The street looked abandoned and there were few lights. Even the full moon was dim due to clouds.

When Seda was out and standing next to Ryoko and me, Argus and Blaze shut the doors and turned their heads toward each other. I tried not to laugh at them—they looked so ridiculous in their sunglasses when it was night time. The two nodded and walked over to the front of the car, where they scanned the street, Raid playing his part by following and keeping watch next to Argus.

Raikidan placed his hand on my back and led me toward the house in front of us. I suddenly realized how quiet everyone was. Ever since we had poured into the limousine, all conversation had ceased. Realizing this elevated my anxiety about this assignment.

Rylan knocked on a low point of the door, and after waiting a few moments, someone opened the door. Rylan grinned at the man inside the house and shook his hand.

"Good to see you could make it, Jay," the man greeted.

Rylan chuckled. "I'm glad you contacted us, Mason."

Mason turned his eyes to Raikidan. "This the Big Boss?"

Rylan nodded. "It is."

Raikidan held out his hand. "Raiden."

Mason excitedly accepted Raikidan's offer and shook his hand. "A pleasure to finally meet you, sir. Please, come in."

Mason moved out of the way so we could enter, and led us deeper into the house until we reached a large, well-decorated living room with several couches and chairs. Most of the furniture was filled with the male residences of this house, save for two blonde-haired women who were on either side of a muscular man with white hair and almond-shaped crystal eyes.

"Ergren, sir, Jay and his company have finally arrived."

The white haired man smiled. "Ah, welcome. It's good to see you again, Jay, and it looks like you brought some friends."

Rylan gestured to Raikidan. "This is my boss, Raiden."

Ergren nodded. "Nice to meet you. Not to sound rude, but you weren't the friend I was referring to."

My gaze stopped wandering around when I realized this guy was referring to me and the other two ladies.

Raikidan rested his hand on my lower back. "This is Xephrya. Xephrya, say hello."

I made eye contact with Ergren. "Hello."

Ergren nodded with a grin and then looked at Ryoko expectantly.

"This is Jasmine," Rylan introduced.

Ryoko smiled. "Hello."

"And the psychic behind you?" Ergren inquired.

"My name is Crystal," Seda introduced. "A pleasure."

"Such beautiful names for beautiful ladies. Please, tell me how you found them."

"We didn't find them," Rylan corrected. "We had them made in another city."

"Except me," Seda said as she ventured toward a window. "I found them."

Ergren continued to grin. "I see."

Raikidan touched me under the chin. "They make for great guards— and even better companions."

I grinned at him and slowly turned to walk away. "Our host isn't very hospitable, Master. He has yet to ask you to sit down and relax." I made my way over to a window Seda stood in front of.

"Though Xephrya has yet to master manners," Raikidan said. "I do apologize."

"No need. She is right, after all. I should have been more hospitable. Please, sit down."

Raikidan and Rylan moved to accept his offer, but by the sounds of it, Ryoko had stayed where she was—or close to it. I was too preoccupied with looking out the window to pay much attention. I observed Blaze walk around the car with Raid following. Argus sat on the hood of the limousine, playing with the sunglasses on the tip of his nose, bored with his job in this assignment.

He looked our way and gave a reserved wave, but my calculations indicated it wasn't me he was waving at. I glanced as Seda to find her waving her fingers slowly at him. She stopped when she realized I was watching, her cheeks tinting a light shade of red. Argus turned his face away, but I caught a glimpse of the color change in his face. I grinned and made my way back to the main part of the living room. *Cute.*

I leaned on the couch behind Raikidan and scanned the room. I didn't know what they were talking about, and frankly, I didn't care. Growing bored, I ran my hands down Raikidan's chest and hung over him.

Raikidan chuckled. "What is it, Xephrya?"

"I'm bored. Are you almost done?"

He chuckled some more. "No."

I pouted. "Why not? This is boring. You promised it wouldn't be boring."

He touched my chin. "I know, and I'll make it up to you when we get home."

I grinned as I stared into his eyes.

Rylan cleared his throat. "I think it's time you two cooled it."

I put out a fake sigh and pulled away from Raikidan, although Ryoko was more than happy to encourage the situation. "I'm bored too, Master."

I grinned when I noticed Rylan having a hard time swallowing and keeping himself under control. *Oh, so he's that kind of guy.*

"You'll have to wait," he finally managed.

She huffed and tightened her grip on him. "But I can't wait that long."

"You'll have to at least make it to the car."

She pouted. "Fine."

I snorted as I walked around the couch. "No one wants to see you naked, Jay."

Rylan glared at me, and Raikidan chuckled as he pulled his arm over the top of the couch to invite me to sit next to him. I did, and then noticed Ergren watching me in an unusual way.

I leaned over to whisper to Raikidan. "Master, why is he looking at me like that?"

Raikidan's intense gaze didn't leave Ergren. "That's a good question."

Ergren grinned. "Impatient little assassin you are."

I narrowed my eyes. "How did you know I was an assassin?"

He gestured to the two women who were now sprawled out against him. "Zena and Niccola are assassins as well. They're handy in many ways, just like you seem to be."

I chose not to respond. I didn't like what he was implying.

Zena gazed at Ergren. "Sir, you looked parched. May we get you something?"

"Yes, please do, and something for our guests as well."

"Of course, sir," the two responded.

Ryoko looked at Rylan. "May I go help them?"

Rylan smiled. "As long as you don't cause trouble."

Ryoko giggled and followed the two women.

"You are welcome to go with them," Raikidan told me.

"Thank you, Master." I slid off the couch and followed the women into another room behind a swinging door. I could feel Ergren's gaze follow us, making me uncomfortable. The moment the door stopped swinging, I relaxed, as did the other three.

"Zena, Niccola, do you have any information for us?" I asked as they searched cabinets for glassware.

"Sorry, Commander, nothing useful," Niccola replied. "I'm surprised you recognized us. We've done our best to change our appearances without permanent reconstruction."

"And you've done well hiding your true identities, but remember, I trained you. I'd be able to recognize you even if you'd had reconstructive surgery."

Niccola smiled. "Well at least someone does. It's hard not being able to be myself now that we work for Ergren."

"Ergren seems like a real creep," Ryoko commented as she grabbed a pitcher out of the fridge. "Why do you put up with him?"

"It's our assignment," Zena stated. "We were to arrive here and pretend we were a gift from one of the other groups. While here, we're supposed to grab whatever information we can and put our assassination skills to good use. Of course he's not with Zarda like we thought, so that really screwed things up. Luckily, another group that comes here shows some signs, so we're hoping to get more information from them soon."

"So you don't mind working for him?" Ryoko asked.

Zena chuckled. "Not at all. We get great sex when we want, with whomever we want, and all we have to do is assassinate targets Ergren wants out of the picture. Though, we have more of a say in our targets than he seems to realize."

Niccola grinned. "We have him wrapped around our fingers. Though, you two look to be doing well too. Especially you, Commander."

I snorted and accepted the two glasses Ryoko handed me. "I have no idea what you're talking about."

"Oh, c'mon, Commander. You two look pretty close."

"It's called acting."

"They're just friends." Ryoko waved a hand. "Trust me, I've tried this route. It is what it is."

"Well if you don't want him, I'll gladly take him," Niccola said.

Ryoko and I exchanged a glance and chuckled. "Trust me, you don't want him."

Niccola tilted her head. "He doesn't seem like a bad guy."

"He's not," Ryoko said. "He's great, actually. He's just complicated and filled with secrets."

Zena grinned. "I like complicated."

I shook my head and left the kitchen with my two glasses. Raikidan smirked when he saw me, and I handed him his drink. He nodded his thanks and invited me to sit back down next him. Just as I became comfortable, I noticed Ergren staring at me.

"Master, why does he keep staring at me?" I whispered to Raikidan.

"It's nothing. Don't worry about it."

"Master, I don't like you keeping secrets from me."

Ergren chuckled. "So you're sure you don't wish to trade her for a short time?" I narrowed my eyes. *I guess we're going down that route.* "My girls would be an excellent trade for you."

"I already told you no." Raikidan rolled his arm over my shoulders. "There's no replacement for her."

A smile crept onto my face. I knew he was playing his part, but his words made me feel good, even if they were a lie.

Ergren looked to Rylan. "The same for you, then?"

Rylan narrowed his eyes. "No. Now can we please get back to business?"

"Of course, of course." Ergren leaned back and made an attempt to place his arms around Zena and Niccola, but they weren't there. Instead, sat near the edges of the couch, next to some of the other men of the house, keeping their distance. "Ladies?"

Neither spoke to him. They just sipped on their drinks.

"Zena, tell me what is bothering you." His words sounded like an order rather than a request.

Zena glared at him. "You planned to trade us."

"Not for long." I didn't like the fact he saw nothing wrong with what he had wanted to do. "So why don't you come back over here."

"No."

He frowned and switched his gaze to his other assassin. "Niccola?"

She stuck up her nose in response.

Raikidan chuckled. "You won't get them to listen if you don't respect them."

Zena smirked. "Maybe we'll just go with them anyway, without a trade."

Zena rose to her feet, her movements unnaturally fluid, and sat next to Raikidan, curling close and resting a hand on his chest. My eyes narrowed while a sudden possessive sensation called me to rip her off him. Niccola followed her lead, choosing Rylan.

Zena touched Raikidan's chin lightly with her finger. "He's handsome and respectful."

Raikidan pulled her hand away. "That won't be happening. Xephrya wouldn't be happy, and she may attack you."

My upper lip curled, a growl escaping my throat. I placed my hand on Raikidan's chest. "I don't share."

"Tell her not to," Ergren said. "I don't appreciate the idea of my ladies being harmed unnecessarily."

"Xephrya has free will. There's no controlling her. If she isn't happy about something, she takes care of it herself, even if I'd prefer her not to."

"Free will?" Ergren laughed. "Why in Lumaraeon would you give her that?"

Raikidan cupped my chin. "I have no need to control her. She chooses to stay with us, even though she was made."

I grinned. "I like it where I am."

Ergren folded his hands together. "Very interesting."

Zena pouted and went to sit next to Ergren. Niccola slowly followed her. Ergren, happy to have his toys back, began discussing things with the boys again. I tuned them out and looked around the room again. My focus kept drifting to the other men in the room. They were exceptionally quiet. None of them spoke or put an opinion into the discussion. It was even hard to hear them breathe. It was as if they were statues, or ordered to be silent and still.

A muffled thumping noise caught my ear and I stopped looking around. It happened again, sending Ryoko and me into full alert.

Raikidan's eyes snapped to me. "What is it?"

"Crystal?" Rylan said.

"We have uninvited guests," she stated.

Before anyone could react, the kitchen door broke off its hinges, and soldiers stormed through the doorway. Everyone jumped to their feet as the soldiers held their guns up.

"Everyone freeze," a helmeted general ordered. "You're all under arrest for conspiring against Lord Zarda."

"Sorry, not going to happen." Seda forced out her arms, and the soldiers flew back.

In the moment it took them to fly back, I had removed my shoes and sprinted their way. Zena called out to me and tossed me an assassin's dagger. I had no idea where she had gotten it, or where the men in this house obtained the guns they now carried, but right now wasn't the time to question it.

The soldiers tried to get back up, but I wasn't having it. Choosing the nearest body, I jumped on him and thrust my dagger into his chest. I poised to go after the next soldier, but Zena took him out and Niccola took out another on my other side.

The three of us took out a few more soldiers before someone called out behind us. "Ladies, get back here before you get hurt!"

I shared a glance with the other two assassins, who nodded at me as we fell back. We barely managed to get back into the living room before a group of men opened fire on the kitchen. I looked around for everyone, noticing that Ryoko was gone and Seda was standing in the doorway of the front door.

"Watch it!" someone yelled.

I didn't need to turn around to find out what they were yelling about. Small black objects rolled past me out of the kitchen and filled the room with smoke. *Smoke bombs!* The smoke was thick and dark, more so than normal smoke bombs, clogging my senses. I choked on the smoke and stumbled. *This isn't good…*

Someone seized my arm and chuckled. "You're coming with me. The large-chested wench is out of my reach, so I'll just have to settle with only having you."

"Fight it! Don't let him handle you like this."

Ergren. Instinct kicked into gear, making me struggle against his grip without a second thought. "No way in hell."

"You don't have much of a choice. Unlike you, I'm not affected by this smoke in the same way you are. I know because Zena and Niccola are the same way. Of course, I've already had them moved somewhere safe. Now you'll join them, and you're too weak to fight me."

"Keep fighting!"

I tried to struggle, but he was right. "No…" I used the strength I had left to fight against him as he dragged me off somewhere. "Let go…"

Ergren chuckled. "There's no way I'm passing up the opportunity to add another to my—"

Ergren's grip disappeared suddenly, and it sounded like he fell to the floor. "I told you, you can't have her!"

"Raikidan?" I whispered.

His strong arms wrapped around me and held me up in my weakened state. *"Lry ul suvy."*

My eyes widened. *Did he just—He did not just speak in his tongue!*

How could he do something so risky? It was one thing for him to be protective, and to act possessive for this assignment, but for him to speak like that… *Why am I so angry? It's not like the guy knows what Draconic sounds like. He probably didn't even recognize them as words.*

Raikidan hoisted my body and cradled me. I stayed quiet as he carried me out of the house and into the running limousine. Raikidan set me down, and Ryoko handed me the oxygen mask she was using. Rylan and Seda jumped into the car and looked around in panic.

"Hit the gas, guys!" Rylan ordered.

Argus slammed on the accelerator. Seda rolled down and window and threw psychic energy behind us. Things crashed about on the street and people shouted, but no gunfire followed. She rolled up the window. "That'll stop them. They won't follow us anymore."

We all let out deep relieved breaths. I handed the mask to Ryoko so she could use it again, and I coughed violently. The coughing irritated my throat some more, and I did my best not to use my voice. I knew any talking would only aggravate my condition. Ryoko handed me the oxygen mask and I sucked in as much fresh air as I could, hoping the ride home would end quickly.

I held my throat as I coughed. By the time we had gotten home, Ryoko had started to feel better, but I wasn't so lucky since I had inhaled more smoke than she had. My throat had gotten worse, even though I hadn't spoken a word since the attack. Shva'sika had been unable to help me with her healing ability, and with no modern medicine downstairs that would relieve any of this pain, she left my room. I coughed more and curled up. At this rate, I wasn't going to be able to sleep, and that wouldn't help my condition.

Raikidan sat down on my bed. My eyes flicked to him. "Can you help me?"

He hesitated. "My healing fire may be able to help… but I'm not comfortable trying to use it on your throat. I don't want to do something wrong, and seriously hurt you."

I smiled at his thoughtfulness, and then had an idea. I coughed some more before speaking. "Do you think you can create some healing fire near me, and I take control of it to eat? I don't know if me controlling it will change the properties"—I coughed some more—"and change it back to regular fire, but it's worth a shot. Regular fire would help me too, especially with how powerful your flame it, so either way is a win for me."

"That's right… you can eat fire…" he murmured to himself. "Uh, do you think you're strong enough to harness my flame? Even a small one will be pretty strong." I nodded. "All right, let's give this a shot then."

I sat up as he took a deep breath and then exhaled out a small flame. I reached out and beckoned the flame to bend to my will. The flame's strength proved a bit difficult for me, and I worried Raikidan may be right about me not being strong enough in my condition, but my will proved stronger, and the flame came to me.

When I held it in my hand, while difficult to maintain, I inspected the fire instead of eating it right away. The red flames flickered and occasionally turned white, showing its power, even in such a tiny form, but that wasn't what caught my eye. There was an unusual glow around it, almost whitish-green, like the aura you'd see with a healing shaman. This had to be the look of healing fire when examined so close. That meant the transfer of wills didn't affect the properties, indicating the property was locked in the fire itself and not the will of the user.

The flame flickered wildly and I shoved it into my mouth. Not used to seeing others do this, Raikidan flinched, but smiled when I looked at him, signaling he was handling it better than most. I sucked in a deep breath as the flame did its magic, and then went into a coughing fit. Raikidan grabbed my shoulders in a panic, but relaxed when he realized the flame wasn't killing me.

He let out a slow exhale when my fit subsided. "This is really nerve-racking, you know that?"

I flopped down on my back as strength came back to me in strong waves. "I think it's amazing."

"I suppose he's not so bad…" the voice said, rather uncharacteristically. *"But don't trust him. Could be a trap."*

Raikidan lay on his side next to me. "Seriously?"

"Your flame is just amazing," I said, relaxing, almost dreamily. "Its strength is like nothing I've embraced before. And it works so fast. I feel so much better already. It tastes pretty good, too."

"It tastes good?" He laughed. "You really are something else." He reached over and brushed my bangs out of my face. "How are you feeling?"

I swatted his hand away. "You fuss too much."

"You don't take care of yourself, so someone has to look out for you."

I glanced up at him. "Like earlier?"

He smiled. "Yeah." He then frowned. "Since we're on that topic, sorry about speaking in my tongue. I know you heard, and it wasn't my intention."

"Why did it happen?"

"I was caught up in the moment," he admitted. "Caught up in my anger. I was furious he'd try to take you like that—that he'd try at all."

"What did you say? You haven't taught me those words yet."

He avoided eye contact. "It was… possessive… caught up in the assignment…"

I rolled over to face him. "That doesn't answer my question."

"Lry ul suvy," he said slow enough for me to catch the words a little better.

That last word... why does that sound so familiar? It didn't matter right now. I could figure it out later. "Rai, that isn't answering the question I'm asking. I want to know the translation."

Raikidan hesitated. "It... it means... 'she is mine.'"

My brow rose. "As in..."

"As in, mine and no one else can have you. As in... my bond partner... my mate..."

My heart's pace quickened, but as I thought about it, I realized it fit the situation of the mission and why he'd say it by mistake. I pursed my lips. "That's not so bad, actually."

His brow rose. "Really?"

"Yeah. It makes a lot of sense with that situation. I thought it was more like a property-ownership type claim."

Raikidan snickered. "No, that'd be Rylan to Ryoko."

My eyes widened and then I laughed uncontrollably. "Did you see how red his face got when she called him Master?"

He rubbed his nose. "Didn't need to. His testosterone kicked into high gear."

We continued to laugh, but it was cut short when someone knocked on the door, instantly irritating me. I sat up. "Come in."

The door opened and Shva'sika poked her head in. "I can hear you laughing. You should be—"

"I'm fine. Rai figured out how to heal me."

She eyed the two of us suspiciously. "Even still. You should rest."

"I'll b—" My brow rose as we heard something heavy bump into a wall. "What the hell was that?"

Shva'sika peered out into the living room. "I have no idea."

I slid off the bed when I heard it again. Shva'sika and I ventured into the living room. The sound happened again, and I pinpointed Ryoko's room as the source. Rylan ventured out of his room, so I knew he wasn't the cause.

"Ryoko?" I called. "Ryoko!"

The only response I received was more thumping. The soundproofing her room had gotten would prevent her from hearing me, that much I knew, but if we could hear her so well, something was up. I stepped closer to her room. I stopped dead in my tracks when the door shattered and a large, brown, hairy beast crashed out of Ryoko's room.

The beast shook its large head and slowly rose up on its large back feet, towering over everyone. It had a long snout, with snarling white teeth and long claws, and was barrel-chested with slender hips and a fluffy tail. The beast's chest, although covered with extra fur, had breasts, defining this creature as female.

"What the hell?" Blaze shouted. He had come around the corner of the hallway just as this beast had crashed out of the room. "What's with the wogron?"

Unfortunately, Blaze's yelling caught the wogron's attention and angered her. She snarled and took a step toward him.

"Ryoko, stop!" I ordered.

The wogron stopped and turned to face me.

Rylan's brow furrowed. "What?"

Ryoko snarled and advanced. I didn't move. She towered over me, and I still didn't back down. It wasn't until she roared and swiped her giant claws at me that I finally reacted. I ducked and dodged her swipe, and then attacked her. She howled and yelped. I forced her back and then stopped my attack.

"Ryoko, you will listen and you will behave." She snarled in response and held eye contact. "That's enough!"

She roared and came at me again, but this time I knew I'd get her to submit. I dodged her attacks, and once I found an opening, I attacked her again, using all the strength I had. I went at her until she whimpered and lowered herself to the ground. I stared her down and waited to make sure she was going to stay submissive.

Rylan took a step forward. "That was all a bit harsh, don't you—"

I shut him up with a flick of my hand. I didn't need him ruining this. Slowly, Ryoko lifted her head and gazed up at me. She didn't look vicious anymore. Her eyes now only windowed to the fear inside.

Placing my hand on her head I smiled and scratched her. "Much better."

Ryoko's thick tail thumped on the floor and then she began happily whining and rubbing herself against me. I laughed and tried to keep her from plowing me over, but it was hard.

"All right, all right, Ryoko." I finally managed to push her away. "Enough, Ryoko."

Her ears drooped, but when she noticed I wasn't angry she perked up a little. I spun around when I heard someone I didn't recognize breathing heavily. My eyes narrowed when I saw the culprit standing on the stairs of the front door hall. Normally I would be happy to see Ryder, but he had brought a friend along, and that made me unhappy.

I stalked toward the pair, but just as I reached them and was about to throw out a bunch of threats, Ryder stopped me. "Easy, Mom. He's one of us."

I grunted and pointed at the kid. "You tell and I'll make you wish you hadn't."

Ryder's friend held up his hands. "I won't, I promise. You can trust me."

I snorted and walked away.

"I thought you said she was friendly," Ryder's friend whispered.

"She is, when she knows you… and isn't stressed out."

Ryoko happily greeted me upon my return. Rylan ventured closer, out of curiosity, and Ryoko turned her eyes on him when she noticed his approach. Her tail wagged a little, and she left me to greet him. He chuckled as she rubbed herself against him and I allowed myself to relax. She was now calm, and instinct wasn't telling her to defend herself from everything.

"Is someone going to tell me what the hell is going on?" Blaze demanded.

He spoke too high an octave, and that did not sit well with Ryoko. She bared her teeth, a deep rumbling growl emanating from her throat. Both Rylan and I narrowed our eyes. Before I could react, Rylan threw his arm out, and an ice shard went flying at Blaze. The shard never hit Blaze, though. Instead, it hovered in the air just in front of his face, thanks to Seda, who had walked out of her room just in time to stop it.

"That's enough, both of you," she said in a calm tone. "This fighting is going to trigger Ryoko's defensive instincts, and we won't be able to calm her if she goes into it a second time. To answer your question, Blaze, Ryoko has stopped taking her medication. It was preventing this transformation."

Rylan looked at me. "Did you know about this?"

I nodded. "At first it was just the full moon that triggered it, but as time passed, it became more sporadic and uncontrollable. Jasmine believed with time and training, Ryoko would be able to control it and transform at will, as well as act like a typical wogron, such as being able to speak and keep herself under control in this state. But we didn't have that kind of time in the military, so they put her on the anti-transformation pills."

"So if you knew, why did you get mad at her when you found out she was still taking them?"

I sighed and scratched my head. "Before I left, she promised she'd get off them and learn to control it." Ryoko whined and nudged me with her nose. I smiled and scratched her on the head. "Rylan, you might as well bring her into your room. This could last a while, and we need to get her door fixed before she can sleep in there again."

"All right, I'll grab some clothes for her." He headed into her room and rummaged around until he found some clothes he liked. He came back out with them folded under his arm. "C'mon, Ryoko."

She sniffed the air, but didn't move. I chuckled and pushed her toward him. She resisted, but when Rylan touched her shoulder, she immediately stopped fighting, nearly landing me flat on my face. I pointed at Ryder when he chuckled, and he stopped with a sigh. Rylan pressed on Ryoko's shoulder and she stood, towering over everyone again.

Once he had gotten her in his room and had shut the door, I walked over to Ryder. "What are you doing here? It's late."

"Well I had come by earlier, like I had promised, but you weren't here."

I scratched my head. "Oh, yeah, sorry about that."

He chuckled. "It's cool. I figured you'd be back later so here I am. Jon just chose to tag along." I eyed Jon with obvious skepticism, and Ryder rolled his eyes. "C'mon." He spun me around and led me down the stairs to the basement. I kept glancing back at Jon as he followed, and Ryder scolded me. "Just relax, will you?"

"We were attacked today by the military while on a non-military-related assignment. Hard to relax after that."

His gaze lowered. "Sorry, I should have figured that was the reason."

"It's all right, Ryder," Jon told him. "I didn't expect open arms and smiles the first time I met them. Of course, had we come at a different time, it might have been different."

I chuckled. At least he wasn't dumb. I opened a cabinet and pulled out some supplies. When I came back, Ryder had a few drawings laid out on the workbench. Placing the items down, I examined the illustrations. They were crude sketches, but I got the idea of what he was thinking when designing them.

I went to get more supplies that would help us, but Ryder stopped me. "Before we make these, do you mind teaching me how to carve?"

My brow rose in question. "Teach you how to carve? That's not something I'm sure I can teach you. At least, not in one session."

He pulled out a block of wood from a pouch. "Then can you carve something so I can watch you? I'll still learn."

I smiled. "All right."

When he handed me the wood, I inspected it. *Good quality… A few imperfections on the surface, but nothing I can't work around.* Sitting down on the workbench, I drew my dagger and willed it to change into a carving tool before getting to work. I wasn't sure what I was going to carve, but I knew something would come to me as I worked.

CHAPTER 42

A light breeze rustled my hair as I sat on the small balcony while Ryoko played with my hair. It wasn't often I let her do this, but every once in a while, when I was in an exceptionally good mood, I let her. She hummed a tune I was sure she was making up on the spot, but then it suddenly stopped. It wasn't just her humming, either. She had stopped playing with my hair completely and this piqued my interest.

Turning to look at her, I found her looking down the street with a nasty scowl on her face. Peering around her, I saw why. A tall buxom woman with tanned skin and bottle-blonde hair was making her way down the street. Normally a person walking down the street wouldn't bother us, but we knew this woman, and she wasn't welcome here.

When she drew closer to the house, it was clear she was making a visit, and Ryoko didn't refrain from being rude. "Cheaters aren't welcome here."

"She's right. This woman doesn't deserve to live for what she did," the voice snarled.

The woman gazed up at us with a frown. "I'm just here to speak with Argus. Can I please come in to do that?"

"No."

She took a quick breath. "Well then, can one of you let him know I'm here?"

"No, now clean out your whore ears and listen. You're not welcome here, so get lost."

"You should break her neck!"

She glared at Ryoko. "I just want to speak with him."

"I said—"

"We'll tell him she's here," I said.

Ryoko's brow wrinkled. "Huh?"

"You heard me. Argus can decide himself if he wants to talk with her," I said.

She huffed. "All right. I hope you know what you're doing."

I ducked my head inside through the window. Argus and Seda sat on the couch working on one of his projects. Seda appeared to be enjoying herself. I felt bad for taking him away. "Argus, there's someone here to see you."

He looked up. "Who?"

"Go outside and you'll find out."

His brow furrowed. "Um, okay." He put down his half of the project and headed for the front door. Seda turned her attention to me as if she was going to question me, but I ducked back outside.

"Why didn't you tell him who it was?" Ryoko whispered.

"I didn't realize Seda was helping him," I said. "I didn't want to upset her."

"Fair call." She snapped her gaze down at the street. "He's coming down, so you might as well be at the door when he gets there."

The woman smiled. "Thank you."

We snorted and watched her stand at the front door.

"You do know what you're doing, right?" Ryoko whispered.

"It's time to see if he's managed to get over her."

The front door opened. "Lyah." His shock was apparent from the breathiness of his voice.

She smiled a little. "Hey, Argus."

I noticed out the corner of my eye how the moment Lyah's name had been uttered, Seda halted her work to listen.

"W–what…" He took a second to collect himself. "What are you doing here?"

"I just wanted to see you…" She scratched the back of her neck. "And I wanted to apologize for what I did."

Argus crossed his arms. "You waited all this time to tell me you're sorry. You really expect me to believe that?"

Lyah frowned. "Argy…"

"Don't call me that."

She sighed. "Argus, I really am sorry. What I did was wrong, and I know that."

"What you did was wrong? You cheated on me with five other guys, three of them at the same time—and that's what I walked in on, and you're now just admitting that what you did was wrong?"

"Yes, I did do that, and I'm sorry. I don't know what I was thinking. You were the best thing that'd ever happened to me, and I was stupid to give that all up."

Seda put down her work and grab Argus' dog tags to fix them. They had broken at some point and Argus had planned to fix them, but he had been distracted by Seda's offer to help him with invention plans. *What is she up to?*

"What do you want me to do about it?" Argus said. I was surprised at how well he was doing. I didn't think he was this well-mended from what had happened.

Lyah flung her arms around his neck and buried her face into his chest. "Give me another chance. Let me make it up to you. Let me prove we're still right for each other."

Argus forced her away. "It's been over ten years, Lyah."

"Please, Argus. You told me once you wanted to marry me and spend the rest of our lives together. We can still have that."

I frowned. She would bring that up. She knew how to play Argus. I could see how difficult it was for him to deal with that reminder. He had invested everything he had into her, and she repaid him by being unfaithful.

My gaze shifted to Seda when she stood and played with her watch until the mask disappeared, showing her blue eyes. She grabbed Argus' crystal necklaces he had taken off earlier and put them around her neck before stalking over to the front door. She didn't look happy.

Ryoko looked at me with a small grin. "This is going to get interesting."

I nodded and watched as the events unfolded.

"Argy…" Lyah touched his face. "Please."

He sighed and turned his gaze away as he removed her hands. "Lyah, I can't."

"But, why?"

"Argus, who are you talking to?" Seda called as she reached the stairs.

Argus gazed back and smiled as Seda descended. Lyah on the other hand, wasn't thrilled at the sound of Seda's voice, and her eyes widened when she got a better look at Seda. Tall, natural blonde and blue eyes, Seda had all the characteristics Argus' tended to gravitate to. Lyah had been an odd choice from the start, given she had none of those naturally, and even her personality wasn't appealing compared to the other women Argus had shown interest in prior to her.

"Seda, this is Lyah. Lyah, this is Seda," Argus introduced.

Seda smiled. "Nice to finally meet you. I must say, I pictured you to be a little taller."

Lyah's insipid smile gave away her. "Hello. I'm afraid I've heard nothing about you, so I can't have an opinion."

Seda chuckled and wrapped her arms around Argus' arm, clearly trying to upset Lyah. But it wasn't her actions that upset the woman. It was something Seda was wearing.

"Are… are those…"

Seda touched the crystal necklaces around her neck. "Oh these? Argus gave them to me. I know how special they are, so I never asked to ever wear them, but he just up and gave them to me."

"You never let me wear them…" It sounded like she was talking more to herself than Argus. "You never—"

"Oh!" Seda put Argus' tags on him. "I finally fixed them."

He smiled. "Thanks. I knew you'd do a great job."

Seda wrapped her arms around his neck and grabbed his chin lightly. She gazed into his eyes for a moment before looking at Lyah, who appeared distraught.

"I'm sorry, Lyah, but like I said, I can't. I've already moved on," Argus explained. "And I'm happy now."

Lyah backed up, crushed she wasn't going to win. "I… I have to go. I'm sorry to have bothered you. You won't hear from me again."

She ran off, tears streaming down her face now.

"Good riddance," Ryoko muttered as she watched Lyah run away.

I, on the other hand, didn't care about where Lyah ran off to. Instead, I continued to focus on Seda and Argus.

Seda pulled away from him and removed his necklaces and offered them to him. "Thanks for letting me use them. I hope you're not mad. I know how important they are to you."

He accepted her offering. "Not at all."

"She's going to be fine after a few days," she whispered. "You made the right choice. She was just bored, and figured you might still want her back. She just has to come to terms with the idea that she didn't get her way."

Seda disappeared from my sight as she headed up the stairs. Argus soon followed, so I moved to sit on the windowsill. Just as she walked into the living room, she deactivated the cloaking watch. I stayed quiet. Argus reached the living room seconds later.

"Hey, Seda?"

She turned to look at him. "Yeah?"

"Um, thanks…" He rubbed the back of his neck and avoided eye contact. "For helping back there."

She smiled. "You're welcome."

She turned to head off somewhere, but Argus stopped her again. "Um, Seda?"

She giggled and looked at him again. "Yes?"

He hesitated and then grabbed his dog tags. "Thanks for fixing this. You didn't have to."

She shrugged. "It's no big deal. It was a real easy fix."

Seda headed down the hall and Argus sighed, disappointed with himself. I shook my head and climbed inside. I didn't say anything until I was about to pass him. "Chicken."

He didn't look at me. "You don't know what you're saying."

"I know and understand you better than you think. I see how you look at her. I see the chance you're not willing to take."

He sighed. "Do you think I'll ever make the right choice? The right one that'll actually make me happy?"

"Yeah, I do."

He looked at me then, but I continued on to my room to do… something.

I crouched down in the shadows when the warehouse came into

view. Then Ryoko, Rylan, Raikidan, and Raid caught up and waited with me. We watched the warehouse for movement, but saw none.

"Something doesn't feel right," Rylan murmured.

I nodded and continued to scan the area. We had received an anonymous tip that something was going on here. Normally we didn't take anonymous tips, but the Council believed this one might be true. It wasn't looking that way.

I motioned for them to follow me. "We'll still check it out."

Keeping low, we snuck over to the building. Ryoko located an unlocked window and the five of us climbed in. The place was dead quiet, aside from our breathing and movement on the metal grate.

"We'll split up," I whispered. "Ryoko and I will go right and you guys go left."

They agreed and we split up. Ryoko and I wandered around, but we found nothing but an empty warehouse. We ended up splitting up to cover more ground. I stopped searching when I noticed a large crate that wasn't marked. It was required for all crates to be marked for inventory and safety proposes. My curiosity got the better of me and I took a look.

Pulling out my special dagger, I changed it into a crowbar and pried open the box. I tilted my head when I moved the lid to the side. There was nothing in it. Not even packing straw. What was an empty crate doing in an ammunition warehouse?

"Find anything interesting in there?"

I turned to see Raikidan leaning against a stack of crates. "How long have you been there?"

He shrugged. "Not long."

"Shouldn't you be with the guys?"

"Shouldn't you be with Ryoko?"

I leaned on the edge of the crate and peered in again. "There's nothing in here."

"That's a problem?"

"Why would there be an empty crate in a warehouse?"

"Maybe they used whatever was inside."

I shook my head. "The crate was sealed. Why reseal a crate after using it? It wouldn't make sense."

Raikidan leaned on the crate, boxing me in. "Maybe they did it to confuse a smart person like you."

I turned and pushed him away from me. "Raikidan, you know not to do that."

He held up his hands and backed up. "All right, all right. Should we go looking around more?"

I nodded. "Let's go this way."

"Sure."

We snuck around looking for more weird crates or anything else out of the ordinary, but I was having a hard time focusing because of Raikidan. He was walking far too close to me, and attempting to grab me inappropriately at times. For him to walk close to me too much was normal for him, but for him to grab at me, that wasn't like him.

Pretending to find interest in a marked crate, I pried it open with my crowbar. Before I could pry the lid completely off, Raikidan stopped me.

"What the hell?" I demanded.

"I don't think you should do that," he told me.

"And why the hell not?"

He boxed me in against the crate. "Because I don't."

I pushed him away but he came right back. "What the hell is with you all of a sudden?"

He grinned. "I don't know what you're talking about."

"The hell you don't. You know to give me my space and you definitely weren't acting like this earlier."

He leaned closer to me. "I just have something better on my mind than this lousy, pointless assignment."

My eyes widened with shock and I tried to move away from him, but he grabbed me by the wrist and pinned me against the crate. His eyes locked with mine and my breath caught. He continued to lean closer, and I froze. No matter how hard I tried, I couldn't move. It was like his gaze hypnotized me.

Then, just as he was about to get too close to my face, he was pulled back and thrown. "Don't touch her!"

I blinked in stunned silence as I stared at—Raikidan? Were there two here? How were there two of him? What the hell was going on?

Ryoko's heavy boots clomped on the concrete floor behind me. The Raikidan who had been thrown took off, and the Raikidan who had done the throwing pursued him, leaving me standing alone in confusion until Ryoko arrived.

"Laz, I heard Raikidan yell. Is everything okay?" She waved her hand in front of my face. "Hello, Laz?"

I shook my head. "What the hell did I just see?"

"What are you talking about?"

"Raikidan… and Raikidan…" My fingers crossed each other as I tried in vain to piece it all together.

"Are you saying you saw two of him?" She laughed. "Hon, you feeling okay?"

I blinked a few times for my mind to finally clear, and then I became very serious. "No, I didn't just see two of them. I felt one of them, and saw the other grab the one I felt."

"You know that sounds really wrong, right?"

"Ryoko, this is serious!"

She held up her hands. "All right, all right, sorry. Let's just go find them and get to the bottom of this."

"Not without us, you aren't." Ryoko and I looked behind her at hearing Raid's voice, to find him and Rylan approaching. "We don't know what's going on here, so it's best if we all stick together."

"We also know that if this imposter Raikidan targeted Laz first, then she's his intended target," Rylan stated. "It's not a good idea for her to be on her own."

Ryoko smiled. "Then we can use her as bait."

Rylan scowled. "That's not a good—"

"No, it's a great idea," I interjected. "I won't leave your sight, but if this imposter has escaped our Raikidan's grasp, I can bait him without him knowing you're there to back me up."

Rylan crossed his arms. "I don't like this."

"I don't either," Raid agreed.

"Well I do, so that makes this vote a tie and we're out of time to negotiate," Ryoko stated. "We're the women, so what we say goes, and we're going with this plan. If you don't like it, you can just not follow us."

I chuckled, and the boys just stared, mouths agape. It was a terrible justification to exercise power, but the boys weren't arguing it either. Ryoko grabbed my wrist and dragged me off in the direction both Raikidans ran off in. The brothers didn't take long to follow.

It was easy to find them. They were making a loud enough ruckus.

I watched as the two went at it on each other with no holds barred. There were damaged crates and blood everywhere. I worried one of the crates could be filled with explosives, but I didn't know how to help. I didn't know which Raikidan was the real one.

"What do we do?" Ryoko asked.

"What can we do?" I replied.

There really wasn't anything we could do. We couldn't just up and attack him, and Raikidan was in a bind as well. His shapeshifting would be too slow, and he couldn't use fire, due to the supposed explosive nature of the contents of the warehouse. It was all up to him to get this imposter dealt with and then convince us he was the real one.

"There has to be a way to help…" Ryoko whispered.

I worked my jaw. How could we? It wasn't like the imposter was easy to spot. That's when I noticed how different the two were moving. One was moving with fluid, almost snake-like movements and the other with strong, more focused movements. The question was, how did Raikidan fight?

He was strong and protective whenever I was around him. He never let anyone close enough to harm me. He was focused…

"That's it!"

Ryoko cocked her head. "What is?"

Without explaining myself, I bolted out into the open and headed straight for my target. The two men stopped fighting when they noticed me, only making my job easier. Swinging my crowbar, I struck the fake Raikidan over the head.

He stumbled backward. "Shit, Eira, what was that for? Do you really not believe it's me?"

"I know you're not."

Before he could right himself, I changed the wrench back into a dagger and ducked underneath him. He went to grab me, but I plunged the dagger into his chest, stopping him dead. He twitched a little and gazed down at the weapon, choking on any words that may have come to his mind.

He stumbled backward, but as he did, he began to change. Surprise overtook me when the person collapsed and finished transforming. The man was actually a sultry woman with pale skin and black hair.

Ryoko ventured closer. "Is that… is that Rana?"

I nodded. "Looks that way."

"But I thought she escaped Zarda's clutches, too," Ryoko said.

"No, she chose to stay," Rylan said. "As long as she did as he asked, she was treated quite well, so she saw no reason to leave."

"Yeah, I remember her having her own room and everything," Raid complained. He rubbed his stomach. "She even got to eat whenever she wanted."

"Who is this Rana woman?" Raikidan asked.

"She's one of only two successful tank-created shapeshifters in any city," I explained.

Rylan rubbed his chin. "But I don't remember her being able to shift into anything of the opposite sex."

"She probably figured out how to." I shrugged. "It doesn't matter, though. She's dead now."

"Isn't it a little suspicious?" Rylan asked. "How did she know about us and our connection to the rebellion?"

"I don't think she knew about us specifically," Ryoko said. "I think she was sent to ambush anyone who came. It just happened to be us this time."

"But that means Zarda knows how to get to us," Raid said.

I shook my head. "No, Rana wasn't under Zarda's orders this time."

"How do you know?" he asked.

"She had a habit of doing things behind his back and then only telling him if she succeeded. It's what helped her position with him. Though I can't be sure if she told anyone else what she was doing. She had a friend who she confided in a lot, even with her failed ideas."

The others scanned our surroundings to see if there was anyone else lurking in the shadows.

Raikidan approached me. "Eira?"

I looked at him. "Yeah?"

He rubbed the back of his neck. "Thanks... for knowing I was real."

I smiled. "Sure. It wasn't that hard when I was able to compare you two. Now let's get out of here."

He grinned and then nodded. We regrouped with the others and left. I didn't double check to make sure Rana was dead, like I should have. Knowing who she was, and some of the more secret traits she possessed, I should have.

Raikidan stayed quiet when I messed up again, being far more patient with me than I deserved. He was teaching me two words at the same time, without telling me what they meant until I got it down. It wasn't something he normally did, but I was determined to complete the challenge. I needed to know what these two words meant. He called me this in the Library entry. I needed to know.

I licked my lips and thought of how they were structured and pronounced. I had caught on quickly how possessive their tongue was, not that I was surprised. The way Raikidan acted, I had half expected it.

"S… *Sa* dnvk…" I groaned. "I suck at this."

Raikidan chuckled. "Try again. *Sa dnuyvk.*"

I took a deep breath a tried again. "*Sa* dn… *sa* dnoyk." I laughed with embarrassment and hid my face. "I'm terrible at this. I sound so stupid!"

He touched my arm. "You don't sound stupid." I glanced at him through my lashes. A meek smile crept onto my face when I caught the sincerity in his gaze. He grinned. "Now try again. You had the first word, so you have half of it down."

"Yeah, the easy half," I muttered.

He chuckled. "Just try again, *sa dnuyvk.*"

My eyes narrowed. He would taunt me by using it that way. I took a deep breath and ran his words through my head, trying to figure out how the words were forced out. When I had first heard him speak his tongue, I thought the words mainly sounded like grunts and growls, but now that I'd had the chance to learn it, it wasn't completely true. Grunts and growls were used, but it still took proper tongue placement and, oddly enough, how much force you put in your voice.

Exhaling slowly, I tried again. "*Sa* dnoyvk."

"Almost. Try again."

Taking a deep breath, I tried again. "*Sa dnuyvk.*"

I blinked and then looked at him. He nodded in approval while smiling, and I smiled back. When he didn't translate, my brow rose in question. "Well?"

Raikidan chuckled and thumped me on the forehead with two fingers before getting off the bed. "My friend."

I stared at him as he walked out of the room and shut the door behind him. *His friend?* Did he really trust me enough to call me a friend? Better question, did I trust him that much to do the same?

The early evening sun warmed my skin as I sat on the edge of the roof, thinking. Raikidan had taught me a lot today, and I was honestly having fun with learning his tongue. Even though it was difficult, it wasn't as hard for me to learn as other languages I had tried.

Though I wasn't sure, I suspected he liked teaching me, based on how patient he'd been. It was nice of him to do this. He could have kept it all a secret, but he chose to let me in on it. I smiled. *It's really nice of him…*

My mind went back to the last set of words he had taught me. He saw me as a friend. He liked the type of closeness we shared, even though I was human. I know we had our spats, and sometimes I felt like he didn't care about me, but he still stuck around. If he didn't want to be here, he would leave, that's just who he is. I touched the necklace he had given me. *He wouldn't have gone out of his way to give me this…*

So, could I see him as a friend? Could I have an attachment to him? *Who are you trying to fool, Eira? You already do…*

I spun around when I sensed someone standing behind me. I half expected it to be Raikidan or one of the others trying to sneak up on me, but I was surprised to see a beautiful, translucent, slender woman with flaming red hair. Her eyes were a magnificent green with a strange golden ring circling the pupil, and freckles scattered across her skin like paint on a canvas.

I tilted my head respectfully. "Can I help you?"

She smiled at me. "I'm glad I can finally meet you. I've wanted to meet you for so long."

I liked her voice. It was soothing, but I didn't know who she was, although she did feel a little familiar for some reason. "I'm sorry, but I don't understand. Why have you been waiting to meet me? I'm not all that special."

She continued to smile. "Our paths are more connected than you know, Laz."

I lowered my gaze. "Please don't call me that…"

"There's so much hate that surrounds you. It pains me to see it. You could have had such a happy life, if he had—"

I scowled. "Don't bring him up."

She frowned. "I'm sorry. I didn't mean to upset you."

"Please, just tell me what you want with me."

"I come with a warning. Beware of our greed, for we are dragons, and even the purest of hearts can be swayed by the smallest coin."

I narrowed my eyes. Well now I knew she wasn't human. "Why are you warning me? What do I have to watch out for?"

"Be wary." She smiled. "And be good to my son. It's been some time since I've seen him so happy."

Before I could get anything out of her she faded. "Hey, don't go!" I reached out to her, but she disappeared. "Who is your son?"

The roof door opened and Raikidan poked his head out. "Eira, who are you talking to?"

I sighed and leaned back. "Just a spirit."

He came out and shut the door behind him. "Must have been an interesting talk if you didn't want him to go."

I gazed at the ground. "She said something, but left before explaining, so I don't know what she was trying to tell me."

He sat down next to me. "I don't know if you're allowed to, but you could tell me and I could try to help."

I scratched my head. "I don't think you want to know."

"Try me."

"It was a warning…" I swallowed. "About dragons."

Raikidan snapped livid eyes one me. "Who did you talk to?"

I shrugged a little, shrinking away from his anger. "I–I don't know. She didn't give me her name. I just know what she looks like."

"And?"

I averted my gaze. "I knew I shouldn't have told you…"

He sighed. "I'm sorry, Eira. I shouldn't take my annoyance out on you. I just need to know who has something bad to say about my kind."

"She was a dragon; that much I can say with confidence."

"W–what?"

I scratched my head. "And she had taken the form of a human. Tall, slender, amazing green eyes and stunning, flaming red hair—gorgeous is the only way to describe her."

Raikidan tensed. "Her eyes, did they have a golden ring?"

I blinked. "Yes."

"And her hair, did it make it look like she was made from a piece of the sun."

"I–I guess so."

"And her voice, is it so soothing it could make a grown man cry?"

I tilted my head. "Raikidan?" He didn't answer. He just stared at the ground. He looked shaken to the core. I rested my hand on his arm. "Raikidan, do you know her?"

He exhaled slowly. "If I'm right, her name is Xephrya and she's… she's my mother."

I froze. He was joking. He had to be joking. But as I watched him, I knew he wasn't, and that meant the son she referred to had to be him. It only made sense. I took a small breath as I was about to tread dangerous waters. "Tell me about her."

He blinked and then gazed at me as if trying to determine if I was messing with him. "You really want to know?"

I nodded. "I'll tell you about mine after, if you'd like."

A smile crept onto his face and he nodded. "All right, I'm just not sure what to say about her."

"Anything. Whatever comes to mind."

"Well, she was caring, but that's to be expected, and smart"—He chuckled—"and beautiful. But the biggest thing about her was that she understood the rationale for everything. She understood me and everything I did better than I even knew myself. My mother didn't care that I was a half-color. She thought it made me better than everyone else. She was the only friend I had who stuck with me until the end."

He worked his jaw. "Someone once tried to tell me she was psychic, since she had a great deal of awareness about the future, but I never believed it. Psychic dragons have always been rare, but even more so since the War of End. What about your mom?"

I scratched my head. "Well she wasn't much different, except for the psychic theory part. She cared the most about me, and she did what she could to make me happy. She was a bit overprotective sometimes, but I'd give up everything to have her back."

"Even give up your son and your friends?"

I nodded slowly. "She was the only one who ever understood me. She knew exactly what I was and why I acted the way I did, but it didn't matter to her. She still loved me the same. I'd even give up my freedom to have all that back…"

Raikidan placed his hand on my shoulder and, instinctively, I rested my hand over his. *There's another point making us more the same than the surface would claim.*

"Raikidan, what exactly happened to her?" I asked.

He removed his hand from my shoulder and leaned on his knees. I waited to see if he'd tell. I wasn't going to press him. This was a delicate situation, not one I would pry about, but now that she had come to me, and told me we had a connection in some way, I felt the need to see if Raikidan was ready to face that part of his past.

He clasped his hands together. "She was killed by humans… soldiers, to be flat out honest with you." My heart stopped. "I remember the insignias on the uniforms as clear as day. The soldiers were from this city."

I stared at him, my jaw going slack. He wouldn't look at me, but it didn't matter. I couldn't believe he had just said that. "Then why… why are you here? Why are you helping us?" I searched for the right words to say. "Why don't you hate us?"

Raikidan turned his gaze to me slowly. "Because you didn't do it. You didn't kill her."

I shook my head. "You don't believe that."

He turned away and ran his fingers through his hair. "You're right. I didn't, at first. I thought you were all the same. I thought I could just hate and blame any of you." He shook his head. "But it didn't take me long to see it wasn't like that. I couldn't blame any of you because none of you could stomach anything you were forced to do."

"Then why offer to help me? You knew what I was. What were you thinking?"

"I was thinking I could avenge her. I thought if I could pretend to like something you wanted, then I could learn everything about you guys so I could figure out the best way to take my revenge. The truth is, Eira, we don't enjoy confrontation. We like to keep things peaceful, and will only act to settle an issue quickly so it can just go away. The only exception to that would be issues related to territory. So my supposed like for revenge, was just me, but I can't do it. I don't... I don't hate you."

"Then who do you hate?"

"No one."

"You have to hate someone."

"I don't hate..." He sighed. "Myself..."

"Why?"

"Because I couldn't protect her... Because I couldn't live up the name she gave me. She told me I was supposed to do something great. I was supposed to protect something important. But I couldn't even protect her."

I didn't know what to say. To feel like you failed the one person who had the most faith in you, I didn't know how that felt. I never failed my mother and her expectations. But then... maybe I did. I wasn't able to stop my mother's death, either. I had been powerless.

I reached out and grabbed his hand. He held my gaze and I could tell he saw the unspoken words. He understood what I went through.

As I held eye contact, I noticed there was something else he wasn't saying. "It's not just yourself you blame, is it?"

He shook his head. "No. I blame my father, too."

"What did he do?"

"He wasn't there. He stayed home."

"I don't understand."

He leaned forward, clasping his hands together. "When I was still with my family, our lair was close to a small human village. My mother, well, she was fascinated by humans. She wanted to know everything about them, and liked to mingle without them realizing what she was. My father, on the other hand, he didn't like that. True to his color, he wanted nothing to do with them, but because my mother did, he went along with her."

"Then how is he at fault?"

"Well, unlike what I told you before, I've come into contact with humans many times in the past. When I was old enough, and had my shifting down, my mother started bringing me along with her on her trips into the village. My father continued to put up with it, but when he found out that the humans knew what we were, he wanted us to stop. The villagers didn't hate us. They actually really liked us, but he didn't care.

"He tried to convince us to stop going to the village, but my mother wouldn't listen. Then, he just refused to go at all—but she continued, and I went with her. He tried to blame me for what happened. He tried to make it seem like it was all my fault. I felt like it was, so it was hard to not believe it. But he wasn't at the village when it happened. He had refused to come with us, just like every other time. He didn't see how upset it made her when he refused. He didn't see how much it hurt her…"

"It's because he didn't love her," I mumbled.

His eyes widened. "What? Of course he did!"

My focus drifted. "He wasn't there for her. He didn't support her. How could he love her?"

"Because he gave up everything for her. He tried to make her happy when he could, even if he failed at it."

"He didn't try enough if he couldn't see just how much he was hurting her by refusing to go somewhere with her."

"He did care!"

I stood. "He didn't love her because he couldn't—because love doesn't exist. It's a lie!"

Raikidan grabbed my wrist before I could walk away from this. "It's not a lie."

I whirled on him. "Yes it is. If it existed, I wouldn't have lost my mother! If it really existed, I wouldn't be here, fighting for my own freedom!"

Raikidan's brow furrowed. "Eira, what are you talking about?"

I stared at the ground. "He promised her he'd come back for us... He promised he cared and would save us. It was all a lie..."

Pain started to come back. The buried emotions squeezed me everywhere. I stalked toward the door. This was not a memory I wanted to remember anymore. But Raikidan stopped me. "Eira, who are you talking about?"

"My father!" My eyes burned into him but then softened as the pain took over. "He tricked her, and got her to believe in his lie. He got her to believe in something for so long, when it was never going to happen!"

The pain controlled me. I needed to let it all out. My fist hit metal, and then pain raked through my arm as it pierced the door.

I rested my other hand against the metal surface and hung my head. "He was an outsider caught up in Zarda's web, and had more than his own life at stake. He met my mother because of it, and eventually told her his cared about her. He made all these promises about how he'd come back for us both, and we'd all be together like a family should... He lied. He never cared! It was all a lie..."

"Eira." He rested his hands on my shoulder. "Calm down, *my friend*. Please, just calm down."

His use of Draconic for those specific words jolted something deep inside me. I gasped for a calming breath and then braced myself as I pulled my hand back through the door. I stared at my bloody arm. "He killed her... Zarda pulled the trigger, but she was gone long before that..." I threw myself at Raikidan, and he wrapped his arms around me. I squeezed my eyes shut as hard as the pain constricted my body. I wished, in that moment over any other, I could cry to take the pain all away. "She's gone because of him and his lies..."

"I'm sorry, Eira. I didn't mean to make you feel this way. I won't bring it up again."

"Thank you..."

"He doesn't know what he's given up, you know. He gave up something really good. It's his loss, not yours."

I pulled away and smiled. "You're right. It is his loss."

He smiled back at me and held my gaze until something came to mind.

"Raikidan, I'd like to ask you something, although it might bring up unwanted memories. Is it still okay to ask?"

He nodded. "Sure."

"The soldiers who attacked you that day, they obviously were there for a purpose. They knew where to find you. But you didn't say if they acted alone, or if someone led them."

"You're right, they had known we were there, and no, they hadn't acted alone." He motioned me to follow him as he went to sit back down. "There was a single man who led them. He wasn't a soldier, though."

"He was the other human you told me you met?"

He nodded. "The only other nu-human. The humans in the village had been just normal humans, and at the time, the soldiers' identities had been hidden thanks to the helmets, so I hadn't realized they were nu-human until I met you. I just assumed the man leading them was some sort of elf or halfling of some sort."

"What did this man look like?"

Raikidan's brow furrowed as he thought about it. "Well, he was tall, clean shaven, had black hair, and had these sinister topaz eyes."

My gaze darkened. "So you have met Zarda."

Raikidan's brow furrowed. "What? No. This man's name was Taric."

I tilted my head. That didn't make any sense. That sounded exactly like Zarda. Sure, someone could share some of his features, but all? There was only one man who shared such similar traits with Zarda, but he had been dead for such a long time.

"Are you sure it was Taric?"

"Yes."

"Raikidan, I really need you to think hard about this."

His lips pressed into a line. "Eira, what is your problem?"

"Because the name you gave me was the leader of this city before Zarda, but he wasn't an evil man. Lord Taric was incredibly peaceful. He went out of his way to keep peace, and make peace with those who didn't want it. He didn't make experiments like me and the others. Those were all Zarda."

"Well that's the name he gave, and he wasn't peaceful. He was quite hostile, and was looking for something from us."

Something wasn't right about this. "Raikidan, how long ago did this happen?"

"Why?"

"Just answer the question."

"It was about eighty-five years ago, I think."

I shook my head. "That wasn't Taric. Taric was long dead by then. That man lied."

Raikidan threw his hands in the air. "Why the hell would he do that, Eira?"

"Why not? He had a plan. He wanted something. Why not hide his identity by using another name with those who didn't know him? At that time, Zarda was still trying to take control of whatever he could. He didn't have a fearsome identity of his own. Besides, he'd feel he was the only one who should be allowed to use that name."

"Why? Why him?"

I took a deep breath. "Because Zarda is Lord Taric's son."

Raikidan narrowed his eyes. "Excuse me?"

"It's exactly as I said. Zarda is Taric's only son."

"But you told me once that Zarda killed his predecessor."

I nodded. "Great son, right?"

"But…" Raikidan shook his head. "But why?"

"Why not? Zarda craved power, even as a kid. He was nothing like his father, even if they did look a lot alike."

"How much alike?"

"Many claim Zarda is a clone of Lord Taric, since Taric's wife struggled to bear children. Some believed it was impossible for her. That's why it can't be Taric you encountered. Because he was dead before then."

"You're wrong. It was him."

I shook my head. "I'm not going to waste my breath anymore."

Raikidan sighed and looked down at my arm, seeing that was still bleeding. "Let me fix you up."

I let him take my arm and burn away the wound. When he was done, I figured it was okay to ask him one last question. "Raikidan, why did he attack you guys?"

He shook his head. "I don't know. My father and my mother's friend, who had come to visit her that day, had sent me away before I could find out."

"They never told you after?"

He shook his head again. "I'm not sure my father knew either. He ended up arriving back at the lair soon after I did, but my mother's friend never showed up at the lair after I was sent away from the scene. I feel as though he was the only one who found out, and I never saw him again after that day."

"Did your mother leave a clan to be with your father?"

Raikidan nodded. "It was one of the largest out there, but she chose to. As much as my father didn't like the idea of living alongside other dragons, he would have for her, but she didn't want to. She wanted to live a different life, not that I blame her much. From what she told me, she didn't fit in too well, so when my father found her, she didn't play as hard to get as most would have."

My gaze lowered to my lap and I rubbed my previously injured arm.

"You should get some sleep," Raikidan said.

"What I need is food."

He rose to his feet. "I'll get you that. Just go lay down."

"Raikidan, don't."

"I said I'll get you something. Now go to your room and lay down."

I exhaled a playful sigh. "Yes, mother."

He chuckled and flicked me on the nose, making me laugh. He headed for the door, and I took the alternate and more direct route to my room.

The hot summer sun beat down on my skin, but it was the least of my concerns now. The man standing before me was. He was tall and lean, with flaming red hair. His eyes were a bright green, with a golden ring around the pupil, reminding me of my peculiar eyes. I didn't want this man here. He brought bad feelings up from their locked-away places.

I narrowed my eyes. "What do you want?"

"Eira, there's no need to be so hostile. I'm not here to start a fight of any sort," the man defended.

"You are not welcome here. My mother told you to never come back."

"Yes, I know, but I bring news from—"

"I don't care what you bring. You aren't welcome here, now leave!"

The man sighed. "May I please speak with Amara then? I know she'll at least hear me out."

"No."

"And why not?"

I stared at the ground and my hands clenched. "Because she's dead."

"W—what?"

My gaze snapped up at him. "She's dead! No thanks to my father, she's dead. Go bring that message back to him, errand boy."

The man didn't seem to know how to react to my news, not that I was surprised. He hadn't come here in eleven years. But it didn't matter. It didn't change the past.

"Mom?" I turned to see Ryder running toward me. A small smile spread on my face when he latched onto my hip. "Mom, who is this man?"

I rested my hand on his head and then glared at the man. "Someone who isn't welcome here."

The man didn't say anything, too curious about Ryder to realize I was speaking. Ryder hid behind me. "I don't like him."

"Good, you shouldn't."

The man's gaze eased when he could no longer see Ryder. "I'm sorry, I'm just trying to process everything."

I snorted. "Well, process it after you leave."

His lips pressed into a thin line. "I came here with a message, but I can see I'm far too late to reason with you in order for you to hear it. So, do you have one for me to give?"

"Yeah, tell my father he's not welcome in my life." I turned away, with Ryder in tow. "Not that he ever wanted to be a part of it to begin with."

CHAPTER 44

I played with my earrings while Ryoko and Shva'sika argued over what dress I should wear. I wished they'd just stop and finally let me get dressed. I didn't see why they had to fuss over me like this.

I sighed. *It's because I'm Raikidan's date.* They always fussed when it was like this, and I wished they wouldn't. Sliding off the bed quietly, I snuck out of my room, knowing full well if they knew I was leaving, they'd protest. But I needed something to do, so I figured I'd check on Seda. Genesis was out somewhere with some of the Council members and Seda hadn't gone with her, meaning she was going to be alone tonight while we were at the party—and I wasn't happy about it.

I poked my head in her room, only to find it empty. *Where could she be?*

"She went to do laundry."

I looked at Rylan as he strolled down the hall. He fussed with his suit jacket, as if it wasn't fitting right. "Something wrong with your clothes?"

"The jacket is tight again. I think someone washed it, instead of dry cleaning it."

"Well that could be true, since you're not all that good at cleaning your clothes and putting them away properly," I snickered—"or you could just be wearing it inside out."

"I'm what? Are you serious?"

I began laughing when he did a frantic search and found out he was, in fact, wearing the jacket inside out. How he hadn't noticed was beyond me. Leaving him to his fixing, I ventured through the maze we called a hallway until I came to Blaze's room. I could hear someone rustling with something near our open laundry room, but before I could keep going, I noticed Argus coming out of his room and down the hall.

These halls were a little small, so I leaned again one side for him to be able to pass, but he didn't come down this far, nor did he seem to notice me. Instead he stopped right at the laundry room.

I noticed his hesitant posture, and it tugged on my curiosity. "Hey, um, Seda?"

The rustling stopped. "Yeah?"

"Well, I was wondering…" He rubbed the back of his neck, struggling with his words. "Well…"

Seda chuckled. "Just spit it out, Argus."

"Would like to be my date for the party?"

My brows rose in surprise. That was definitely not what I had been expecting him to ask.

"Me?" Seda sounded just as surprised. "Well, if you really want me to, then sure."

I watched as he smiled. "Yeah, I'd really like you to."

"All right then. I'd like that. I'll see if I have something to wear after I get this load done."

"One thing, though. I'd prefer if you didn't use the cloaking watch."

Seda pursed her lips. "Argus, you know I can't go out in public unless I do."

Argus pulled something out of his back pocket and handed it to her. He scratched the back of his head when she took it. "I, um, fixed this up for you so you could…"

"An identification card?" She giggled. "I'm a registered Battle Psychic, and my name is… Crystal?"

His face reddened. "If you don't like that name, I could always change it, or you could just not use it. It's up to you."

"No, I like it. Thank you. I should finish this load so I can see if I have anything to wear."

"I'll leave you to that, then."

I shook my head while smiling as he went to go hide in his room.

It's a start, at least. When I figured I had given Seda enough breathing time, I walked over to the laundry area.

"Hey, Seda?"

She jumped out of her skin when I spoke. "By the goddess! How long have you been standing there?"

I chuckled. "I just got here. I came to make sure you were going to be okay being on your own tonight, but from what I caught on my way over, that won't be an issue."

Her cheeks reddened. "You heard all of it, didn't you?"

I removed my earrings. "Yeah I did, and you'll need these more than me."

She smiled. "Thanks. You're not going to say anything else about this?"

I shrugged. "Nothing else to say. He's a good choice, that's about it. I'll leave you alone now so I can let the girls know what's going on. Maybe they'll help you with your wardrobe and leave mine alone so I can finally pick it out myself for once."

She chuckled. "I think they've already decided, and you're not going to like it."

I groaned. "I'd better go put a stop to it then."

She giggled. "Have fun with that."

"I'll send them over to you next."

She placed a hand on her chest. "Aw, thank you. That's so kind."

I laughed and headed back to my room, bracing for a fight.

Discomfort plagued me as I stood in the crowded room. Although I was uncomfortable, I knew I'd have been even more so if I hadn't had the choice in my current wardrobe.

I had prepared myself to fight to get my way when I had reached my room, but I hadn't prepared myself for the heart attack they nearly gave me. The dress they picked out was hideous, and they weren't happy I'd spoken my mind about it, either. I fought with them over it and barely won, but I couldn't give myself all the credit. I had Raikidan's help.

He had walked into the room to break up our squabble, and the moment he saw the dress he put an end to it, right then and there. The girls had been so surprised he hadn't liked it, but disliking it had been an understatement. He hated it more than me.

But that didn't matter now. I was in the shimmery, ruby red dress I had worn many times before, and I was quite comfortable. I could hardly believe I was admitting it to myself, but I actually liked wearing this particular dress. I felt… pretty. Nowhere near as beautiful as the other ladies around me, but that was okay.

I stayed quiet as the others around me mingled with loyal civilians and soldiers. Raikidan stood next to me, his hand resting comfortably on my hip and keeping me calm. We never mingled, and luckily no one ever questioned it. Seda was also keeping to herself, but after she threw another psychic across the room, I didn't blame her. He deserved it of course, but it had made others in the party hall wary of her.

Argus, on the other hand, didn't notice the lack of attention. He didn't even react much when he had been picked on numerous times. Seda was the only thing he could focus on. It was cute, to be honest.

I gazed around as the music slowed, drawing partygoers to the designated dance floor. Even our friends left, leaving Raikidan and me alone.

"Do you want to dance?" Raikidan whispered. "You don't look like you're in the mood to be here, but I figured I'd ask."

"No, I'm good, thank you."

No conversation happened after that. It had been like that all night, not that I minded. He had been right. I didn't want to be here. A bad vibe screamed at me the moment we arrived, and it made me want to leave.

"Eira, are you all right?" Raikidan whispered.

"I'll be fine."

"What's bothering you?"

"I'm just getting a bad feeling, that's all. Nothing—"

"Like something is lurking about?" I turned a curious gaze on him. "I'm getting it too. It's not something friendly, either."

"At least I'm not crazy," I muttered.

"Or we could be both crazy."

"Better to be crazy with someone than by yourself."

We laughed, but our laughter was cut short when the music player providing the dance music started skipping and then died. The room went quiet, but then erupted with loud laughter when someone began swearing at the machine. I shook my head as I tried to quiet my laughter to a chuckle.

I smiled when I noticed Ryder making his way over to us. "Hey there, stranger."

He smiled back. "Hey, Eira."

I looked him up and down. "You look good in a suit."

His cheeks flushed. "Um, thanks."

"So what brings you our way? Or are you just here to chat now that they're making a fuss over that broken music player?"

He chuckled. "Well honestly, I have something to ask you."

I eyed him. "What is it?"

He held out his hand. "Would you mind playing a few songs for us until we can get that thing fixed?"

"I'm not sure…"

"You don't have to sing. Just play the piano."

I sighed and took his hand. "All right, but only because you asked me."

He smiled and pulled my arms around his, leading me to this supposed piano. I was surprised by the size of it when we finally made our way through the party hall. It was definitely a grand piano, but it looked even bigger than your average grand. I sat down when Ryder pulled out the seat just enough for me. I moved my fingers to loosen them up as I took a deep breath. *It's not that bad. It could be worse. It's just until they fix the music player.*

Ryder sat down on the seat next to me and whispered in my ear. "You can do it. It's just a few songs."

I took another breath and began playing a quiet tune. It was slow, but appropriate for the atmosphere that was needed, and no one complained. As I played, I realized why this piano was so different than the other pianos I had seen. It wasn't a typical piano. It was electric, and had been modified to be able to sound like a regular piano, or an electric one when desired. The modification was requiring it to be larger than normal.

My gaze changed from looking over the piano to watching Rylan as he strolled past the piano and picked up a guitar. *What is he up to?* It was obvious he was going to play something, but what did he know that would go with my playing? Of course, knowing him, he had found some of my current writings and memorized them, including the one I had been working on, that had been inspired by my talk with Raikidan the other day.

Blaze and Argus strolled over to the other set up instruments just as Rylan began to play. My fingers began to play along without a thought, which startled me a bit. If I played without thought, then it was possible I was going to sing without a second thought, either, which is exactly what happened.

Once Rylan finished his verse, I took up mine in the duet. I could feel so many pairs of eyes on me, but I didn't care. They didn't make me want to run and hide. They didn't make me want to stop. I felt nothing from their stares. It felt good to let this feeling out easier than I ever had before.

My fingers slowed as the song came to its end, but the song didn't get a chance to end properly, thanks to someone's slow, loud clapping. I ground my teeth in anger. *This guy has a lot of nerv—*

"Beautiful. Simply beautiful," a smooth, yet commanding voice said.

I froze. *It can't be.*

The voice in my head stirred, hissing and thrashing as if it were an agitated animal rather than a voice at all.

I looked up. My heart stopped and my blood ran cold at the sight of the olive-skinned man with black hair and piercing topaz eyes, confidently strolling toward us with a malicious grin on his face. *Zarda...*

His topaz eyes burned into me as he advanced. Each thump of his boots on the stone floor vibrated into my very being. I wasn't afraid of him, but I didn't trust him.

This is bad. It was more than bad. It was terrible. Never had he appeared here before. Zane had even assured me once that Zarda never showed up. I glanced at Rylan and the boys, and they appeared to be struggling to stay calm as well.

"Such a talent you have, Eira. To be able to do that in a room full of people you don't know, how do you do it?"

He reached out and ran his fingers through my hair, a displeased scowl on his face. "You disobeyed. I explicitly told you to complete that assignment at any cost."

I eyed him and played dumb. "How do you know my name?"

"I know many things." His sharp gaze flicked to the group of soldiers who had been fixing the music player. "Is that thing running yet?"

One of the soldiers saluted. "Yes, sir."

"Good, then get it playing something." Zarda held out his hand to me. "May I?"

The voice stirred again but uncharacteristically didn't speak.

I gazed at him warily through my lashes. A battle raged inside me. A part of me wanted to run and hide, while another told me to stand and fight and end this once and for all, but the most logical side told me to act as normal as possible and accept his offer like any citizen would. After all, who wouldn't want to take the chance to dance with the Lord of the city? I accepted his offered hand and reluctantly allowed him to pull me onto the dance floor.

"High casualty loss is illogical. Resources and time cannot be replenished quickly," I said. *"To deplete such resources so carelessly, would be seen as an imperfection"*—I held his gaze—*"and all imperfections must be eliminated. Isn't that right, sir?"*

He chuckled. "I love to hate that snarky attitude of yours."

"You're quite the talk among my men," Zarda said. "Many of them are quite fond of you. Quite the change from when you were one of them."

I blinked. "Excuse me?"

"Did you really think you could keep hiding from me, Eira? Did you really think I wouldn't find you?"

I tried to pull away from him. "Lord Zarda, I think you're confused."

Zarda chuckled. "Oh I am? Then tell me, how do you know me?"

I smiled at him slyly. "Are you not the Lord of this city? Are you not the talk of these parties?"

He grinned and forced me to dance closer to him. "You've always been far too smart for your own good."

The back of his hand crashed into my cheek. "Don't you dare disobey me again."

I glared at him. "I told you, you have the wrong person."

He chuckled. "You've always been good at lying. You've always been good at manipulating to get your way, but not with me. I've always been able to see right through your lies, my pet."

I ground my teeth. "How many times do I have to tell you, you're confusing me with someone else!"

He grabbed me by the throat. "I own you. I tell you what to do and you do it. Fail, and you will be the next eliminated imperfection. Do you understand?"

He pulled me closer and spoke into my ear. "You can keep pretending to be the feeble, memory lost immigrant all you want, but I will have you again. I made you and I will have you. I enjoy this little game. It's more fun when you—"

"May I?" I looked to see Raikidan attempting to cut in.

"About time he showed up," the voice hissed.

"You know, it could be considered rude to cut in on a dance with the Lord of the city," Zarda sneered.

"It would be considered rude if I didn't dance with my date before the night is over," Raikidan said, his tone even.

Zarda chuckled and let me go. "Very well, she's all yours."

Raikidan took my hand and pulled me across the dance floor. He didn't speak until Zarda had disappeared into the crowd. "Are you all right?"

I swallowed. "Keep dancing until the end of this song and then get me the hell out of here."

Raikidan nodded and gripped me carefully as we danced. He held my gaze and I found myself smiling a bit. He smiled as well, and it made it hard to stop. As he spun me on the dance floor, I didn't feel the least bit out of place, and even though dancing wasn't my strong suit, I found it easy to keep up. All the worry I had felt while under Zarda's malicious gaze faded away.

A part of me felt as if I could do this forever, but the song ended, and just as I had asked, Raikidan led me out onto the balcony. I leaned on the stone railing and took several deep breaths as the tension returned.

"Eira, are you all right?" I clamped my eyes shut and shook my head. He placed his arms on either side of me. "It's going to be okay."

I shook my head again. "No, it's not. It's not okay, Raikidan. He knows. He knows…"

"It's going to be okay. You have to believe me."

"No, it's not going to be okay. He's known all along. It's just a game to him. We've already lost this. It's o—"

He leaned his head against mine. "Enough. It's not over. We can still do this. You just need to keep going and you'll see."

I sighed stared out into the city. He was wrong. It was over. This… game… it was all over now that he knew.

"Eira, I thought you should know, I think you look really nice tonight." My face flushed and I didn't answer. He chuckled. "What, not going to argue with me this time?"

I played with my finger. "In all honesty, a part of me wants to accept your compliment and the other part, well, doesn't."

"Well you should listen to the part that wants to accept it, because I'm being completely honest with you."

I looked at him with a tiny smile and he smiled back. I held his gaze for a few moments, until I had to pry myself away. A strange feeling stirred from that shared moment and it didn't feel right.

The voice roused in my mind but didn't make a comment. I wasn't sure how to take the behavior today. I half expected it to compel me to lash out at Zarda the moment he touched me. And then it seemed to calm the longer I was with Raikidan. Until that moment at least.

We remained silent for a few more moments before Raikidan spoke. "How are you feeling now?"

"I'm all right. I'll be better once we get out of here."

"Well you can stop waiting." We turned our focus over our shoulders to see Seda walking toward us. "Zane has the car ready. The others are heading down there now."

I nodded. "Thanks for letting us know."

"Sure. I have to admit, I'm surprised you didn't attack him."

"We were in a room filled with soldiers, and I'm wearing a dress." I shook my head. "I know better than to do something so stupid. I am surprised you didn't attack him, however."

She grunted. "I already had my chance, and I blew it."

Raikidan looked at her in confusion. "What?"

I chuckled. "Seda attacked Zarda once."

Raikidan's eyes widened and his mouth hung open. "Why?"

"Because I witnessed Zarda kill Lord Taric." Seda sighed, holding one arm close to her body with the other. "Lord Taric was a kind man. He was more than kind. He was the most caring man I had ever met. He cared about his people and about all of the experiments he made, but he had a special liking for psychics. He was fascinated with our abilities and tried to find ways for us to put them to their best possible use to benefit others. He liked us so much he kept a group of us in his company most of the time.

"I was one of those psychics and I enjoyed my time with him, but it wasn't meant to last forever. You see, Lord Taric wasn't blind, nor was he stupid. He knew what Zarda was trying to do, but with his failing health, there wasn't anything he could do. In the end, Lord Taric released every last psychic from service, in hopes Zarda wouldn't be able to get a hold of our powers, since no soldier can be forced back into service once dismissed on honorable terms."

Her lip quivered. "The day Taric let me go, I didn't leave. I refused to leave him alone, and he didn't argue. I spent most of my time with him unless he sent me on quick errands. The day Lord Taric died was one of those days. He had sent me to run down to the laboratories to collect some reports for him. I came back just as Zarda killed him. I had been so angry I dropped everything I had and attacked Zarda. But due to my training, I didn't have the heart to kill him, even though he had taken our former Lord's life. Instead, I called for help, even though I knew it was too late."

Her hands clinched into fists. "Zarda tried to blame me. He tried to convince everyone I had done it but no one believed him. They knew I couldn't have done it, but without any other psychics to help prove either one of us right, Zarda was never charged with treason and got the power he had wanted for so long."

"You could have stopped all of this," Raikidan stated. "You could have made it so all of this never happened. But you didn't."

"Had I stopped him then, Laz and the others would never have existed," Seda reminded him.

Raikidan nodded in understanding, but I wasn't so accommodating for her reasoning. "One life isn't worth the thousands Zarda has taken."

Seda took a moment to find the words to speak, but she didn't speak about the current topic. "We shouldn't make the others wait any longer."

I didn't allow Raikidan to go anywhere when she left. "Raikidan, can I ask you something?"

"Sure."

"You now know who Zarda is. Does he look like the man who killed your mother?"

Raikidan crossed his arms. "To be honest, I'm not sure. He feels familiar, but there's something about him that isn't the same as the man I met."

"You don't believe I'm right, then."

He shook his head. "I can't believe your theory right now. I just can't be sure he's the same man."

"Very well. We should get home. I don't want to be here any longer than I need to be."

I was sure it had been Zarda. It could only be him. The time frame fit. No one else had a reason to ruin Lord Taric's reputation. No one but his own son who could never live up to the man his father was.

I dug my nails into his soft flesh until he bled and pulled away. I spun on my heels and headed for the door. "No one owns me, Zarda. That would be too big of an imperfection to ignore."

CHAPTER 45

E*verything was dark, and the thick fog clouded my good vision. I didn't know where I was, or why I was here. I wandered around, but the fog remained just as thick as before. I whirled around when I sensed something behind me, but found nothing there.*

"Hello?" I waited a second before calling out again. "Hello? Is someone there?"

I spun around when I sensed the presence behind me again, but again, there was nothing there. Feeling sure I wasn't alone here, I ventured further into the fog until I stumbled across a shadowy figure. It was moving about like me, as if it was lost—and it looked like a man, but I couldn't figure out much more than that.

"Hello?" I called.

The figure stopped and turned my way. It didn't speak or run away, so I ventured closer. As I advanced, the fog between us became thinner, and I noticed this man was wearing some sort of uniform.

"Who are you?" I asked him.

Instead of replying or being as curious as me, he ran off.

"Wait, don't go!" But it was too late. He was gone, and I was alone in the darkness once more.

The book flipped another page as I searched. My dream had been so strange. I wanted to know who that man was and what it all meant.

I had read through shaman theories and dream symbols, but nothing had told me anything about the dream or had been relevant to what happened.

My brow furrowed when the book stopped showing me what I wanted, and began searching for something else. I had never seen anything like it before. Never had I heard of a book changing topic unprompted.

Words flowed through my mind when the book finally found the information it was searching for, and I couldn't believe what I was hearing. It was a treaty between the city of Dalatrend and the dragon clans. It sounded old, a few decades at least, and it was a long one. I had never heard of such a long treaty. *Why is it so long?*

My brow furrowed when the book read off some information that was strange, so I reread it. It spoke about how as long as dragons stayed away from this city and kept an extremely low profile, their existence would be kept secret, and they would stay safe. I put the book down. Did Raikidan know about this? No, he couldn't. He wouldn't have come here if he had known.

I read the treaty some more, and pain formed in my chest. The treaty stated if a colored dragon was to be caught, the treaty would immediately break, and all dragon clans would be attacked. This was bad. Dragons weren't creatures to be messed with. Human lore spoke about how hard it was to kill one, and having been around Raikidan for so long, and with Zaith's clan for a short duration, I knew that to be true. So for them to be forced into a treaty like this, Zarda had to know a way to kill them.

I thought about Raikidan's mother and how she had been killed by humans. I was still convinced Zarda had something to do with it. My heart slowed. *Maybe he does know how to kill dragons.*

I didn't know the details of Raikidan's mother's death, I knew better than to ask, but I did wonder what type of form she had been in when she died. If she had been in a dragon form and Zarda had killed her, he would have had the leverage to convince the dragons to bend to his will. With the technology we have, it wouldn't be hard to mass-produce the weapons needed. This meant Raikidan and all of Zaith's clan were putting the dragons in danger. *All because of me…*

I put the book down and searched for the other book I owned. This had to end. I couldn't risk a genocide for the sake of my own wants. Raikidan, Ebon, and Zaith's clan needed to see this. I wrote three letters, one being more personal for Raikidan, and I also had three copies of the treaty made.

I wrote a small note and left it on my bed before heading out of my room. It was now time to enlist some help.

> *Raikidan,*
> *Meet me at our spot outside the city walls. It's important.*
>
> *Eira*

I tracked Ryoko down and showed her the treaty. "I need your help with this. I need to get Raikidan out of here."

She hesitated. "I don't know, Laz. It's not like Zarda knows he's here or anything. We're pretty good at hiding."

I stared at her with hard eyes. "He's been seen in his dragon form in battle. Do you really think Zarda doesn't know? It took a lot of planning for us to throw them off about me, and Zarda didn't believe it. He knows Raikidan is here somewhere, and he's just playing games."

"His sightings will be passed as mass hysteria or trauma from battle," she insisted. "Everyone in this city thinks they're all dead. Zarda was pretty convincing about that."

"Yeah, key word there is Zarda. He made those lies. He spread them. He'll believe a group of soldiers if they all claimed to see a dragon in the city. He'll play it off as trauma or hysteria, but he'll secretly believe it."

"Laz, you're overreacting," she said.

"Overreacting? Worrying about genocide is overreacting? Worrying about Raikidan's safety is overreacting?"

Ryoko let out an aggravated breath. "Seda, care to give me a hand here?"

"I'm sorry, but I don't have much input here," she messaged us both from the safety of her room. *"You both have valid points."*

"Well who is right?" Ryoko asked.

"I don't know," Seda said.

"Can't you just do your psychic thing and look into the future?"

Seda sighed. *"It's not that simple, Ryoko. I can't just conjure up any future I want."*

"Can you at least try?"

"Give me a moment."

We waited a few minutes before Ryoko got impatient. *"Well?"*

"His future is dark."

My heart stuttered. I didn't like the sound of that. *"What's that supposed to mean?"*

"Yeah, that sounds really bad," Ryoko said.

"Oh, sorry," Seda said. *"We psychics use different terms with each other than with ordinary people, and for a moment I forgot you two were ordinary."*

I grunted. *"Ordinary, right."*

"Ha ha, very funny, just tell us what's going on," Ryoko grumbled.

"It means his future is uncertain. His future depends on this choice."

"So what you're saying, is neither of us is right or wrong," Ryoko tried to clarify.

"No, not necessarily. One of you could be right and the other wrong, both could be right, or both could be wrong. His future and his future choices are just dependent on the outcome of this particular one."

"So will you know once we make a choice?" Ryoko asked.

"I might be able to find out twenty-four hours after the choice is executed."

"Well I vote Raikidan stays," Ryoko said.

"And I vote you're wrong," I muttered.

"Seda?" Ryoko asked.

"As much as I like Raikidan, I'm going to side with Laz," Seda said. *"I don't want any harm coming to an entire species because of our selfish choices."*

Ryoko scowled and I waited for her to create some sort of argument, but to my surprise she didn't. She just sighed in defeat. "All right, fine. We'll do it your way. Let's get this plan you have cooked up in your head on the road."

She wasn't going to be happy with this decision, but it wasn't like I wanted this outcome either. *I need to do what's right in this situation.*

Raikidan,
I'm sorry it had to be this way. I wish it didn't...

I stood in the shade of a tree and waited for him to arrive. He'd be here, but it was all a matter of when.

> *Thanks for offering your help. I'll never forget what you've done for us… for me. Maybe someday we'll meet again, during a better time.*

My ears perked when something rustled the bushes. Raikidan pushed his way through the underbrush and made his way over to me, a smile plastered on his face. It pained me to see how completely unaware he was.

"So what's this all about, Eira? Why did you have me come here and not just wait to tell me back at the house?" His brow pulled together with concern. "Eira, what's wrong? You look so upset."

I tried to take slow, steady steps as I walked toward him, but the situation had a tight hold on me and I ended up running to him. I threw my arms around his neck and buried my face in him. "I'm sorry."

"Sorry?" He grunted but it came out as a partial chuckle. "Sorry about what?"

I pulled away from him and gazed into his eyes, taking in the sight one last time. "Goodbye."

"Wh—"

I caught him as he fell. I studied his unconscious form before looking up at Ryoko. She handed over a small envelope and then took Raikidan from me. I took great interest in it, but didn't peer inside. If it was important, she'd tell me.

I stood once she had him securely on her back and pulled out a portal. Thinking of one place in particular, I activated the portal and led Ryoko through.

> *You can't come back. I can't allow you to put you and your kind in harm's way for our cause. I've already sent a message to Zaith's clan, letting them know the alliance is over, and I sent a message to your brother to relocate to another city. None of you can come back here…*

We came out of the portal and stood beside a slow running stream, the lack of rain this summer being the culprit for its state. Even though it was a different time of the year, I still recognized this place, that day still so fresh in my mind. As I took in the scenery, I couldn't keep those memories at bay.

"Is this where we're leaving him?" Ryoko asked.

I nodded. "Not in the open, but this is the place."

"What's so special about this place?"

My chest tightened. "This… is where we first met."

"Laz…"

I motioned her to follow. "There's a cave up stream. We'll leave him there."

"Okay."

She followed until we came to the cave Raikidan had slept in that same night. I climbed the rocks that were not as wet as they would have been, had more water been flowing from the falls. I glanced back to make sure Ryoko was doing okay, and then disappeared into the cave.

I helped her lay Raikidan down and then knelt next to him. Ryoko bent over and slipped the envelope I had handed back to her under Raikidan's hand.

"I'll give you a moment," she whispered.

I nodded and remained quiet until she left. I look down at Raikidan and then ran my fingers through his hair, trying to memorize the texture one last time. "I hope you can forgive me for this someday. It's honestly for the best. For you… and… for me. No matter how much I try to lie to myself—try to hide from the truth—it continues to surface and stare me in the face. I care for you too much. This distance between us will be for the best. You'll be happier." My lip quivered. "And me…"

I sighed and stood. Stalling didn't do me any good. Spinning on my heels, I headed for the cave entrance. Prolonging this goodbye stopped nothing anyway. I'd get over all this quickly, and Raikidan would be better off. It's how things needed to be.

When I reached the bottom of the rock face, Ryoko greeted me with a sad attempt of a smile. I took out a portal and opened it in front of us instead of responding. But, before I entered, I couldn't stop myself from looking back up at the cave one last time—hoping he'd wake up and stop me from making this choice. The cave remained still and I knew I needed to continue on with my mission.

Goodbye, my friend.

Entering the portal, I felt like I was being torn apart from the inside out. *Goodbye…*

I jolted awake and looked around the cell. It was dark and everyone was asleep, for now. I rested my head against the wall and stared up at the stone ceiling—those memories buzzing in my head... and in my heart.

A soldier came by the cell, but he only peered in long enough to make sure we were all accounted for before moving on. More would soon come, and they'd take us away again to see if we'd crack. I could only wait. Wait for the inevitable cycle of them wasting their time and then crawling back into this corner only to remember more. Fate was funny like that.

GLOSSARY CHARACTER

DALATREND

LEADERS

Taric – Former ruler of Dalatrend, nu-human, father to Zarda, deceased

Zarda – Ruler of Dalatrend, nu-human, son to Taric

MILITARY

Rana (*RAH-nah*) – Nu-human experiment, assassin, trained under Eira, vendetta against Eira, deceased

Rick – Nu-human experiment, general, deceased

Verra – Nu-human experiment, general, vendetta against Eira and Amara, deceased

Zo – Nu-human experiment, General, Interested in Eira

REBELLION

COUNCIL

Adina (*ah-DEE-nah*) – Oversees Team 7, nu-human experiment, first Dalatrend shapeshifter experiment

Akama (*ah-KAH-mah*) – Oversees Team 5, nu-human experiment, first Dalatrend Seer experiment (not planned), twin to Enrée

Eldenar – Oversees Team 4, nu-human experiment, first Dalatrend war experiment

Elkron – Oversees Team 6, nu-human experiment, first Dalatrend elementalist experiment

Enrée (*EN-ree-ay*) – Oversees Team 2, nu-human experiment, first Dalatrend Battle Psychic experiment (not planned), twin to Akama

Genesis – Oversees Team 3, first nu-human, necromantic abilities

Hanama (*HAH-nah-mah*) – Oversees Team 1, nu-human experiment, first Dalatrend anthropomorphic experiment

TEAM 1
Assassin based

Evynne (*Ev-een*) – Nu-human experiment

TEAM 2
Recruitment based

Dan – Nu-human experiment, former lieutenant to Eira

Innon (*EYE-nin*) – Battle leader, nu-human experiment, former commander

TEAM 3
Income based, former Brute and foot soldier mostly

Andariel – Nu-human experiment, double ear prototype, brother to Azriel, former medic, strip club owner: Midnight

Argus – Nu-human experiment, inventor

Aurora – Nu-human experiment, Underground computer tech

Azriel – Nu-human experiment, double ear prototype, brother to Andariel, former medic, night club owner: Twilight

Blaze – Nu-human experiment

Eira (*AIR-uh*) – Nu-human hybrid experiment, battle leader, former commander, mother to Ryder, assassin, Shaman of the Rising Sun. Alt names: Laz, Laz'shika (*laz-SHEE-kah*)

Lena – Nu-human, partner to Zenmar

Orchon (*OR-con*) – Nu-human, bouncer at Twilight

Raid – Nu-human experiment, brother to Rylan, experimental shapeshifter: dog, interested in Ryoko

Raikidan (*RYE-ki-DAN*) – Black and red dragon, cousin to Corliss, son to Xephrya, Guard in training

Rylan (*RYE-lan*) – Nu-human experiment, brother to Raid, experimental shapeshifter: wolf, former captain, artificial mental bond with Eira, ice elementalist, interested in Ryoko

Ryoko (*Ree-OH-koh*) – Half-wogron experiment, clone of Peacekeeper Ryoko, Brute, former lieutenant, best friend to Eira, interested in Rylan and Raid

Seda (*SAY-duh*) – Nu-human experiment, psychic: Seer, twin to Nioush, sister to Saléna and Nyra

Xantar (*ZAN-tar*) – Nu-human experiment

Zane – Nu-human experiment, uncle to Eira, brother to Jasmine and Amara, former soldier, mechanic

Zenmar – Nu-human experiment, crippled in a skirmish, partner to Lena

TEAM 4
Reconnaissance based

TEAM 5
Psychic based

Vek – Nu-human experiment, psychic: Battle Psychic, registered

TEAM 6
Research and development based

TEAM 7
Reconnaissance based

Chameleon – Nu-human experiment, molecular fusion ability, former assassin

Doppelganger – Nu-human experiment, temporary cloning ability

Ezhno (*EZ-no*) – Nu-human experiment, Underground computer tech

Mocha – Nu-human experiment, anthropomorphic: cat

Nioush (*NEE-oosh*) – Nu-human experiment, psychic: Battle
Psychic, twin to Seda, brother to Saléna and Nyra

Raynn (*rain*) – Nu-human experiment, battle leader, former
general, clone if Peacekeeper Raynn

MOLES
Nyra – Nu-human experiment, psychic: Battle Psychic, twin
to Saléna, sister to Seda and Nioush
Ryder – Nu-human experiment, son to Eira and Rylan
Saléna (*sah-LEY-nah*) – Nu-human experiment, psychic: Seer,
twin to Nyra, sister to Seda and Nioush
Talon – Nu-human experiment, bone spike ability

MERCENARIES
Arnia (*ARE-nee-ah*) – Nu-human experiment, twin to Jaybird,
metal elementalist, former mole, interested in Ven'lar
Jaybird – Nu-human experiment, twin to Arnia, air elementalist, former mole

SHAMANS

NORTH TRIBE
Fe'teline (*fey-TELL-een*) – Nu-human – Shaman of the Rising
Sun
Ven'lar (*ven-LAR*) – Nu-human, Shaman of the Cleansing
Spirit, interested in Arnia

SOUTH TRIBE
Ir'esh (*EAR-esh*) – Chief, elf, father to Tla'lli, Shaman of the
Fractured Crystal
Ne'kall (*nay-CALL*) – Elf, son to Del'karo, father of four,
Shaman of the Rising Sun
Tla'lli (*teh-LAH-lee*) – Elf, daughter to Ir'esh, Shaman of the
Whispering Winds, interested in Talon

EAST TRIBE

Nela – Nu-human, lightning shaman, Shaman of the Dancing Lights

Se'lata (*say-LAH-tah*) – Elf, spice merchant, Shaman of the Fractured Crystal

WEST TRIBE

Alena – Elf, wife to Del'karo, mother figure to Eira, mother of Ne'kall and twelve other children, Shaman of the Cleansing Spirit

Daren – Human, Valene's adopted father, inn keeper, former partner to Valessa

Del'karo (*del-CAR-oh*) – Elf, mentor and father figure to Eira, husband to Alena, father of Ne'kall and twelve other children, Shaman of the Rising Sun

Ken'ichi (*ken-EE-chee*) – Nu-human, friend to Eira, Guard and Shaman of the Cleansing Spirit

Maka'shi (*mah-KAH-shee*) – Leader, half-elf, Shaman of the Frozen Waste, widow

Me'kunar (*may-COON-are*) – Elf, scholar

Mel'ka (*mel-KAH*) – Elf, elder, storyteller, Shaman of the Fractured Crystal

Shva'sika (*sh-VAH-see-KAH*) – Elf, sister to Xye, mentor and adopted family to Eira, Shaman of the Dancing Lights. Alt names: Elarinya (*ell-are-IN-yah*), Danika

Valene (*Vah-LEEN*) – Human, daughter to Valessa, Eira's and Daren's adopted daughter, plant-based Shaman of the Fractured Crystal

Valessa – Human, mother to Valene, former partner to Daren, Shaman of the Fractured Crystal, deceased

Xye (*zeye*) – Half-elf, brother to Shva'sika, attempted to court Eira, Shaman of the Cleansing Spirit, deceased

DRAGONS

Corliss – Green and black dragon, cousin to Raikidan

Xephrya (*zef-RYE-ah*) – Red dragon, mother to Raikidan and Ebon, deceased

VELSARA WILDS CLAN

Anahak (*an-ah-HAWK*) – Black dragon, mate to Xaneth, father to Rimu and six other offspring

Rimu – Black and red dragon, son to Anahak and Xaneth

Xaneth (*zan-ETH*) – Red dragon, mate to Anahak, mother to Rimu and six other offspring

Zaith – Clan leader, red dragon

GODS

Anila (*ah-NEE-lah*) – Goddess of air

Arcadia (*are-KAY-dee-ah*) – Goddess of spirits, daughter to Solund and Lunaria, sister to Phyre

Genesis – Goddess of life, partner to Zoltan

Gina – Goddess of health and healing

Halcyon (*hall-SEE-on*) – Goddess of the sea

Imera (*eye-MEER-ah*) – Goddess of literature and knowledge

Jin – Goddess of refined earth

Kendaria – Goddess of water

Koseba (*koh-SAY-bah*) – God of shapeshifting

Le'carro (*ley-CAR-oh*) – God of lightning

Lunaria – Goddess of the moon, partner to Solund, mother to Phyre and Arcadia

Nazir (*nah-ZEER*) – God of death and corruption

Phyre (*fire*) – God of fire, son to Solund and Lunaria, brother to Arcadia

Raisu (*RAY-sue*) – God of dreams

Rashta (*RAH-sh-tah*) – Goddess of judgement and rebirth, currently missing

Rasmus – God of love and fertility, partner to Savada

Satria (*sah-TREE-ah*) – Goddess of war

Savada (*sah-VAH-dah*) – Goddess of sex and seduction, partner to Rasmus

Sela – Goddess of psychics, sister of Tyro

Solstice – Goddess of ice and winter

Solund – God of the sun, partner to Lunaria, father to Phyre and Arcadia

Tarin – God of nature, partner to Valena

Tyro (*TIE-roh*) – God of psychics, brother of Sela

Valena – Goddess of earth, partner to Tarin

Zoltan – God of life, partner to Genesis

MISCELLANEOUS

Alyra (*all-EYE-rah*) – Nu-human experiment, former soldier, partner to Lakon, mother to Eyri, musician

Devon – Nu-human experiment, former assassin, musician

Eyri (*EYE-ree*) – Nu-human, Lakon and Alyra's daughter, musician

Lakon (*LAY-con*) – Nu-human experiment, former assassin, partner to Alyra, father to Eyri, musician

Rosa (*ROH-sah*) – Succubus, mated to Zaedrix

Voice – Mysterious voice that speaks to Eira inside her head. Malevolent

Zaedrix (*ZAY-driks*) – Incubus, mated to Rosa

SPIRITS

Amara (*ah-MAR-ah*) – Nu-human experiment, general, mother to Eira, grandmother to Ryder, sister to Jasmine and Zane, water elementalist, deceased

Anir (*ah-NEER*) – Black dragon, claims to know Eira, deceased

Jade – Nu-human experiment, former soldier under Amara, deceased

Jasmine – Nu-human experiment, aunt to Eira, sister to Amara and Zane, geneticist, deceased

Lazei (*LAH-zay*) – Human, ancient swordsman, protector of the Eternal Library, deceased but active by use of spiritual crystal

Tannek – Nu-human experiment, former soldier under Amara, deceased

Zeek – Nu-human, Brute, former soldier under Amara, deceased

PEACEKEEPERS

Assar – dwarf, deceased

Pyralis (*PIE-ral-iss*) – Red dragon, former Velsara Wild Clan leader, deceased

Raynn (*rain*) – Human, deceased

Reiki (*Ray-KEY*) – Green dragon, deceased

Ryoko (*Ree-OH-koh*) – Half-wogron, Shaman of the Fractured Crystal, deceased

Varro – Elf, healer, deceased

ORPHANAGE

Lyra (*LIE-ruh*) – Matron, Nu-human

Myra (*MEER-uh*) – Nu-human, attached to Raid

Orphans (Elara (*el-ARE-ah*), Jakcel (*JACK-sell*), Elsa, Levi, Panga, Nari, Kelcen (*Kell-SEN*), Alson, Ellie)

GLOSSARY LANGUAGE

ELVISH

Elvish is an eloquent language, light on the tongue with an airy sound. Even the usual consonants of common don't hold the same harshness in Elvish. Many elves and other humanoids raised with Elvish as their mother tongue carry this light speech over in their common.

While not the easiest language to learn, Elvish is a favorite among the linguistically gifted. Those who seek to learn this language seek out elves before any other race and are taught by full immersion. Some elves will provide a few words for the humanoid to start with but it's not common to do so. The elves believe this technique is the best way to learn and creates a better understanding of the language for everyday use.

Written Elvish is just as elegant as spoken, usually written in script by native speakers. Non-natives tend to forgo the script, which is accepted by native speakers, though the handwriting is still expected to be neat, and flourished on important documents. Sloppy writing is considered an insult.

Phrases used in the series:

Éan ag eitilt – Flying bird

DRACONIC

Draconic is a guttural language made up most of grunts and growls with the occasional tongue flick, exhales, or teeth clatter. It's difficult for a non-dragon to learn, as the formation of these words are foreign to most humanoids. Some sounds are impossible for non-dragons to create so other sounds are substituted as an alternative. Even dragons taking a humanoid form must make these changes. Rarely is a humanoid able to perfect the speech, even when raised among dragons.

Those attempting to learn are always taught single words before attempting sentence structures. Draconic sentence structure is similar to Common, but with a possessive edge due to the mindset of dragons. There are no contracted words in Draconic, as such, dragons who don't speak common often, tend to use the same sentence structures of their mother tongue when they do speak common.

It's not common for dragons to write in the current age but there is a basic written form of the language that was used more extensively in the past. This written form is comprised of glyphs easily created with dragon claws and easy to decipher for most dragons no matter the cleanliness of the script. Non-dragons find this writing easier to learn than the spoken language and most of the time will stop learning after they've master it.

Words Raikidan has taught Eira in the series:

Aio – You	*Duny* – Fire
Aion – Your	*Din* – For
Aionl – Yours	*Dnis* – From
Ayl – Yes	*Dnuyvk* – Friend
Cyyg – Keep	*Ev* – An
Diik – Food	*Evk* – And

Finna – Worry
Frem – What
Fryzg – Whelp
Fulkis – Wisdom
Fuzz – Will
Gzyely – Please
Id – Of
Ion – Our
Iv – On
Ki – Do
Knewiv – Dragon
Lgunum – Spirit
Lisymruvw – Something
Lmnyvwmr – Strength
Lry – She
Lynyvuma – Serenity
Lyy – See
Mi – To
Mii – Too
Mioxr – Touch
Mrevc – Thank
Mruvc – Think
Mryny – There
Ol – Us
Pnyemry – Breathe
Py – Be
Rel – Has
Rety – Have

Rl – He
Rosev – Human
Rovwyn – Hunger
Rul – His
Rus – Him
Ryn – Her
Ryzzi – Hello
Sa – My
Suvy – Mine
Sy – Me
U – I
Ud – If
Ul – Is
Um – It
Vi – No
Vim – Not
Vyyk – Need
Wiikpay – Goodbye
Wym – Get
Xivvexmyk – Connected
Yem – Eat
Ytyv – Even
Ziaeza – Loyalty
Zity – Love
Zoxca – Lucky
Zudy – Life
Zulmyv – Listen
Zutyl – Lives

Phrases translated to Eira in the series:

Ion cuvk – Our kind

Lazmira, sa xruzk – Lazmira, my child

Zity, gyexy, lgunum, ziaeza, lynyvuma, lmnyvwmr, fulkis – Love, peace, spirit, loyalty, serenity, strength, wisdom

LOST LANGUAGES

Thought the history of Lumaraeon, language has developed and died, but some have left a more notable impact on the races. These forgotten languages hold important information lost during the millennia of turmoil making them important topics for scholars.

OLD TONGUE

Old Tongue, also known as God speech, is the most ancient form of speech that was replaced by the various languages of Lumaraeon, ultimately dying out among the mortal races. Much of the language was lost during the War of End and with no one but the gods around to remember, the language was thought dead. Until a large find of books in the Eternal Library turned up after a new entryway was found, eight hundred years ago.

Scholars have done their best to decipher the old language and have since found new discovery sites all over Lumaraeon to help with their research. But while the tongue is researched, it is not know if the translations are quite right, and no one has thought to ask the gods, not even Imera, the goddess of literature and knowledge.

Words used in the series:

Mukarna – Makers

ABOUT THE AUTHOR

Shannon Pemrick, is a full-time USA Today bestselling author, and fuller-time geek and dragon obsessed. She also has too many novelty mugs, not enough chocolate, and a forbidden love-affair with all things shiny.

Shannon resides in Southern New Hampshire with her overly sarcastic husband and one too many pets who steal all her bed space. When she's not burning her fingers across a keyboard or trying to squeeze into a spot on the couch for movie night, she's rolling dice and getting lost in RPGs or searching for brides for her dragon overlords.

You can learn more about Shannon by visiting her website at:
Shannonpemrick.com